ANGELS

of the

RESISTANCE

Also by Noelle Salazar

The Flight Girls

ANGELS

of the

RESISTANCE

NOELLE SALAZAR

mira

ISBN-13: 978-0-7783-3360-9

Angels of the Resistance

For questions and comments about the quality of this book, please contact us at CustomerService@Harlequin.com.

Mira
22 Adelaide St. West, 41st Floor
Toronto, Ontario M5H 4E3, Canada
BookClubbish.com

Recycling programs
for this product may
not exist in your area.

Printed in U.S.A.

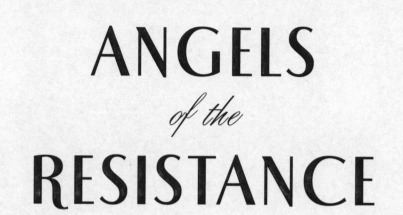

ANGELS
of the
RESISTANCE

1

Haarlem, Netherlands
April 1940

Sunlight dappled through the green leaves, scattering golden light across the blanket where I sat, my back against the trunk of a tall birch tree, while I kept watch over the Aberman children.

The rain that had kept me up the night before, pummeling the roof above the third-floor bedroom I shared with my older sister, scented the air with the smell of damp grass, stone, and bark. I breathed in, soothed by its familiarity, and yawned, my eyes blurring with exhaustion as I tried to stay present. Too many late nights and early mornings were beginning to take their toll, and the clatter of dice being shaken and rolled by tiny hands before me, accompanied by laughter, shouts of outrage, and harrumphs of frustration, were almost soothing, lulling me into a false sense of security.

I glanced down at the book in my hand and the paragraph I'd read at least a dozen times without retaining one word. Unfortunately, sometimes running from my own thoughts by feeding my brain new information didn't work. Guilt and fear, it turned out, loved a quiet moment, whispering in my ears at night as I tried to sleep, and nudging at me while I sat at my desk in class, trying to focus on what the teacher said. Which was why I'd decided two months ago that I needed noise. Noise would distract me and help me escape the thoughts running through my mind.

Going, doing, and helping was what led me to taking the Saturday afternoon childcare job. It was why I'd suddenly began offering to run errands or clean for my mother, rather than complaining when she asked. It was why I'd begun staying after school, poring over books I knew I'd be assigned to read the following year in an attempt to get a head start. I'd been determined to become a barrister like my father had been since I was a little girl, and the extra studying filled my head with new and complicated words, lofty ideas, and imaginings of grandeur— which were a much-needed diversion from my otherwise too quiet world. And Haarlem, our sweet little city by the sea, was more than just quiet. It was practically silent, as if all sound emitted was whisked from our homes and carried by the near-constant wind out across the water where it dissipated into the gray clouds above.

"You cheated!"

"I did not!"

I blinked, startled out of my thoughts, and turned my attention to Isaak and Lara, whose earlier mirth had become something less friendly. At six and eight years old, I knew their moments of getting along would become less and less frequent as their interests changed and their peers' desires began pressuring them in other directions. But for now, they still got along for the most part. Until someone inevitably cheated at a game.

"Lien," Lara, the younger of the two whined, her wide brown eyes staring up at me, "Isaak cheated."

"I didn't!" the older boy protested, his mop of brown curls vibrating with his insistence.

I crossed my arms over my chest, becoming a miniature version of my father when he'd been alive as he'd solved similar skirmishes between me and my elder sister, Elif.

"Well," I said. "I wasn't watching to say either way so what shall we do? Quit? It would be a shame. You were both having such a good time. Perhaps have the roll in question rolled again? What would be fair to the two of you?"

Like my father had always done, I gave both participants a choice, rather than accusing or taking sides. If they were having fun, the one at fault would usually feel bad and acquiesce, so as not to ruin the day.

Isaak huffed. "I'll roll again," he said.

I hid my smile. Isaak nearly always cheated; Lara was just finally catching on. Keeping my expression thoughtful, I nodded.

"Sounds like a sensible plan," I said, and then shot to my feet as a sudden shriek split the air in two.

I leaped over their game and stood at the edge of the blanket, a human barrier between whatever trouble was brewing and the children I was responsible for.

"What was that?" Lara asked beside me.

Without looking, I corralled her behind me, my eyes scanning the park around us.

Haarlemmerhout Park covered sixty hectares of land in the southern part of the city. Beech, horse chestnut, linden, and silver maple trees towered above lush green blankets of grass and mossy winding paths where lovers were often caught stealing a kiss by young families out for leisurely bicycle rides. In a park so big, on any given day, one could find a spot to spend several hours in and not be bothered by others. It was strange enough to hear sounds besides ours, but sounds of distress were especially surprising.

Movement on the other side of some nearby shrubbery caught my eye, and I glanced over my shoulder.

"Isaak," I said. "Watch your sister for a moment. I'll be right back."

Heart thudding in my chest, I marched across the soft, damp grass, intent to stop whatever danger was in motion. But as I rounded the tangle of budding green plants, all I saw were two boys in the middle of the walking path bent and staring at a small lump on the ground between them.

One of the boys prodded the lump with a stick and the lump shifted and lifted its small head, hollering again at his aggressor. I sucked in a breath, pinpricks of anger and sorrow mixing behind my eyes, making them burn.

"Stop that!" I yelled, trying to make all 162 centimeters of me look taller than they did. "Get away from that bird!"

Two pairs of wide eyes met mine, and then the stick was dropped as the two boys ran off and out of sight.

I hurried to the bird, tears clouding my eyes.

"Hello, little love," I whispered, looking for an obvious injury. "Did those mean boys hurt you?"

He eyed me from where he lay, and I chewed my lip as I looked him over best I could without touching him. The wing I could see seemed intact, his spindly legs curled into little enraged fists.

"Is he okay?"

I wiped my eyes and glanced up at Lara, who was standing with her brother beside me, their small faces pinched with worry, dark eyes full of concern.

"I'm not sure," I said, and pointed. "This wing looks okay, but I can't see the other one without moving him."

"Should we take it somewhere?" Isaak asked.

I sniffled and leaned back, getting hold of myself before my emotions erupted from the place I kept them shoved inside. It was only a bird after all. Not worth the tremors of despair threatening to burst.

"No," I said. "But maybe we could move him out of the way."

I pointed to the shrubbery beside us. "Why don't the two of you build him a little nest over there?"

As they ran off to gather leaves and small branches, I stared down at the creature.

"I'm sorry you're hurt," I whispered, my eyes once more filling with tears.

There was something so awful about seeing a creature, fragile and vulnerable, unable to help itself, left to the devices—or torture—of others. To feel and be so powerless...

"We're done," Isaak said, kneeling beside me, his cheeks pink from the effort. "Are you crying?"

I shrugged.

"It's just a bird, Lien."

I pursed my lips. "It's a living creature, Isaak," I said, my voice soft. "We should always do everything we can to help others. Even if they're just birds."

I pulled the scarf from my neck and stared down at the gull. "You ready?" I asked him, and then swooped the fabric over it and wrapped my hands gently around its body.

"Do you think it will live?" Isaak asked as I set the bird in the nest.

A glimmer of sadness pressed at my heart. I knew that sometimes even when the best efforts were made and all the prayers were whispered, they were still not enough.

"I hope so," I said, setting the grumbling fowl on the nest the kids had made. "The two of you did a great job. It's a handsome nest. He should be very grateful."

"He doesn't sound it," Lara said, and I managed a laugh.

We watched the gull for a while longer as he warily eyed us back and shifted his small body on the pile of foliage and sticks, and then I shepherded the children back to the blanket and their games.

"Play with us," Isaak said, holding up a well-loved deck of cards.

I nodded and took a seat, happy for the distraction.

As the afternoon passed, the children, easily bored, moved on from card games to running through the grass, twirling until they were dizzy, and a game of tag until, tired out, they lay side by side, Isaak reading and Lara drawing, while I opened my math book and studied for an exam the following Monday.

A breeze kicked up and I shivered, noticing the light around us had changed from golden hued to dismal. I glanced at the sky to find the sun, tired from her brief exertion, had pulled up her blanket of clouds and disappeared beneath a dark gray cover, giving the cold wind permission to sweep in and scatter the papers Lara was busy drawing on.

"Hurry," I said, and the three of us took off in different directions, chasing down pictures of dogs, horses, and trees, all the while laughing as papers somersaulted and cartwheeled across the vast lawn.

As I pulled a gangly giraffe drawing from the branches of a budding shrub, and a rotund elephant from a springy bed of moss, I heard the telltale buzz of a plane in the distance. I searched around me for more drawings and then lifted my eyes to the clouds again, listening as the sound amplified, the airplane coming into view, heading in our direction.

"Kids," I said, my voice a warning. I gestured for them to come closer and then took hold of their arms and pulled them beneath the cover of a tall birch tree.

"It's just a plane," Lara said.

But no plane was just a plane when a war was going on.

Lara pulled on my arm and I gave her what I hoped was a smile as a light rain began to fall, tapping on the leaves above us before sliding off and peppering us with drops.

The planes had come more and more often in the past several weeks, but I'd never given them much thought before today. Had never felt even a glimmer of fear, assuming they were headed to France or England where the war was actively happening. But for some reason today, the sight and sound of this one put me on edge and the closer it got, the harder my heart beat.

The drops of rain grew in size with every second I stood with my eyes glued to the plane, watching and waiting, but for what I didn't know. And then I saw a door open.

"Isaak," I said. "Lara." I pushed them behind me, causing Isaak to trip over a large root. He recovered and grasped my hand, his eyes wide with fear as I placed my body in front of theirs, the rumble of the engine above like thunder, shaking the air around us.

But no guns discharged as it flew by. No bombs were dropped. No damage was done at all, save for the fraying of my nerves and a cascade of fluttering white.

"What is it?" Lara asked.

We watched as the wind caught and scattered the overturning debris, sending it floating through the air across what looked like the whole of the city.

"I don't know," I said, letting go of their hands and taking a step forward, watching as one of the items landed softly on top of a shrub near where our blanket was laid out.

Isaak reached it first, snatching it from where it lay and turning it over, a frown on his handsome face.

"What's it mean?" he asked, handing the paper over to me.

I took it and frowned. Vibrant blues, reds, and whites glared back at me as I tried to make sense of what I was seeing. A white bird on a flag. A drawing of a young, blond man in uniform with a large drum strapped over his shoulder, and words. Dutch words with a German message that sent a shiver down my spine.

I swallowed, my fingers trembling as I held the paper. Because they weren't just a German message. They were a Nazi message.

A Nazi invitation.

"For the good of your conscience," it read. "The Waffen SS is calling you."

My fingers tightened, crumpling the paper. It wasn't the first

time I'd seen one these garish signs. I'd spotted them a couple
of times over the past several months, adhered to light posts and
once, shockingly, in the window of a small shop. Was this where
they had come from? Or was this a new tactic? Were we to be
inundated regularly with this raining down of terrible requests
for our men to join the German forces?

Of course, I knew all about the war Germany had started. It
was all anyone talked about since the news the year before that
Hitler had invaded Poland had come not so much as a shock as
it had with a sigh of acceptance. And when England and France
quickly declared war on Germany in retaliation, no one was
surprised. Scores of Jews had been entering the Netherlands for
the past two years in hopes that our neutrality during the Great
War would extend to whatever this war turned out to be. But
the poster in my hands made me worry that perhaps they were
wrong. Perhaps this time we wouldn't be so lucky.

Because if we were to stay neutral, what was that plane doing
here?

"What's it say?" Lara repeated her brother's question, reaching for the poster.

"Nothing." I folded it and shoved it in my coat pocket. "It's
trash." I checked my watch, noticing a thread had come loose
on the worn, too-big brown band, making it sag on my wrist.
I tucked it inside the cuff of my sweater. "We should get you
two home. Your parents will worry if we're late."

The three of us packed away the items we'd brought in a
cloth bag, and then I stood by trying to quell my impatience as
I watched the two of them take the corners of the blanket and
try to fold it into a neat square.

"Here," Isaak said, handing me the lumpy heap with a proud
smile.

I grinned as I tucked it under my arm and took a last look
around for stray toys, papers, and drawing implements.

"Ready?" I asked, and the two nodded. "Shall we check on our bird friend before we go?"

"Yes," they said in delighted unison.

The gull was just as we'd left it, and in fact looked to have made himself more at home, burrowing deeper into his new nest of leaves and twigs, his narrow beak nestled down into his puffed white chest.

"See?" I whispered, glancing at the children crouched beside me. "I told you you made him a handsome home. Look how happy he is."

Convinced the bird would live, we walked across the grass to the sidewalk. I glanced at the sky and then moved in closer, making sure I was at most an arm's length away from both kids should I need to protect either of them from an oncoming bicyclist or any other dangers that might befall them. I knew how fast the unthinkable could transpire. I'd seen it happen before.

"That was a bad one," Lara said as we walked.

"What was a bad one?" I asked, looking around to see what she was talking about.

"The plane," she said. "It was a bad one. I saw the spiders."

Spiders. It was what she called the Nazi insignia.

I nodded. They were the bad ones indeed. I'd never felt that more than I did now, a seed of doom planting itself in the pit of my stomach as I wondered if that plane, its engine noise still reverberating through my body, was just the beginning of something more. The warning crack of thunder before a storm.

2

"Lien saved a bird!" Lara announced as soon as the front door of the Aberman house swung open, revealing a very pregnant Mrs. Aberman who stood aside to let us in.

"I can't wait to hear all about it," she said, winking at me over her children's heads. "After the two of you wash up."

As the children ran upstairs, I followed their mother into the sunny kitchen to wash my own hands, noting the colorful drawings hanging from nearly every surface with a bittersweet smile. Not long ago, the kitchen of my own house had looked similar. Now though, the only art left was a family portrait, painted by a child's hand in primary colors and propped up on the mantel over the fireplace, and some mature, stark and colorless images of the countryside that were more gloom than joy. The rest of the happier pieces had gone in a box that had been placed in the third floor closet, set among other items that had once had a place in the main parts of the house, but were now relegated to this one space, in the dark, with the door shut.

Noticing the cloth bags filled with groceries on the counter,

I dried my fingers on a towel and reached for the closest one, pulling out a bouquet of deep purple beets.

"Oh, Lien," Mrs. Aberman said, easing herself into a chair. "I should say no, but my feet are killing me. I swear the market was more crowded than usual. Of course, that's probably just because I'm the size of a house now."

"You're not," I said, glancing at her as I set a large bag of flour on the floor of the pantry.

Mrs. Aberman was the most beautiful woman I'd ever seen. The natural flush that graced dewy skin flecked delicately with pale freckles didn't need even a dash of rouge for enhancement. She wore her glossy dark curls swept off her face, and held herself with the grace of a ballerina. I'd often found myself staring at her in admiration as she spoke with such patience to her children, or laughed at her husband's jokes. The fact that she'd attended university and held a degree in teaching made her even more spectacular in my eyes, especially since I'd decided I too would pursue higher education. It was rare to know women her age and older who had sought something besides marriage and a family. And while she had given up the one for the other, much as my own mother had done, knowing she'd aspired to more was both fascinating and inspiring.

"Were the children good for you today?" she asked.

"They're always good for me."

There was silence, and I met her eyes across the table. We shared a smile.

"They're *mostly* always good," I said. "We had a nice time. There were a lot of card games."

"There always are."

Heavy footsteps coming down the stairs announced the arrival of Mr. Aberman, who entered the kitchen with his shirt sleeves rolled up like always, his feet bare and pale against the gleaming dark hardwood floors, and his ever-present grin in place.

"Well?" he said. "Are you quitting? Were they terrible?"

"I was just telling Mrs. Aberman how good they were," I said, placing five apples in the bowl on the table and folding the cloth bags I'd emptied.

"They're upstairs chattering away about an injured bird," he said, looking around. "I'm almost afraid to ask."

I smiled at my favorite teacher. Mr. Aberman taught ninth grade literature with patience, grace, and a lot of humor, which I suspected was needed when dealing with the antics and hormones of fourteen-and fifteen-year-olds.

"There was a bird," I said. "We did not bring it home with us."

He gave a great and comical sigh, and his wife and I laughed as I passed him a small block of butter to be put away.

"It was a fun afternoon," I said.

"You are a godsend, Lien," he said. "I was able to get every paper on my desk graded."

"Good," his wife said, with a mischievous smile. "That means you can cook the dinner tonight."

"It would be my pleasure," he said, and she turned wide eyes to me.

"I think maybe you're also a miracle worker!" She reached over and slapped Mr. Aberman's hand. "Pay her well before she decides to never come back."

As I pocketed the money I'd earned a few minutes later, the kids came barreling down the stairs to tell the tale of the bird and how they'd painstakingly picked each leaf, stick, and blade of grass for its nest.

"They did a wonderful job," I said. "Despite whatever injury the poor thing was nursing, he seemed quite happy in his nest when we checked on him before heading home."

"I daresay you three are heroes," Mr. Aberman proclaimed. "Which deserves…" He opened a cabinet and peered inside as the kids jumped up and down, clearly knowing it was the cupboard treats resided in. A moment later their father proffered three wrapped chocolates, one for each of us.

"Thank you," I said, pocketing the candy.

"Thank you!" Lara and Isaak yelled before running off to another part of the house.

I checked my sagging watch. "I'd better go," I said, my voice filled with regret. "I have homework."

"On a Saturday?" Mrs. Aberman looked to her husband, who raised his hands in surrender.

"Don't look at me," he said. "I'm the nice teacher."

I left the happy household with a grin that began to fade as soon as the door closed behind me, shutting their joyful voices inside while I stood just beyond reach on the other side. I began the short walk home.

Each step led me away from the light and airy feel of their family, and closer to my own, where laughter was rarely heard these days and a pall lay over the house, dark and heavy and oppressive. Where words that used to fill the space were barely spoken, and we moved about like ghosts, together but alone.

At the corner I turned right and found myself ignoring both the ticking on my wrist and the windows of the famously forward-tilting shops, which, when I was younger, made me feel as though I were being watched over, but recently had begun to feel like they were glowering down at me, disappointed and full of accusation.

But rather than skirt to the outside of the city center like I often did these days, I stayed within the shopping area, taking in the familiar sounds of Haarlem, letting the noise fill me up in hopes it would linger when I returned to the silence of my house.

Bicycles squeaked past with chains in need of oiling, little faces in wood carts smiled up at me, their parents at the helms. Teenagers on handlebars, their friends pedaling, some recognizable from school, others not. Restaurants teemed with people looking for a late lunch or early dinner, patrons spilling out the door or sitting at tables, the candle centerpieces lit, the flames dancing in the breeze.

As I walked past my mother's shop, I slowed my step and glanced inside. It was rare to find her alone, and today was no different. As she examined a piece of clothing with one woman, another browsed items on a rack while still another sat in one of the plush, purple velvet chairs, a garment folded in her lap as she waited her turn.

My mother, who had gone to university to become a nurse, had found a class by accident for clothing design. Already a talented seamstress, she added the design class to her roster "for fun" she'd told her father, and fell in love with creating her own pieces. Despite her love of sewing, though, and obvious talent, she did as was expected of her and graduated with a nursing degree, followed quickly by marrying her college sweetheart at the end of the First World War, and got a job at a local doctor's office. But two years later, her inability to stay away from fabric and design had littered their home with other people's clothing brought in to her on the sly for hemming, taking in or letting out. With reams of fabric shoved in every nook and cranny, father convinced her to give up her nursing job and open her own shop. He'd just made partner in a law firm, and they could afford to lose her nursing salary. She never looked back.

I hurried past the window and didn't realize I'd taken a right instead of a left at an important street until it was too late and I found myself walking toward the spot I'd been avoiding for eight months. Horrified at my mistake, I gasped and stopped in my tracks, leading a cyclist to almost run into me.

"Watch out!" he shouted as he rode past.

But I didn't respond, my eyes glued to the spot.

That spot.

I stood rooted to the cobbles, their uneven surface digging into the heel of one foot, the arch of the other, as I pictured a pale face emerging from the canal, wet and lifeless. The sound of the water licking at the stone walls, the wind whistling around the nearby bridge, the muffled voices of people milling about on a Saturday afternoon, filled my ears as the memory assailed me.

"Miss? Are you okay?"

I jumped and turned to find a woman looking at me, her brow furrowed with the question. I shook my head and stumbled around her, hurrying as fast as my legs, suddenly wooden and not my own, carried me home.

On Sundays my mother, sister, and I cleaned the house from top to bottom. It was a weekly ritual that saw us up early, quietly working in our designated areas until it was all done and we were free to spend the rest of the afternoon as we wished until our dinner guest arrived as she always did at exactly six o'clock.

Finished with my chores, I put the supplies away and trudged up the stairs to the third-floor loft bedroom I shared with Elif, who had finished moments before me and was already standing in a paint-splattered apron before her easel, a blank expression on her face.

I lay on my bed and stared up at the sloped ceiling, mentally ticking off the things I needed to do before school the following day. Anything to keep my mind from becoming too empty and quiet like my sister's seemed to have gone.

I glanced at her again. She hadn't moved and, from what I could tell, had yet to blink. She peered hard at the paper before her, which had the vague outlines of an idea. A seascape, it looked like, with clouds above and what looked to be the shape of waves unfurling onto a shore below. It was as if, if she stared at it long enough, the picture in her mind would appear without her having to raise a brush.

It was odd to see her fingers, forearms, and chin, where she inevitably scratched an itch with a paint-smeared finger, not covered in vibrant colors, or a world or scene not emerging as if by magic on the sheet before her as her hand moved deftly from palette to easel. There was usually a constant flow of creation. Flowers and bicycles, little smiling faces, baskets, and windmills. Reds over oranges and greens over blues, bright yellows and searing pinks that turned into sunrises or sunsets depending on her mood.

Her side of the room used to be covered in paintings. Some adhered to the walls, others hanging on a cord to dry. But now the cord hung mostly empty, with only a half dozen pictures clipped to its length. The rest had been rolled and stowed beneath her bed. Our room, once filled with color and joy, was now as dull and drab as the rest of the house, as though the life had been sucked out and all that remained were whispers of what once was.

She set down her paintbrush, covered her palette, and removed her apron, having painted nothing, and moved to the closet, pulling out clean clothes for dinner. With a sigh, I stood and did the same. I felt her eyes on me as I pulled my dirty frock over my head and tossed it in the laundry bin. As I reached for a clean dress, I met her gaze.

"You're okay?" she asked.

I inhaled, held the breath, and then exhaled with a nod.

"I'm okay," I said. "Are you?"

She nodded, pulled her dress on, tied the tie around her waist, and went to the bathroom to wash up.

It was our way of checking in with one another. Careful. Not too much. For fear that one or both of us would break. And we couldn't break, because if we did, we'd be just one more thing our mother had to manage. And we couldn't do that to her, not after all that had happened in the past few years. So we took our sadness—the deep wells of pain—and buried them as best we could, pretending they didn't exist as we walked through our lives numb with shock and hollow with grief.

In the kitchen we donned clean aprons and began the task of peeling and chopping. Mama finished her dusting, changed clothes, and joined us. For the next thirty minutes or so, we moved around one another as though doing a choreographed dance, completely in sync, as if anticipating the move of the other and complementing it with one of our own. The normalcy of it made me feel almost like we were okay. Still who we'd been before. Rather than what we now were; splintered, each of us pointed in a different direction.

"Lien," Mama said. "Will you get the plates, please?"

I pulled the small wooden step stool from its spot in the corner and set it down on the floor, and then climbed the two steps and grasped the knob of the uppermost cabinet door where we kept the nicer plates used for company. The shortest of the three of us, I could just barely reach and had to stand on tiptoe and count with my fingertips, feeling the four edges of the plates before carefully removing them from the cupboard. But as they cleared the edge, something else came tumbling out and fell to the floor.

"Oh no," I said, hurriedly stepping down and placing the dishes on the countertop before turning to see what had fallen.

"What is it?" Mama asked from where she stood at the stove top placing potatoes into a pot of boiling water.

"I'm not sure," I said, getting to my knees and looking beneath the chair in the corner where the item had rolled. From where it hid in the shadows, all I could see was that the object was small and rounded. As my fingers wrapped around it, I noted that its surface was smooth with small notches in it. I pulled it out and into the light of the kitchen and sucked in a breath.

"Oh."

A hush fell over the kitchen as three sets of eyes took in the small wooden cup in my palm.

Madi's cup.

"Mama," I whispered, unable to look at her. "I'm so sorry."

At her silence, I risked a look and saw that she was standing stock-still, staring at the item in my hand.

"I forgot I put it up there," she said, her voice quiet. "I found it a few weeks ago and couldn't bear—" She shook her head. "I thought if I couldn't see it…"

I stood, holding the cup awkwardly in my hand, unsure what to do with it. Put it back in the cabinet from which it fell? Back into the dark like so many other things that used to grace the rooms of this house? Or put it back with the rest of the cups, where we'd see it every time we opened the cupboard door for something to pour our tea into?

"She loved that silly thing," Elif said, twisting the towel in her hand.

I stared down at it. None of us had understood her attachment to it. It was a cup. It had been in the cupboard for years, unused, until she found it and made it hers. Her little teeth marks dotted the lip of the cup all the way around. The handle, once slender and flat, had been chewed into a strange shape that reminded me of a gnarled tree root.

"Remember how she carried it everywhere?" I asked. "Always keeping it half filled with water or milk?"

"'*But I'm thirsty,*'" Elif said, repeating Madi's constant complaint.

And when she'd finished drinking whatever was in it, she'd start to chew, until our mother or father reminded her gently to stop. After which she'd go refill it and start all over again.

Mama held out her hand and I placed the cup in her palm. She ran her fingers over the teeth marks, a small, sad smile on her face, and then pressed it to her chest, a tear rolling down her cheek.

"I miss her," she whispered.

The pit in my stomach that had opened eight months ago widened once more and threatened to pull me in. Guilt and shame washed over me like a wave. Though everyone promised it wasn't my fault, I didn't believe them. I was the one who had been there with her. I was the one who didn't see until it was too late. I was the one who had watched as she was pulled from the water, pale and lifeless. Sweet Madelief, full of fire and laughter. So different from both Elif and I, with a spirit so big in a body so dainty and small. She'd loved us all with a ferocity. She was unabashed in her wants and needs, joy and fury.

"I don't know where she came from," I'd heard my mother once say to a friend about Madi as we watched her run headlong across the sand into the frigid North Sea. "She's so much. So much louder, funnier, and more spirited than any of the rest of us."

"There's always one," the woman had said with a grin.

Madi was our one. And her absence from our home—from our lives—left a stark and shuddering silence.

Mama held out the cup to me.

"Put it back, please," she said, and turned back to the stove.

"Yes, Mama."

I stepped back up onto the stool and then looked down at the cup in my hand. Inside it was one of my mother's tears. With a sigh, I placed it back in the cupboard and closed the door.

Our dinner guest, Mrs. Vox, or Aunt Liv as we called her, was an old friend of my parents'. Her brother, Henrik, had served in the Great War fighting for the Queen of England as part of the Royal Army with our father. Through him, our father and Mr. Vox met and, despite a decade and a half of age between them, they became fast friends.

The men's friendship lasted throughout the war, subsequent injuries, and a return home to Haarlem for the two—Henrik went elsewhere before finding his way back years later. My mother and Mrs. Vox took a liking to each other as well, and the elder couple became like a great-aunt and -uncle to us. And then, in a strange twist of fate, the two men died within a year of one another. Mr. Vox from a heart issue, my father from an automobile accident.

After Mr. Vox died, father had implored Mrs. Vox to come for dinner on Sundays.

"Hugo would have my hide if I didn't burden you with our too loud dinnertime chatter and common food," father had told her, to which she cracked the tiniest of grins.

When father died that following year, she arrived the following Sunday with her butler, her cook, and three wooden crates of food.

"It's time to return the favor," she'd told our mother, wrapping her in her arms.

She came most weeks, with the odd one spent at home or with other friends. But when Madelief died, she ingrained herself in our lives, taking over care of Elif and me, the household, and most importantly, our mother, who found she couldn't leave Madi's bed most days, her grief hollowing her. Were it not for Aunt Liv, I feared we wouldn't have made it through as well as we had. And I was positive our mother would've been the next to perish, leaving my sister and I orphans. But thanks to our gracious aunt, who wasn't our aunt at all, we were fed and watched over until eventually mother began to emerge from Madi's bedroom. And then participate in conversations again. And then allow us to hug her, albeit briefly, the contact almost too much for her. As though she were afraid if she let herself enjoy our presence, we might be ripped away like father and Madi. And she couldn't bear it.

The knock on the door came at exactly six o'clock, and Mama greeted Aunt Liv at the door while Elif and I finished setting the table. As always these days, I tried not to notice that not all the spaces had place settings.

"Girls," Aunt Liv said, entering the room with a restrained flourish. We hurried to kiss her cheek and take her coat and the telltale box from the fancy bakery in town.

Her perfume enveloped me like a comfortable and familiar blanket as I delivered the bakery box to the kitchen counter before being ushered into the sitting room, where we'd only moments before removed the coverings from the rarely used furniture.

"Tell me about your week," she said, her voice a mix of inviting and demanding. "Elif? How's school and what are you painting?"

Elif smiled politely and quietly rattled off the details of her week. As she spoke, I noted the large ruby brooch our guest wore at her throat, the fine silk of her dress and stockings, and the quality of the leather on her shoes. Olivia Vox was wealthy in a way most weren't, both her and her late husband descendants of prominent families, and they themselves using what they'd come from to create more. As they had no children, their money was often given to universities for funding, museums, orphanages, and...us. Nothing so obvious as a basket full of cash or a new wardrobe at the beginning of each school year. They would never want us to feel as though we were a charity—and we weren't. At least not while father was alive and his law firm, which he took over several years before his death, was thriving. No, the Vox money came to us in subtle ways. Mrs. Vox would say it was earned.

If it was manners she thought we lacked, she fed us in her dining room and taught us how the well-bred ate, drank, and kept a house. If we weren't cultured, memberships to museums and passes for the trains so we had no excuse not to go. Our palate not varied enough? A culinary expedition of all the finest restaurants in Amsterdam. She often "accidentally" bought too much fabric for a piece she wanted made, and then insisted my mother use what was left to make something either for herself, us, or to sell. It was why there was now a rack of premade clothing hemmed loosely to be sized for the purchaser.

Sometimes she had a pair of shoes made and the cobbler somehow made them too small, "forcing" her to offer them to one of us.

"But how did he manage to make them two entire sizes too small?" my mother would ask. "Perhaps you need a new cobbler."

But we knew. We always knew. And while our pride would never let her lavish us with gifts, and hers couldn't keep her from trying, we all pretended we didn't know that she was taking care of us in a most frivolous fashion that wasn't needed for survival, but did something wonderful for all our souls.

When Elif was done reciting her activities, Aunt Liv turned to me.

"How did your test go this week?" she asked. "And what are you reading?"

She also remembered everything. Her mind, she'd once told me, was oftentimes a burden.

"No matter how much information I cram inside my brain," she'd said one afternoon, a few weeks after Madelief's death, "I can never make it forget all the previous things it learned and saw. On the one hand, it's a gift. On the other…" She'd wiped a tear from her cheek then, surprising me with her rare show of emotion. "It can make life awfully hard."

"I got an A," I said. "And I'm rereading *The Hobbit*."

"Again?" She laughed.

I'd read it so many times my copy was worn, and some of the pages had come loose. I had to keep tucking them inside so I didn't lose them. Aunt Liv had bought me a new copy last year, but it was too shiny. The pages too stiff. And it lacked something else I didn't have the heart to tell her—it hadn't been given to me by my father as the other had. I didn't care how terrible its condition was. His hands had held it, and for that reason alone, I doubted I'd ever read another copy.

"I can't help it," I said. "I love it. I love the adventure and the friends Bilbo makes. The journey… But mostly I love his heroism, even though he's so very afraid."

"I suppose sometimes in fiction we find the thing we need

to raise our spirits, help us escape, and even teach us how to be brave." She reached for my hand and gave it a squeeze. "But just in case you need something new, I brought a new book for you to read. And Elif—" she turned to my sister "—a fresh set of watercolors for you." She sat back and smiled at us both. "Your father would be proud."

My chest puffed and I smiled. It was the greatest compliment she could pay.

"All the—" Mama stopped and blinked, pasting a smile on her face. "*Both* girls are doing wonderfully," she said, her voice soft as she stood, signaling it was time to move to the dining table. "They make their mother proud as well."

"But of course they do," Aunt Liv said. "And so they should strive to. Not many children can boast they have a university graduated mother. You're a rare pearl, Katrien. Both Mr. Vox and I always said so. And of course your Willem knew. That's what happens when girls are born to intellectuals. They are pushed to succeed themselves. It's so important and doesn't happen enough if you ask me. More girls should be encouraged to be educated past high school. Then fewer women would feel the need to populate the world with dimwits!"

Mama pressed her lips together, but they didn't hold. As always, Aunt Liv could lighten the mood and brighten our day. We all laughed at her opinionated view of her own gender. She loved kids, she'd often told us. She just didn't understand why there had to be so many of them, especially when there were some whose parents could barely afford to clothe or feed them.

"If the mothers would just educate themselves first, they'd learn economics and how often less is more."

"Says the woman who brought a box of desserts that could feed two families," Mama said, raising an eyebrow.

"When it comes to dessert," Aunt Liv said, "less is more has no place in the conversation."

After dinner we returned to the sitting room with a fresh pot of tea and a set of dessert plates gifted to us by our dear aunt at Christmas.

"Dessert deserves a proper pedestal," she'd declared.

I had to admit, it did seem tastier when presented on white porcelain with hand-painted blue flowers and scalloped edges.

"Not to put a damper on the evening," Aunt Liv said, taking a bite of her little cake, a confection covered in white icing with the tiniest of pink flowers cascading over the side. Aunt Liv never did anything halfway, including picking out desserts. "But have you been listening to the news?"

The two adults exchanged a glance, and a shiver pricked up my spine as my mother gave the elder woman a nod. "I have," she said.

"I fear we might not be so lucky as to stay neutral this time around," Aunt Liv said.

"But," I started, "the queen said—"

"I know," she said, holding up a manicured hand, the band of her wedding ring gleaming under the light of the lamps. "I've heard her speeches as well. But this war, I fear, will be on a much grander scale than the last one. And our country's location could be key. We, unfortunately, stand between two major battling countries. Either one may want access to our beaches and airfields, giving us a terrifying front row seat this time around."

I glanced down the sofa to Elif, who sat stock-still at the other end, her worried gray-blue eyes staring back. But frightened as I was by this information, experience with feeling helpless spurred me to rise and hurry to the foyer where my coat hung. I pulled the crumpled flyer from my pocket and returned to the room.

"What's that?" Mama asked.

I stared down at the paper in my hand, my thumb playing with the corner, and then handed it to Aunt Liv who lifted her brows as she took it and opened it.

"Where did you find this?" Her voice was quiet.

"In the park. It fell from a plane."

"Liv?" Mama said, getting to her feet to come see.

"Do you know what it says?" I asked. "Does it mean something that there are Nazi signs here? Are they—here?"

Elif's gasp was almost inaudible and I felt the cushion we shared shift, but my eyes were on the adults whose demeanor, though slight, had changed with the question, and I got the sneaking suspicion they were both working hard not to exchange another look. .

Aunt Liv smoothed her hands over the skirt of her dress.

"Well, I certainly don't know," she said. "But should I hear of anything, I'll be sure to inform your mother. Until then, please be careful. Watch what you say and who you say it around, understand?"

I nodded.

Not long afterward I retrieved Aunt Liv's coat and bag, and the four of us walked single file to the front door and took turns hugging and kissing her, before the walls and windows began to tremble around us.

"I wish they'd stop!" Elif said, her brow furrowing as she placed her hands over her ears.

It was a common complaint by her these days, but this time there was something besides the usual annoyance in her voice.

Fear.

Mama reached for her, then me. And as the engines of the low flying warplanes rumbled overhead, shaking us to our very cores, Aunt Liv wrapped us all in her perfumed embrace.

3

A brittle wind crackled over the curved rooftops, unfurling down their tilted faces before slipping beneath my layers. I shivered and tucked my chin farther into my scarf, gripping the handlebars of my bicycle and pressing harder on the pedals.

"Slow down!" Elif yelled from behind me.

I eased off my pedals a touch. In the past many months I'd become driven in all things, focused on the task at hand. I made everything a purpose, no matter if it were homework, running an errand for my mother, or riding my bicycle to school.

"Sorry," I said, giving her an apologetic half smile when she caught up.

"It's fine," she said, panting a little. "I'm used to it."

Guilt sliced through me. I knew Elif was hurting as bad as I was after the loss of our younger sister. I knew my pulling away was not only hurting me, but her as well. No matter how different we were, we'd always moved and made choices as a unit. It didn't matter that I liked schoolwork and she didn't. That she was creative and I was more logical. That I liked to be outdoors, playing, the wind in my hair and on my skin, and she'd rather sit with a cup of tea and her paintbrushes. But then Madi was gone, and we'd found our ways of coping were not the same. She withdrew while I pushed forward.

"I won't do it again," I said, reaching over and placing my hand on her arm before returning it to my handlebars.

She smiled and nodded.

At school, we waved goodbye to one another and hurried off in different directions. I pushed through the heavy doors into the school and strode through the halls.

"One minute late," a teasing voice said as I rounded the corner to where every morning I met my two best friends.

I met the dark brown eyes of Tess, whose grin faltered when I checked my watch in a panic.

"I'm early by at least three minutes," I said.

"It was a joke."

Her voice was quiet as she glanced at our friend Fenna, in hopes of exchanging the same commiserating glance they'd been sharing for months now. But Fenna was busy digging through her book bag, her brow creased in frustration.

"What's wrong?" I asked.

"I can't find my assignment that's due first period."

"Are you sure you did it?" Tess asked, earning a glare from our friend.

"Of course I *did* it," Fenna said, her voice tight. "And I know I put it in here. I just can't find it."

"You will," I said.

She took in a long breath and then exhaled, her shoulders relaxing. Her eyes met mine and filled with tears.

"My father..." she said, and I nodded.

Fenna's parents were strict, expecting nothing but the absolute best from their only child. Fenna constantly voiced her incredulity that they ever decided to have a kid, since neither of them seemed particularly interested in her as a person. Only in her as an extension of them. And since they were prominent members of society, missing assignments would not do.

"Found it!" she said, pulling it free, her body seeming to wilt in relief.

"Of course you did," I said, and she flashed me a grateful smile.

We meandered down the hall then in the direction of our first-period classes, chatting about the evening before and the planes that had shaken the city.

"We were in the middle of dinner," Tess said. "Mama dropped her glass and got water everywhere."

"We were seeing Aunt Liv to the door," I said. "That sound startled me nearly to death."

"I don't know why they have to fly so low," Fenna said. "If they're not attacking us, it just seems a cruel trick." She looked at me. "Did your mom or Aunt Liv say anything about it?"

I wondered what the two older women would think if they knew how often my friends asked about their thoughts and opinions. If they knew how they were revered. It used to bother me, making me feel as though they cared more about my relations than me, that they liked them better than me, until I witnessed how little time Tess's parents had for her, her father a busy family doctor, her mother raising three kids. And Fenna's father was a barrister like mine had been, but found himself far more important than he was, while her mother ran his office. They worked late hours, often through the weekends, and expected that their only child take care of herself so they didn't have to be burdened.

But then I realized. They didn't not care about me—they envied me. The interest and time paid to me by these intelligent, older women. My opinion mattered. My company was enjoyed and wanted. I was privy to information, ideas, and plans. And so I stopped feeling jealous of their inquiries. Stopped holding the knowledge I'd gained so close to my chest, and shared what was shared with me, bringing them into the fold and delighting in their excitement at being included.

I leaned in, causing the two of them to step closer, bowing their heads to hear my lowered voice. "Aunt Liv said she doesn't think we'll be able to stay neutral this time. She thinks the queen is wrong and that Germany will want to use our airfields."

Fenna's eyes widened and Tess sucked in a breath. I reached out and squeezed her arm. We'd heard rumors of Jews being arrested in Germany for reasons we didn't understand and couldn't quite believe. Whispers of a manifesto written by the country's leader years before had made the rounds in the school hallways more than once, prompting several teachers to touch on the subject, to educate, inform, and to try and quell any worries.

"The Netherlands will remain neutral," was practically drilled into our heads.

But one began to wonder, and it was hard to deny the possibility of our country having to take a side, which then begged the question: Were we better off siding with England, or Germany? Which led to a more horrifying question. Should we side with Germany, a prospect too terrible to comprehend, and the Gestapo came here, what would that mean for our Jewish community?

We'd learned through newspaper articles and reports on the radio of countries being attacked and German soldiers moving in. But it was through Aunt Liv that we'd heard worse rumors. Whispers of the unthinkable. Of Jews, men and women alike, elders and children, forced to leave their homes and sent off to work camps in remote destinations. It sounded absolutely terrifying, but it was the look on our aunt's face as she told us in a lowered voice that bothered me most. A look of not just worry, but fear. And if Aunt Liv was scared, we all should be.

"Mrs. Vox isn't the final word on anything, though," I said, hoping to lessen the worry now etched on their faces.

"But she hears things. She knows people who know things," Tess said, digging in her bag.

I couldn't deny it, and most things Aunt Liv had warned about over the years due to her connections had proven true. But I had to believe that this time our queen's word would prevail over my aunt's cursed ability to always be right.

"It's high time she was wrong," I said, and offered what I hoped was an encouraging smile.

Tess pulled out her green enamel compact and stared in the small round mirror, dabbing at her eyes, trying to distract herself from what this could mean for the town, and for the Jewish community she was a part of.

"Do you think freckles fade with age?" she asked, staring at the tawny spots she always complained about sprinkled over her straight nose and pretending she wasn't upset by what I'd just said.

Fenna and I looked at one another. Her earlier irritation disappeared behind a familiar twinkle of mirth that nudged at my hardened heart. "Yes," she said. "I hear once you reach eighteen they completely disappear."

Tess's bark of laughter filled the hall, and Fenna and I joined her. As she slipped her compact back into her bag, she changed the subject to the upcoming weekend.

"We should go to the beach," she said. "It's been ages."

Both girls glanced hesitantly at me, waiting for me to turn down the idea, as I had most ideas since the tragedy that had struck my family eight months ago. I couldn't remember the last time we'd spent an evening giggling well into the night, filling our mouths with treats and talking about boys we thought were cute. But since that day, I hadn't been able to stomach allowing myself to have fun. I didn't deserve lightness and laughter, no matter what anyone else said.

"Maybe," I said, and checked my watch.

"She said maybe," Fenna said, her eyes wide.

"It wasn't a no!" Tess said.

I rolled my eyes. "It wasn't a yes," I said.

"Close enough for me," Tess said.

"We'll just...see." I began backing away toward my first period class. "Don't get your hopes up, okay?"

"Too late!" Fenna said.

I shook my head and turned, hurrying through the bodies that now filled the hall, my heart heavy. There was no way I could go to the beach. I'd made plans to take Madelief there three days after the accident. I'd promised her. And then she'd died and the thought of going without her made my stomach twist into a knot. I'd failed her. I didn't deserve to forget and move on. To have fun in her absence.

It felt like dancing on her grave.

As soon as I entered the door to Mr. Aberman's literature class, my friends and the beach were forgotten.

"Good morning, Miss Vinke," Mr. Aberman said from where he sat at his desk at the front of the classroom.

"Good morning, sir," I said, my eyes taking in the words on the chalkboard.

Every Monday morning a quote was written across the board, which we were meant to use as inspiration to compose a short essay. We didn't have to know where it came from, we only had to interpret what we thought it meant, debate it, or describe how it related to our own life. It was one of my favorite exercises.

I hurried to my seat, pulled out a sheet of paper and pencil and got to work. I was five sentences in when the bell rang, several stragglers flying in the door at the very last second.

As I gathered my things at the end of the class hour, my mind returned to the essay. Was my argument strong enough? Since I'd decided to pursue a career in law like my father, arguing a point was something I'd taken pride in improving on and I was determined to put it into practice whenever the occasion presented itself, much to my mother's irritation.

"You don't have to argue every point" was her new constant phrase.

But I wanted to win. I wanted to do as he had done; stick up for those who couldn't stick up for themselves. Prove innocence. Save the downtrodden. Never mind that I was a woman, some of his brilliance must be in my genes. And combined with my mother's own university triumphs, surely I was destined for greater than just a small town life by the sea. Surely there was something inside me that would get me far, far away from here and all the pain that resided in this place.

I waved to Mr. Aberman as I left the classroom and hurried down the hall to my science class where I slid into my seat while some of the previous class was still exiting.

Ignoring the noise around me, I pulled my textbook out and reread the first page of the chapter we were starting today, which I'd already read the night before when the memory of the low flying planes was still vibrating in my bones, keeping me awake. Never one to waste an opportunity to study, I'd grabbed my book and made myself comfortable on the floral settee in the library.

"Have you memorized the entire chapter already?"

I looked up and felt my cheeks warm.

Most of my classes were with peers from my own grade, but this one was a mix of ages, which included Diederik Claasen, a senior boy I'd recently noticed and had developed a small crush on.

It wasn't much of a crush, to be honest. Not like the full-blown "I'm going to marry him one day" monthly episodes Tess had, scribbling her name next to some boy's surname in her notebook—until her interest died and she moved on to the next one. Fenna and I could never keep up.

No, I had other more important things on my mind than boys. But Diederik had caught my attention a few weeks before when I'd dropped my pencil and it had rolled between his feet.

"Here you are," he'd said, handing it back.

When I'd met his eyes, I was startled by the crisp blue of his irises. The square line of his jaw. The way his blond hair swept off his forehead, the comb lines visible in a gleaming and perfect wave.

"Diederik Claasen is strange," Tess had said when I'd mentioned the encounter that day at lunch.

"Strange how?" Fenna had asked.

"I've heard he has no friends."

"That sounds sad, not strange," I'd said.

"He's been here over a year. He barely talks to anyone, and when he does, he's curt and not very friendly. And his parents never attend social events."

Fenna and I had exchanged a look. While my mother rarely attended social events, not enjoying going without my father, her parents always did.

"Any opportunity to show off what their money can buy," she'd bitterly said once.

"Maybe he's just shy," Fenna said now.

"Maybe he's not good with people," I said. "Not everyone is a social butterfly like you, Tess."

"Which is unfortunate," Tess said. "Life would be so much easier if everyone were more talkative."

As she'd said that, the object of her own affection walked by, completely oblivious to her charms and the clothing ensemble she'd painstakingly put together.

"It's the freckles, isn't it?" she'd asked, causing Fenna and I to roll our eyes at one another.

I didn't spend much time thinking of Diederik Claasen outside the science classroom. But while we were in class, there were times I found my gaze blurring out the teacher, my mind wandering as I wondered what it would be like be asked out by the older boy who sat so stoically behind me. What we would talk about if he did. And what it would feel like to hold his hand, which I'd noticed was large and strong-looking.

When the bell rang at the end of class, I was so intent on the passage I was reading I jumped, knocking my pencil to the floor where it rolled beneath his desk once again.

"This seems to be becoming a habit," he said with a smile as he handed the writing utensil to me.

His fingers were cold, his gaze piercing, and I swallowed, unsure why I felt unsettled.

I gave him a small grin and took the pencil from his hand. "You must think me clumsy."

"I think several things about you. Clumsy does not happen to be one of them."

With that he stood, grabbed his things, and gave me a parting smile before leaving.

"Tell me again," Tess said at lunch when I told them what had happened in science class.

I sighed and finished chewing my bite of sandwich, and then repeated the entire short exchange once more.

"Well, I still think he's weird," she said. "But at least he's interesting *and* weird."

"He's nice to look at too," Fenna said.

"True," Tess said, running a hand over her dark brown curls, held in place by a pearl clip. She was wearing one of her usual outfits of expensive sweater over paint-stained and untucked blouse with a mostly wrinkled navy skirt, a pair of stockings, and oxfords. By contrast, the pale blue headband that held back Fenna's straight, black hair perfectly matched the skirt she wore. Her blouse was white, starched, and was one of at least a dozen matching ones that hung in her closet, and her shoes were so shiny I could probably see my reflection in them. I continuously marveled at how two girls could present so differently.

"But are good looks and being interesting enough to get past the weird bit?" Tess asked, unwilling to give up the subject.

"Honestly, Tess," I said. "I couldn't care in the least."

She stuck her lower lip out in a pout and turned to Fenna to discuss the matter further while I pulled out my math homework to look it over one more time before I had to hand it in during my next class.

"There she goes again," I heard Tess say. I looked up, prepared to defend myself, but Fenna was already elbowing her.

"Give her a break," she said, throwing me a wink. "One of us has to pass the ninth grade, and the way you keep staring at boys rather than studying, it sure isn't going to be you."

I gave her a grateful grin while Tess pretended to be wounded, which lasted all of a few seconds because a handsome face walked by, drawing her attention, making Fenna and I shake our heads just as the bell signaling lunch's end rang.

It was an unspoken agreement that every day after school Elif and I would ride home together. There was a sweet comfort to the routine that I counted on. Even if we were so different, the fact that one of us was always waiting for the other, that I could look ahead or behind me as we rode and find her familiar form, was a salve on the tender underside of my emotions that I kept so tightly bound.

Today she rode ahead of me and a few blocks in, slowed so that we were riding side by side.

"How was your day?" she asked, her expression earnest and caring.

I was reminded of all the years previous when she'd so often owned her older sister role with such seriousness, her eyes constantly watching my every move. And then Madelief's, until Madelief was no longer there. For reasons unknown, with our younger sister's death, Elif had become less attentive to my comings and goings, rather than more so. As if she'd somehow disconnected herself from me with the loss of our other sibling.

If I were to let myself think about it too much, I might be lonely. And so I didn't.

"It was good," I said and then smiled, thinking of my unexpected exchange with a certain blond boy in science class. "How was yours?"

"Boring."

We laughed then, just two sisters thrilled by the mediocrity of our days. No drama. No worries. Just a day. There was something to be said for it, and even something to celebrate about it.

At home we made ourselves a snack before settling in the library with our homework.

As usual, Elif sprawled out on the floral settee, creating a mess of papers around her. I never knew how she found anything working that way, and shook my head as she flipped furiously through a textbook before making myself a nest out of throw pillows and blankets on the floor and pulling a notebook from my bag.

Chewing the end of my pencil, my gaze moved around the beloved space that was our home as I contemplated the report I was assigned to write.

As always, the white walls, wood floors, and spare but pretty furniture in shades of blues and pale greens soothed me. There were large rugs to sink our toes into on cold mornings, which was most mornings, brick arches that led from one room to another, wood beams and corbels that gave the space character, and various objects my parents had collected on holiday before they'd had children, including a silly porcelain dog my mother always shook her head at but that my father had loved for reasons no one understood.

Despite my father's death three years ago, and Madelief's more recently, this house, filled with too many memories to name, still brought peace despite the accompanying pain. No matter that they were no longer here, that their places at the table were bare, that Madelief's bedroom door was always closed. It was because they had once been here, that I could still hear the echoes of them, his laugh and her giggle, his heavy footfalls and her bare feet whispering across the hardwood, that brought me comfort—even when those same things threatened to shred my heart to pieces.

"Lien?"

"Hmm?" I said, looking up at Elif beside me.

"You're crying."

Surprised, I reached up and touched the tears I hadn't felt streaking down my face.

"So I am," I said, meeting her frown with a reassuring smile.

But I could see she was still worried. Always the big sister fretting over her younger one.

I tore a blank page from my notebook, crumpled it, aimed, and threw it. It bounced off her nose.

Her jump of wide-eyed surprise made me laugh and she drew her own weapon, sending a ball of paper flying my way—and missing by a good half meter.

"Sure Shot," she said with a grin before returning her focus to her work.

"Sure Shot," I whispered.

It was a nickname bestowed upon me by our father. He'd always proclaimed an extreme distaste of war, and the time he'd spent fighting. The loss of life around him, and the loss of life he'd personally been responsible for. But he'd also found he had a talent for shooting.

"I hated that I was good at it at first," he'd told Elif and me the first time he'd taken us out for target practice. "But later, after the war—after I was safe at home, your mother beside me—I learned the value of the skill. Not the killing. But the protecting."

And so he'd taught us to protect ourselves. To respect the power of weaponry. The feel of the cool metal in our hands, and the sharp lurch as the gun kicked back into our palms. I thought it was fun. A game. I loved shooting the targets he set up for us. Like him, I had a natural talent for it. I hit my target nearly every time, earning me the nickname that had stuck until the day he died.

"You couldn't miss if you tried," father said time and time again.

I stared at the crumpled paper that had bounced off Elif's nose. We'd stopped going shooting after a while, when I began to complain. I didn't want to stand in the woods for hours when I had friends to spend time with. And Elif, who'd never quite taken to the sport anyway, looked thrilled at the prospect of not going. And so, with a look of disappointment I pretended not to see, he agreed. No more target practice. When he died, though, I regretted it. If anything, it was time we got to spend together while he told us stories, taught us bad words out of the earshot of our mother, and learned about the daughters he'd always dreamed of raising. I regretted taking those moments from him. And was ashamed I'd robbed myself of them.

We were still working when Mama arrived home after work, laden with reams of fabric and a cloth bag filled with meat from the butcher and a fresh loaf of bread. Setting our homework aside, we washed up to make dinner, shooing her to the library to relax with a cup of tea.

After we ate, the three of us, as we so often did, returned to the library, Elif and I to finish our homework, mother to work on some pieces she'd brought home from the shop. The hum of the sewing machine was the soothing, ever-present background noise of our lives. It was almost startling when the needle stopped for a thread to be cut or a garment to be turned, causing me and my sister to look up every time as if to make sure all was still right with the world.

As the evening went on, one by one we finished up our tasks. First Elif, who began gathering her papers, organizing them in her bag. I was next, closing my notebook and setting it and my pencil in my own bag. And then mother, snipping a thread, shaking out the garment, and sliding it onto a hanger.

"I forgot to tell you," Mama said as we gathered in the kitchen to make tea. "Olivia came by the shop today."

There was something in her voice that made my sister and I turn, but her back was to us as she poured water from the kettle into the pot.

"Is Aunt Liv having something made?" Elif asked, her eyes darting to mine as if perhaps I knew something, but I just shrugged. It wasn't odd for Aunt Liv to go by the shop. What was odd was it being mentioned.

"No…" Mama turned and gave a hesitant smile at the sight of us standing and watching her. "She came by to inform me that the flyer you found, Lien, is not the first of its kind seen around here. There have been others. Not many, but they've been spotted, and quickly removed."

"But—" My mind reeled as I tried to latch on to a thought. "Does that mean, someone from the Gestapo came and hung them?"

She pursed her lips. "It is more likely that someone here hung them."

The room was quiet.

"You mean," Elif said, "one of us? Someone… Dutch?"

"That's exactly what I mean." She looked from Elif to me and then waved a hand at us. "Come. Let's bring this to the library."

We quickly helped her load the teapot, cups, and biscuits onto a tray and made ourselves comfortable in the small, cozy room.

"Why would one of our countrymen hang such a thing?" I asked.

"Don't be naive," Mama said. "It could just as easily have been a woman."

I turned wide eyes to Elif.

"Perhaps," Mama said, "their views align with *his*."

Hitler. I shuddered to think that anybody—any *Dutch* anybody—could possibly agree with the German führer. A man who believed he was part of a "superior" race and justified to send Jews off to work camps, the conditions of which we had recently heard were appalling.

"How could anyone—"

"People are blind. Desperate. Willing to believe lies if they can find something in that lie that says their life will be better for it. Even if people get hurt in their pursuit of that life."

"Tess…" I said, my eyes filling with tears.

"I know." Her voice was soft as she rose from her seat to sit beside me on the floor and take me in her arms. "But let's try not to worry too much. Nothing's happened yet, and may not."

But my mind told me I needed to act. To make a plan. I leaned into her, smelling her lavender perfume, the familiar curves of her body, so soft and warm and comforting. Hugging, once common in our household, had become a hesitant action. All of us afraid to allow ourselves the simple pleasure of holding and being held. It had been weeks since the last time I'd allowed her to be close to me. And in truth, it had been weeks since she'd tried.

"I'm scared," I whispered.

"Me too, Lien," she said. "Me too."

4

For the next couple of weeks, the sun made a daily appearance, brightening the oft gray skies and warming the near constant wind to a manageable temperature.

The nicer weather brought out shoppers in droves, and our mother's shop was a welcome recipient of women looking to have new dresses made for the warmer season, old ones hemmed or refashioned to reflect the newest styles, and a few men whose professional wardrobes needed alterations.

An uptick in business meant Elif and I were needed after school to help with sales, making deliveries, and running constantly to the back room for thread, fabric, or orders being picked up.

"And bring the navy thread," Mama called to me as I raced to the back to grab a suit jacket for a male client. "And the tan!"

I nearly collided with Elif as she hurried out with a pale green frock in hand.

"Oof!" I said, bumping into the doorway.

"Sorry!" she called over her shoulder.

Sifting through a rack of men's jackets, I found the one I was looking for, pulled it free, and hung it on the end before going in search of the needed thread colors.

An old bureau held hundreds of wooden spools in different sizes, their color schemes listed by drawer. I knelt and pulled out the second to bottom drawer and removed the navy. Three drawers up was every shade of brown imaginable. Shoving a tan in my pocket, I turned, my heel catching on the chair at the table behind me where a stack of fabric, folded and waiting to be put away, teetered. I reached out to steady it and then slid it over to rest against the wall, but it bumped into something and the top half spilled over.

"Darn it," I whispered, staring at the mess, but I didn't have time to clean it up now.

I returned to the storefront with the items my mother needed.

"What a mess," I heard Mama say an hour later from the back room.

I hurried through the door, my arms laden with garments brought in for alterations.

"Sorry, Mama," I said, cringing to find her staring at the pile of fabric on the floor. "I knocked it over earlier and haven't had time to clean it up. I'll do it now."

The bell on the shop door chimed, and she sighed and swiped the back of her hand across her brow. She'd been staying late to keep up with orders for over a week and working all day on the weekends. At night, Elif and I kissed the top of her head before climbing the stairs to bed as the sewing machine hummed its song. I never knew what time she finally went to bed, but she was often back in her seat when we came down for breakfast in the morning.

She gave me a distracted nod, her eyes taking in the mess once more, and then slid past me to greet whoever had come in.

I hung the clothing in my arms on the "To Do" rack in the order of the dates on their tags and turned my attention to the material that had been knocked down and trampled on in our hasty comings and goings.

As I bent to pick up the fabric, I noticed the culprit that had led to the tipping of the tower. A slender box was on the table between the stack of still folded remnants and the wall. Sliding it from its hiding spot, I lifted the lid and frowned at the contents.

Inside was a small stack of blank identification cards, pencils, an ink pad, pens, and a stamp. For a long moment I stared down at the items, trying to make sense of them. But having no idea what they were for or why they'd be in the back of my mother's sewing shop, I put the lid back in place with a shrug and slid the box back where it had been.

My hand was on the doorknob when it hit me. I turned and scanned the room, looking for anything that seemed out of place or like it didn't belong. But it wasn't easy in such a small space. There were boxes, reams of fabric, clothing... If there were things to be hidden, this was both a great space and a terrible one. There was no room for anything extra. It was packed to the gills.

Deciding I was wrong about what my mother may or may not be doing with a bunch of blank identification cards, I moved back to the table and began folding the mountain of fabric.

"How are you doing back here?" she asked a little while later, poking her head in.

I wanted to ask her about the cards, but the slivers of dark beneath her eyes, little bruises of exhaustion, stopped me.

"Almost done," I said.

"Good. I've locked the doors and Elif is sweeping." She stopped talking and stood in the doorway, watching me.

"Is there something else?" I asked.

Her smile was wan and she shook her head. "No. I was just thinking, how about we eat at a restaurant tonight?"

"Really?"

It had been ages since we'd eaten anything but a home-cooked meal, and the thought of sitting at a restaurant and being served sounded wonderful.

"Really. It's been a long week, and I think we could all use a nice meal out. Even though I may fall asleep at the table before the food arrives."

She did not fall asleep at the table, though she was quieter than usual as she listened to Elif and I prattle on about our day at school.

After we ate, we hurried home beneath a clear sky streaked with shades of orange and pink, the wind off the North Sea whisking alongside our feet.

Once we were safe inside our house, Mama lit a fire in the fireplace while I put on the kettle for tea and Elif cut thick slices of the sweet dikke koek we'd baked a few days before, and slathered butter on them for dessert.

As I sank into my nest of blankets and pillows in the library, I noticed the cloth bag our mother used to tote scraps of fabric home, full and sitting on the floor near her feet.

"Mama," I said, a whine in my voice, "I'm never going to be as good a seamstress as you. Please don't make me try."

"Hmm?" she said, finishing a sip of tea and following my gaze to the bag. "Oh. Those aren't for you." She looked at Elif and shook her head. "Nor you. I'm using them to make blankets."

I looked down at the pile I was sitting on. We had plenty of blankets.

"Not for us," she said, her voice quiet.

"Then for whom?" I asked.

"For whomever might need them," she said. "In war, it's always the basic needs people lack desperately."

"But we're not at war, Mama," Elif said.

"You're right, Elif," Mama said. "But should that change…"

I met my sister's worried glance with my own and took a bite of my cake, forcing myself to turn my attention to Elif's newest creation, a muted painting of a field of pale tulips spread out before a windmill. She'd brought it down from our room the night before, and it sat propped against one of the bookcases.

"I think it's your best yet," I said, and she smiled.

After school on Friday, Elif and I rode our bicycles to the shop to help out.

Mama was on her knees on the floor with straight pins in her mouth as she adjusted the hem of a pair of trousers for the woman standing on the pedestal. She nodded as we came in the door and hurried to the back room to drop off our bags before returning to the storefront to help out.

"How was your day?" she asked a while later as I counted the money in the till.

"Fine," I said.

"And the science exam?"

"It was fine. I got an A."

"Of course you did," she said. "You've stayed up so late studying all week. I knew you'd do well."

"Thank you, Mama," I said, my voice quiet.

"You know," she said, straightening the items on the counter beside the register, "you should really have that watch fixed." She looked around the room, which was empty now, save for the two of us and Elif, who was sweeping scraps of fabric and thread from the floor. "Why don't you run over to the Ten Booms and have them take a look."

I looked down at the threadbare strap, sagging on my wrist. "Are you sure? What if the shop gets busy again?"

"You won't be gone long. Go ahead. You don't want it to fall off your wrist and get lost."

It was true. I'd be devastated if I lost my watch.

"Okay then," I said. "I'll be back soon."

The Ten Booms watch and clock shop was only a few doors down from my mother's store. A little bell on the door announced my arrival and Casper, the owner, looked up from where he was seated at the counter repairing a clock.

"Well, hello there, Miss Vinke. How can I help you?" he asked, setting his tool aside.

"My watch strap needs mending," I said, removing it and setting it before him.

He lifted it and turned it over in his hands. "Looks like it needs an entire new band."

My breath caught. "Is it possible to save the band? It was my father's."

"Hmm. Well, the stitching is coming undone and the leather where it's sewn is pretty worn."

"Can you sew it in a different spot? It's big on me anyway. Maybe you can make it smaller?"

He peered through his glasses and nodded.

"That would work, yes. But you might be able to see where the old stitches were."

"That's okay," I said, smiling. "I think I'd actually like that."

"Well, okay then. It will be a few days until I can get it done. We recently got several pieces in that need fixing."

"I'm fine with that," I said.

"Alright then. Come check in with me next Tuesday. Oh—" He stood. "I almost forgot. Can you take something to your mother?"

"Of course."

He bent, disappearing behind the counter for a moment. When he stood again, he was holding a plain, slender box. I peered at it for a moment, wondering why it looked familiar.

"Please give her this," he said, handing it to me. "And I will see you next week."

I waved as I left and had barely gone ten steps when it hit me. The back room of my mother's store. That was where I'd seen a box like the one in my hands before.

Stepping out of the way of foot traffic, I looked around and then quickly lifted the lid. Sure enough, inside was another small stack of blank identification cards. I replaced the lid and hurried on my way.

"That was quicker than I thought," Mama said as I came in the door, her gaze taking in the box under my arm.

"Mr. Ten Boom wanted me to give this to you."

"Oh?" she said, averting her gaze. "Well, why don't you just set it in the back room for now, and I'll take a look at whatever it is later."

I did as I was told, a dozen questions racing through my mind as I set the box on the table amid a tape measure, pins, and a beautiful piece of brocade fabric. Tracing my fingers over its woven floral pattern, the metallic threads running through it winking up at me beneath the desk light in the corner, my brain landed on a single thought: a memory of my grandmother after she'd witnessed Elif and I hedging at doing something we'd been told.

"De Lange girls don't stand idly by. They take action. Always have. Always will."

Even at eight years old, I'd wanted to challenge my grandmother. To tell her we weren't de Lange girls. We were Vinke girls. But I'd feared her piercing stare and hadn't dared. Instead, I'd nodded and scurried off behind Elif.

The words had stuck with me, though. They'd made me see my mother in a different light. One I'd forgotten about in the past few years as tragedy struck our family not once but twice in too-quick succession. I remembered now, though.

My mother was a woman of action.

But what action was she taking?

I searched the table for the other box, finding it tucked beneath a small case of sewing supplies on the floor. When I opened it, I found all that remained inside were the writing implements. The blank documents were gone.

At the end of the day, we locked up the shop and rode our

bicycles to Bloemendaal for dinner at Aunt Liv's home. Normally, I rode ahead. This evening, though, I lagged behind her and my sister, my eyes watching our mother with curiosity. She was doing something, I was convinced. Keeping a secret. Holding back information. Not that it wasn't allowed. She was our parent. But I did find it intriguing. And possibly a bit frightening. What could she be doing that she felt the need to keep it from us? The only times I'd known her or our father to keep Elif and I in the dark was when they'd thought something too dangerous or salacious for our ears.

We glided along the curving streets of the wealthy community by the sea Aunt Liv resided in, and my attention turned to the massive homes with their gated properties and pristine lawns. As we came around the bend to her street, my attention gravitated to one house in particular.

I'd always known the gray-painted wood-and-brick home on the corner belonged to the family of the quiet blond boy from my science class. But today, after our last encounter, my heartbeat quickened at the sight of Diederik Claasen's house, and I found myself wondering what he might be doing within the walls of the handsome, if not austere, residence. But the many windows were dark, leaving me to conclude its occupants were away.

We coasted through the gates of Aunt Liv's home and parked our bicycles next to the large, gleaming black flower boxes filled with cascading vines and budding plants before climbing the steps and knocking on the arched front doors.

As always, I stood with my head tilted in awe. The house was made entirely of brick with elegant white trim and shining black shutters flanking each of the many windows alight with a golden glow. It was at once overwhelming and inviting.

The landscaped property that stretched out around it was green and lush with sculpted shrubbery, small clusters of flowers in every color imaginable, beautiful weeping ornamental trees, their gently waving branches sweeping down over ornate stone benches, and tall cedars and pines beyond, encasing the entire property, making it feel like a world unto itself.

The front door opened, and we were let in by Alard, Aunt Liv's longtime butler.

"Good evening, ma'am." He nodded to our mother before turning to us. "Ladies."

"Good evening, Alard," we said.

"Kat." Aunt Liv's voice floated down the staircase to us as she greeted our mother, and then us. "Elif. Lien. I'm so glad to see you. How is everyone doing?"

As usual, she was dressed with understated elegance in a navy blouse, crisp, white trousers, a string of large white pearls around her neck, and a pair of flawless, white high-heeled shoes. Her gray hair was swept back in an elegant updo held in place by a pearl-encrusted comb, her sharp green eyes accentuated by a thin line of brown, and her lips painted the most delicate pale mauve.

As she led us through the house, she and mother spoke of their days while Elif and I looked for any new additions to the grand home. There were always one or two details that had changed, and it was a favorite game of ours to see who could spot them first.

We walked through a sitting room, another smaller sitting room, the library, and a study before finally reaching the dining room. Each room was painted or decorated in the color of a jewel. Emerald, ruby, citrine, pearl...but the dining room was my favorite. With pristine blue walls the color of sapphires, and rich velvet curtains, napkins, candles, and lamps in the same deep hue. Above us were two large chandeliers dripping with crystals and creating prisms of color on the gold tablecloth with its blue jacquard runner and a floral arrangement so large and exotic-looking, I imagined, as I always did as we took our seats, that this was what it felt like to dine with royalty.

"Will Henrik be joining us?" Mama asked.

Aunt Liv's mouth twisted in amusement. In all the years my

sister and I had been alive, neither of us had ever met Aunt Liv's younger brother. We knew only that he'd been a school friend of our mother's, and later a war buddy of our father's. But war had left him injured and disfigured, and with no desire to socialize, even with those who knew and loved him. He lived on the property, though I wasn't sure where. I assumed in one of the many bedrooms on one of the three floors. And whenever he made a rare appearance in town, word spread like wildfire.

"Did you see him?"

"He's frightening to look at."

"He made a baby cry."

But whenever we mentioned it to mother, she just waved a hand and smiled. "Oh, Henrik," she always said. "Always one to play up the rumors."

"You ask every time," Aunt Liv said and then sighed, a sadness creeping in to her expression. "Could I but drag him here… But I could promise him new fingers and he still wouldn't come."

"I know," Mama said. "But I have to ask. It's been so long since I've seen him."

"I reprimand him every time you leave. He acts properly contrite at least." The two women laughed. "He did say, when I invited him earlier today, to give you his love."

"Oh, he did not," Mama said, snorting delicately. "Now you're just lying."

Aunt Liv grinned and covered her mouth with a manicured hand, a giant yellow stone glinting in the lights of the chandeliers. Not many people could get away with calling Olivia Vox a liar. Her standing in the community was one of great respect, and most people assumed that because of her position, she probably wasn't any fun to be around. I loved overhearing people whisper as she walked by, in awe of her intelligence, wealth, and flawless attire.

"You're right," she said and then waved to the table. "I don't know why I bother trying to fool you. You know him too well.

Anyway, let's have a drink, shall we?" She signaled to one of the kitchen staff standing by and he poured wine for the two women, and tea for my sister and I.

While we talked about school and things we were looking forward to this summer, Alard appeared to murmur something to Aunt Liv.

"Frans is here?" she said, glancing at our mother in surprise before dabbing at her lips with her napkin. "Well, invite him in." She turned to another member of the staff and pointed to the table. "Bring in another setting, won't you, Max? And a glass of whiskey."

"Of course, ma'am."

Frans was actually Frans van der Wiel, or Uncle Frannie, as Elif and I called him. Like Aunt Liv wasn't really our aunt, Uncle Frannie wasn't really our uncle. He had fought in the Great War with our father, Mr. Vox, and Henrik, and afterward had kept in touch with the three. He visited as often as he could when father and Mr. Vox were still alive, making special trips to see Henrik wherever he was hiding out. Father used to tell us he considered the men his brothers. And like a brother, after father passed, he made sure we were looked in on and sent packages filled with treats and clothing and books from wherever in the world he was.

We didn't see him much these days, though. I never understood what he did for employment, but it seemed to be affected by this new war, and the last time we saw him was at Madi's funeral.

A moment later the man himself entered the room ahead of Alard, an exhausted smile on his face, his dark, wavy hair longer than usual and a bit unkempt.

"Livvie," he said, going to Aunt Liv to kiss her cheek, before planting one on our mother's, and then rounding the table to kiss the tops of my sister's and my heads.

"Take your coat off and put that case down," our hostess said.

"Max has fixed you a drink, and the first course has yet to be served. Your timing, as always, is impeccable."

"My apologies for barging in uninvited," he said, handing his coat and briefcase to Alard. "I wasn't expecting to be in town."

"Well, we're glad for your company," Mama said. "As always."

"You're doing well?" he asked, the simple question carrying the weight of two deaths in it. He leaned across the table and reached for mother's hand, which she placed in his with a smile.

"I'm doing as well as can expected, I suppose," she said and then looked to me and Elif. "We all are."

He sighed. "It's hard traveling so much sometimes. I want to be here. For all of you."

"We know, Frans," Aunt Liv said. "Which just makes the times you are here that much sweeter."

The first course arrived then and we caught Uncle Frannie up on all things school, mother's shop, and Aunt Liv's many soirees and rumors. Rumors that we all knew were never just rumors when it came to Olivia Vox.

"You could run your own division of the police force with all the information you're able to obtain," Frans said.

"I can't help it if the town's women feel the need to spill their secrets as soon as they walk over that threshold."

Mama and Frans shared an amused glance.

"When you bestow that golden invitation to dine here, how can they help themselves?" Mama asked with a wry smile.

Aunt Liv merely shrugged her innocence.

Second and third courses arrived on china so beautiful, it felt almost a shame to eat and ruin the beautifully presented food. But the aromas rising off the plates quickly took any thoughts of my abstaining away and I dug in with ill-concealed hunger, my manners barely kept intact.

As the evening wound down, small silver platters with gleaming silver cloches were placed before each of us. The domed lids were lifted to reveal a dessert of aromatic and delicate custard decorated with bright, edible flowers.

"Elke, this looks scrumptious," Aunt Liv said to her cook, who served the last course with the help of Max. "Thank you."

"Of course, ma'am," Elke said before taking leave again.

"Frans," Mama said, "you haven't told us yet what you've been up to. How is work?"

I never understood what Uncle Frannie did. I just knew it was something in government.

"Lots of things happening these days," he said. "Sleep is no longer a priority. And my pride in a freshly starched shirt and combed hair have fallen by the wayside, clearly. My apologies, ladies, for arriving in a most unkempt fashion."

"Don't be silly," Aunt Liv said. "You are doing important work. Which grows more important by the day. Who cares about starched shirts and combed hair?"

"Can you tell us anything?" Mama asked.

There was a look exchanged around the table, causing Elif and I to exchange one of our own. This was normally the point in adult conversation when we, the children, were sent to another room to amuse ourselves with a game or treat provided with a conspiratorial wink by the cook. But apparently we'd graduated, because for once we were not sent away.

"There are rumors," he said. "Of course you know that. We've been discussing it for years. But now we think it's inevitable."

"What's inevitable?" Elif asked.

"That the Netherlands will enter the war," Uncle Frannie said.

A tremor of fear swept quietly through my body, threatening to unmoor the feeling of safety my country had always provided me.

"Would we side with the Germans?" I asked, my voice low.

"We might not have a choice," he said. "If Germany decides to use force, attacking us…well, there are many more of them.

Our chances of beating them are slim. They would then most likely occupy us. Use our resources, push our people out while bringing their people in, and recruiting able-bodied boys and men, if they don't force them into work camps like they are doing in other countries."

"Can't we do something?" Elif asked, her eyes wide like saucers in her pale face. "Can't the queen…" She trailed off, her gaze going round the table, waiting for someone to speak up and reassure her.

Aunt Liv gave a little wave of her hand, and Max and the other gentleman waiting to be of service exited the room.

"My love," Mama said in a quiet voice as she reached for Elif's hand, "that's what Frans is doing. He's gathering information, finding people to trust, working against Germany right beneath their noses in some cases."

"Your father and I used to discuss the possibility of this happening," Uncle Frannie said. "Hitler's supporters, even after he was imprisoned, still believed in him and his ideas. For years we monitored this, working with a small band of men and women, inserting them into these groups of rabid followers, to report back to us. We worked from the point of view of, 'what if?' What if he was released and somehow gained power again? And that's exactly what he did, starting with publishing a book. As he rose in ranks, we began putting more people in place. We wanted to be prepared. We didn't know what was coming, but we both felt it would be big—and bad. And your father, like I, believed strongly that the Netherlands would not be prepared or able to resist the power that is Germany. He worked every spare moment he could to help me seek out those who would be good at finding information, planting information, and lying for information. He assisted in setting the stage for the networks that are already fighting secretly, right beneath the enemy's nose."

Father. Of course he would have looked ahead. Prepared. Defied evil. I sighed. How I missed his larger-than-life presence.

His humor and kindness. The way he would notice us quietly struggling and offer guidance and advice, but always stopped before doing too much, letting us find our way on our own. His absence had left an emptiness, and the three of us had been scrambling ever since to fill it. So many times I'd wondered how life could be so cruel. How life would be different if he were still with us. Lighter. Sillier. Less stark. And Madelief, she would still be here too. If he were alive, I wouldn't have been the only choice that day to walk with her to school.

I stopped myself, as I always did, when I started to place blame anywhere but on myself for what had happened.

I couldn't look at Elif. Couldn't raise my eyes to meet my mother's across the table. If I did either, I would cry. Instead, I looked to Uncle Frannie.

"What do you mean 'networks' and 'fighting secretly'?" I asked.

"Just that," he said. "A group of people doing their part to disperse information, hide individuals and families, transfer important items, alter papers, hand out pamphlets and newspapers, and put up posters, among many other things. It's dangerous work done right under the noses sometimes of the Gestapo, and there are people doing it in every country Germany has invaded so far. With the help of brave individuals willing to risk their safety, they are able to get information to the British. Important locations, names of high-ranking officers, dates of attacks, and more. In fact..." He turned his attention to Elif. "I was wondering if you might be interested in helping, Elif?"

She frowned and looked around the table as if checking to be sure he was speaking to her. "Me?" she asked.

"Frans..." Mama's voice was a quiet warning.

"What about me?" I asked, sitting up in my chair.

"Elif is sixteen," Uncle Frannie said.

"So?" I said, mentally building a list of reasons why I should get to help too, despite being two years younger.

"It can be dangerous work."

"Sixteen isn't much different than fourteen," I argued.

"In some respects, no," he said. "But for this work…it's about maturity and—"

"Frans," Mama said again, this time her voice sharper.

"It's what we've always talked about, Kat."

"I know but…" Her eyes filled with tears. "Not now. Please?"

But I wasn't finished fighting for my chance to be part of whatever Elif was being asked to do.

"You think I'm not mature enough but I get straight As, help out at the shop, watch the Aberman children," I said. "I'm going to go to university to be a lawyer. I'm plenty mature and I want to help too."

"Lien," Aunt Liv said.

I wanted to ignore her but my manners wouldn't allow it. Crossing my arms over my chest, I turned sullenly to look at her.

"It's not only us who make the decisions," she said. "There are rules regarding these things. I promise, as soon as you're of age, if the war is indeed happening here, your assistance will be asked for. Until then, it is important you keep doing what you've been doing."

I huffed and pushed my dessert away, not allowing myself to look across the table at Elif who was nudging my foot under the table with hers. I didn't want to hear any more on the subject, and apparently the adults had come to a silent conclusion that discussing it further while I was around wasn't the thing to do, so they moved on to other subjects until it was finally time to leave.

I hurried to the front of the house and took my coat from Alard, giving him a stiff thank-you as I shoved my arms into the sleeves.

"There are different levels of helping," I heard Aunt Liv quietly telling Elif. "But it is up to you if you want to."

I set my jaw and watched Elif give her a placating smile before turning to retrieve her own coat from the butler.

"Thank you for dinner, Aunt Liv," I said, stepping forward and kissing her cheek before turning to Uncle Frannie. "It was good to see you, Uncle."

"It was good to see you as well, Lien," he said, and reached out to tussle my hair as he'd always done. But I stepped out of the way, as if to prove only children had their hair mussed, and I was no child.

We rode home in silence, Mama in front, Elif in the middle, and me once again bringing up the rear. At home, we hurried inside and shed our coats.

"Tea?" Mama asked.

"No, thank you," I said at the same time Elif said, "Yes, please."

"Lien?" Mama said as I headed for the stairs.

I spun around. "Are you going to let her do it?" I asked her.

She sighed, her shoulders rounding with the weight the world had set upon them these past few years, my question an extra brick.

"I don't know," she said. "It can be dangerous work. I'm not sure I'm ready to say yes—despite the previous conversations your father and I had. But if I do, it's not personal, my love. It's just timing."

"Hmm," I said, and then turned and hurried up to my room.

I was peeling off my blouse when Elif entered the room and shut the door behind her.

"I don't want to do it," she whispered. "Whatever it is—I don't want to."

She stood before me with eyes full of fear, tears welling up, threatening to fall. I fought the urge to run from her. To retreat and hide. To look away before the disappointment and pain of my inability to close the divide etched its way across her face.

Before I let her down, like I'd done Madelief.

"You'll do great," I said, offering a half smile.

"But I don't want to," she said. "I'm not like you, Lien. I'm not brave."

I peered at my older sister. "I'm not brave."

"Yes, you are," she insisted. "After Madi…you picked yourself up and worked harder, moved forward. I…" She looked at the bare walls where so many of her paintings used to hang, and now only a couple did. "All I do is try to cover what I feel with bright colors, as if somehow by painting happy scenes they'll seep into my skin and take the dark and gray away. Or at the very least, cloak them. And I've barely been able to do that."

"You did nothing wrong, though," I said, my voice soft as I stared down at my socked feet. "You don't need to hide or prove yourself. But I did, which is why I need to do whatever it is Aunt Liv and Uncle Frannie were talking about."

"But Lien," Elif said, her brow creasing at its center. "You didn't do anything."

"Exactly," I said, meeting her gaze finally and fully. "When it mattered the most, I did nothing."

5

At school the following Monday, I was still distracted by the opportunity just out of my reach, the wheels of my mind turning, trying to find a way to convince my mother, Aunt Liv, and Uncle Frannie that not only was I mature enough to take on such a task (despite not knowing the task), I was ready.

"Oh!" I said as I ran into the back of someone, and then felt my face warm as I looked up into the eyes of Diederik Claasen.

His amused grin caused an unfamiliar flutter in my belly.

"Good morning to you too, Miss Vinke," he said.

"Good morning. I'm so sorry. I didn't see you."

He raised his blond brows and my face grew hotter. Diederik was built like a man. Tall, broad, the hint of pale whiskers across his jaw. While he might be quiet and seem odd to some people—most people—no one could deny the fact that he was a formidable presence. And one certainly didn't miss spotting him. It was near impossible.

"I was distracted," I said.

"Well," he said, "I hope you're distracted enough to run into me again sometime."

I raised my own brows now and watched as his cheeks reddened.

"See you in class, Lien," he said, and turned on his heel. But as he walked away, he looked over his shoulder, giving me one last smile before disappearing down the hall, causing my chest to squeeze in an unfamiliar manner.

"Are you okay?" Tess asked when I arrived at our meeting place.

"Mmm-hmm," I said, thinking about the exchange that had just happened and that parting smile.

"Is something wrong?" Fenna asked.

"Hmm?" I blinked out of my stupor. "No. I…"

My voice trailed off when the color drained from Tess's face as she stared past Fenna and me. We turned to see what she was looking at, and a pit opened in my stomach at the sight of two men in the familiar Dutch military gray-green uniform, field hats tucked under their arms, striding through the school's hallway.

Fenna grabbed my arm. "What are they doing here?" she whispered. "Is something… Did Mrs. Vox say they would be coming?"

I shook my head. If Aunt Liv or Uncle Frannie had known anything about an appearance by the military at the high school, neither had breathed a word of it, which led me to believe they hadn't known, because the two of them always seemed to know everything happening in our small town.

The five-minute warning bell for first period rang, but still the bodies lingering in the halls didn't move, everyone waiting for what we didn't know.

"We should get to class," Fenna said. "I'm sure if there's anything to know, the teachers will tell us."

The three of us looked at one another and then nodded, worry mirrored in each of our faces.

"I'll see you both at lunch," I said and then reached out to squeeze their arms before turning and hurrying down the hall to Mr. Aberman's classroom.

There were only three other people in the room when I entered. Several stood at the door looking up and down the hallway, others were nowhere to be found.

"Good morning, Miss Vinke," Mr. Aberman said, his usual smile nowhere to be found.

"Good morning," I said. "Do you know…" I waved vaguely in the direction of the open door, but he shook his head.

"I assume if there's anything to know, we'll hear soon enough," he said.

I nodded and took my place at my desk, removing my notebook and the new novel we were reading, and listening for something…anything. But the next sound I heard was the ringing of the first period bell, which startled me, the chimes reverberating through my body as the rest of my classmates finally came filing in.

By the end of class, we still hadn't heard anything. As I made my way to second period, I caught slivers of conversations in the halls, the soldiers all anyone could talk about.

I barely noticed Diederik when I arrived, my mind, like everyone else's, on the soldiers we knew were still in the building. At least that was what was being whispered as no one had seen them leave.

"Exciting day," he said as I took my seat.

"How do you mean?" I asked.

He shrugged. "I just mean that everyone is in a bit of a tizzy."

"Yes, well," I said, dropping my bag to the floor and taking my seat. "It's not every day we have soldiers in the school. It's worrisome."

"Is it?" he said, tilting his head as if considering this.

"You don't think so?" I asked. "The Netherlands stayed out of the last war. I'd like to hope we'd stay out of this one as well. The alternative would be frightening."

"Perhaps your country will, in a manner of speaking, stay out of the war."

Before I could ask what he meant, the teacher began the lesson and I had to turn back around in my seat.

"By the way," Diederik whispered behind me, his warm breath on my neck. "You look lovely today, Miss Vinke."

A shiver of something that felt remotely like fear skittered down my spine, and when the bell rang at the end of class, I was the first one out the door.

By lunchtime the soldiers had left, but we still hadn't heard a reason for their visit, and most people had grown bored of the mystery and moved on to other subjects.

It wasn't until my last class of the day that the mystery of the soldiers was finally solved.

"As you all know," Mr. Smit, my math teacher said, standing at the front of the class, "we had some visitors to the school this morning. I have been tasked with telling you the nature of their visit."

He went on to explain that the government had stepped aside to allow the military to make decisions on the behalf of the country. Martial law was to go into effect immediately.

"In fact," he continued, "it is my understanding that when you leave school today, you will notice several members of the military stationed around town."

He raised his hand to quiet those who had begun whispering.

"These are merely safety measures. Nothing has been reported. No attacks that they are aware of are on the horizon. They just want to be cautious. Responsible. Questions?"

Several hands rose and Mr. Smit went about quelling fears.

"For now the only measures being taken are a curfew and possible blackouts during the evening. Other than that, I believe it should be business as usual. Now, please take out your textbooks and turn to page two hundred and thirty-eight."

The roar of voices in the halls at the end of the school day was deafening as everyone discussed martial law and what it might mean for the country.

"I might not be able to go to the beach this weekend after all," Tess said as we bumped and weaved our way through the hallway and out the doors. "I can't imagine my parents letting me go anywhere without them now."

"It's just precautionary," Fenna said. "I actually feel safer knowing there are soldiers about."

As much as I wanted to share in Fenna's optimism, I didn't. There was something foreboding about the presence of military on our streets. And with Aunt Liv, my mother, and Uncle Frannie convinced the Netherlands wouldn't be able to stay neutral this time around, I had a feeling this was just a precursor for what was to come.

"See you girls tomorrow," I said as they got on their bicycles, waved, and rode away.

I rolled my own bike out of the way of the others and waited for Elif. When she stepped over the threshold, her eyes met mine with a solemn expression.

"Are you feeling what I'm feeling?" she asked, grabbing hold of her bike and swinging a leg over the seat.

"That it's starting?"

She nodded.

"Yeah," I whispered.

As promised, the appearance of soldiers was prominent, but not obtrusive. They stood like statues every few blocks or so, or walked in pairs, their dark uniforms like a warning as they cast long shadows along otherwise bright streets filled with the flowers the Dutch were famous for. And should you happen to meet their gaze, they were quick to offer friendly if not curt smiles.

"They are Dutch," Elif reminded me, trying to ease my concern.

"The one at the end of my street is very handsome," Tess announced that Friday, causing Fenna and I to roll our eyes.

"Of course you think so," Fenna said. "He's male, isn't he?"

My laugh was sudden and loud, making both of them stare at me in surprise. I pressed my lips together.

"I don't think I've heard you laugh like that since—" Tess stopped herself, her cheeks reddening. "Well, for a while," she finished saying.

"I haven't had much to laugh about, I guess," I said, my voice soft.

"What do you mean?" Fenna said, a mischievous grin on her face. "You're friends with Tess."

"Hey!" Tess said, and then we all laughed. She turned serious after a moment though. "I was right about my folks. They don't want me to go to the beach. At least for now."

"I have to work at the shop anyway," I said.

"I did dreadfully on my math exam," Fenna said. "I have to work all weekend on an extra assignment to try and make up for it."

"Maybe you two can come over next weekend," Tess said. "We can go to *De Blauwe Jurken* and look for dresses, and then spend the day in my room trying new hairstyles. I still can't get my curls to obey." She pulled on a strand of her hair in frustration and then let it go, watching it bounce back into place.

"That sounds nice," I said, and Fenna nodded.

On Saturday I woke early, dressed, and followed Elif down the three flights of stairs to the kitchen, the scent of the *ontbijkoek* mother had baked the night before wafting over us.

"I warmed some bread for you both," she said, placing a slice for each of us on plates.

We ate quickly, gathered our things, and rode single file through the streets of Haarlem to the shop, the early-morning sun shimmering through the fog that hadn't quite lifted from the night before.

As we passed two soldiers making their way down *Barteljorisstraat*, they nodded and called out a friendly "Good morning."

"Goedemorgen," the three of us replied, and then looked at one another, bothered by the normalcy of the greeting.

We arrived at the shop, parked our bicycles, and Elif and I bounced on our toes while we waited for Mama to unlock the door and let us in.

"Lien," she said, "turn the heat up a tick, please. Elif, I have some work I need you to tend to in the back before we get started today."

"Yes, Mama," we said, and scattered to do as she'd asked.

After I turned up the heat, I walked through the small shop with the feather duster, swiping it across picture frames hung on the wall, counters and tabletops, and over lamps. It was a bright, sunny space with daylight pouring through the large front windows, the walls covered in a shimmering off-white wallpaper that had been offered to mother after Aunt Liv had had one of the rooms in her home covered in the same paper.

"I purchased too much," she'd said, signaling to Alard to place the box of rolls on the counter. "I can't return it, and it would look so lovely in here. I can send Abel to hang it for you. He's bored right now since all I have for him to do is paint touchups. By the look on his face, this is an abysmal use of his talents."

Abel was responsible for all the maintenance at the Vox residence.

Looking around at the dull gray walls, mother did the smart thing and said yes.

Staring at it now, I had to admit the shimmer added something glamorous but warm to the space.

I finished up dusting, straightened a stack of magazines on the coffee table, and went to the back room to put the kettle on for customers who wanted tea, stopping as soon as I crossed the threshold at the sight of Elif bent over the table, the box of blank identification cards before her.

"What are you doing?" I asked, accusation clear in my voice.

She jumped, not having heard me come in, and smeared the ink she'd just been painstakingly making into letters.

"Mama asked me to do this," she said, her voice flat, refusing to look up and meet my eyes.

"Do what?"

"Ask her."

"I thought you didn't want to be a part of this."

"I don't," she said. "I mean, I don't know if I do. But this didn't seem too dangerous so… I said I would."

I leaned over to look at the card. There was a photo attached of a young woman I didn't recognize, a date of birth, some other numbers, a town name.

"Who is she?"

"I don't know," Elif said, carefully removing the photo and a blank card to begin again. "I don't know who she was, only who she will be." She pointed to a piece of paper with a name on it, as well as the information my sister had already added to the ID. "She was Jewish. Soon she won't be."

"Is this the first time you've done this?" I asked.

"No. I did two others three days ago. They were my first."

"Why didn't you tell me?"

"I knew you'd be mad. I know you want to do this, Lien. And honestly, I'd prefer it were you and not me. But since they're not letting you and I can, I feel obligated to at least do this one small thing for them."

Them. I narrowed my eyes.

"You mean Aunt Liv and Uncle Frannie?"

She sighed and leaned sideways, looking past me out the door. "Yes and no. Apparently this work is part of an underground movement called the Resistance."

I filled my chest with air and held it, anger and jealousy flooding my veins. Elif didn't want to be part of any underground groups working to help Jews leave the country, and yet she got to. I did want to be part of one—and wasn't allowed. It wasn't fair.

"Lien—"

I let out the breath I was holding. "It's fine," I said, and moved to the small counter where the kettle was perched and plugged it in. "Absolutely fine."

While mother unlocked the front door, letting in the first customer of the day, I stood behind the cash register and folded a stack of fabric over hangers to be hung on a rack for people to peruse. Normally I'd enjoy the task, the new batch of material lighter and brighter than the previous month's selection as summer was fast approaching and most people were wanting new items to take on holiday.

Elif appeared eventually and I ignored her as we moved about the store, cleaning up scraps, running for thread or fabric similar in color to this one but not as heavy as that one. It wasn't even noon, and we'd already had a dozen customers in and out our doors.

"Lien," Mama said from where she was perched at her sewing machine, mending a hole in a jacket a client had brought in. "I need to you deliver some items to Aunt Liv, please."

I wanted to be disagreeable, angry at her for not entrusting me with the same tasks she was Elif, but the opportunity to get out of the shop for an hour or two was too tempting.

"Where are they?" I asked.

A few minutes later I was bumping over the cobblestone streets of Haarlem, beneath the blanket of silver clouds that had moved in, the wind in my face, two gulls gliding through the air above me, calling out to one another in their distinctive, high-pitched screech.

As I exited the city center to the outskirts, and then coasted onto the road leading to Bloemendaal, my shoulders relaxed and the anger I'd been holding in dissipated. My attention turned to the fancy yards blooming with all manner and color of flowers,

the trees bright and green with new growth, the lawns practically preening with their short, smart cuts.

I came around the corner to Aunt Liv's street and sucked in
a breath at the sight of Diederik outside his house. Of all the
dozens of times I'd ridden past before, it was the first time I'd
seen him outside and wasn't sure what to do. I'd never told the
girls how he'd reacted to the soldiers being at school. Or the
strange thing he'd said about "your country" and staying out
of the war "in a manner of speaking." The brief conversation
hadn't sat well with me, and his closeness, the feel of his breath
on my skin, had frightened me for some reason.

I ducked my head, hoping he wouldn't see me now, but luck
was not on my side.

"Lien!" he called out, waving to me.

My heart sank. I slowed as I rode closer to the house and he
strode toward the front gate.

"Hello, Diederik," I said, coming to a stop at the entrance
of the driveway.

"Hello," he said, his eyes sweeping over me, seeming to take
in every detail, from my hair twisted into one long plait hanging down my back, to my pale yellow blouse and navy trousers.
"Are you— Do you live near here?" he asked, looking surpris-
ingly flustered. "I've never seen you out this way."

"I'm delivering some items to Mrs. Vox. Do you know her?"
I asked and then pointed. "She lives in the brick hou—"

"Of course," he said, his voice short as he cut me off and
crossed his arms over his chest. "Your parents are friends of
hers?"

I felt suddenly uneasy, making me want to put my guard up
and not tell him more than I had to.

"She's a customer of my mother's. I'm delivering some clothes
she had made."

"Ah," he said, his expression relaxing, arms dropping to his sides. "Well then, that's very kind of you. Seems she could at least pick up her own clothes, though. Or send the help."

"I think my mother was trying to get me outside. I've been spending a lot of time indoors lately." I was surprised at how easily the lie rolled off my tongue.

"Well, I'm glad she did," he said. "It's nice to see you outside of school."

I pasted a smile on my face. "You too," I said as I tightened my grip on the handlebars. "Well, I should go."

"Do you come this way often?" he asked. "For deliveries?"

I shrugged. "It depends."

"Maybe next time you can some inside for a visit. We could have tea or...lunch?"

"Maybe."

"I'll take that as a yes." His smile was almost smug. "I guess I'll see you at school Monday then?"

"See you then," I said.

As I rode away I couldn't help but feel I'd escaped something, but what I didn't know. His response to my going to Aunt Liv's house gave me a queasy feeling. As if I were missing something important that was right in front of me.

6

Diederik was standing by the front doors of the school on Monday morning. He waved when he saw me, and I hesitantly lifted my arm and waved back before glancing at my sister with a nervous smile.

"Is he waiting for you?" Elif asked in a hushed voice as we slowed our bicycles.

"I think so," I said, my palms dampening.

After running into him the Saturday before, I'd told Aunt Liv about his odd behavior when I mentioned her name. She in turn told me what she knew about the Claasen family, which I then shared with my mother and Elif with great concern. Though the attention he'd paid me had been flattering, piquing my interest for the handsome, quiet boy, it now made me uncomfortable and I wanted nothing to do with it. Or him.

I parked my bike next to Elif's and dismounted.

"I have to get to class," she said, both of us noticing him making his way toward us. "I have a test, and I want to go over my notes. Will you be okay?"

"Of course," I said, giving her a reassuring smile. "I'll see you after school."

She lingered a few seconds more, a doubtful look on her face. But after a moment she slung the strap of her schoolbag over her shoulder and raced off to her first period class while I grabbed my own bag from its basket.

"Good morning," Diederik said as he approached.

"Good morning," I said, mustering up what I hoped looked like a genuine smile.

"Can I take your bag for you?" he asked.

"Oh. That's nice of you but no, thank you. I've got it."

He was quiet as we walked toward the doors of the school and I peeked up at him, only to find he was watching me, his usual bland expression focused, as if determining something about me. Or perhaps studying me. He caught my eye and smiled. I fought the shiver that raced up my spine.

"It was such a nice surprise to see you Saturday," he said. "I was hoping to ask you to come back this weekend."

My stomach gave a little lurch.

"But," he said with a sigh, "we're going out of town Friday."

"Oh," I said, hoping my relief wasn't obvious. "That's a shame."

"Maybe when I get back?"

I didn't want to get his hopes up and was relieved when I looked down the hall and saw Fenna was already here.

"I'm sorry, Diederik," I said. "I really need to talk to Fenna about something. I'll see you in science class."

I hurried away, each step closer to my friend and farther from Diederik making my nerves settle and the sick feeling in my stomach dissipate.

"Hi," Fenna said, her quick smile turning to a look of concern. "Are you okay?" She looked past me, and I wondered if Diederik was still standing there but couldn't bear to look.

"I'm fine," I said.

"Good morning!"

I jumped and turned as Tess joined us.

"Did I see you walking in with your handsome crush a minute ago?" she asked, elbowing me in the rib cage.

"Please don't call him that," I said in a soft voice.

Both girls stared at me, their brows furrowed.

"Did something happen just now?" Fenna asked.

"No. I just don't want the two of you to call him that. I don't like him like that."

They exchanged a confused look. "Alright," they said.

I was glad I had Mr. Aberman's class first, his humor and eagerness to keep his students engaged a welcome distraction from my thoughts. But science class was something different. With Diederik sitting so close to me, and an assignment on the board we were to do quietly at our desks for the duration of the hour, I was distracted and uncomfortable. The soft breaths of the boy behind me did nothing to help. Nor did his "accidental" brush against my arm as he walked past me, or the dropping of his paper, which settled beneath my seat, causing him to get out of his and kneel down beside me.

I was relieved when lunchtime finally rolled around and I sat at the table where Fenna and Tess were waiting with a sigh.

"So?" Tess asked.

I looked from one friend to the other. "You can't repeat any of what I'm going to tell you, okay?"

"Of course," Fenna said, and they both leaned in.

I took a look around to make sure no one else could overhear, and told them about my weekend activities, seeing Diederik at his house and the strange way he reacted when I said I was going to the Vox residence. I told them how something hadn't felt right. That I'd felt fearful. And that when I'd arrived at my aunt's house, I'd told her about the experience.

"What did she say?" Tess asked.

"Well, apparently both Mr. and Mrs. Claasen have been

watched since they moved to town. They're both of German descent and the timing of their relocation raised, as Aunt Liv said, some red flags."

"What kinds of red flags?" Fenna asked.

"Mr. Claasen worked in international relations until a few years ago when he started a job consulting in law enforcement, which somehow brought him here. No one knows why the Netherlands, but Aunt Liv has her suspicions."

"How does she know all that?" Fenna asked. "It's like she's a spy in a novel or something. And why was his job change deemed so strange?"

"She hears stuff from Uncle Frans," I said. "And I think she has other connections as well through her late husband. Anyway, I guess the job move is what alerted people to him because one doesn't normally upend a great career for one they have no training in. And, apparently in his circle, where Aunt Liv has acquaintances, his allegiance is well-known to be with Hitler. Taking a job in law enforcement makes one wonder if he was placed there for a purpose."

Fenna chewed her lip, and Tess wrapped a strand of hair around a finger. All three of our lunches sat before us, barely touched.

"You need to stay away from Diederik," Fenna finally said.

"I plan to."

"I mean it, Lien. I knew something was off about that boy. I fear now it's worse than I thought."

For the remainder of the week, I kept my head down and my studies at the forefront, ignoring Diederik in class as much as possible and no longer rushing to second period, preferring instead to take my time walking, entering the classroom as the bell rang so he wouldn't have a chance to talk to me. When our hour was up, I made sure all my things were gathered and hurried out the door to third period. And while he could still talk to me during breaks in our lessons, I engaged in the bare minimum of conversation before giving him a polite smile and turning back to my work.

By the end of the day Thursday, I was so exhausted I begged off working at the sewing shop after school.

"Are you okay?" Mama asked, feeling my head for fever.

"Yes," I said. "I just have a lot of homework."

"Lien." Her voice said she knew I wasn't telling her everything, a power that I'd always felt equal parts annoyed by and thankful for.

"Avoiding Diederik all week has been tiresome."

"You have seemed extra tense." She smiled and rubbed my back. "Go on home. We'll see you in a little while."

"Thanks, Mama."

Despite the billowing gray clouds threatening rain, I took my time riding home. I'd spent the entire week bound up tight, afraid to look up in case it was Diederik's eyes I met in the halls, and it was nice to breathe in the crisp air, knowing that the following day there would be no rushing to class, no constant evasion, no fake smiles. But as I turned a corner I nearly ran into a couple walking by, my eyes glued to the tall, blond boy standing on the opposite side of the street.

My first thought was to hurry away, but the backpack at his feet and something I couldn't identify in his hand got the best of my curiosity, and rather than leave, I pulled down the nearby alleyway and watched as he knelt, pulled a sheet of paper from his bag, and adhered it to a lamppost. When he was done, he picked up the bag and moved down the sidewalk, doing the same to the next lamppost with another piece of paper from his bag. I stayed in my hiding spot until he'd moved out of sight, and then hurried across the street to see what he'd posted.

"No," I whispered, looking at the sign that moments ago had been in his hands. It was the exact same poster I'd found flying about the park weeks ago when I was watching the Aberman children.

Diederik was a Nazi. There was no other explanation.

I rode home as fast as I could. I wasn't sure if it was the chill in the air or the feeling of fright in my body that made me so cold. All I knew was I couldn't stop my teeth from chattering or my body from trembling.

I built a fire in the fireplace and put the kettle on, holding up my hands to the stove top to warm them. I was standing in front of the fire, empty teacup in hand when Mama and Elif arrived home an hour later.

"That feels wonderful," Mama said, shivering a little as she came and stood next to me. "Darling, are you okay?"

I turned to her, tears spilling down my cheeks.

"Oh," she said, pulling me to her. "Lien, what's happened?"

I told her and Elif what I'd seen. The sickness in my belly when I'd looked at the poster. The fear filling my body now.

"He's one of them," I whispered.

"You need to stay away from that boy," Mama said, her voice terse.

"I know, Mama. I know."

She grabbed my arms and I yelped in surprise.

"Do you?" she asked, shaking me a little.

"Yes," I said, frightened by her reaction, more tears streaming down my face.

She pulled me to her in a tight hug and then set me away from her again, her eyes fierce as she looked into mine.

"Stay away from that boy, Lien," she said. "Promise me. And keep Tess even farther away. Do you understand?"

I nodded and sucked in a trembling breath, looking to my sister whose pale skin had turned an almost gray hue watching our exchange.

We spent the evening the way we always did, with dinner around the table followed by tea and dessert in the library. But afterward, instead of scattering to our separate spots and disappearing into our own little worlds, we kept close, talking about the day we'd each had. Mama had a new customer come in, a particularly fussy woman, and my heart swelled to hear my mother's laughter as she recounted the detailed demands of the customer. Elif told a funny anecdote about something that happened in one of her classes, and I talked excitedly about a new assignment.

"And how are Tess and Fenna?" Mama asked. "I've barely seen them lately."

She didn't say why she hadn't seen them. She didn't have to.

"They are exactly the same," I said, keeping a lightness in my voice that I didn't feel. "Tess is still boy crazy and trying new hairstyles, and Fenna is still counting down the days until she can leave home for university."

"You should have them over. I miss them."

"I'll tell them you said so." But even as I said the words, I knew I wouldn't. I wasn't ready to allow myself to return to the way things had been before.

We slowly began to wander off, finding other tasks to do around the house before heading upstairs for the night.

"See you two in the morning," Mama said, pulling a swath of fabric from her cloth bag.

"Don't stay up too late," Elif told her as she leaned down to hug her.

"I'll try not to."

Her eyes met mine and held. She gestured for me, and I pulled in a long, deep breath as I stepped toward her.

"Come here," she whispered, holding out her arms.

I didn't want to be held. Didn't want to feel the acceptance of her embrace. She may have forgiven me, but I hadn't forgiven myself. And yet I craved to be near her. I may not have felt deserving of her love, but I wanted it.

I wrapped my arms around her waist and exhaled, sinking into her familiar frame. I was shocked to feel how much thinner she was. As she held me tight, I tucked my chin, burrowing into her shoulder.

"You're okay," she whispered.

It wasn't a question, nor was it a compliment. It was a permission.

A permission I wasn't ready for.

I kissed her cheek and pulled back. "Night, Mama."

"Good night, sweet girl."

As I climbed into bed after washing up and changing into my nightgown, I noticed Elif watching me.

"It's going to be okay," she said.

"I hope so," I said, and turned out the light.

7

On Friday morning we kissed Mama goodbye and took up our bicycles for the usual ride to school. As we pedaled through the narrow alleyway from our house, bumping along and veering around puddles left from last night's rain to the main road, I saw Elif ahead of me looking around as if confused. A minute later she stopped.

"Do you hear that?" she asked over her shoulder, her brow furrowed.

I stopped too, listening, but all I could hear was the jingle of bike bells and the murmur of morning voices.

"I don't hear anything," I said.

I noticed a few others looking around now as well, and I strained to hear what they heard, but the rumble of a trash bin being rolled down the sidewalk obscured anything out of the ordinary. It passed, the sound getting farther away. And then I heard it. A rumble. Deep, low and reverberating. Like thunder, but different.

"Lien! Elif!"

We turned at the sound of our mother's voice and saw her

running toward us, her eyebrows knit, no jacket against the bitter chill of the spring morning.

"Come home," she said, looking over her shoulder to where the noise was growing louder. "Now!"

"What's happening?" I asked.

I looked at Elif, who frowned back at me as the sound grew louder still, the air around me shaking with it, causing my heartbeat to quicken and my fists to squeeze the handlebars of my bicycle. And then I watched as my sister's eyes rose to the sky and a look of horror stretched across her face.

"Mama?" Elif whispered.

I turned and saw that the sky had darkened. But not with the usual clouds. No, this was a different sort of cloud altogether, the rumble turning to a roar as dozens of planes flew toward us.

"Girls!" Mama said. "We have to go now!"

Elif spun her bike around and I followed, staring at the sky as I did. There were so many of them, they seemed to go on forever.

We pedaled hard, our mother running beside us, dodging pedestrians, their children in their arms, and bicycles swerving this way and that as people hurried to get off the streets.

"It was on the radio," Mama said as we hurried down our alleyway. "They mean to attack."

"Us?" I asked.

"Yes."

I met Elif's eyes as we pulled up to the house, dismounted our bikes, and hurried inside.

"Help me block the doors," she said. "And then we need to close all the curtains."

We dropped our schoolbags and helped her move a chest to barricade the front door and a bookcase to block the door in the library that led to the garden.

I hurriedly followed Elif up the stairs.

"I'll get our room," she said, and kept climbing upward.

I rushed to our mother's room, my eyes taking in the familiar images on the walls, the bureau still filled with my father's clothes, the jewelry box with etched glass that I used to think was filled with pirate's gold when I was a girl.

I closed the curtains, making sure no light could get in, and then returned to the second floor landing where the two other rooms were the bathroom and Madelief's room. I entered the bathroom.

The window was small, the white curtain over it not much for keeping light in or out so I grabbed a bath towel and flung it over the rod.

Elif's footsteps thundered down the stairs.

I exited the bathroom and met her eyes before looking past her to what used to be our younger sister's room.

"Do you want me to—" she started to ask.

"No," I whispered. "I'll do it."

"I can wait for you."

I shook my head. "Go help Mama."

She reluctantly left me standing there staring at the door, my chest tight, my mind trying to stay blank as an image of dark water rippling in a canal flashed in my mind. A strand of blond hair. A cracking sound.

I squeezed my eyes shut and shook my head. "No," I whispered and reached for the doorknob. I didn't have time to think of that day now.

The smell hit me first. Madelief's scent, the memory it induced so powerful it stung my eyes with tears. The perfume of a young girl's soap and the lavender sachets Mama put in our drawers and closets and under our beds.

I took in what had been the essence of my little sister. Dolls, drawings of flowers, necklaces woven from fabric scraps, and the pink dust ruffle and matching curtains she'd begged for after seeing them in a shop window last spring. Her music box sat atop her bureau, porcelain ballerina figurines given to her by

Aunt Liv next to it, and everywhere were the butterflies she'd drawn and cut out and placed on her walls, mirror, and window.

The window.

Taking a breath, I stepped inside the room and crossed quickly to it and pulled the curtains shut, the material beneath my fingertips reminding me of so many nights coming in here at her request to lie beside her and tell her about my day, my friends, the things I was learning about in school. So many nights I pulled these same curtains closed, removing dolls and paper scraps from beneath me before giving her the stories she wanted.

Her absence hollowed me and left me breathless.

"Lien?" Mama called from downstairs.

Inhaling, I wiped a tear from my face, closed the door, and hurried downstairs.

"The pink curtains are too thin to keep light from being seen," I said.

"Did you close the door?"

"I did."

"Then there's nothing to fret over. No light gets turned on in that room anymore."

I sucked in a breath and looked to Elif whose eyes had gone wide with shock and sorrow, the brutal truth shaking us both.

"What do we do now?" Elif asked our mother quietly.

"We wait and listen," Mama said, turning up the volume on the small radio she kept beside her sewing machine.

For a moment static filled the room, and then a voice broke through.

"What did he say?" I asked, leaning forward. "Amsterdam?"

Mama hushed us.

Elif and I took a seat on the settee, our legs touching, neither of us wanting to be too far from the other, while Mama sat in her usual spot in front of the sewing machine. We listened to the report in terrified silence.

Seaplanes had landed in Nieuwe Maas River in Rotterdam,

and men in boats were pulling up on the shores and taking the bridges that weren't being guarded. Other bridges to the north were being held strong by the Dutch, having heard the planes coming in and being able to get men on them.

I imagined the bridges being overrun with men in uniform, red patches on their arms, that horrid black insignia that promised nothing but misery and pain. What would happen if they made it across those bridges?

As the morning stretched into afternoon, we began to move about the house, tidying and making tea, anything to keep us occupied while we continued to listen to the news. Eventually I got out my schoolbooks. If I wasn't going to have class, I could at least read ahead and be prepared.

The phone rang just after one and we all jumped. Mama shot to her feet and ran to answer it, Elif and I close behind.

"Hello?" she said, her body rigid. A moment later, though, her shoulders relaxed. "Oh, Liv. Yes. We're okay. Are you— Oh, you're kind to offer but I think it's best we stay inside." She was quiet as she listened, and then, "We have enough candles for a few days, and I have extras at the shop. Are you okay there? Of course. Okay. Speak soon."

"What did she say?" I asked.

"She offered to send Alard for us, but we both agree staying inside is the safest option right now. She may send him with supplies, though. Just in case."

The three of us cooked dinner together, moving about the small kitchen quietly as we continued to listen, the radio now perched on the countertop, our nerves on edge.

As night fell, we lit candles and turned off the lights.

"We'll need to buy more," Mama said. "What we have won't last long. And I'll need to sew new curtains with whatever dark fabric scraps I have."

"Why?" I asked.

"Pilots can see light," she said. "Even from hundreds of feet in the air."

We ate biscuits and drank tea by the fire as usual, and then Mama suggested we wash up and change into our nightclothes.

"Gather your pillow and some blankets too. We'll sleep downstairs tonight."

"Why?" I asked.

"When there's the threat of bombs falling, the safest place is closest to the ground."

I trembled as I brushed my teeth before climbing the stairs to Elif's and my bedroom to change clothes and gather my things. I'd never before thought about how the only thing between us and the outside was the roof. If a bomb were dropped on us while we slept in our beds, there was no way we'd survive.

I pulled on my nightgown and then decided to don a pair of trousers as well, in case we needed to leave the house for some reason in a hurry.

"What are you doing?" Elif asked, the front of her hair wet from splashing water on her face.

I had pulled out the small bag I used whenever I slept overnight at Fenna's or Tess's house and was throwing underclothes, socks, a sweater, and a book inside.

"I just thought...if we have to leave quickly for some reason, I'd have some things ready to go."

Elif studied me for a moment before pulling a bag out from under her bed and doing the same.

We returned downstairs, our arms laden with pillows and blankets, our bags hanging from our shoulders. We dumped the bedding on the floor and hung our bags on the coatrack, which was now standing in front of the entryway cabinet that had been shoved in front of the door. Afterward we joined our mother, who was standing in the dining room surveying the space.

"I was thinking we'd move the two small sofas to the library.

Then we'll each have a bed where the fire is. I just feel safer back there near the kitchen. And it will be cozier."

"Almost like a campout," Elif said. "Remember when Papa used to take us camping?"

"I much prefer camping in the library to outside," Mama said with a small smile, pressing a finger to her lips. "Don't tell."

We chuckled and then grew serious as we began the task of moving furniture around, each of us lost in our own thoughts. As we grew tired, the day's tension wearing on us, we made our beds and snuggled in.

Sleep was hard to come by. The fire turned to embers too quick for my liking, leaving us in an inky blackness, the only sounds in the house coming from our breathing and the planes that seem to grow in number due to nightfall. In the distance there were large booms that shook the air, even from miles away. Eventually, I fell into a fitful sleep, my arms wrapped around my pillow, my face pressed against it as I cried silent tears.

The following day we woke and immediately turned on the radio. The newscaster repeated what we already knew; De Kooy airfield had been hit, as well as Amsterdam–Schiphol, and Ockenburg and Ypenburg in The Hague. At one point the evening before, paratroopers had fallen from the sky in a surprise attack, and the Willemsbrug, a bridge in Rotterdam, had been taken in an attempt by the Germans to get into Belgium.

"I'm going to call Aunt Liv," Mama said. "Will you two start breakfast please?"

I wasn't hungry, but the task would at least distract me for a little while.

We quietly went about pulling out the dishes, trying to hear what was being said on the telephone but only catching every other word or so. Eventually we both stopped and stood in the middle of the kitchen, listening.

"No," we heard her say. "I'm not going into the shop. I can't imagine anyone will come by and if they do, they'll just have to wait. Who needs new clothes at a time like this? I'm not risking my life. And I'm certainly not leaving the girls." There was a long pause. "I promise I'll call if we need anything. Stay safe. You too."

"May I call Fenna and Tess?" I asked after she'd hung up.

"After we eat. And as long as you keep the conversations short. I want to keep the phone line open in case someone calls needing something."

We spent the day as we had the day before, with the added tasks of going through the cupboards and pantry, making a list of what we had, and another for what we needed.

In the late morning, Mama hurried out to the neighbors' on either side of us to make sure they were safe and to ask if they needed anything.

"Is everyone okay?" Elif asked when she returned.

"Yes. Just frightened. I'm going to bring a couple of our extra blankets to the Hoeks and..." She looked hesitantly at the two of us. "Maybe a toy or two of Madi's. The young ones are hard to keep entertained when they can't go outside to let some energy out. A new toy will help distract them, don't you think?"

I looked to Elif, who sighed and then turned back to Mama.

"It's a good idea," she said.

Mama looked to me and I nodded. "Madi would've liked that," I said, my voice soft.

We ate lunch at the dining table, which now resided in the sitting room, the radio the only noise in the room. Afterward, as promised, I was allowed to call my friends.

"Mama's terrified," Fenna said. "I can't remember the last time she spent any time with me, but since yesterday she practically won't leave my side. The only break I get is when I use the bathroom. And father of course thinks it will all be fine. I wish I was at your house. Your mother I can tolerate at least."

Tess wasn't nearly as talkative, her worry coming through in the words she did manage to say.

"Mama wants to leave," she whispered. "But Papa says we need to stay and help. He says it's our duty to our country. But Lien, I'm scared."

The tremor in her voice stayed with me the rest of the day.

By late afternoon a broadcaster, whose voice I feared would now fill every one of our waking and sleeping moments, announced what we all inherently knew—we were to stay inside and to not go out if at all possible.

"Additionally," he said, "schools will be closed until notified."

For the next couple of days, we lived in a state of constant panic, with scant periods of boredom. The news only got worse. Nazis dressed as Dutch military policemen had been found bringing in what they claimed was a group of German prisoners they'd captured, all in a ploy to gain access to a police station. Some of the men were actually Dutchmen though, members of what was called the Nationaal-Socialistische Beweging, which was apparently a Dutch Nazi party.

"It's terrible," Mama whispered, just as the phone rang, Aunt Liv on the other line.

When she hung up, she hurried to the foyer and put her coat on. "I have to go out," she said.

"What?" Elif and I practically shouted.

"Alard's left something for me at the shop, and I need to retrieve it."

"But Mama…" I said, looking to Elif who had a horrified expression on her face.

"I'll be fine. There are soldiers still out on the streets. *Our* soldiers. The Nazis haven't come here yet."

"We can't be sure of that," Elif said.

"I know, my love," Mama said. "But this is part of the job."

"What job?" I went still, waiting for her answer.

"The job I signed on to do," she said. "For our country."

She pulled a knit hat over her dark blond waves, knotted a scarf around her neck, and kissed us both on the cheek.

"Help me move the cabinet?" she asked.

Elif and I each took one end of the cabinet, sliding it out just enough for mother to squeeze through.

"Lock the door behind me and move the cabinet back into place once I've gone. I won't be long so be listening for my key in the lock to let me in, okay?"

"Please be careful," Elif whispered, her pale eyes filled with tears.

I was paralyzed where I stood, unbelieving that she would go. That she would leave us right now. But in the next instant she was gone, and Elif was locking the door and shoving the cabinet in front of it.

Anger filled every inch of me. "Did you know about this?" I asked.

"About what?" Elif said.

"About whatever it is she's going to get."

"Of course not," she said, twisting her fingers. "What do we do if something happens to her? I'm frightened."

I didn't say anything as I stalked to the library and sat on the sofa I was using as a bed. I knew exactly what I'd do. I'd make Aunt Liv let me part of the underground operation. I'd fight.

But Mama returned, as promised, not more than twenty minutes later. I heard the key in the lock and shot to my feet, Elif on my heels as we hurried to let her in.

"Did you get what you went for?" I asked, still mad she'd left, but mostly that she was doing dangerous work but wouldn't allow me to.

"I did," she said.

"And? What is it?"

She removed her hat and scarf and turned to face me, her gaze wary. "Lien—"

"You won't let me do the things Elif is doing, which as far as I can tell is just some simple copying and pasting. And now you're going out to retrieve things when we have no idea if or when our town is next." My voice caught on a sob. "You're a mother. You're supposed to stay home. I should be the one going out. I don't have kids to take care of, and if something happens to me it won't matter."

"What do you mean it won't matter?" she asked quietly.

I bowed my head, angry at myself now for the tears blurring my vision.

"I'm just a girl," I said in a flat voice. "No one's counting on me."

Her breath was warm on my hair as she carefully wrapped her arms around me. As if afraid if she moved too fast I'd run.

"Is that what you think?" she asked. "That no one's counting on you? That no one can?"

I let her hold me for another few seconds and then stepped back, wiping at my face with the cuff of my sleeve.

"I know I'm capable. And no one will give me a chance. Just because I'm young doesn't mean I can't be responsible." Again my voice broke, but I powered on. "Papa told us that story once, remember?" I looked to Elif. "About the little kids in England during the first war that carried messages? I could do that."

She took off her coat, hung it, and turned to face me again. Hanging from her neck, previously hidden from sight, was one of her cloth bags. Whatever was inside it was thin and flat. She pulled the straps over her head and set the bag on the cabinet behind her.

"I know, Lien. And you already have."

I frowned. "No, I haven't."

"You have. You just didn't know it."

She motioned for us to follow her to the library where she sat on the sofa she'd been sleeping on and curled her legs under her while Elif and I each perched on the edges of our own temporary beds and waited for her to continue.

She sighed and rubbed her face. I noticed suddenly how tired she looked. How pale and unkempt in her rumpled sweater and trousers when she was normally dressed smart, her hair styled, her cheeks colored with rouge.

"Your watch," she said, meeting my eyes. "I had slipped a note inside the band that needed to be delivered to the Ten Booms." She sighed. "The clothes you delivered to Aunt Liv had forged ID cards sewn into the lining. The reams you took to Mrs. Timmerman had information stored inside. You've been doing the work, Lien. I just didn't tell you."

Confusion then anger surged through me. "But—*why* didn't you tell me?"

"Because if you didn't know and were stopped and searched, you wouldn't be lying when you said you knew nothing about it." She closed her eyes for a moment and then met my eyes again. "I should've told you, but it was safer this way. For the deniability it allowed you."

"But wouldn't they figure out it was you who put it in there?"

"Most likely. And that's okay. I'm prepared for that."

"You're prepared for that," I repeated. "You're prepared to maybe go to jail, or worse, and leave us on our own?"

She took a deep breath and nodded. "I am prepared to deal with the consequence of my actions for my country. The country of your father. The country of my daughters."

I sat up straighter. "Well, I am too."

"Lien—"

"Why can't I? Elif is only two years older, and she doesn't even want to do the work. *I* do. And apparently I already have been. Please, Mama. Let me help."

She sat back and closed her eyes again. "I'll think about it."

"Mama—"

"Lien!"

I jumped in my seat, and from the corner of my eye saw Elif press a hand to her chest. Mama rarely raised her voice to us, and was hardly ever cross. But the sharpness in her voice exposed the fragility of her emotions at this time.

"I will *think* about it," she said. "For now, let it go. *Please.*"

It was in my nature to push. To assert myself. To present my reasons calmly and with information to back up my ideas. But I had no information. All I had was my stubborn determination to do something. To help. Because without that, I felt I had nothing. I was worth nothing.

"Okay, Mama," I said, my voice quiet.

The room was silent for a moment and then mother spoke again.

"The item I retrieved from the shop," she said, her voice quiet. "They're posters. They look much like the one you found in the park that day, Lien. And then again with your friend."

"He's not my friend," I whispered.

"They look similar so that at first glance they'll go unnoticed by those who placed the others."

"What do they say?" I asked.

Her eyes met mine, the exhaustion in her gaze momentarily gone and replaced by a more familiar steeliness. She got up, disappeared into the foyer, and returned a moment later with her bag. She pulled free one of the posters and turned it so we could see. Emblazoned across the bottom was a single word.

Resist.

8

With a strict curfew in place at night, and Dutch soldiers suspiciously monitoring and moving people along during the day, putting up the posters was going to be near impossible for our mother.

"Let me help," I begged. "Please, Mama. I can do it."

It had taken much convincing on my part, and finally Elif agreeing to help, to get her to allow us to go.

And so, before our sleepy little town awoke the following morning, the three of us skittered silently across the cobblestones, splitting up at the mouth of the alleyway.

Mama went alone, Elif and I together. We would hang one poster each and then go home. It was all our mother would agree to after I'd hounded her the night before.

"Keep to the shadows," she'd said before we'd left, as we slid into our coats, our blond hair tucked out of sight beneath our collars and hats. "And watch out for one another."

Our story, should we get caught, was that we had snuck out of our house and were going to a friend's house. Mama's story was that she was looking for her daughters who had absconded.

"Always keep your story simple," Mama said. "It's easier to believe if you don't embellish."

"And if we're caught in the act?" I asked.

"Don't be. But if you are…" She sighed and rubbed her eyes.

"I'll say it blew off in the wind and I'm just putting it back."

Her eyes narrowed and then she nodded. "Simple and straight-forward. That should work."

Haarlem, even at its most bustling, was a quiet town. But in the early-morning hours, with every window covered, and every townsperson sequestered inside their homes, the silence combined with the absence of light was downright eerie.

As our mother had directed, we kept close to the buildings and under the cover of the shadows they cast. Our goal was to place our posters as near to the market square as possible, as that was where foot traffic was always at its heaviest.

I took the lead and Elif stayed close behind me, her fist gripping the back of my coat. At each street's end we stopped, our breath held as we looked for soldiers standing guard, and back-tracking if we saw one to find a different way around. As we neared the square, my hands began to sweat and I paused at the end of the street we were on.

"Is there a soldier?" Elif whispered.

I shook my head and pressed my back to the brick wall behind me. "I think this is the spot."

"Here?" She looked around.

There were two lampposts only a few meters away. I pointed first to one, then the other. She nodded and we both pulled the posters from their hiding spots beneath our coats. I grabbed the roll of adhesive tape from my pocket and tore off two pieces for Elif and two for myself. As I was putting the roll back, we heard sharp footsteps striking the cobblestones not far from where we were situated. Grabbing my sister's sleeve, I pulled her behind a cluster of bicycles and we crouched down. The footsteps slowed, paused, and then seemed to go back the way they'd come. I stood, held up a hand to signal for Elif to wait, and stepped quietly back to the wall we'd just abandoned. Holding my breath, I peeked around the corner.

Three soldiers stood, their backs to me, only a stone's throw away. They were smoking cigarettes and chatting quietly in the early-morning light that was growing brighter with every passing second.

I ducked out of sight and motioned for Elif, who hurried to my side.

"There are three of them," I said. "Facing away from us for now. We'll have to be quick."

The lampposts we'd targeted were only steps from where we hid, but we would have to step out into the open to reach them. If any of the three men turned while we were on the move, we'd be caught. I had no idea what kind of punishment would be handed out to two teenage girls hanging posters at dawn— and I certainly didn't want to find out.

"I'll go first," I said, attaching the adhesive to the top and bottom of my poster. After a quick look around the corner of the building to make sure they were still facing away, I stepped into the clearing, moving from shadow to shadow until I reached the post, pressed the tape to the cool metal, and hurried back, again keeping to the long stretches of dark shapes.

My heart pounded in my chest as I returned to my sister's side and once more pressed my back to the wall.

"My turn," Elif murmured, peeking around the corner, her poster ready in her hands.

She slipped from my side before I could say a word, and for the briefest of moments I had the urge to pull her back, unwilling to have another sister in harm's way. But before I could act on my instincts, she was gone and back.

"Done," she said, her eyes bright with triumph. "Let's go."

We left the way we'd come, and when we arrived home, Elif

reached for the door handle, only to have it pulled open before she could touch it.

"Thank goodness," Mama breathed as we entered. "It went well?"

"When can we do more?" I asked.

She gave us a small smile and shook her head. "Soon."

We spent the rest of the day inside, the radio on, trying to distract ourselves with chores and schoolwork, of which we had nothing new since we'd yet to return to class. In the evening we learned the German Wehrmacht was trying to take the *Afsluitdijk*, a major dam and causeway in the north.

The next morning, as we ate breakfast in the library, we learned the Dutch were still holding strong. It was hopeful news that prompted mother to set out a plate of biscuits.

"We must celebrate the small things," she said.

In the afternoon, Elif helped me slide the bookcase just enough from in front of the back doors so I could slip out to check the garden. It was early yet, several of the vegetables not ready for harvest, but there was spinach, garlic, onions, and turnips to be had. I picked a few of each and then spent some time pulling weeds and luxuriating in the fresh air and warm spring sun that had parted the clouds. It was a beautiful day. The early-morning fog had lifted to reveal a crisp blue sky dotted with white, fluffy cumulus clouds, and the cold breeze off the water had been filtered and warmed by the dunes on the beach, the trees of the forest, and the homes of the town. It seemed almost cruel we couldn't be out in droves to enjoy it.

Reluctantly, I got to my feet, wriggling my toes in the grass, and picked up the basket filled with fresh vegetables sure to find their way into our dinner tonight. As I took a step toward the house, something bright and red at the edge of the back porch where it met the fence line caught my eye. I padded barefoot toward it, and bent to get a closer look, lifting the leaf partially obscuring it.

"Oh," I whispered, staring at the little red bird whittled out of wood.

It had been Madi's, given to her by our father. I remember when he'd made it, sitting on this same back porch in his favorite chair, worn from weather and use, the wood faded, the fabric thinned. He'd contemplated what color to paint it for days, finally deciding on red because Mama kept complaining how much she kicked inside her belly.

"She'll be a little fireball," he'd said.

As soon as she was old enough to know better than to eat the paint off, it was always in her sticky little hands. She'd carried it everywhere when she was little, making it nests in the garden and beds out of her clothes in her room. It perched on the table during meals, and sat on the sink watching over her bath times. As she grew into a precocious seven-year-old, we saw that little bird less and less. In the days before she died, she'd torn her room apart looking for it, but had never found it.

"Hello there, little bird," I said, picking it up gently, as if it were real. "We were looking for you. You're so naughty to hide out here. I— Madi's gone." My voice broke on the word, and I quickly brushed away the tear tracing its way down my cheek. "But I'll take care of you. I know she'd want—"

I stopped, the next words forgotten as I stood and looked up, the air around me vibrating.

"Mama?" I called out, slipping the bird into my pocket.

I looked around for the basket I'd abandoned when I'd seen the red bird, finding it at the edge of the patio a few feet away. I grasped the handle, the buzz of engines starting to sound like a low roar.

"Mama?" I called again, searching the sky as I stepped onto the stone porch.

She poked her head out the door. "What is—"

The sound increased suddenly and she gasped and stepped outside, looking up while motioning for me to come toward her.

"Get inside," she said, her voice low and steady. *"Now."*

Her last word was drowned out as a squadron of low-flying Luftwaffe planes blackened the sky above us.

We rushed into the house and she slammed the back door.

"Help me," she said, pulling on the bookcase.

Elif and I got on the other side and pushed until the door was once more obscured and the room was dark again. For a moment, the three of us didn't move, listening as still more planes flew overhead, the windows rattling around us.

"Elif, the radio," Mama said.

She turned it on, and we huddled together on the sofa mother had been sleeping on, staring at the speaker...waiting.

It didn't take long for the reports to start coming in. Rotterdam, a large port town about an hour's car ride south of us, was the subject of what was being called an unrelenting aerial attack by the very planes that had crossed over our house. The bombs they dropped could be felt for miles...even in Haarlem where the floorboards of our home quaked beneath our feet.

As we listened to the broadcaster's increasingly worsening news, we forgot dinner. Forgot to light candles. Forgot almost to breathe as we sat holding hands, not uttering a word, until night fell and we could barely see one another anymore.

The ringing of the phone startled us. Elif whimpered in response as Mama felt her way along the furniture and picked up the receiver.

"Hello?" she said, her voice hushed. "Liv, yes, we've been listening... What?... But they haven't... Okay. Yes, okay. Goodbye."

"What did Aunt Liv say?" I asked.

I could see her shape moving carefully about and heard the strike of a match. She lit a few candles and came back to the library, taking a seat this time at her sewing machine.

"Queen Wilhelmina and her family have left the country." Her voice was low, her eyes serious. "They've traveled to London."

I felt the blood drain from my face, my limbs go cold.

"She's deserted us?" Elif asked.

"Let us not pass judgment yet, my loves," Mama said. "The queen would not leave without good reason to do so."

But at fourteen, there was no reason I could think of good enough for the queen to leave her countrymen and women behind. Had she fled out of fear? Duty? Had she looked at the situation and decided it to be hopeless? Whatever the reason, she'd abandoned us. Left us to fend for ourselves without her guidance. Left us to hide or fight, or whatever it was we'd need to do…alone. I felt sick, and suddenly very, very frightened.

"I think I'll go wash up," I said. "And change out of these clothes."

"Wash down here," Mama said. "We'll all just wear what we have on to sleep in tonight."

"But why?" Elif asked.

"Who knows if there's another attack planned. It's best we stay away from the upper floors for now." She smiled in an effort to reassure us, but even in the flickering light of the candles I could see the fear that resided in her eyes. "How about we make dinner? Lien, grab the basket, won't you?"

I'd forgotten the basket, which I found tipped over near the bookcase by the back door. I gathered the vegetables that had rolled out and carried it to the kitchen, where my sister and I prepared to chop and peel while mother put on a pot of water and, like the well-choreographed dance we'd performed hundreds of times before, we began to move around the kitchen as if we were one, a woman and her two girls, the eldest with paint flecks in her hair, the youngest with a little wooden bird in her pocket.

I woke to the sound of talking. Disoriented, I pushed up onto my elbows and looked around. The covered windows made it impossible to know if it was still night, or if morning had come.

I peered through the dark to see that Elif and my mother were still asleep, the latter with her head positioned near the radio, which was still on, the volume turned low.

On tiptoe I moved across the cold wood floor, my quilt wrapped around my shoulders, and knelt before the cabinet the radio sat atop. I turned it up and sat on the floor, my back resting against the sofa my mother slept on as I listened to the grim news: the center of Rotterdam had been destroyed. Fires burned throughout the city. Thousands of homes had been destroyed. Hundreds were dead.

"Lien?"

Mama's whispered voice startled me and I sat up, sniffling and wiping the tears from my face.

"What is it, love? Are you okay?"

I shook my head. She gathered her own quilt around her and sat beside me on the floor. Without giving it a moment's thought, I sighed and leaned into her. She wrapped her arms around me and rested her cheek against my head.

"We will have to be strong," she whispered. "I fear the worst is yet to come."

As much as I hoped, uttering pleas to the universe under my breath that she was wrong as we folded our blankets, opened the curtains, and sat down to breakfast, that afternoon, as the sun shone down and the tulips we were famous for tipped their colorful and oblivious faces upward, the radio once more crackled to life to announce the country had surrendered.

9

"I don't want to go," Elif said, her arms crossed over her chest as she stood beside the dining table, her breakfast untouched.

School, it was announced over the weekend, would resume. We would have two weeks to turn in any assignments already done, take last exams, and then we'd be let out for summer and the seniors would graduate.

The argument between my mother and Elif had been going on from the time it was first announced until now, when we needed to be hurrying to get to school on time.

"What if they drop bombs on the school?" Elif asked for what seemed like the one millionth time.

"They could just as easily drop bombs on our house," Mama responded, as she had one million times before. "Elif, go. See your friends. See your teachers. Germany has already defeated us. They won't drop bombs on land they need."

Elif sighed. "I'm not talking about Germany. I'm talking about England."

We were all silent as we contemplated this. It was something we hadn't thought of before. At least, my mother and I hadn't.

"England is not going to bomb us when we've done nothing to them," Mama said. "Besides, our queen is there. Surely they are all consulting with one another about steps to take."

I didn't know if it was true or not. Didn't know if she was making it up, or believed it. What I did know was that I wanted to see my friends. I craved the normalcy and distraction of the school day.

"What if they arrive while we're in school?" I asked quietly when Elif ran upstairs to brush her teeth, shouting behind her that she still didn't want to go.

"The Wehrmacht?" she asked, and I nodded. "Then you will do as your teachers say and go straight to the shop. I'll be there all day with the radio on so I know what's happening. Okay?"

"Okay."

In the end, and with great reluctance, Elif agreed to go to school, but not without much grumbling. As we swung our legs over our bikes, though, our eyes met.

"It will be okay," I said. But even I didn't buy the confidence in my voice.

It was the strangest ride to school I could remember. We were officially occupied by Germany, and yet there was no sign of the enemy as the doors to shops opened as we passed by. The smell of bread filled the air, and we passed person after person on the street. Lots of them. Walking, and riding, and chatting. Their faces were more serious than usual, their eyes darting this way and that, but they were there, leading their lives like always.

The schoolyard, while busy, was emptier than I'd expected, the lineup of bicycles half of what it normally was. I glanced at Elif as we walked across the grass to the doors. She looked like a statue. A statue trying not to cry.

"It will be okay," I said again, more for myself than her this time.

"If anything happens," she said, looking over her shoulder at me with steel in her eyes, "don't leave without me."

I stopped walking, shocked by the thought, but she went ahead without looking back. For all my forward thinking and trying to be prepared at all times for all things, how had I missed setting a plan for what to do should our school come under attack?

Tess shouted my name as I walked in a daze down the half-empty hallway to where we met every morning.

I sighed with relief at the sight of my two friends.

"Hi," I said, looking the two of them over as though it had been years, not days, since I'd seen them last. "How are you?"

But neither answered as we all took in one another's appearances. It was clear how wc all were by how we looked.

Fenna's normally put-together ensemble was wrinkled, her ever-present headband pushed haphazardly into dark hair that may have been brushed the day before, but certainly not this morning. Tess's clothes looked as they always did, but it was the pallor of her face, the smudges of dark under her eyes, and the way her shoulders were hunched, as if waiting for an assault of some kind, that would haunt me for the rest of the day.

We barely spoke as we stood there, waiting amid a throng of students, the usual volume in the halls muffled in light of the events of the past few days. When the warning bell rang the three of us were startled, looking to one another in a sort of panic, none of us wanting to leave the others' sides.

"See you at lunch?" Fenna said in a small voice.

"See you at lunch," I said with barely more conviction. I gave Tess a faint smile I hoped was encouraging, and we turned to go to our classes.

Mr. Aberman was sitting at his desk when I arrived, and I was shocked by his appearance. Normally flipping through a book in search of a passage, or writing text on the blackboard, a little grin of mischief on his face, today he sat staring blankly at the back of the room.

I'd never considered my favorite teacher's age before, but

thought he was maybe in his early thirties. This morning, though, he looked older. Haggard. Like Tess, there were dark half-moons beneath his eyes, and his hair looked like he'd combed half of it and then forgot to finish the other side. His clothes were pressed but his shirt was only half tucked in, and when he shifted in his seat, I noticed one of his pant legs was stuffed inside his sock.

"Good morning, sir," I said, my voice quiet.

His eyes shifted to me and for a brief moment brightened.

"Good morning, Lien." He went back to staring.

When the bell rang, he got up from his seat with such reluctance, such defeat, that for a moment I thought he was going to pick up his briefcase, walk out the door, and not come back. Instead, he glanced around at the empty seats, gave a short, lackluster lesson, and then had us read until the bell rang.

I stopped at his desk on my way out. "Mr. Aberman?"

"Hmm?" He looked confused, as if he didn't know where he was. "Oh. Lien. Yes?"

"Are you okay, sir?"

"Of course." But his smile said otherwise. "Just tired. Not much sleep when you have two kids and a wife who can't get comfortable." His eyes focused then, and for the first time all morning he seemed to really see me. He sighed. "It's just been a stressful few days, as I'm sure it's been for you as well. Have a good rest of your day, okay? I'll see you tomorrow."

I hated leaving him. I'd never seen him in such a state before. I wondered if someone should call his wife. If perhaps I should go to the front office and speak to the principal. Maybe they'd ask me to stay, which seemed a better option than having to sit in front of Diederik for the better part of an hour.

But Diederik never showed up to class that day.

I wondered if anyone else noticed his absence, which was glaring to me, his presence having become so prominent in the past few weeks. But if they did, they didn't mention it. And with so many others not attending, it probably didn't stand out.

With no incident that first day, we returned the following day with less apprehension, and a slightly larger student body in attendance. The third day went much the same. I even heard some laughter in the halls again, which further helped calm my anxiety.

I was sitting in math class that afternoon when the sound of feet running outside the open classroom door made me look up from the equation I was working on. At first only a few of us noticed, and subsequently ignored it. But then the number of shoes striking the tiles grew and we started shifting in our seats and looking around at one another until eventually the teacher got up from his desk and peeked out the door. A moment later the teacher across the hall came into view, and the two of them spoke too quietly for us to hear.

"What is it?" a boy in the front row asked.

Mr. Hoek bowed his head and rubbed his eyes. The other teacher left and we all sat staring at the man in the doorway, waiting.

"They're here," he said, his voice catching.

A moment later we were all on our feet.

I shoved my textbook and paper into my bag as I hurried out of the classroom and into the hall, heading for Elif's fourth-period classroom.

I saw Fenna weaving through the crowd toward me, and told her I had to find my sister.

"I'll look for Tess," she said. "Meet by the bike rack?"

I nodded and we split up. A moment later I was standing in the doorway of Elif's empty classroom.

"Damn," I whispered, looking up and down the hallway for her.

Thinking she might've headed for my classroom, I started back the way I came, dodging people left and right. Some were standing in the middle of the hall talking, faces etched with fear. Others were huddled together, some crying, some shouting, "Let's go get 'em!" I was so busy taking it all in while at the same time searching the faces around that I didn't see Elif until I ran into her.

"There you are," she said, her eyes wide with fear as she grabbed hold of my arm and spun me around. "Let's go."

"I told Fenna we'd meet her and Tess by the bicycles," I said as we rushed down the hall and out the doors.

"That's fine. Ana will be there too," she said of her best friend, her step quickening.

There was a crowd of people standing near the dozens of bikes trying to decide if they should go watch the spectacle or head home. The five of us girls decided home would be best.

"I don't want to ride home alone," Tess said, her eyes rimmed in red.

"We'll take you," I said, looking at the others. "And then Ana. And then Fenna. Okay?"

It made the most sense since Elif and I would be going home together. Everyone nodded and we grabbed our bikes and extricated ourselves from the mob, most of which had started to dissipate as people headed off in different directions.

Tess's mom was standing outside the door waiting for her. Both of Ana's parents were watching for her. But when we arrived at Fenna's home, her parents hadn't returned from work yet, and all the lights were off and the door locked.

"Come home with us," I said.

She sighed. "Thank you. But I'd best not. When they do come home, they'll be worried if I'm not here. I'll be fine. I'll light some candles, turn on the radio, and sit by the phone just in case I need you."

"Promise you'll call if they're not home by six," I said.

"I promise."

We watched her go inside, listened for the click of the dead bolt sliding in place, and then rode our bicycles toward the shop.

Unfortunately the shop was near the square, which was where a parade of military personnel and vehicles was gathering, from what we heard from people we passed on our way.

"What do we do?" Elif asked when we came to a second group of people blocking the exit of the alleyway we'd gone down.

"Keep going," I said. "Eventually we should be able to get through."

But I wasn't so sure.

As we rounded the next corner, the ground began to shake. We looked around and then up, searching the sky for planes. But the rumble was earthbound this time. Instead of turning again at the sight of people crowding the street, I rode closer to them.

"Where are you going?" Elif shouted at me.

"I need to see," I yelled back.

Jumping from my bike, I rolled it off to the side and leaned it against a building, then scampered onto the top of a metal trash bin. It shook and I looked down to see Elif climbing up beside me.

"Can you see anything?" she asked. I shook my head, staring over the heads of the people lined eight and ten deep in front of us.

"Nothing yet," I whispered.

The rumbling grew louder, the window behind me beginning to shake. And then we heard it. The sharp stomp of boots striking the cobbled streets.

A moment later they came into view. Crisp, dark uniforms, impassive faces, guns strapped to their backs. They reminded me of a windup toy soldier I'd seen once in a store. But these men weren't toys. And their weapons weren't either.

After several had marched by, a massive tank, the steel plates of its track clattering against the street, rolled into view. I shuddered. Elif's fingers snaked through mine and held fast.

"Can we go now?" she whispered.

"Yes."

She hopped down, but as I turned to follow, something across the street caught my eye. I stopped and peered, my stomach twisting as I waited for the next wave of soldiers to go by. For a break in the spectacle. And when it finally came, I sucked in a breath.

Diederik, separated from the others watching by standing about a foot in front of them, an island of acceptance in a sea of disbelief, watching as Haarlem was occupied step-by-step, tread-by-tread, his arm held straight and high in salute.

10

By the end of May, Austrian born Arthur Seyss-Inquart had been assigned to govern our country. In his inaugural speech he claimed they wouldn't oppress us, our land, or our politics.

"What does that mean?" Elif asked our mother, her brow furrowed with skepticism. "They want to be our friends?"

Mama shook her head. "It's meant to subdue us so we don't rise up and fight them."

He kept his word initially, but that summer of 1940 was fraught with tension, disbelief, confusion, and fear.

The German military commandeered city hall and took offices in several other buildings in town, as well as took up camp in the few small hotels. There were uniforms everywhere. Every store we went into, every street we walked down, and every park we visited was dampened by their presence.

But it was hard to complain too much. While other countries' economies were being stripped, Dutch businesses flourished. Restaurants overflowed with soldiers wanting to taste the local cuisine. They bought clothes, books, tulip-inspired gifts to send home to their girlfriends, wives, and mothers, and stood in queues that went out the doors of our chocolate shops, a treat, it had been overheard, that they'd long been deprived of.

And yet despite the business burgeoning with customers, one was never able to forget the truth of the matter. We were occupied, and those men opening doors for us, smiling as they passed us on the street, and heard flirting with any pretty girl who walked by, were the enemy. Weren't they?

Every time I left our house I was struck by the oddness of it. There was none of what we heard was happening in other countries; the constant barrage of attacks, people forced from their homes and sent away on trains, bombs falling, citizens trying to leave and getting trapped or, worse, killed upon escape, machine-gun fire raining down on them. I wasn't complaining about the lack of aggression, but I also didn't understand it. Why were we different? Is this how it started in all the cities? Were they nice until they weren't?

I was on guard at all times. I didn't trust their manners and often hurried to beat them to opening the odd door for me. I didn't want their favors. I refused to meet their eyes or their smiles with my own. I was careful not to seem rude, but I refused to be like so many others being taken in by these inadequate gestures. I had not forgotten, nor would I ever, that they weren't visiting. They were occupying.

Summer came, bathing us in warmer days and carefree moments that allowed us to forget at times what was happening in the world around us.

Most flocked to the beach in droves, undeterred by the soldiers Fenna and Tess informed me sat nearby, their shirts folded neatly beside them on their blankets, eyes darting from person to person. While I missed spending long afternoons in the sun, the waves lapping at my toes, I still couldn't fathom being there without Madi. And I certainly didn't care to go and have my day marred by the presence of the men occupying my peaceful home.

Other than their constant presence, the only real change we saw in town was at the theater, where American-and British-made films were removed, and only German-made films were now shown, and on the radio, where the few broadcast stations now played German music or reported German news. Thankfully, though, the BBC was still able to transmit, and many of us tuned in nightly to hear updates on the war, with the rare appearance by Queen Wilhelmina on Radio Oranje, where she kept us apprised of what our government in exile was doing, boosted our morale, and prayed with us for better days ahead.

"I knew she wouldn't desert us," Elif whispered the first time we heard our sovereign address the nation over radio waves.

It was mid-August when we got the next shock to our collective system, with an announcement that Jewish teachers would not be allowed to return to their positions in the fall.

"Why?" I asked my mother. But I knew why. It was what I had suspected from the beginning. They would treat us well, until they didn't.

The next time I was to watch the Aberman children, I arrived at their house early, anxious to see my favorite teacher and his family.

"Oh, Lien," Rachel said when she opened the door, their new baby in her arms. Little Bo was born in June and was a quiet baby with a sweet disposition. "I forgot you were coming. We're a little…" Her voice trailed off, and she waved vaguely at the front hall. "Come in. Please."

I followed her to the kitchen where Mr. Aberman was sitting at the table looking much as he had that first day back at school after the attack in May. He'd grown thin. There were hollows in his cheeks that hadn't been there before, and his shirt hung from his body. Even his wife, now that I looked closer, looked thinner than a woman who'd had a baby not long before should.

"Hello, Lien," Mr. Aberman said, giving me a wan smile that

disappeared as fast as it had come. "How are you? What are you up to today?"

"I came to take the kids to the park..."

His eyes moved sharply to his wife.

"Oh. I'm not sure we— Maybe you could play with them inside?" Rachel said. "We just... We're not comfortable having them out of our sight. Or even outside right now."

"Of course," I said. "I'm happy to play upstairs with them. Maybe read a book?"

Mrs. Aberman's eyes filled with tears. "They would love that, Lien. We haven't felt much like reading or playing lately. They'll be so thrilled to see you."

I nodded, placed my finger in the baby's pink palm, watching as her tiny fingers curled around it, and then hurried up the stairs.

When we returned to school in the fall, it wasn't with the usual first day of school excitement. Mama had made us a few new items of clothing, but not as many as she normally did, preferring to reconfigure some of our clothes to reflect current styles rather than sew entirely new pieces. Her mind, like ours, was elsewhere.

We'd managed to hang the remaining few posters in that initial stack she'd received in May, but there'd been an increase in identification cards needing forgery, and it was hard to keep up with demand with a shop to run. Elif and I had helped her during the summer months, but now that we were set to return to school, she'd have to do most of it herself, or wait for us to help after the last bell rang.

The new, stern faces on the staff at school were a jarring addition, and the lessons they taught, all heavy on Nazi ideology, were discussed in hushed voices in between classes and at lunch.

Even the regular teachers, the ones allowed to stay on, whispered in dismay. But no one was comfortable or brave enough to question it.

"I heard Mr. Van Rossum ask Mr. Nagel what he thought of the new lessons," Fenna said. "He didn't even answer. He looked like he wanted to cry."

I glanced across the table at Tess who was quieter than usual. Fenna and I had kept close to her all summer, going to her family's home for overnights, dinners, and leisurely afternoons spent in their small but lovely garden.

It felt almost normal as we lay around her room in our usual spots: Tess propped up with pillows against her headboard; Fenna sitting at the vanity brushing her long, dark hair, and me lying on the floor beneath the window, watching the clouds drift by and smiling, as I always did, at the fading red paper heart I'd given Tess the year we'd all turned ten. I'd put each of our initials on it and told her, after her latest crush had dismissed her affections, that the three of us were all the love she'd ever need. She'd affixed it to the window where it had stayed all these years.

But that sweet feeling of normalcy left the moment we convinced her to go out anywhere. She frantically pulled her hair back so tight no curl had a fighting chance, and wore a hat and clothing that looked like it had come from Fenna's closet, rather than her own.

"She's trying to blend in," Mama said when I told her of the change in my friend. "Trying to hide the physical traits associated with being Jewish." She'd sighed and shaken her head, whispering, "Poor thing."

Tess had two of the new teachers at school. Fenna and I each had one. Classes with them were quiet, no one daring to speak out of turn. No one wanting to even breathe.

It was the second week of school when I had to retrieve a book from the library, taking me past Mr. Aberman's old classroom. Once a space filled with lightness and laughter, when I hurried by I was startled by the silence, the heads bowed over papers, the teacher's eyes watching like a hawk.

Elif, in her last year of high school, was thrilled to be on her way out. Something I found almost unfair, and more than a bit daunting. I didn't like the idea of being at school without my sister. There was comfort in knowing that, should anything happen, I could run down a hall and find her. But next year that wouldn't be the case, and the thought that I may somehow be trapped and separated from my family should there be an attack or a bombing, frightened me.

"Maybe the war will be over by next year," she said, trying to soothe me.

But from what we heard on the news every day, I doubted it.

It was October before I saw the Abermans again. Mr. Aberman had taken to teaching the older two kids at home, along with a handful of other children whose parents were too scared to send their kids to school.

The living room had been turned into a classroom, with a blackboard on the wall where a painting of the seashore used to hang, and several chairs had been added for seating. There was a new coatrack in the entryway, a cup filled with extra pencils, and shelves with paper and books.

"It's different," he told me on the Saturday afternoon when I'd come by to watch the kids. "But the parents are willing to pay, so I'm actually making more than I was, and I don't have to walk in the rain and cold to get to work."

I smiled, happy to see him finding the good in a situation that had cramped their once tidy home and made him and his family scared in their own town.

Mrs. Aberman walked in then, Bo—who was four months old now and had the longest eyelashes I'd ever seen on a child—on her hip, smiling, her little pink fist wrapped in her mother's dark hair.

"Can I hold her?" I asked, and was handed the child, who squealed and drooled and pumped her arms, making us all laugh.

"Just one more Aberman kid who loves you," Mr. Aberman said as I smiled down at the tiny girl whose downy hair was paler than her other siblings and curled softly over the delicate shells of her ears.

I both loved to hold her, and ached at having her near. I could remember holding Madelief at this same age. I'd been much smaller then, only allowed to hold her with the help of a parent, but I'd adored her impish grin, her eyes the same gray-blue as Elif's and mine. "Vinke blue" our father had called it. Like the sky before and after a storm.

It was late December when I came again, braving the biting cold winds off the North Sea that streaked down the streets and rushed inside as soon as Mrs. Aberman opened the door. This time it was Bo I was watching, while the older children went with their parents to get cocoa and pastries at their favorite bakery.

They'd been venturing out more these days, they'd told me. It was hard to stay inside when the town was decorated so festively for the holidays. I'd been chasing after Bo, who was crawling everywhere, for the better part of an hour when the rest of the family came home, the kids looking happy, the remnants of chocolate on their faces, their parents looking as though they'd seen a ghost.

"You're back early," I said, shifting Bo to my other hip as I first checked the clock, and then noticed their expressions. "Did something happen?" I asked, my voice lowered.

Bo reached for her mother, who took her and left the room, shooing the older children upstairs to wash their hands and faces. I glanced at Mr. Aberman, who met my eyes.

"There were soldiers at the bakery," he said, his voice solemn. "They kept looking at us and sneering. When they left, one of them ran into Rachel. Hard enough to make her spill her tea. It was clearly on purpose, but of course we kept our heads down and mopped up the mess. They lingered, though, and then the one uttered something—" He stopped and looked away, but not before I saw something in his eyes that made me uneasy.

He looked scared. "He said something deplorable. A slur. It was quiet, the kids didn't hear, and wouldn't have understood if they had. But Rachel and I did." He sighed. "I have been afraid ever since there were rumblings about war, and then fearful when countries began to fall. But now...now I'm truly frightened. There has been much talk in our community. I didn't want to believe it, but I don't think we have a choice now."

"You mean, our community of Haarlem?" I asked, and he gave me a grim little smile.

"No, Lien. In *our* community. The Jewish community. There are so many of us here, and so many more have come from other countries, assuming our previous stance of neutrality would keep them safe. But now we know better, don't we? Nowhere is safe. There are rumors of networks in other countries. People trying to help us, hide us, get us out safely. My brother told me..." He stopped and sucked in a breath, shooting me a worried look. "Never mind. It's not impor—"

"I know about the underground," I said, my voice low. "I've helped put up some posters."

A cavalcade of emotions washed over his face. Surprise, wonder, understanding. And then again, worry.

"Be careful, Lien," he said, placing a hand on my arm. "It is dangerous work. Not a job for young girls. And you should be just that, young girls. Free and happy without a worry, except for your grades of course."

I smiled, but then looked toward the stairs where his kids had gone up only minutes before.

"And your girls, sir?" I asked, my brows knitting together. "And Isaak? Don't they deserve the same things?"

He crossed his arms over his chest, his large brown eyes filling with tears as they moved around the happy kitchen filled with framed photos, finger paintings, a stray toy truck tucked among the cookbooks on a low shelf...

As I headed home a little while later, my hat pulled low, my scarf over my mouth and nose to block them from the icy wind coming off the sea, I took a detour and rode past Tess's house.

Her family had gone to Hoorn for the day to visit an elderly aunt. Normally I wouldn't think twice about it, but after hearing Mr. Aberman's account of the incident at the bakery, I was suddenly concerned that they were so far away. What if something happened and they couldn't get back home? Or weren't allowed. Or were taken elsewhere against their will?

As my imagination began to branch out, creating scenarios and situations, my legs pumped harder, my bicycle speeding up.

A gentleman yelled as I zipped around a corner, our arms brushing as I sped by.

"Sorry!" I said, and pressed the brakes. My heart pounded in my chest, my breath coming in short puffs.

Impending war had always been frightening, the implications and rumors terrifying. But until it had landed on Dutch soil, I hadn't believed we'd be affected. I hadn't taken it seriously or been as afraid for the safety of my loved ones as I was in this very moment. The childlike veil I'd hidden so comfortably behind had been lifted, the ugly grown-up truth flooding in.

I needed to do more than just put up a few posters.

"How were the Abermans?" Mama asked as I entered her shop a few minutes later.

As usual, she was bent before a customer, pins in her mouth, a tape measure draped over her shoulders. Another woman browsed the fabric samples on the rack.

"Good," I said. "Fine."

She gave me a curious look, but didn't say more.

"Where's Elif?" I asked.

"In the back. Perhaps you can see if she needs help?"

It was the way she said it that got my attention.

"Of course, Mama," I said, and hurried towards the back room.

"Your girls are so responsible, Katrien," the woman standing still on the pedestal said.

Elif was sitting at the table, the desk light shining down on the identification card before her, her brow knit in concentration.

"Mama said to help you," I said.

She finished a letter and sat up, scrutinizing her work before looking up at me.

"There are three that need to be done today," she said. "And then we need to get them to the Ten Booms. There's no time to teach you the writing part, but you could attach the pictures and do the stamps."

"And the delivery," I said.

She peered at me.

"I've done it before," I said.

"But you didn't know you were doing it."

"So I'll pretend I don't know I'm doing it."

"Fine. Here." She passed me a card. "This is an example. Practice the stamp on a piece of paper. It needs to be faded so it looks old, not fresh."

I did as she told me, and when she was done filling out the card she was working on, she handed it to me.

"Well?" she said as I stared down at the card. "What are you waiting for?"

I took a breath, raised the stamp, and pressed it to the paper. Holding my breath, I raised it back up.

"Perfect," my sister said. I exhaled.

We worked side by side, me watching as she carefully filled out the cards and then practiced the faked signature on a spare piece of paper before finally writing it on the card. Me affixing the photos while saying a prayer for the face staring up at me, and then applying the official stamp, all the while wondering how my mother got an official stamp.

When we were done, Elif gathered the cards and pulled a slender, square-shaped box with the Ten Boom logo on top from a shelf behind us. Turning it over, she pressed one side of the bottom and its opposite end popped up just enough for her to slip her fingernail in and slide the false bottom out a few inches. She placed the cards inside, slid the bottom back in place, and turned the box over and set it on the table. I picked it up and opened the top. Inside was a beautiful gold pocket watch. Elif pointed to the chain, and I leaned in for a closer look. Where the chain attached to the watch, the link was broken.

"If you're stopped," she said. "That's your excuse."

I stood and grabbed one of the cloth bags our mother kept on a hook and put the box inside. The scent of smoke startled me, and I turned to see Elif standing over the metal trash bin, holding a lit match to the papers she'd practiced signatures on.

"What about the stamp?" I asked.

She put the extra ID cards, the stamp, and glue in a box, and then bent down and reached beneath the table we'd been working at. As I watched, she pulled one of the floorboards up and set the box inside and put the floorboard back.

"Wow," I whispered.

When she stood again, I noticed something different in her eyes. There was still fear. Fear of war. Fear of the unknown. And now the fear of getting caught. But there was also pride. At some point in this back room, she'd gained a certain kind of power. Power I ached to have as well.

I flung the straps of the bag over my shoulder.

"See you soon," I said.

11

By year's end, Haarlem was at once the same, and yet altered in small, subtle ways. A vein of worry set just beneath the skin of the town connected us all as we waited for something we couldn't quite fathom.

Shops in town were as busy as ever, though, food in abundance, and the holidays unfolding in their usual fashion. There were a few modifications, like the omission of any decoration that portrayed the Dutch flag or was considered religious. The strangest part of the season for me was the absence of the bell in the tower of the great church in the square, the warm, hollow tolls the background music to every day I'd been alive. It had been ordered to stop ringing days after Germans occupied our small town. But it was hard to complain about something so insignificant when the streets were bustling with people, some familiar, others filtering in from other places, looking for refuge.

Mama suggested having Fenna, Tess, and Ana over for dinner on New Year's, and each girl's parents gave consent, with the stipulation that they were home before curfew. And so, for a few precious hours, we gathered and toasted the new year with the tiniest pours of champagne and cakes sent by Aunt Liv, who was hosting a party in a far grander scale at her home.

"One day I'll get an invite to one of her parties," Tess said.

I exchanged a look with Elif, who pasted on a smile and turned back to her friend Ana.

Normally we would be attending the party, but in a secret that was shared with us just days before, Aunt Liv's soiree this year would host not only an array of our country's wealthier inhabitants, but several German officials as well. And while we were disappointed to miss out on the festivities, none of us much fancied being in the company of the enemy.

We'd sat around our dining table like we always did on Sunday, our mouths open as she explained before we got wind of who'd been invited through classmates at school, or in the local paper.

"I will seem a traitor to some," she said as we ate, though I'd lost my appetite with the announcement. "There will be rumors, reports, and lies spread. Ignore it all. You will know the truth—but you cannot speak it. Ever. Do not correct anyone with the knowledge I'm about to give you. Not even your closest friends." She'd looked at me when she'd said the last part. "It is integral that everyone believe...well, whatever they feel they must about me. But thinking I am aiding the enemy will only help me do my job better."

"And what is your job?" I'd asked.

"Getting as many details out of those privy to important information as I can," she'd said, dabbing at the corners of her mouth with a napkin. "I have always kept one finger swirling in their business. It was a decision Hugo and I made long ago, during the first war. It makes others look at us a certain way, but those in the know understand. What we do is purely for our country. And so, what looks traitorous to some is a sacrifice we have always been willing to make. One day, if you decide to do more for the underground movement, you will have to accept that some of the things they say about me will be whispered about you behind your backs because of our association. To succeed, you must turn the other cheek. Pretend you didn't hear. Ignore, smile, and say nothing. Most will never know what we did. One day I may even be punished by those I helped. I'm okay with that. But I want you girls to know, because it is inevitable stories will circulate. Having favor with the enemy is no small feat."

Elif sat back at that, a look of distaste I didn't understand crossing her features.

"Elif," Mama said, reaching for her hand. "Not that kind of favor."

"Oh," she said, her cheeks reddening. "I thought…"

Aunt Liv laughed. "Oh my dear," she said. "Not many men would be interested in that with this old woman."

I felt my own cheeks warm as understanding dawned, which only seemed to make the older women that much more amused.

"There are some who will be desperate enough to get themselves in those positions," Aunt Liv said. "For some, it will feel like it's the only way to survive. For others, it truly will be. And still for others…one never knows who's working for whom. Don't cast stones upon those willing to do whatever they can to get lifesaving information out of the enemy. Some of the strongest women I've known used their bodies like tools to save the ones they loved. Be kind, my dears."

She left us that night with minds full of thoughts that we may never have pondered previously. Questions we couldn't form well enough to ask just yet. And the knowledge that our gender possessed a power we found unfathomable. Frightening. But awe-inspiring.

The month of January brought with it the disturbing news that all people of Jewish descent were to be registered.

"They're separating us," Tess said, her voice low as we ate lunch one day.

As much as I wanted to deny it, she wasn't wrong. There were rumors of maps being drawn up identifying name, age, gender, marital status, and the location of all Jews living in each city across the Netherlands. As I'd long suspected, our German occupiers had drawn us in, fooling us with their talk of the Dutch being part of the "master race." What they'd failed to mention was that that didn't include Dutch Jews. The seed of doubt in my stomach had grown into a pit, and I couldn't help but wonder what came next.

I was returning from an errand delivering a new coat when I glanced down at a stack of newspapers outside a corner market. The headline made me trip over my own feet. "My Honor Is My Loyalty," it shouted. It was what we'd come to know as the battle cry of Dutch men joining the Waffen SS. I picked it up, bile rising in my throat as I skimmed the article, which encouraged enlistment, the photos below showing Hitler Youth riding motorcycles and a group of young men in a glider club showing how well off one could be if only they joined the ranks.

Shaking, I paid for the paper, looked around to make sure no one was watching, and shoved it in a nearby trash bin.

"How did Mrs. Hummel like the coat?" Mama asked when I returned.

"She loved it of course," I said, and moved on to my next task without prying for information.

As I was still only fourteen, nearly fifteen, Mama hadn't changed her mind about me being too young to do much of the underground work Elif was getting to do, like forgeries and information exchanges. If the items I delivered had information sewn in them, I was kept in the dark about it. If a box I was to take to the Ten Boom watch shop was hiding identification cards, I was none the wiser. But I liked to imagine every job I did outside the shop was a secret mission for my country. I wanted to believe I was aiding our fight for freedom, even if a skirt was just a skirt and a box held only a broken watch. I was determined to be taken seriously about my want to help, but realized throwing tantrums wouldn't get me there. I would bide my time and then make my case.

In late February, a strike in Amsterdam by Dutch workers lasted two days in retaliation of a program by the Germans that saw over four hundred Jews brutally seized and deported. The strike spread to other cities, including Haarlem, causing panic that had everyone fleeing the streets for their homes, blackout curtains pulled shut, doors locked. We were kept home from school and not allowed to use the telephone.

"But I need to see if Tess and Fenna are okay," I said tearfully to my mother.

"Their parents are sure to have them home as well, Lien. You will see them again soon."

A few days later it was announced over staticky radio airwaves that over 300,000 Dutch citizens went on strike, bringing part of the country to a standstill and notice to the rest of the world of the unrest that was happening. To prevent another strike from happening, security forces chose at random eighteen protesters and publicly executed them. It was a shock to our small, peaceful country, and there were many nights I had trouble sleeping, for fear that at any moment on any day, me or someone I knew could have the same done to us for something we'd had no part in. I was terrified the protest had set something worse in motion.

Spring of 1941 snuck in with its usual blustery start, the sun peeking through the clouds on a more regular basis, the wind off the water not quite so jarring. And with the warmer weather, more and more people were out and about, timidly enjoying the parks and outdoor spaces of restaurants, nervous smiles on their faces as they clung to any happiness they could find in the darkening days we worried were coming.

While the Abermans didn't call on me as much these days, preferring to keep the groups they associated with small, their only visitors the students my old teacher taught, every so often I was still asked to watch the children.

On one particular Saturday afternoon, I left my mother's sewing shop to walk the few blocks to their home. It was sunny, a rare cloudless day, and for a moment I forgot myself. Forgot the world we were currently living in, and just breathed in the warm air, feeling the rays on my skin.

I let my mind wander, away from my responsibilities at school and the assignment waiting to be finished as soon as I got home. Away from the forgeries Elif had been diligently working at in the back room before I'd left. Away from the jacket mother had been sewing in a rare pause between customers, a folded square of paper beside her waiting to be placed inside the lining.

I hated being left out of the important work they were doing. Of wondering but not getting to know for sure if the items I delivered hid important information. But I'd argued my point so much, my mother no longer heard me. She didn't care that I said I was ready. That I was just as responsible at nearly fifteen as Elif was at nearly seventeen. That I was prepared for the worst, while never really knowing how bad the worst could be. I wanted to help. I'd begged, and then threatened. But all that had earned me was extra chores and time spent alone in my room.

"I don't see why you're in such a rush," Elif had said one day as we changed out of our school clothes. "Forging documents isn't exactly fun."

"Maybe not for you," I said. "And anyway, that's not the work I want to do. I want to do deliveries."

"You are doing deliveries."

I'd sighed and rolled my eyes. "Important deliveries."

"For all you know, you are," she'd said.

But I wanted to know for sure.

I turned down the next street, two blocks from the Aberman house, and stopped. A small crowd had gathered outside the corner market. Past the wall of bodies I could hear two men

arguing over something that had happened in the store and a
woman pleading with both of them. Part of me wanted to stay,
to find out what was happening, but I'd be late if I did. Hurrying around the bystanders, I heard some of the voices rise in
warning and someone stepped backward into me. As I stumbled, a sound I hadn't heard in years made the hairs on my arms
raise. A distinctive click.

I turned as a scream rang out, followed by a shout and then
the discharge of a gun.

Footsteps of the bystanders thundered away and I stood stock-
still, staring at an older man I recognized as the owner of the
shop who was kneeling, his now dead wife in his arms.

"Call someone," he said, his voice hoarse and broken. One of
the onlookers still standing nearby hurried into the store.

Shaking, I looked around, wondering who had taken the shot.
Several meters away I saw the back of a soldier walking away,
unhurried, two bottles of beer in one hand, the other shoving a
pistol in its holster. I took a step toward him, not knowing what
I would say should I confront him, but a moment later he disappeared around a corner and my moment of bravery vanished.

I looked down at the older man rocking his wife's body back
and forth, his shirt and pants soaked in her blood. The two were
a familiar part of my walk to my teacher's house. Often she was
out front arranging the bouquets of flowers for sale, or he was
straightening the bins of fruits and vegetables. They were always
friendly. What had gone wrong?

"They're Jewish," Mr. Aberman said in a low, sad voice as
we sat at the kitchen table after I'd arrived near tears at his front
door.

Mrs. Aberman set a cup of tea before me and leaned down
to wrap her arms around my shoulders.

"Why does it have to matter?" I asked.

"Sometimes people just get an idea," Mr. Aberman said. "And

for them, that's it. The answer to some terrible question in their minds."

They let me sit until my hands stopped shaking, and then Mr. Aberman offered to walk me back to my mother's shop.

"If you don't mind," I said, "I'd like to still watch the children. It will help calm my nerves."

The two adults exchanged a warm look.

"I think we would all like that," Mrs. Aberman said. "I'll call them down."

We played in the garden out back, Lara and Isaak challenging me to several races before I collapsed onto the blanket their mother had provided. I urged them on as I sat with Bo, whose father had brought her out to watch her siblings' antics.

As I rolled a ball to the littlest Aberman, I noticed the older children seemed clingier, each one demanding my attention in a way they never had before, their desperate pleas confusing me.

"Lien, look at me!"

"Lien, see what I can do!"

"Lien, watch this!"

"Lien! Lien!"

Even Bo, who could say a handful of words now, including "Leen," her name for me, was grabbier than usual, her pudgy fingers gripping handfuls of my hair when I wasn't giving her my full attention.

At one point I looked up and noticed Mr. and Mrs. Aberman standing in the back doorway, watching us. I waved and then watched in surprise as Mrs. Aberman raised a hand to cover her mouth and disappeared inside.

When it was time for me to go, Bo wrapped her arms around my neck.

"No no go, Leen," she said. "No go."

"I'll see you again soon," I said, gently extricating myself from her sticky grip and kissing her downy-soft cheek before setting her down. "Be a good girl."

I waved goodbye to Lara and Isaak, who stopped playing a board game they'd brought outside and threw themselves at me in an enormous hug.

I mussed their hair. "See you soon."

It wasn't until I walked back inside that I noticed the boxes tucked in a corner and the bare shelves and walls.

I turned, my gaze landing on Mr. Aberman, who stood watching me from the entryway to the kitchen.

"Are you…" I looked around the room again, trying to make sense of it. "Moving?"

"We're…just sorting through some things," he said, clearing his throat to cover the break in his voice.

Mrs. Aberman came down the stairs then and looked from her husband to me. She sighed and stepped into the room.

"Lien," she said, her voice soft. "Thank you for coming today. Thank you for—" She looked to her husband and wiped a tear from her cheek. "Thank you for taking such loving care of our children. They sure do love you."

"Of course," I said. "I love spending time with them."

I sucked in a breath, trying not to let on that I knew. I knew what they weren't saying, and I understood why. They weren't safe here. Not in this town. Not with the neighbors they'd shared bread and wine and laughter with. Not in this home where they'd made so many memories together.

They'd asked me here today, I suddenly understood, not to babysit, but to say goodbye. The realization hit me in my center, and all at once an image of dark water filled my mind. Cold air. A small gasp before I heard the splash.

I fought to push the sound away, focusing on the couple before me once more.

Mrs. Aberman opened her mouth to say something else, but when no sound came out, Mr. Aberman walked to her and placed his hand on her arm. She ducked her head and raised her fist to her lips, her chin trembling.

"You've been a godsend to us, Lien," he said. "Thank you."

"I was happy to do it," I said. "Thank you for allowing me in your home. It was an honor."

After school that following Monday, I rode to the Aberman house. The bicycles that usually stood outside the front door were gone, the curtains on all three floors closed. I knocked on the door but there was no answer. When I walked down the street and around to the narrow alleyway that ran behind their home, I saw that the toys usually littering the patio and grass were gone, the curtains on the back windows drawn as well, the little shed that housed their garden supplies closed, a padlock on the door.

They were gone. I had no idea if I'd ever see them again.

My heart ached as I rode to the shop, tears blurring my vision, the sound of Bo's baby voice in my head telling me, *No no go, Leen. No go.*

I hadn't gone. But they had.

12

As another school year came to an end, we celebrated Elif's graduation with a small party in our backyard. Ana and her family came, as well as Tess, Fenna, and Aunt Liv, who received some strange looks from the other guests.

"I have heard rumors," Tess said, noting the uncomfortable look on Ana's mother's face as she watched Aunt Liv sip from a teacup from her chair on the patio.

"Don't believe everything you hear," I said, my voice soft but stern, causing her and Fenna to eye me with curiosity. But I moved away before either could question what I meant.

That summer was different from the one prior, with even less time spent with my friends as everyone was keeping to themselves more and more to prevent any run-ins with soldiers. But on a rare late summer's afternoon, Fenna and I sat on the floor of Tess's bedroom as we'd done hundreds of times before, gabbing about the new upcoming school year and what we'd been doing to keep busy.

Like me, both girls had been put to work at their parents' businesses. Tess's dad, a family doctor, had been forced to leave his practice due to the restrictions put in place by the Nazis. Rather than fret, he began seeing patients in their home, and Tess had become his part-time receptionist, taking calls and reminding patients when they were due to come in.

Fenna was also now employed by her father, doing filing and other office tasks three times a week. His law firm was busy as ever and was in need of the extra help.

They complained about their jobs, wishing they could work like me in my mother's sewing shop so they could spy on some of the more glamorous clientele.

"It's not very fun, to be honest," I said.

"At least you're spared the smells I have to deal with," Tess said. "The other day someone came in with a festering boil. I couldn't eat dinner after that!"

We dissolved into giggles and then sobered as we moved on to other subjects, like how much emptier the streets were these days. It was common knowledge that any able-bodied man between the ages of eighteen and forty-five was being required to give up their lives here to fight for the Germans, or live and work in Germany so that their men could fight in the war. We'd heard recently of several boys who had been in Elif's class being sent away.

When we returned to school that fall, the class ahead of mine, which was one of the biggest to date, had been depleted by many of the boys who were already eighteen being sent to prepare for war, or to the work camps. Four of the male teachers were gone as well, replaced by stern German men and women with no smiles to give but punishments at the ready. By winter, I had set aside my dreams of becoming a lawyer like my father and planned to swap my education for a job.

"I could work with you and Elif here," I pleaded the Saturday after *Sinterklaas* as I stomped around the very shop I was begging to work at. "Or maybe at one of the markets. Or a café."

"Love," Mama said, looking up from a pleat she was sewing,

"No one is hiring. It's the slow time of the year. And with the war and so many citizens leaving—"

"You mean being forced out," I said.

"Many places have no need to hire anyone," she continued. "Go to school. Learn. See your friends. Try and retain some sense of normalcy in these strange times. Please."

"What if the school is bombed?"

Several in the country had been by then, and those schools left standing were overflowing with packed classrooms as students were being moved around from one facility to the next. Even ours had seen an influx in the early days of the war, though recently with some families moving on, whether by choice or force, it had resumed more normal class sizes. And still, some schools we'd heard weren't even bothering to try and educate their youth.

"They'd rather their citizens not learn Nazi ways," Aunt Liv reported one Sunday evening when she'd come to dinner. "They're studying from the books they have and hoping to resume classes sometime in the future."

But no matter how much I pleaded that there was no point in me getting an education at such a time when I could be doing more important things like Elif was doing, my mother wasn't hearing any of it, even when the next evening we received the news that the United States had entered the war.

"In the early morning hours," the broadcaster announced, "Japanese planes bombarded Pearl Harbor on the island of Oahu, dropping bombs and sending entire battleships to their graves on the floor of the Pacific Ocean."

I looked to my mother as if to say, *See? There's no point to school right now.*

Her eyes held a warning before they returned to her sewing.

By the time the country had thawed from winter that following spring, it was clear we were headed the way other countries had already gone. An announcement went out that all Jewish citizens were now required to wear a yellow star on their clothing, making sure it was visible at all times.

The first day Tess showed up with one sewn to her jacket, her face burning with embarrassment and fear, I pulled her to me and hugged her fiercely in the school hall, startled when she whispered in my ear, "Be careful, Lien. People are watching you."

Nearly every day now a truck was spotted loading men into it. Old, young, it didn't seem to matter anymore. What mattered was that they were Jewish.

"Why do they need so many of them?" I asked my mother one day as we made dinner. "How many factories do they have to fill?"

During the summer I was finally allowed to do more work. I was sixteen now, old enough by my mother and Aunt Liv's standards, and ready. And so, one blustery afternoon I followed Elif into the back room of the sewing shop and learned the delicate art of falsifying documents.

That night, my fingers and the cuffs of my sleeves ink stained, my mother, sister and I rode our bicycles to Aunt Liv's for dinner. Our meals at the grand house happened less often now since she was entertaining the enemy more and more often as a way to gather information to be passed on.

Even more disturbing were the slight but noticeable changes to her decor. Photos had emerged and been placed where they would be seen. Pictures of Mr. Vox and several important members of the National-Socialist German Workers' Party from WWI. There was even one of Hitler, by himself, positioned prominently on a table by itself.

"Once Hugo had settled into a small position of power among the men of the party, we held dinners, much like I'm doing now," Aunt Liv explained. "Dinners where information flowed freely. We had to be careful, of course. To share every detail learned at those gatherings would raise suspicion among the attendees. We could only choose one or two pieces of information to pass on. It was quite terrible, to be honest. Virtually choosing who got to live and who did not. But the small consolation was that people were indeed getting to live *because* of those dinners. Just not as many as we would have liked."

It was then that I realized the danger she was putting herself in. And not only herself, but her staff.

"They are given a choice," she said when she saw me glance at the kitchen staff after they'd served the first course and retreated once more. "Should they choose to leave, I provide safe passage wherever they desire and a month's pay. Should they decide to stay, I double their salary and encourage those who have a family to support to send them away so that if we are compromised, their families will remain safe. It is not for everyone, which is why I thoroughly question every person I hire. They know coming in that this may be a choice they have to make and papers are drawn up and signed for everyone's safety."

From that day on, I looked upon her staff with a newfound respect.

When the talk at the table turned to matters of the underground movement, as I'd hoped it would, I took the opportunity to push my belief that I was fully willing and able to do whatever Elif was going to be doing. Not just the safe back room activities I'd finally been given.

"You said when I was sixteen—"

Mama held up a hand.

"I know what I said. But like your sister, you will start small. With the less dangerous assignments."

"But she doesn't even want to do the dangerous assignments," I said. "She's told me."

"That was before," Elif said, her voice low.

I turned surprised eyes on my sister, and for the first time in a while took a long look at her. She'd changed in the past year and somehow, in the distractions of school and the shop and living in an occupied city, I hadn't noticed. The roundness in her face had slimmed, leaving more prominent cheekbones and wider eyes. We still looked remarkably similar, but the babyish round cheeks I still had were gone from her face, giving her a prettier, more elegant look. Like our mother. And while she hadn't grown any and was still only an inch taller than me, she now held herself with more confidence and maturity, making her seem taller.

"You're not afraid anymore?" I asked.

"Of course I'm afraid," she said. "It's dangerous work, and I don't want to die. But I also realize how important it is. We're saving lives. And that makes it worth the risk."

I turned to our mother. "I'm willing to take the risk too."

She sighed and glanced at Aunt Liv, who kept her expression blank.

"I know you think you are, my love," Mama said. "And I'm proud of you. But you're only sixteen, Lien. Elif is technically an adult now. Legally, she can make her own decisions without my interference."

I pouted through the next two courses, not speaking to anyone and avoiding Elif's eyes, which I could feel urging me to look at her. But I was angry and felt left out. They were treating me like a child, and it infuriated me.

Mama and Aunt Liv moved on in quiet voices to the subject of an upcoming dinner party the latter was having in hopes of gaining information.

"I wish you were available, Kat," she said. "You used to be so good at this sort of thing."

I stared across the table at my mother, wondering what Aunt Liv meant. What kind of thing had my mother been good at? But then the conversation changed again.

"Do you know where to go tomorrow?" Aunt Liv asked Elif, who nodded. "Henrik and Frans will be there, as well as a few others you'll be working with once you're all trained."

"And the weapons?" my sister asked.

"They'll be provided."

"Weapons?" I said, looking around the table. "What weapons?"

"It's just a precaution," Aunt Liv said. "For now. One never knows how a situation will turn out. Better to be armed and ready to defend yourself than caught defenseless."

"You said 'for now,' though."

The two women exchanged a look.

"There are other jobs that need to be done," Mama said. "We just want to be sure they're prepared for anything that might come up."

I was silent on the ride home, lagging behind my mother and sister as I bumped along the cobblestones, the smell of the rain that had fallen while we'd eaten dinner at Aunt Liv's filling my nose.

"Lien," my mother said over her shoulder. "Keep up."

I was sullen the rest of the night, moving about the house without speaking as my mother made tea and Elif hurried upstairs to wash and get ready for bed. I passed her on the stairs as she came back down and I headed up, and refused to look at her. When I returned to the main floor, I ignored the cup of tea set out for me, the aromatic steam enticing, but not enough to give in to.

I climbed onto the sofa I was still using as my bed, pulled the blankets over my shoulders, and turned my back to the two of them. If they spoke at all, I heard not a word.

In the morning, the three of us rose, dressed, and quickly ate before Elif and mother left for the shop and I prepared to spend my day studying for final exams.

"If you finish early or need a break," Mama said, slipping into her jacket, "I'd love to have you at the shop."

"Mmm-hmm," I said, barely looking up from my textbook.

As soon as I heard the front door close and the lock slide into place, I ran up the stairs to my mother's room.

The guns my father had taught Elif and I to shoot with were still in a wood box beneath his side of the bed. I pulled it out, unlatched it, and opened the top, letting the familiar smells wash over me. I had once thrilled at the feeling of holding these guns. The power at my fingertips, the aiming, my breath, the cool metal beneath my fingertip as I pulled back, and the kick to my palm that reverberated up my arm to my shoulder. We'd go out for hours, lining up targets, taking our shots, examining and comparing. Elif had loved spending time with our father, but hated the shooting. It was too loud, too exhausting, not feminine or soft. But I had thrived. I was a natural, my aim impeccable. And I was going to prove my skill set was too valuable to be turned away.

I placed what I needed in my book bag and then sat back at the table, keeping an eye on the clock. At eleven, I grabbed the bag, put on my coat and shoes, and hurried out the door. I'd overheard mother reminding Elif that she'd have to leave the shop by eleven thirty so as not to be late for training. At eleven fifteen I sat on my bike two doors down, hidden from view and waiting for her to appear. When she did, I followed her at a distance.

The training spot was in a wooded area northwest of where Aunt Liv's home was in Bloemendaal. I watched from behind a grouping of trees as Elif rode into a clearing, greeted whomever was already there, and dismounted her bicycle, leaving it with three others.

It didn't take long for the shooting to start and, with the noise as my cover, I crept closer, walking my own bicycle up the narrow path and setting it down quietly. Closer and closer I moved, careful not to step on downed branches, listening as directions were shouted.

"Not bad," a voice said. I recognized it as Uncle Frans. "Try relaxing your arms a little."

Another shot. Then another. A grumble from nearby.

I looked around the thick trunk of a tree and saw a man leaning on a cane watching the guns being fired. His body was hunched and gangly, his clothes hanging off him. Graying dark hair that looked as if he'd barely just remembered to comb it before leaving the house, and a profile that reminded me of someone I revered and loved. This was Henrik, Aunt Liv's brother that no one ever saw but gossiped about aplenty.

I watched him for a moment more as he peered at the others, and then turned just in time to see Elif hit her mark. I smiled and looked to see who else was part of the group.

Aside from her, Uncle Frans, and Henrik, there was another younger man, and a girl whose bright auburn hair shone like a beacon through the trees.

Several shots discharged one after the other.

"Nice, Charlie," Uncle Frans said.

I took a step from behind the tree I was using for cover to see this Charlie's shots, and trod right on a branch, which cracked and broke, the sound echoing through the trees.

"Who's there?" Henrik called.

A second later I heard a click and for a moment was looking at the wrong end of the pistol before it was pulled away.

"Jesus, Lien," Uncle Frans said, lowering his gun. "You could've gotten yourself shot. What are you doing here?"

My face burning, I stepped out from the brush and followed him hesitantly toward the others.

I couldn't look at Elif, nor the other two trainees, and one glance at Henrik made me wish I hadn't come.

"What's in the bag?" he practically snarled at me.

I looked down at my side, having forgotten it was on me.

"A gun," I said.

"What?" He held a hand up to his ear.

I sighed and then shouted. "A gun!"

"What kind?"

I looked at Uncle Frans.

"Is it your dad's?" he asked. I was surprised to see that he seemed to be fighting to keep from smiling.

"It is," I said. "The one he taught me with."

"Well, might as well get it out. Henrik won't stop barking until you do."

"What's that?" Henrik yelled, making Uncle Frans chuckle quietly.

I pulled the slender case from the bag, opened it, and pulled out the gun.

"That a 9 mm FN?" Henrik said, moving closer.

Uncle Frans nodded. "It is," he said.

"Well, the little girl brought it. Let's see what she can do with it."

"I don't think—" Elif spoke up, but Uncle Frans raised a hand.

"It's okay, Elif," he said. "Henrik's just being Henrik. We'll let her take a shot or two, and then she'll head back home before your mother catches wind of this. Right?" He looked to me again and I hesitated, not wanting to agree, but nodding obediently.

"Tell her where to stand," Henrik said, bending to grab something and then limping across the grass to hang a fresh target.

Uncle Frans led me to where the young man was standing. My eyes met his, and I was surprised that rather than look annoyed by the interruption like I noticed the redheaded girl was, or bemused by the fact that a young woman was taking his place, they held a look of genuine curiosity. He gave me a small smile and a nod as he stepped aside, and I felt my cheeks warm as I ducked my head and took his place, wishing suddenly that I'd stayed home with my textbooks. Maybe I was wrong. Maybe I didn't belong here after all.

But then, as Uncle Frans moved away, he gave Henrik a look I recognized from being a girl. From being small. From being underestimated always. He was just humoring me.

I glanced past him at Elif, who had seen the look as well. Her eyes met mine and I sucked in a breath. *Show them*, her expression seemed to say.

And so I did.

I turned toward the target, raised my hand with an inhale, and as I exhaled, I pulled off three shots without hesitating. Each bullet landed at the center, forming a triangle my father had called "Lien's symbol."

The echo of the shots reverberated around us until the wind swept them away, whispering across the blades of grass, leaving us in silence as a stillness fell over us.

"Jesus," the redheaded girl said.

"Damn," the young man beside me said.

"Papa called her Sure Shot," Elif said, walking toward me and Uncle Frans, whose brow was furrowed as he stared at the used target that Henrik took down with a mangled hand before hanging another.

"I remember," Uncle Frans murmured. "I thought he was just being a doting father."

"Again," Henrik shouted, and stood aside.

And so I did it again. Same pattern. Same dumbfounded response by everyone but Elif, who moved to stand by my side.

Uncle Frans nodded, a distant look in his eyes. "I'll talk to your mother," he said.

13

As promised, Uncle Frans spoke with our mother.

"She's a great shot, Kat," Elif and I heard him say from our perch, out of sight, at the top of the stairs.

"She's sixteen, Frans."

"There are boys younger than that signing on to fight in this war," he said.

I waited for her to say, "but those are boys," forgetting for a moment that my mother had never put restrictions on our interests or activities based on gender. Rather, she and our father had always encouraged us to try things not "typical" for girls to enjoy. There were trucks in our toy chest. Pride at our target shooting. Cheering us on during our brief stint playing football, the only two girls on an all-boys team. I knew my gender wasn't the issue.

"She's my baby," I heard her whisper.

Elif's fingers laced through mine.

That was it. With Madi no longer here, I was the baby again. Elif was an adult; she could do as she pleased. But I... I'd lost that middle child independence I'd enjoyed when a new baby had arrived, moving attention off me and focusing it on the neediest member of the family. Until that member died, shifting focus once again.

"She'll be trained well and we'll ease her in," Uncle Frans said. "Keep her to the lighter, less dangerous jobs until she's gained more experience and is closer to being of age."

Elif and I leaned in, straining to hear our mother's answer. But it didn't come until much later, after we'd been sent off to bed for the night, where I lay in my bed, staring at the ceiling until my eyes could no longer stay open.

In the morning, our mother, looking as though she'd aged years, told me she'd agreed to let me join my sister.

"You will do exactly as you're told," she said, her eyes fierce, her grip strong on my hands. "You will listen and train and not do one job unless you understand perfectly what you are to do. Do you understand me, Lien? Because so help me, if you get hurt, it will be nothing like the punishment I will incur for your sloppiness."

"Yes, Mama," I said, a tremor in my voice, my heart quickening in excitement.

The summer of 1942 was different from any before it. As I pedaled beside my sister through the streets of Haarlem on a warm June morning, our reflections undulating across the glass of the shop windows we passed, a mixture of determination, fear, and mischief swirled in my belly. I'd finally gotten what I wanted: purpose. But would it come at a price?

What it did immediately come with was responsibility, and so rather than race like I wanted to the field where we'd begun training in earnest with Henrik, I made myself keep a leisurely pace with my sister so as not to draw attention while wearing a skirt with a secret pocket mother had sewn into it to hide the pistol I was carrying.

In fact, to anyone watching, we just looked like a couple of young girls out for a morning ride. Every detail, from our plaited hair, simple clothes, our eyes wide with the fabricated innocence Mama had made us practice in the mirror, was meant to disguise us in plain sight. Not that anyone looking at the two of us would ever guess that we were up to anything nefarious. Being small in stature and always looking much younger than our age had its advantages for this job. No one would guess we were on our way to learn how to set fires, derail trains, or kill another human being. No one would even think it possible the idea of doing such things would cross our minds.

As we glided around the last curve, I caught sight of one of the lookouts who gave a little wave, the signal that all was clear. I cut into the brush beside a large oak, and bumped along the narrow path tamped down by bike tires and feet just enough to see if you were really looking, but not enough if you just happened along that way.

We reached the clearing and rode our bikes behind the rundown house at the far end of the property. Most of the windows were broken and the front door was missing. For all intents and purposes, the place looked abandoned and forgotten, the owners long gone, the four outer walls barely standing upright. But it belonged to Henrik. He had lived here, Aunt Liv told us after our first time seeing it. It had been his home.

"Aunt Liv," I asked over one of our now rare Friday night dinners at her home, "is it okay if I ask—" I shot a look at my mother before continuing "—what happened to Henrik?"

"Oh," she said, a small, sad smile on her lips. "Henrik was always headstrong. When England went to war, he packed a bag, left the key to the front door in an envelope for me, and got on a ship. He's never wavered in what he believes in, and never balks at standing up for those beliefs. But that war…" She sighed, and my mother reached over and took her hand.

"He was such good fun to be around when we were kids," Mama said. "It's hard to see the boy he was beneath the scars, but he's still in there."

"Planning kidnappings of my dolls and whispering lies to the boys I fancied," Aunt Liv said with a little laugh that caught and broke. But ever the lady, she put her smile back in place and moved on with the story.

"After the war," she said, "I didn't see him or hear from him for a long time. Your father returned. Frans…and of course my Hugo, but Henrik was nowhere to be found. No one had seen him. No one could tell us a thing. And then one day I was in my office and I heard voices at the front door. Angry voices, and then a murmur. The familiar timbre of a voice I'd been afraid I'd never hear again." She laughed. "Alard had almost shot him. Thought he was trying to rob us. He looked a mess. He was filthy, his hair matted, his clothing hanging off his body. He was missing fingers, and there was a dirty bandage wrapped around his head covering the eye he'd lost. There were other injuries too, but he wouldn't discuss them with me. Eventually though, he healed. He had the glass eye placed, the fits of paranoia lessened, he put some fat on his body, and learned to live a new normal. I'd fixed up his house for him, but he didn't want to go back there and wouldn't say why. I think he didn't want to be alone. And he didn't want to stay here." She waved a hand at the house around us. "Which I understood. It was too much. And I was too intrusive, always watching, always wanting to help. Henrik didn't want help. He wanted to be forgotten.

"Hugo came up with the idea for the barn. I of course thought it preposterous. He couldn't live like an animal in a barn. But he loved the idea." She snorted and shook her head. "Of course he did. It was an adventure and men are still boys at heart. The barn was built with a small basement residence for Henrik. A month after he moved in he brought home chickens, then a cow. Then more cows. He built himself a farm back there behind our fancy house. And I couldn't have been happier."

Two weeks later we saw the barn for ourselves.

We arrived to the Vox residence as instructed, riding past the house first and circling to the back where we hid our bicycles in the brush beside the fence that ran along the property line. After we walked all the way back around, we knocked on the glossy black front doors and waited to be let in.

"Ladies," Alard said, standing aside. "Good morning."

"Good morning, Alard," we said.

Appearances were everything, which was why every few weeks Elif and I had breakfast at the Vox residence. Should Aunt Liv's new friends in uniform be watching her, she wanted to be sure they saw that we were frequent and welcome guests.

"So that should they find you wandering around the back of the property at any time, they know not to report you…or shoot," she'd told us. "But be aware, should they find me suspicious of anything, they might also look upon you and bring you in for questioning. It is imperative that you insist our meals are family oriented only. We are not blood related, but I care for you as if we are. Which is the truth, minus a few details. Less is more, girls. Remember that."

And so we dined on poached eggs, fresh sausages, and warm sweet breads before each of us checked our watches and my sister and I excused ourselves and hurried out the back door.

It was odd the first time we'd gone to the barn. When we were younger, we'd played in the backyard of the grand house while the grown-ups talked, the barn far off in the distance barely piquing our interest. Back then, the entirety of the property had seemed like a magical place. A fairy-tale land with its many potted plants overflowing with trailing vines and flowers, burbling fountains, and sculpted trees. But the day Aunt Liv walked us out the back door and across the large paved squares, past the black iron tables and chairs and the elegant greenhouse filled with plants and, my imagination insisted, many fae in all shapes and sizes and colors, their wings flitting them from one exotic plant to the next, it was as though a veil was lifted, a curtain pushed aside, and another world—a scarier world—was revealed.

At the edge of the pristine lawn was a gate, beyond it an unkempt bit of land filled with cows, goats, three sheep, chickens, and the barn. Aunt Liv pushed open the gate and stalked across the marshy field in her expensive shoes, past a large black snuffling cow, to the nondescript white structure that housed not only the animals leisurely wandering about, but her brother.

Past the bales of hay, two water troughs, sacks of feed, and various tools, were three large barrels. She stopped beside them, slid her hand down the back wall, and then ducked out of sight.

"Come along," she called from somewhere below.

I didn't need to be told twice. I hurried across the dirty floor, Elif a few steps behind, to see where she'd gone.

Behind the barrels was a rectangular hole in the floor. I peered down into the darkness looking for a staircase, but saw none.

"It's a ladder." Aunt Liv's voice floated up to us. "On the side closest to you."

I lowered to my knees and reached down, my hand disappearing into darkness. I found the top rung and turned my body, easing myself down. It was clever, placing the ladder on the near side and out of sight. Anyone who approached it as we had would miss it and most likely assume it was either a trap, storage, or perhaps a place to dispose of hay.

Elif followed a moment later, and the three of us stood in the dark at the bottom of the ladder.

"Is there a light?" I asked, my eyes straining in the minimal light coming from above.

"No," Aunt Liv said. "Having a light here would defeat the point of this space."

She placed her hands on my arms, turned me, and moved me a few steps. She then did the same with Elif.

"In front of you is a false wall," she said. "There is a knock that will alert whomever is inside that you're friendly. When you hear a series of clicks, that means the locks have been disengaged and you can enter."

"How do we open it?" Elif asked.

"It slides."

I felt movement beside me and then heard a sharp rap of three knocks, a pause between two of them. A moment later four clicks echoed through the small space.

"Go ahead," Aunt Liv said.

I couldn't see what Elif was doing, so I reached forward and pressed my hands to the wall, pushing one way, and then the other. The door slid open and I blinked at the sudden light.

Spread out before us was one large room divided into different sections not by walls, but by support posts and furniture. When we stepped inside we were in a sitting area, complete with a small sofa, an armchair, and an oval coffee table with a marble top that looked out of place in a barn basement. I noticed, as I looked around, that most of the other furniture did as well. As though it had gotten its start somewhere much nicer—the main house, I supposed—and was cast off here.

Next to the sitting area was the kitchen. Beyond it, a bed and small chest of drawers. There were two doors on the other side of the room. I assumed one was a bathroom, the other a closet. But it was the center of the room that held one's gaze.

A massive table, scarred, charred, and covered in wires, bits of wood, nails, and more tools than I could count, sat front and center. Standing behind the table facing us was Henrik. Nearest us were the young man and the redheaded girl I'd met previously in the woods when I'd interrupted target practice. Charlie and Annie, respectively. They gave us brief smiles before Henrik barked at us.

"Well, don't stand there," he said. "Come in already."

"Have fun," Aunt Liv said.

As we walked toward the table, I took in the rest of the space. The long wall on the far side had dozens of shelves stacked with spools of wire, metal boxes, buckets, tools, and too many other things to name. Knives in all shapes and sizes hung in rows, guns in another section. Ammunition, gunpowder, and a box labeled Don't Touch were the last things I noted before turning my attention to the table and our host.

"Fireboxes," he said, and for the next few hours the four of us watched and then practiced making our first explosives.

For the next several weeks, we returned to the barn three times a week. Sometimes we made fireboxes, other times we learned how to use the daggers we'd chosen as our own, a process that took far longer than I'd expected it to.

"It is not as simple as choosing the one you think is prettiest," Henrik said the day we arrived to find them laid out on the big table. He was looking at Elif, Annie, and I when he said it. "The weight needs to be light enough to wield, but heavy enough to make an impact. The hilt should feel good in your hand. Natural."

"I can't imagine any dagger feeling natural in my hand," I murmured, eyeing the array of sharp blades.

As comfortable as I was with a gun, I wasn't sure I could actually shoot someone. The thought of stabbing another person made me hesitate even more. Life, I'd learned, was precious. Essential. To take a life… How did one begin to make that choice? Maybe in a moment of trying to stay alive myself it would seem an easy decision, but intentional killing seemed wrong.

I looked at the others who were holding and weighing the evil-looking knives in their hands, none of them seeming to give thought to what it might be like to sink one of those blades deep into the flesh of another. How could they be so accepting of the idea? Maybe I wasn't as cut out for this work as I thought I was.

"Don't worry," Charlie said beside me, his voice low. "You'll probably never have to use it. But it's good to always have one on you and know how to properly handle it."

Charlie already had a dagger, but he joined us in trying out the ones on display. I didn't know what I was looking for and watched Annie, who had a weapon in each hand, her eyes closed as she felt them. Elif, on the other hand, was poking at hilts, running a finger over their wood handles before finally picking one up and then putting it down just as fast.

I wrapped my fingers around a white-handled knife with a wicked-looking blade. The hilt was thick, and I struggled to find a comfortable fit for it in my palm.

"Here," Charlie said. "Try this one."

I glanced up at the older boy. In the past weeks I'd grown used to his presence, but knew little about him, other than that he was originally from The Hague, but had spent the past few years in England going to university. His only family were his mother and older sister, both of whom moved to North America when he left for school. And his father, like mine, had passed away. Other than those details, I had no idea how he'd come to be in Henrik's basement, how he was such a good shot, or why he had a dagger of his own. He didn't talk much, preferring to watch and listen. Henrik called him The Observer, and when his eyes weren't on what we were being taught, I often caught them on me.

I took the dagger he held out, my fingers brushing his, my face warming in reaction. The hilt wasn't large or ornate, but slender and manageable for hands as small as mine. The wood was pale and smooth from being held often in his hand, and there were tiny nicks and scars along its body, and a small, rounded pommel at the end that gave it balance. My thumb slid into an indent worn into the wood, and I realized it must've come from the previous owner's thumb.

"How does it feel?" he asked, his voice low.

"Its weight is good," I said.

"It's a Stormdolk."

Stormdolk. Storm dagger. How one could like a weapon I didn't know, but I did like it. It felt natural in my hand.

I glanced to Elif beside me and saw she was holding a similar knife.

"They are sisters," Henrik said, and I looked up to see that he was pointing to the daggers Elif and I held. "They were made from the same block of wood and came together. Owned by a good man."

"How come he gave them up?" Elif asked.

"He died."

When he didn't elaborate, we turned back to the weapons in our hands.

"The blade seems so long," I said, peering uneasily at the shining silver and its gleaming tip. It was at least eight inches, the double edges sharpened to ensure a lethal result.

"Should you ever need to use it," Charlie said, "you will be glad it's not shorter. If you must resort to using a dagger, you want to make your message clear."

"And what message is that?"

"That you will live, and they will die."

His eyes were like steel, his jaw set. My own eyes moved across his face to the scar that ran across his cheekbone and disappeared into his hairline. He pulled up one of his sleeves and I looked down. Another scar, at least six inches long, was slashed into his arm.

"You didn't die," I said.

"He wasn't very clear getting his message across. I was." His smile was like a glimpse of sun after days of rain.

"Will you show me?" I asked.

"I'd be glad to."

At Henrik's insistence, he ended up showing all of us. From the closet we pulled two hay-filled sacks stuck on metal frames, and Charlie marked the spots we should aim for and showed us how to hold our weapons, how not to, and different ways to strike. Then, two at a time, we stepped up to the "enemy" and began the grueling practice of learning to save our own lives.

"I'm exhausted," Annie said an hour later as we took a much-needed break in the upper part of the barn, out of sight from anyone who might walk by. Her red hair was damp and strands stuck to her face, but she didn't seem to notice as she took a huge bite of the sandwich she'd brought.

Unlike Charlie, Annie was an open book. Born and raised in Haarlem, she was older than Elif and I at twenty-two, and had a confidence about her I hoped to one day have myself. She didn't seem to get embarrassed if she did something wrong, couldn't care less if she sweat through her clothes or exposed a bit of skin, and didn't get flustered when we were told to "aim for the groin." She was funny, feisty, and willing to step in and speak up if Henrik ever forgot his manners or raised his voice—which happened often.

My favorite thing about the older girl was how she treated Elif, who'd never had an older sibling and was used to being the one looking out for everyone else. Annie took Elif under her wing, helping build her confidence. This seemed to take pressure off my sister, allowing her to learn and fail and try again without feeling like we were all looking at her to be an example.

"Using a dagger is definitely more tiring than shooting a gun," Charlie said. "You ladies did well, though."

"It was unnerving," I said. I hadn't liked how close I had to be to the dummy to strike deep enough.

Charlie looked at me from the bale of hay he was propped against, his head tilted as if contemplating my words.

"It's a more personal experience," he said. "You have to get close to the person, and it's easy for the situation to turn and for you to be overpowered. Especially for women who are lighter, smaller, and less inclined to want to inflict pain. There are maneuvers though, ways to move your body, and areas to target to help you get the upper hand. Or just get away."

"Why didn't Henrik have you teach us that?" Annie asked.

"I think he's more concerned with the weapons and didn't consider it. But I'm happy to."

"Now?" Annie got to her feet.

Charlie laughed and tossed his last bite of lunch into his mouth. "Sure."

We spent the next half hour learning the parts of our body that inflict the most pain, and the parts that hurt the most when hit, kicked, or headbutted.

"Lien," Charlie said, stepping to the center of the stall we were in, "will you help me demonstrate?"

There was a fluttering in my belly as I stepped toward him. He turned me so my back was to him, and then wrapped his arms around my waist and pulled me close.

"Try to get away," he said, his breath brushing against the shell of my ear.

I could feel my face heat with something besides embarrassment as I pulled and struggled, working up a sweat.

"Okay, stop," he said, and loosened his grip. "Remember what parts of you are the strongest. Don't think just about getting away. Think about how can you hurt me."

I thought for a moment, my chest heaving from the exertion of struggling against him.

"My heel?" I asked.

"Yes. You can stomp down on my foot. What about your head? You're shorter than me, but your head could cause a lot of pain if you threw it back into me."

To test his theory, I slowly tilted my head back and felt it bump against his chin.

"You do that fast and hard enough," he said, "you'll take out a tooth or make someone bite their tongue or see stars, causing them to loosen their grip on you. All you need is that second of distraction to get away, or to turn and do more harm."

We took turns after that, Charlie moving us around, talking through how we could get away from him.

"Scratch, bite, claw, pinch, poke, stomp, elbow, headbutt, grab," he said as we cleaned up our lunch mess and headed back to the trapdoor. "It's your life or theirs. Fight for your life."

The next time we met, we went through the motions again, with Charlie and each other. Elif and I practiced at home as well, shoving the dining table out of the way and trying to find new vulnerable spots on one another.

Inevitably, one of us got hurt. Mama would just shake her head as someone shouted out and keep on sewing. But the additional training helped. We both felt more confident in our own strength. I'd always thought because I was small, I was weak. But that wasn't the case. In many instances, being nearer to the ground assisted my attacks. My lower center of gravity helped me keep balance easier. I was able to throw my weight around better than someone taller. And I was closer to the groin area.

"Use that to your advantage," Charlie said.

It was mid-July when I found myself sitting on the sofa in Henrik's basement waiting for my turn with the dummies, when Charlie sat beside me. I tried to ignore his presence, but it wasn't as easy as it had once been. Our sessions upstairs had made me too aware of him. His scent—soap and fresh air. His smile—shy with a hint of mischief. His eyes—blue like the deepest part of the ocean. He infiltrated my thoughts when I wasn't expecting it, causing me to stare unseeing at walls. If Elif noticed, she was kind enough not to say anything.

We watched the two women work for a while, Charlie's head turned away from me, allowing me to study his profile privately.

"How's your friend?"

I jumped at the sound of his voice, not realizing I'd let my gaze slide down to his hand resting on his knee. He was looking at me, his eyes filled with concern, and my mind raced, trying to remember what I'd told him about my friends.

"Tess?" I asked.

He nodded.

I sighed. *Tess.*

The situation in Haarlem had escalated in the past couple of months. Jews were being taken by the truckload to the train station every day. We heard about it on Radio Oranje, from our neighbors, and whispered about in shops as we picked up our groceries, meat from the butcher, and bread from the bakery.

It didn't matter if they were of Dutch descent. They were Jewish. They had to go. It was in May I first noticed several familiar faces had disappeared from my morning ride to Mama's shop. Jewish-owned shops were closed, and vendors that had had stands at the Saturday market for decades were gone.

"It's only a matter of time," Tess had told me the last time I'd seen her. "They're taking us at all hours of the day. Just yesterday I heard that the Einhorns were taken in the middle of the night."

I'd known the Einhorns—Tess's neighbors—since we were children.

"What does your father say?" I asked.

She shook her head, her eyes filling. "He's afraid for everyone else. He's worried if he's not here and someone gets hurt, they'll be left in the street for dead. He's talking about sending us into hiding." She grabbed my hands and held tight. "I'm so frightened, Lien."

I met Charlie's eyes, and for a moment couldn't speak. He reached his hand out to me and wrapped it around my fingers.

"She's scared," I said. "Her father wants to stay. He's a doctor, and he's afraid no one will help their people should they need it. But he wants to send the rest of them into hiding. She's worried it's too late, though. The trucks come every day now."

"And we can't even trust our own people to keep us safe," he said, shaking his head as he referred to the Dutch policemen who were now working with the Gestapo. "Have you talked to Mrs. Vox?"

Across the room Annie cheered for Elif, whose jab to the

dummy had hit right on target. I watched them celebrate for a moment and then turned back to Charlie.

"I have," I said. "She's trying to find somewhere for them to go."

"I might know of a place." He squeezed my hand and let go. The feel of his skin remained on mine for a fraction of a second more and then dissipated into the air. "I'll talk to her today."

"Thank you, Charlie."

"Anytime, Lien." His voice was firm, his smile soft, the look in his eyes a promise.

14

True to his word, Charlie spoke with Aunt Liv after we finished training for the day. That evening, after we'd returned home, there was a knock on the front door. For a moment, no one moved, and then we all stood at once.

"I'll get it," Mama said, and hurried to answer while we followed after.

She shoved the cabinet we always kept in front of the door now out of the way just enough to pull it open a couple inches. There was a murmuring of voices, and then she closed the door and slid the cabinet back.

"Who was it?" Elif asked as we went back to the dining room where'd we'd been eating dinner.

"Alard," she said, looking at me. "They found a place for Tess's family."

"Where?" I asked.

"He didn't say, but they are to be ready to move in two days." She took my hand. "Go tomorrow first thing and let them know. They can bring one small bag each, that's it."

My entire body seemed to exhale with relief. The panic that

my friend would be pulled out of school against her will or her family taken under the cover of darkness was quelled, allowing the stress that had stiffened my muscles for days to ease.

But two days wasn't soon enough.

As I rounded the corner to Tess's street the next morning, I gave a start at the sound of a man's sharp voice as he barked orders in German.

I slowed, trying to see through the small crowd that had gathered, and was startled to see the slender Jewish owner of my favorite bookstore stumbling out the door of his house, three men in uniform following close behind.

The man's lanky form was hunched from fear or pain, and he cowered against the outside wall of his home as one of the soldiers threw a stack of papers at him. A gust of wind scattered them in all directions. As the soldier started shouting again, the man shook his head and looked around desperately for someone, anyone to help.

"I don't understand," he wailed.

The soldier spoke again, this time in Dutch.

"You send these papers?" he shouted. "You spread these lies?"

"No! I swear!"

As terrifying as it was to witness, I wasn't here for this man. I needed to get to Tess, whose house was down the street, on the other side of where the argument was taking place. But as I shifted my bike to move around the crowd, I saw it. A truck, and the line of people waiting to be loaded onto it.

A lump rose in my throat as my heartbeat quickened, my fingers clamping around the handlebars. I started riding, pushing against the pedals, willing the tires to spin faster, one of the man's papers stuck in the spokes, crumpling with each turn of the wheel.

As I rode past the scene, I turned just in time to see the man's head bounce off the brick wall of his house with a sickening crack. He fell forward and there was another crack, this time louder, the echo from the gun in the soldier's hand bouncing off the surrounding buildings.

I involuntarily hit the brakes as a spray of blood showered the cobblestones seconds before the man's body collapsed to the ground. The screams from the crowd combined with the shock of what I'd just witnessed caused a chill so violent I could barely force myself to move, pressing heavy feet against the pedals and pushing one after the other. I had to get to Tess's house—had to stop this same fate from coming for her or her loved ones.

I could hear the cries of the people being loaded now, see the fear etched in their eyes. A soldier blocked my way and I hit the brakes.

"You need to turn back, miss," he said, placing a hand on my handlebars.

I ignored him, looked around him, not caring about my safety, only my friend's. But I didn't see her and wondered if she was already in the truck. If it was already too late.

And then the front door of her house opened and one by one the family emerged.

Tess was wearing her favorite blue cardigan, the yellow star emblazoned on its front. Her face was pale, her eyes wide and frightened, her hair damp as though she'd been pulled from the bath.

"Tess!" I shouted, waving an arm.

She turned, her eyes seeking me out. When she saw me she stumbled, dropping the small suitcase in her hands to the ground. It fell open, some of the contents spilling out, but she didn't move, her eyes locked on mine as her mother knelt, shoved the clothing back inside, and handed it back to her, prodding her along.

"Wait!" I yelled, desperate. I looked up at the soldier who was unmoved, his face a mask. "Please. That's my friend. Can I see her? Can I say goodbye?"

He didn't answer, his hand firm on my bike. I swung my leg

over and made a run for it, but he dropped the bike and wrapped strong, cold fingers around my wrist.

"Please!" I cried.

The soldier at the back of the truck turned to see what the commotion was, and my heart nearly halted in my chest.

Diederik.

I hadn't seen him since the day the soldiers had marched into our little town. I remembered how he'd stood apart from those around him, chin lifted, arm held straight out in front of him in a salute of solidarity. I remembered how sick I'd felt at the sight. But nothing compared to seeing him dressed from head to toe in the classic dark gray uniform of the Nazi regime, his cap perched just so on his smooth, blond hair, the telltale SS "Death's Head" badge displayed prominently on the front of it. I felt sick. I wanted to ignore his existence, to pretend I hadn't seen him—but he may be my only chance.

"Diederik!" I shouted.

His eyes narrowed and then widened as he recognized me and took a step in my direction.

"Help! Please! That's Tess!"

I pointed and watched as he looked at my friend, taking her and her family in. I could see her shoulders shaking as she sobbed. My stomach churned as he turned back to me, and then looked past me at the officer holding on to me.

"Stay at your post!" he yelled to Diederik.

Diederik's chin dipped in a clipped nod and my heart sank, my stomach lurching as he turned on his heel and resumed standing guard as Tess's neighbors disappeared into the darkness of the truck.

"Please! They've done nothing wrong," I said to the officer. I tried to pull away, but he only held tighter, using his other hand to take a piece of paper from his uniform.

"See this?" he asked, holding it in front of my face. "Your friends are Jews harboring Jews. A crime punishable by death."

I felt the blood drain from my face, my knees buckling, and stopped trying to loosen his grip for fear I'd fall if he let go.

"They'll be sent to work in one of our camps until decisions are made about what to do with them in regards to their deceit."

"But—"

His grin was malicious. "If you like, I can see to it that you get a seat on the truck as well. I'm sure we can make room."

A shiver ran up my spine, and my eyes filled with tears. But then I heard Tess call my name and threw caution to the wind, more worried about my friend than myself. Ripping my wrist from the soldier's grasp, I ran for the truck.

"Tess!" I screamed.

The soldier behind me shouted something in German to Diederik, who looked from his commanding officer to me. He said something to the other man in uniform before stepping toward me. Maybe he was coming to listen. Maybe he would help after all.

I kept my eyes on Tess, who stopped at the wide, dark mouth of the back of the truck and turned, her eyes meeting mine, empty of hope, an acceptance of what was happening.

The dark waters rose and I heard the sound of a crack, a gasp, and saw an innocent blond head disappear beneath its murky depths—

I shook my head, jostling the images loose and looking to Diederik, inhaling as a small smile tilted the corners of his lips.

He raised his rifle and slammed the butt of it into my head. The last thing I heard was Tess's scream as the pain radiated and the world went black.

I came to some time later in the middle of the street, my bike beside me, a woman I recognized from the Saturday market kneeling over me. Something cold was pressed to my forehead, but it did nothing to alleviate the ache that filled my head, which was nothing compared to the ache I felt when I saw that the truck was now gone, having taken my friend and her family with it.

A low moan of agony grated against my throat, and I curled into a ball on the cobblestones and cried, realizing how horribly I'd failed again.

Eventually, painfully, and with the woman's help, I got to my feet and wiped my eyes.

"Here," she said, holding out the bloody rag that had been pressed to my head. "Take it with you."

"Thank you," I whispered.

She picked my bicycle up and I leaned on the handlebars as I walked, defeated, to Tess's front door. I tried the handle, but it was locked, the curtains in every window on the main floor drawn. I tipped my head back and looked at the upstairs windows. At the faded red heart in the corner of Tess's bedroom pane.

With a heavy sigh, I leaned forward and rested my forehead against the white door, my chest heaving as tears streamed down my face. I stayed like that for some time.

When I pulled back, I saw that my wound had left a red smear on the door. Reaching out, I traced a heart in it, then got on my bicycle and rode home.

"Is that you, Lien?" Mama called from the other room. When I didn't answer, I heard her footsteps quick on the hardwood floor. "Oh. Lien!"

She ran toward me and pulled me to her for a moment before pushing me away to examine my head. "What happened?"

Again footsteps, this time Elif running down the stairs. "Oh my gosh. Are you okay?"

But I couldn't talk. Couldn't say. My head screamed with pain and my heart...

"I was too late," I whispered.

"Too late for what?" Mama asked.

"Tess."

The rest of the day was a blur. They led me upstairs, washed my face, helped me into my nightgown, and laid me on the sofa in the library with a cold compress on my head. Their voices were comforting murmurs as I drifted in and out of a fitful sleep filled with visions of Tess's eyes before she disappeared into the truck, of Madi's face before she was swallowed by dark waters.

I woke with a start some time later and shot up from the sofa, a sob filling my chest as an image of Diederik filled my mind.

"You're okay," Mama said, hurrying to sit beside me. "You're safe, my love. Lie back."

I did as she said, and she leaned over to check the bandage she'd placed earlier.

"You have a nasty bruise that will look worse before it looks better," she said. "I think you've been spared stitches, though. That gash should close fine on its own."

I didn't care about the state of my healing. "I should've gone there sooner," I said. "I should've gone last night to tell them."

"It was too near curfew," she said. "And there was no way to know the truck would come for them today."

But I wouldn't hear it. I had hesitated, and I had failed.

Mama went to get a fresh compress. When she returned, I had rolled over so I was facing the back of the couch, pretending to be asleep. She ran a hand over my hair before moving away. A moment later I heard the familiar hum of the sewing machine.

I opened my eyes and stared at the fabric of the cushion, making a promise, both to my friend and to myself.

I would never hesitate again.

15

When Elif and I arrived at the field for target practice the following day, there was a brief moment of silence as everyone tried not to stare at my pale and broken appearance.

"I'm sorry about your friend," Annie said in her husky voice, giving me a fierce hug. She smelled of gunpowder, tobacco, and cinnamon, the combination oddly comforting. "We fight for her."

I nodded my gratitude and moved to my place between Elif and Charlie. As I passed my sister, she reached out and squeezed my hand.

When I'd awoke this morning, I'd found her lying on the floor beside the sofa I slept on, reminding me of when we were kids and would crawl into one another's beds when we were scared.

I squeezed her hand back and moved on.

"Lien," Charlie said. His voice was a whisper, but I could hear the emotion in those two syllables. He didn't meet my gaze. "I'm so sorry. I should've spoken up sooner. When you first mentioned their troubles. I didn't realize—"

I reached out and wrapped my fingers around his, wishing I could comfort his feeling of helplessness. Of guilt, and failure. I'd seen the same menagerie of expressions only this morning when I'd been unable to look at myself in the mirror. I'd tried to focus on the wound on my head, the bruising and traces of blood, until finally meeting my own eyes as I accepted that once again I'd failed. It seemed I was always just a few seconds too late when timeliness was at its most important. I would never forget that last image of Tess as she stood before the dark opening of the truck, only to climb inside while I lay unconscious on the pavement, and disappear to God knows where.

"It's not your fault, Charlie," I said. "It's mine. *I* should've acted sooner."

Before he could say more, I turned away and pulled my gun from the hidden pocket in my skirt.

That day Henrik had us engage in a more rigorous target practice. Rather than just stand, aim, and shoot, we had to fire from behind trees, lying in the grass, while running, and from not only our bicycles, but from the handlebars of each other's.

We tripped, stumbled, fell, and more than once got launched from our narrow cold metal seat as the driver of the bicycle hit an unseen rock or root. Sometimes we were concentrating so hard on our target, we forgot to pedal or accidentally turned our handlebars, jackknifing our bikes and missing our targets completely. It was an exercise in patience and perseverance.

At one point, Annie let out a stream of expletives. The four of us stood petrified, waiting for Henrik's reaction, and then burst out laughing. It was the release we all needed.

After we'd recovered, Henrik waved a gnarled hand.

"Again," he said. With a collective sigh, we got back to it.

During our break, we split up for lunch in the barn before resuming our training. Instead of doing our usual maneuver practicing, we sat quietly eating on top of the hay bales, Charlie in one corner of the stall, Annie in another, and Elif and I side by side across from them. We were exhausted from the energy exerted running, jumping, rolling, and riding around in the field while Henrik barked orders at us. More than once a gun failed to fire. More than once one of us asked if we could take a break. Several times we crashed into one another. And I was grateful for all of it. Not because I'd learned so much, but because it had provided a much-needed distraction, and built my determination up once more. I may have failed Tess, and Madi before her. But now, with this training, I would never fail anyone again.

"That felt almost cruel," Annie said after a while. "I wonder if that's what it's like when they train soldiers." She looked at Charlie. "How come you aren't enlisted?"

I'd wondered this myself. He was young, physically fit, and knew a lot about combat in its many forms. And he certainly didn't seem the type to shirk that kind of duty. Yet he was here.

"I have a heart condition," he said. "I tried to convince them it didn't matter. I play football, lift weights, and can run for miles. But the military apparently has enough men and doesn't need one they deem defective."

"How did you learn to shoot and—" She gestured to the stall where we'd engaged in mock attacks. "All that."

"I grew up shooting, and I have a couple of university pals who joined the Royal Army. They taught me some useful things." He shrugged and brushed a crumb from his trousers. "I met Olivia through a friend's parents, she introduced me to Henrik, and here I am."

"But, how do you support yourself?" Annie asked, clearly unconcerned with privacy. "Do you have a job? Don't you have to stay out of sight so the Gestapo doesn't make you put on one of their awful uniforms and fight for them?"

He nodded. "Mrs. Vox was kind enough to give me a place to stay. I share a flat with another chap in a building she owns not far from here. The previous tenants..." He sighed. "Well, they're no longer there. She sends food by way of Alard once a week."

"So she basically hired you to do this work?" Annie said.

"She did. I was looking for a way into this war, and she and Henrik handed me one."

I watched him as he spoke. This young man, handsome, self-assured, could probably be anything he wanted. He could flee to America and be with his sister and mother. But he stayed because he believed in something. He wanted to do what he could to help.

After lunch, we moved down into the belly of the barn to begin a new set of lessons. Part of our job would include delivering sensitive information, and sometimes weapons. Elif and I already had experience with the first and knew how to hide small notes within the plaits of our hair, the hem of a coat, the band of a hat, or up a sleeve.

But the weapons. How did one move a weapon? Elif and I were fortunate that our mother was a seamstress and could create pockets beneath pleats, and any other number of creative additions to clothing that no one could see unless they looked under our skirts and in our jackets. But what did other people do?

And then there was the issue of moving people from one safe house to the next. Families that had been hiding for months in one place would need to be moved eventually. And others would need papers as they were constantly shifted from house to flat to building to a train out of the country.

There were disguises to discuss and new identities to be assumed.

"When you're on a job," Henrik said, "you always carry your fake ID. Memorize the information on it. Have your story before you leave the house."

There was no map of the safe houses, in case it was somehow stolen. We were to memorize their locations. Every single one in Haarlem, and a few in Amsterdam near the train station.

"You will need to learn a variety of skills," he said. "Including what to do if you suspect you're being watched, how to evade

someone following you, and what to do if caught with information or a weapon on you. What do you do if your weapon
doesn't discharge? What if someone is coming at you that's twice
your size? What if you're working in pairs and your partner is
caught? Do you give yourself up too?"

He looked around the table. "The answer is no. Get to a safe
house, report what happened, sit tight, and wait."

When Elif and I arrived home after our training session
that day, we hurried upstairs to wash up and change into clean
clothes.

Side by side we stood in front of the sink in the bathroom,
taking turns washing our hands before wiping our faces clean
with warm, wet cloths.

I winced as I pressed on the bruise coloring my forehead. It
had turned a frightening shade of black, and the bandage was
stained with blood.

"Want help changing that?" Elif asked. At my nod, she
grabbed the box of medical supplies Mama kept on hand.

I sat on the edge of the tub and watched her as she stood over
me, her face a mask of concentration. As she peeled the soiled
bandage back, she blanched.

"What is it?" I asked, afraid I'd made it worse with today's
training, or maybe it had gotten infected.

"It looks so painful," she said. "You sure you're okay?"

"Fine as one can be after being hit in the head with the butt
of a rifle. It looks worse than it feels," I lied. "Promise."

She pressed a new bandage in place and I gripped the edge of
the tub, clenching my teeth in an effort not to yell out as pain
stretched its fingers across my skull.

"Done." She put the box back on the shelf, washed her hands
again, and headed for the door.

"Elif," I said, "are you scared?" My voice was small, the bravado I'd felt before seeing my friend step onto that truck the
day before all but gone.

She turned and studied me a moment, a small smile on her lips. "I was."

"But you're not anymore?"

"I mean, it would be reckless not to be scared at all. I don't want to get caught. And I certainly don't want to die." She leaned against the door frame. "But I realize I have a reason for doing this."

I frowned. She hadn't failed Madi. She hadn't failed Tess. Elif had never failed anyone. Besides our mother, she was the most dependable person I knew. She had nothing to make up for. So what could her reasons for risking her life possibly be?

"What is it?" I asked.

"You," she said.

I looked at her, taken aback. We'd been close as young girls, rarely bickering. Her reserved and dreamy nature and my more exuberant attitude somehow only served to complement one another. She made me kinder, empathetic, and observant. I made her daring, assertive, and could make her laugh like no one else.

At the seashore on lazy weekends, she'd stand on our blanket, far from the spray of the waves, until I took her hands and led her to the water where we'd scream with laughter as it swirled around our toes and ankles. At home she'd find me reading, concentrating hard to remember the facts at my fingertips, and would run her own small fingertip down the furrowed line between my eyebrows, smoothing it over and over until my face relaxed into a smile and my body sagged against hers.

When Madi was born, rather than try and make her pick a favorite, we joined forces and split big sister responsibilities down the middle. She read stories, I played blocks, she changed dirty diapers, I cleaned the spit-up. We were so invested in our jobs as big sisters, our mother often pretended to complain.

"I might as well go on holiday," she'd say. "Elif and Lien can clearly take care of everything."

But as we grew, our differences began to separate us bit by bit.

Elif found a best friend to spend time with. Then I did. As we entered our teenage years, the divide grew, our interests leading us in opposite directions. We still got along, but in a more polite and vague way. The paintings I used to fawn over now received a cursory glance and a compliment if I remembered. The tower of books beside my bed that she used to ask about, wondering what they'd taught me, no longer piqued her curiosity.

And then Madi died...

And it was as though the invisible film separating us strengthened and grew edges, becoming a fragile, sharp-cornered window that we could only look through with wary gazes at one another, our voices muffled as we navigated life from our separate sides.

No blame was ever given for what happened. No fingers pointed or accusations yelled, but the three of us each wrapped ourselves in our own guilt, suffering alone, together, within the confines of a home now echoing of ghosts. Mama cursed herself for not being able to take Madi to school herself that day. Elif cried because she'd begged off helping, wanting to meet up with Ana instead. And I agonized that I hadn't been able to prevent what happened. That I'd been so close, yet too far away.

In the weeks and months that had followed, the closeness Elif and I once had fractured, a chasm widening to the point that, for a long while, the only words we exchanged were when we were forced together to help with dinner, clean the dishes, or as one of us climbed into bed and asked the other to get the light. But in the past couple of years, with war on the horizon, and then in our midst, there had been another shift. A reuniting of sorts. It wasn't spoken of and didn't happen quickly, but we began to share our space, our words, and our lives with one another again. Despite that, I never considered we'd be in the position we were in now.

I shook my head and got to my feet, holding on to the sink for balance as pain seized my head in a vise.

"You can't do this for me," I said. "If something happened to you, I'd never forgive myself."

"Oh, it's not all for you," she said. "It's also for our family and this town. And…it's for me, because it's the right thing to do. Isn't that why you want to do it? And Charlie, and Annie?"

I shrugged, not wanting to admit there was something else that drove me. Something personal. A wound no physical bandage could cover.

"I never would've decided to do it without you, though," Elif said. "I knew you'd end up by my side eventually. As soon as Mama allowed. And that's the only reason I had the strength to accept the job. And now that I have, for the first time I feel proud of who I am. I've always been afraid. But learning these new skills… I feel powerful. I am more than I thought I was."

"I've always known that," I said, my voice soft.

She grinned and pulled me into a gentle hug. "Thank you," she whispered.

When she let me go again, she hung on to one of my hands.

"You were amazing today," she said. "I was so proud. And with that gash on your head—you looked like a warrior." She chuckled. "Charlie couldn't keep his eyes off you."

"He was just checking out his competition," I said, and we both laughed.

"Annie probably was," Elif said. "Charlie, though… I think that boy is smitten."

I waved her off, my face warming, and she gave me an impish grin and a little shrug before turning and heading out the door.

As we walked down the stairs to help with dinner, me a couple steps behind her, I stared at my sister, pride filling my chest. In mere weeks she'd gone from sewing shop assistant, to forger, to something much more lethal. Her aim with a gun was nearly flawless now. Her attack with a knife fearsome. She'd mastered every trick Charlie and Henrik threw at her, and her skill at hiding information on her person would make the best magician in the world proud. I'd always looked up to her, even if in the past few years I'd never have admitted to it. But now, in these past few months, that feeling had only strengthened.

At the landing, she stopped and waited for me. When I stepped down beside her, she laced her fingers through mine. Our hands were riddled with small bruises in faded shades of purple and blue, like bits of the watercolors she used to paint, but so rarely had time for these days. Our palms and the pads of our fingertips were calloused from jamming daggers into dummies, practicing fighting maneuvers, and target practice.

As we passed a photo of Papa on the wall, I stopped, halting Elif beside me. Together we stood staring at the image.

He used to call us his angels. Claimed to anyone who would listen that he could always count on us to know right from wrong and to choose good over evil, even from a young age. He was so proud, always, of who we were. Unabashedly loving and supportive of our choices.

I wondered if he'd even recognize us, his two eldest daughters, no longer so well-combed and clothed, but rather bruised and battered. I wondered what he'd think of our choices now.

"He'd be so proud of you girls," Mama said from behind us, her voice soft. "Look at my angels, he'd say. Look at them fly."

16

I didn't return to school that fall. Neither did Fenna or, from what I heard, half our class. Most of the teachers had been replaced, leaving parents to fret about the decisions they had to make: have their kids taught by Nazis with their new regimented curriculum, keep them home and suspend their learning for the time being, or have them attend one of the many classes that had popped up in random spots around town?

Many of the teachers had opted to offer classes from their homes, empty shops, back rooms, or, if it was nice out, in someone's garden. Every so often I'd meet Fenna and we'd walk to the park, noting on the way the groups of young children or teens gathered behind the windows of stores we'd previously shopped in, their owners no longer around, having been taken away by truck.

On the days we met, we always walked by Tess's house. The little heart remained in the window and always brought a sad smile to my face. The smear of my blood on her front door had washed away some by the rain, but a small stain remained, a reminder of my failure to save her.

"Do you think she's okay?" Fenna asked one cool November afternoon as we sat on the front step, our backs against the door.

I'd heard too many rumors recently about the work camps to naively think our friend was okay. I imagined her life had taken a drastic turn from the cozy, warm world that had existed on the other side of the door we were now leaning against, to the cold reality of a stark camp watched over by the enemy. But I couldn't say that to Fenna. She'd grown thin from worry and stress since the previous spring, having been harassed more than once by the soldiers that frequented her street. The only time she left her home anymore was when I came by or on a rare outing with her parents.

"I'm sure they're all doing fine," I lied, and said a silent prayer that someone or something was watching over Tess and her family.

I left my friend at her door a little while later with a smile, and then rearranged the expression on my face as I turned to face the men in uniform dotting the sidewalk.

"Your youthful appearance will serve you well," Aunt Liv had told us one day while we dined on fruit-filled crepes before hurrying off to the barn. "No one will suspect two young Dutch girls to be carrying loaded weapons. And they most certainly won't fancy you know how to use them. If anything, if you're caught and found with anything on you, they'll think you were coerced into it. Threatened."

She'd gone on to teach us how to arrange our faces into what she called "masks of naivete."

We'd stood with her in front of the wall of mirrors in her most glamorous sitting room, practicing widening our eyes slightly, eyebrows raised just so, lips a little bit parted.

"Imagine," she said, "that you have seen a thing of wonder. That is the expression to paste onto your face and hold as you walk past them. Portray youth and innocence, and they will believe it."

We never asked how she knew such things. We merely did as we were told, practicing until it became second nature. And even sometimes using it on Henrik to try and get out of one more round of stabbing.

"Go," he'd say, pointing at the dummy. "That shit doesn't work on me."

Our attempts and Henrik's responses never failed to amuse Charlie.

"You know he was an expert at sniffing out spies, don't you?" he asked from where he was sitting on the sofa reading one of his many comic books after another failed effort by us girls to get out of jamming a blade into the stiff straw.

Our hands were tender, our arms and shoulders ached. But Henrik didn't care. And his reasoning was annoyingly sensical.

"You fight for your life until your very last breath," he told us. "Learn how to keep going, even when you feel like you cannot."

I sat beside Charlie with a little huff, trying to keep the grin off my face. "We still had to try," I said.

"He'll just make you build more fireboxes if you don't do the stabbing."

I made a disgusted noise and he laughed. Building fireboxes was tedious, quiet, and boring work. Given the option of the two, stabbing was better. But still, I was exhausted and sweaty.

"Here," Charlie said. He held out a comic book and I stared down at it, wondering what I was to do with it. Fan myself?

"Have you never read a comic?" he asked. I shook my head. "My sister sends them from the States. They're fun, dramatic, with a lot of action and some good, heartfelt moments. This one has a woman for the hero. Read it. I think you'll like her."

I glanced over to where Annie and Elif were sinking their blades into the crude bags of hay and then took the comic and held it in my hands, absorbing the brightly colored image on the front.

"'*Wonder Woman*,'" I read aloud. "What is she wondering?"

Charlie snorted and continued reading.

Wonder Woman had long, dark hair, a tiara, a red-and-gold top, and a blue skirt spangled with white stars. And there were men shooting at her, which she seemed to be deflecting with bracelets. Curious, I turned to the first page.

I'd never read a story like the one in my hands. Had never seen a woman depicted as a hero, jumping into harm's way to save those in peril. I was enthralled with her confidence and strength, and the way she had no problem telling others in the story that they had done wrong, all the while swinging her lasso and yanking bad guys away from man, woman, and child.

I hadn't realized how absorbed I'd become in the story until I saw a pair of trousered legs standing before me. And a cane.

"Am I disturbing you?" Henrik asked.

"Oh!" I said, and jumped to my feet.

Charlie was already going at the dummies, his comic packed away. I dropped *Wonder Woman* on top of his bag and hurried to my place, pulling my dagger from its sheath as I went.

"Sorry," Charlie said, his chest heaving a little. "I tried to warn you, but I thought you were ignoring me when you didn't answer twice."

"I wasn't," I said, glancing over at Henrik, who stared back. I turned and drove my blade into my dummy's kidney. "I didn't hear you."

"Did you like it?"

I paused, not caring for the moment if Henrik was glaring at me with his one good eye.

"I really did. She's amazing."

"Hang on to it. You can return it to me next week."

This time when I faced my dummy, I pictured the cartoon-ish bad guys from the comic and imagined myself as Wonder Woman, who wasn't wondering anything. She was fearless, strong, determined...she was just a wonder herself.

★ ★ ★

The following week we returned to the basement to find Charlie in his usual spot on the sofa, comic in hand, Annie perusing the wall of pistols, and Henrik standing at his table in deep discussion with a gentleman.

"Uncle Frans!" Elif said.

"Girls," he said, smiling at my sister and me. "Henrik says you've all been doing great work. Think you might be ready to take your newly learned skills outside of the barn?"

The four of us looked at one another. This was what we'd been waiting for, but my heart pounded at the thought of actually putting to practice all the things we'd learned.

"I'm ready," Annie said, stepping over to the mammoth table. "What are we doing?"

Our first job involved dynamite.

"There's a train scheduled to come in," Uncle Frans said, spreading a map out on the table and pointing to different spots. "We need the dynamite set here, here, and here." As he pointed, we all leaned in.

"So you only need three of us?" Annie asked, her brown eyes flicking to Elif, Charlie, and me as if determining who she thought should sit this one out.

"We'll need all four," he said. "While three of you are setting the bombs, the fourth will be the lookout, ready to shoot anyone who tries to interfere, or fires on you."

"I can be the lookout," Charlie said.

"Good," Annie said. "'Cause I wanna blow up a train."

Henrik shook his head and rolled his one good eye. "You're only blowing the rails. Not the train. The train will go off the tracks, though, effectively running it aground and stopping it from getting where it needs to go."

"What's in the train?" I asked, worried it might be people returning home from the work camps.

"Supplies, ammunition, and Nazis," Uncle Frans said.

I nodded.

"When do we go?" Charlie asked.

"Tonight."

We stayed in the barn until night fell. I'd never been out of my house after curfew and that alone made me feel daring, even though I was inside elsewhere.

As soon as Elif and I agreed to be part of the mission, word was sent to mother in the way of a basket of fresh vegetables and fruit from the Vox garden with a note that told her in code that we would be home late.

"You shouldn't have too much trouble the closer you get to the target," Uncle Frans said. "There are a few large buildings they've commandeered for food and weapon storage, but at most there are only five or six guys guarding them and so far they haven't had problems with attackers so the security is relaxed at best. It's the residential areas you'll encounter when you leave Bloemendaal that you'll need to be wary of. And even a few of the homes around here. But we'll tell you which ones."

"Hurry," Henrik said. "But don't be reckless."

Round trip, the mission should only take a little over an hour to get there, set the bombs, and come back. At the allotted time, armed with the explosives and our pistols, we crept out into the night.

We moved in twos, Annie and Charlie twenty paces or so ahead of Elif and I at all times. One group watched ahead, the other kept an eye around and behind.

As we reached the first large home in Aunt Liv's neighborhood occupied by the enemy, we slowed and ducked behind the fence, watching for movement, but apparently whoever lived there felt no threat from their Dutch neighbors as there were no guards out and about. We moved on.

We reached the residential area fifteen minutes after we'd left the Vox residence. It was eerie to see how dark the streets were without the glow of the streetlights or lamplight spilling from the windows of homes.

"It's like a ghost town," I whispered, and shivered at the thought.

We moved in the shadows, which there were many of, and hurried from cluster of bikes to trash bin to alleyway, looking around before each member of the group ventured into the open for brief periods of time. Around us we could hear families moving about inside their homes behind the blackout curtains. I smelled food cooking, and my stomach grumbled loudly.

We were three streets in when we heard voices and stopped, pressing to the wall beside us, Charlie peeking around the corner.

He held up his hand and I squinted, trying to see how many fingers he was holding up and failing. It was too dark. I pulled on Annie's coat and she leaned toward me.

"Three soldiers," she whispered and turned back to watch Charlie.

He motioned again and Annie whispered, "They've gone."

We moved quickly, sliding silently out of the alleyway and back onto the main road. A few more minutes and we were out of the neighborhood and into the farmland that would take us all the way to the railroad.

Keeping low, we crept along fence lines until finally, mercifully, our target was one small shack and a few more meters away.

We stopped at the shack, keeping out of view of a large barn to the west. It hadn't been mentioned in the brief from Uncle Frans, but one could never be too careful.

As the three of us girls knelt to remove our bombs from the bags we carried, Charlie kept a lookout.

"Ready?" Annie asked.

"Wait," Elif whispered. "It's too dark. Remind me what I'm supposed to do."

"We're to follow this track to the bridge. There's another set of tracks that head east once we reach it. If we can't see the tracks, we'll certainly be able to feel them," Annie said. "And then we set up the bombs, one, two, and three down the line—and run."

"Get back to this spot as fast as you can," Charlie said. "Set the bomb and run. Don't wait for anyone else. Follow back the same way you went. From here we'll need to run as fast as we can to the fence line because once we leave this shack, we're out in the open. Got it?"

Even in the dark I could feel his eyes on me.

"Lien?" His hand was on my arm.

"Got it," I said.

"Be careful."

We ran, one behind the other, bent low, our feet quick and silent on the grass.

"Tracks," Annie whispered then changed direction, now running north. Elif and I followed.

It wasn't far to the bridge, but in the dead of night, the whole of the country blacked out, it was disconcerting. I couldn't see my feet in front of me and felt off balance.

I could taste the water before we reached the bridge, the wetness in the air washing over me and dampening my face and hair.

"Bridge," Annie said.

I heard Elif's footsteps ahead of me go right and followed. We had found the second tracks.

I knelt and placed the explosive in my hands on the track and then waited for Annie's signal. The seconds felt like minutes, my heartbeat punctuating every tick of my watch. And then I heard it. A soft whistle carried down the tracks by the wind. I set the explosive and ran.

I could hear Elif's and Annie's footsteps pounding the ground behind me. In my head I was counting. I made it to seventeen when the first blast shook the night, followed closely by two more.

"Let's go!" Charlie said when we reached the shack.

The four of us streaked across the open field, our breath heavy, urging one another until we reached the fence where we ducked down and took a moment to watch and listen.

"No one's coming," Elif said. I hadn't realized until then that her hand was gripping mine.

"The townspeople are probably too afraid to look," Charlie said. "But the Germans will come eventually. Let's keep moving."

We went back the way we'd come, following the same roads, hiding behind the same trash bins and in alleyways until we were running down the dirt road that ran behind the Vox property. We reached the familiar fence and scurried between the pickets.

Taking cover behind the barn, we peered up at the main house. Again, there was nothing to see. It was as if we hadn't just done something that could get us arrested. Or worse yet, killed.

We climbed down into the belly of the barn, knocked, and Henrik let us in.

"Well?" he said, his voice gruff. It was clear by his rumpled clothes and hair that we'd woken him. "Did they go off?"

"They did," Charlie said.

"Great. Go home. Get some sleep. Come back in a couple of days."

The four of us looked at one another. Adrenaline was still screaming through my veins. That was it?

"See you all later, then," Annie said, and disappeared out the door.

I looked at Elif and she stared back at me.

"Should we—" she started but didn't finish.

"Liv is waiting for the two of you. Go up to the main house. Elke will let you in."

"I'll walk you," Charlie said, and gave Henrik a nod. "G'night."

Henrik muttered something unintelligible, and the three of us left for the main house where Charlie left us in Elke's safe hands.

"See you ladies soon," he said before disappearing into the darkness.

Aunt Liv was curled up in an emerald dressing gown in the parlor, drinking something amber-colored out of a crystal glass.

"How was it?" she asked.

"It went well," Elif said.

"Good." She motioned to the sofa and chairs. "Sit. Eat."

We did as she said, the adrenaline pumping through our veins slowly dissipating as we filled our bellies with warm bread and meat, roasted vegetables, and hot tea.

"Have I ever told you two how I got into the business of deception?" Aunt Liv asked.

We shook our heads.

"Well, let me tell you now. I have a feeling some of the things I learned might help you in the future."

I glanced at Elif who raised her eyebrows in return, and then we sat back with warm cups of tea in our hands and listened.

"During the First World War," Aunt Liv said, "while the men were off fighting and the women were left at home to do the things women are told they are supposed to do, I found myself quite restless. My own husband couldn't fight. He was ten years older than I and past his prime for things like climbing out of ditches and running across war zones, but he did a great deal of strategizing that took him to England. Never one to be left behind, I went too. To keep myself busy, I joined a little group that specialized in two particular things. Back then we referred to it quaintly as 'going fishing.'"

At our confused looks she gave us an amused grin and then continued.

"I was known for my proficiency with what is referred to as a sleight of hand. Lure, trap, and kill. One minute I was a flirtatious woman, vying for attention and following an inebriated fellow down an alleyway, the next I was a dagger-wielding murderess. One thing you can count on with me—I'm always armed."

I peered at her sleeves, wondering if there was a dagger hidden inside. Or perhaps in her dressing gown pocket.

"Weren't you terrified?" Elif asked.

"At first," she said. "I got myself into more than one precarious situation, I'll admit. Twice it should've been me that was killed, but luck always seemed to be on my side somehow. You can't count on luck, though. If you decide to do this sort of work, you listen to what you're told and train hard. Any little mistake could be the end of you."

We went upstairs to one of the guest rooms in a daze a while later, our minds filled with newfound respect for Aunt Liv. She wasn't just a woman of means who paid others to do the hard work, she was a woman of courage and strength. A woman who was willing and able to do the hard work herself. But as I changed into a spare nightgown and brushed my teeth, all I could think of was her description of the job.

Lure, trap, and kill.

The phrase repeated in my mind until I fell into a deep and dreamless sleep.

17

Sinterklaas came like a cruel joke that year. The few shops that were still open made some effort to create festive windows, but the usual lights and decorations that adorned every streetlight and storefront were not allowed, casting a pallor on an already bleak holiday season.

Instead of the usual round of parties we attended at friends' homes, Elif and I found ourselves standing on a street corner across from Haarlemmerhout Park one Thursday night, eyeing the pub she was about to go into.

"You ready?" I asked her.

She shook her head.

My hands trembled inside my pockets, and I grasped the little red wooden bird I'd slipped in it at the last minute. Madi's bird. For luck.

Because tonight I would kill someone.

I ran through everything Uncle Frannie had told us days before, Elif, Annie, and I gathered around him like we were sitting around a campfire. Charlie, we were told, would not be joining us for training that day, as the seduction of men was better left to women.

"As most jobs are," Aunt Liv had said with a wink.

Per our uncle's instruction, Elif would enter the pub we'd find our target in alone.

"Order a pint," he said. "You don't have to drink it all. Take a few sips, look toward the door as though you're waiting for someone. Do you have a watch?"

Elif shook her head.

"I'll loan you one," Aunt Liv said.

"Check your watch," Uncle Frannie continued. "Make it look real. You're there to meet a friend. She's late. Look annoyed. Meanwhile, scan the pub. The man you'll be looking for is young, dark-haired, and will be carrying a messenger bag. Once you identify him, make your move."

"My move?" Elif asked, her brows furrowing.

"If he's at the bar," Aunt Liv said, "ask the bartender for something a little stronger than the beer. Smile, but show your frustration. You've been stood up. When the drink arrives, take a sip, shudder, and ask the mark if he wants it."

"What if he says no?" Elif said.

"It doesn't matter, you're just looking for an opening. You're pretty, and there's not much going on in this sleepy town. He'll engage in conversation. Trust me."

"What then?"

Uncle Frannie nodded at Aunt Liv who continued.

"Flirt. Be sweet but coy. But your goal is to get him to follow you out. Either by acting scared and helpless and thus hoping for an escort home—or by promising him something more."

Elif shot me a look, her cheeks pink.

"From there," Uncle Frans said, "you lead him into the park where Lien will be waiting to shoot him. Once the target has been liquidated, you get out of there. Hiding out of sight will be men waiting to dispose of the body."

"How come they can't shoot whomever we bring out?" Elif asked.

"Everyone has their job. To make it quick and efficient, you shoot, they bury. Also—" he had the decency to look remorseful as he said the next bit "—they're seen as more expendable. They don't have the same skill set and are more easily replaced."

"What happens if our target doesn't follow us?" Annie asked. "If they turn around and head back to the pub?"

"You walk away like a woman scorned and report back as soon as possible," he said.

"What if we're grabbed once we leave the pub and the man tries dragging us off somewhere else?" I asked, my voice low. It was my biggest concern. I was the smallest out of everyone. It wasn't strange to think I might be overpowered.

"In that case, you scream. Not only will your teammate hear you, the whole of the pub probably will too, and will come to see what the commotion is. And if that doesn't happen, let him get you out of sight...and then shoot him."

I glanced at the pub and then back at Elif twisting her fingers.

"What if I can't do it?" she asked, her voice small as she seemed to shrink into her coat.

"Then you'll come find me and we'll go home," I said, reaching out and squeezing her hand.

She nodded and stared at the pub. The door opened and an older gentleman emerged, glanced our way, and stumbled away, disappearing a moment later around a corner.

"I've never been on a date," Elif said. "I barely even talk to boys at school. How am I supposed to go in there and flirt convincingly with a man I want nothing to do with and get him to follow me out?"

"This is not a date," I said, my voice firm. "Don't think of it like that. It's a job. An important one. And you're going to do just fine."

"What if he touches me?" she whispered.

My eyes filled with tears and I looked away, staring at the trees of the park where I'd soon be hiding, waiting to do my own part in this mad plan. But these were the risks we'd signed on to take, and why we were working in pairs. It was very likely that at some point a man would try and overpower one if not both of us. It was also the reason I'd been assigned as the shooter for these jobs.

"She doesn't miss," Annie had said one day at target practice. "It's infuriating."

I'd ducked my head, but Charlie caught my eye with a smile.

"Don't be ashamed," he said. "Your skill may save your life. Or one of ours."

"It feels terrible to be good at something that takes lives."

"A life for a life," he'd said. "That's how I think of it. They take one of our innocent, we take one of their monsters. Think of your teacher and his family. Think of Tess."

I'd sucked in a breath and stared at the holes marring the target several yards away. A life for a life.

"I'm ready," Elif whispered, and took a step, her fingers slipping from mine.

"You're sure?"

She nodded and took off her coat. Beneath it she was wearing our mother's clothes, sewn to fit her, and looked quite chic in the low-cut dress with the skirt shorter than she or I had ever worn before. On her feet were a pair of pale blue heels that were a mite too big, but mother had poked another hole in the band to pull the strap tighter around her ankle and shoved cotton in the toes. She could run in them if she had to. We knew because she'd tested them out.

She adjusted the strap of the purse on her shoulder and, exhaling a little huff of breath, stood all of her five feet five inches and gave me a last look.

"You'll be in the park?" she asked.

"I'll be waiting and ready."

She squeezed my hand and I squeezed back.

"Be careful," I said. "I'll see you soon."

I watched her walk across the street and with a last look over her shoulder at me, she opened the door and disappeared inside.

I exhaled and made my way down the block a little ways before crossing to the park. Curfew wasn't for another hour, and I had no idea how long I'd have to wait. Would I get stuck in the dark in the woods? How long would it take her to convince the man she was to lure out to the cover of the woods with a promise of...what? A kiss? A feel beneath her blouse? What did it take to convince a man to follow you?

Aunt Liv had shown us how to touch a man's hand or arm. To laugh, tipping our heads back slightly to expose our necks.

"Move in close. Let your breast rest against his arm or chest. Play with your hair," she'd instructed, demonstrating by wrapping a lock of her own hair around a finger. "Touch your lips, your cheek, your hands." As she named each body part, she showed us what she meant and then nodded for us to try it ourselves. "Men are fascinated by the female form. Bring his attention to yours as much as you can."

I walked along the dirt path I'd previously strolled with Fenna just two weeks before. A couple sat on a bench, his arm around her shoulders, her face tipped up to his. I ducked my head and turned away, quickening my step and praying they'd be gone by the time Elif appeared.

At the gathering of trees I looked around, making sure if anyone was around they didn't see me step into my hiding place in the brush and crouch down, my brown coat and the dimming light helping to disguise me. Leaning against the tree, I checked the time and watched the pub, my heart beating with every tick of the second hand.

At fifteen minutes my legs began to ache. I stood slowly and stretched them as best I could, careful not to make a sound and keeping my eye on the pub. Three men approached the door and opened it. There was what looked like a bit of confusion and my heart skipped as I saw my sister exit, a man behind her, his arm reaching for hers.

I sucked in a shaky breath, my fingers fumbling through the fabric of my coat for the pistol hidden deep in the pocket. Shifting my feet, I sought more solid footing between the roots snaking out of the ground around me, my eyes glued to Elif and the man as they crossed the street and headed toward me, the murmur of their voices drifting softly across the expanse of grass.

"No hesitation," I whispered to myself and squeezed my eyes shut, picturing Madi in the water, and then Tess walking up the steps to the truck. My hand tightened around the grip of my gun.

A life for a life.

But no matter the list of justifications I made for being here, for holding a gun in my hand, for taking a life, my stomach still turned, sick rising in my throat and threatening to spill from my lips. Because no matter all the reasons I'd found to make standing here okay in my mind, my heart questioned the moral implications of what I was about to do. And despite Aunt Liv's advice for tamping down the emotions that came with the job, how could I anticipate which emotions I'd feel? How could I be sure I wouldn't be consumed and destroyed by a guilt so heavy and dark that I'd never recover?

"There is no book we can read that will make us feel one hundred percent certain about the choices we make in war. Or in life," Aunt Liv had told us. "No guiding force to enlighten us. All we can do is our job. For the sake of the greater good. You just have to believe in the cause."

And I did believe, which was why I stood now, my gun in hand, swallowing bile and trying to keep tears of fear from welling in my eyes as their voices grew louder.

Elif laughed and I could tell it was forced. Fake. Higher pitched than usual. And the man's voice... I frowned. There was something eerily familiar about it.

I shifted my stance, careful to stay behind the cover of leaves but trying to get a better angle. My sister had taken the lead, and I couldn't see the man behind her. She knew where I'd be and I hoped she realized that to get a clear shot, she'd have to move.

"Where are you going?" the man asked. My eyes narrowed. I knew that voice.

"Well, we can't very well do anything out in the open, Charlie," Elif said.

Charlie?

My blood ran cold, my grip loosening on the pistol. No. It couldn't be. It didn't make sense. And yet...that was his voice. I knew I'd recognized it. But how? And why? And—

They were so close now. Elif just needed to step out of the way and I'd have a shot. But—Charlie? Our Charlie? My—

Maybe I'd heard her wrong. Maybe I'd heard *him* wrong. But a moment later my sister glanced up, her eyes finding mine through the branches and leaves, and she stepped out of the way, giving me a perfect view of the man with her.

Charlie.

Static filled my ears and I blinked, and then blinked again, confused. Why was he here? Had the target not shown up? Had Charlie been a patron at the pub and was escorting my sister to me?

Elif turned her back to me. They were talking, but I couldn't understand what they were saying through the voice in my head questioning everything I knew—everything I *thought* I knew— about the man who had followed my sister out of the pub.

I watched him smile at her. The same smile he'd given me dozens of times. My heart squeezed as my brain shuffled through facts I'd learned about him that were now, what, lies? Was Charlie a traitor? A pit opened in my stomach.

No hesitation.

He'd said the words to me himself, but I shook my head. This couldn't be right. Something had to have gone wrong. Information confused somewhere along the way. And yet—we'd been warned, hadn't we? The enemy could be anyone. People we knew could be turned. People we trusted. People we even thought we might love.

I exhaled, watching as Charlie stepped toward Elif, and pushed away the static clouding my mind. I heard her hesitant giggle, the desperation in the sound as she took a step back, keeping my view of him clear.

No hesitation.

Holding my breath, I tightened my grasp, set my forefinger on the trigger, and took the shot.

18

Click.

The sound echoed off the nearby trees. No one moved.

I squeezed again.

Click.

I looked to Elif, who was trying to get to her own gun from where it was strapped to her thigh, hidden beneath her skirt, its use not planned.

Charlie slid the bag he carried off his shoulder.

"Don't move." My voice trembled as I pulled the trigger yet again. But it was no use. It was empty.

Fear and confusion warred in my mind. Hadn't I checked the gun before I'd left? No. I'd checked it in the morning, though. How—

I looked at Elif, but she seemed as confused as I and was still trying to retrieve her own pistol, but in her frenzy, she was having a hard time undoing the strap holding it in place.

"Dammit," I said under my breath as I took several steps back and shoved my gun into my pocket and then reached for my dagger, my eyes glued to Charlie.

Charlie.

I didn't understand. All this time…he was working for the other side?

"I have something for you," he said, holding the bag out to me. The same bag our target was meant to be carrying…

I gripped the hilt of the dagger in my waistband and glanced at Elif, who had pulled her gun and was checking to see if it was loaded. Her eyes met mine and she shook her head. I turned back to Charlie, who had taken another step toward me.

"Stop moving," I said, pulling the weapon free and holding it out in front of me. "What do you mean you have something for me?"

"Take the bag. Check the front pocket."

When I didn't move, he sighed and pulled a slip of paper from the pocket he'd mentioned and then held it out to me. I stood rooted to my spot on the path, hoping he couldn't see how bad my hand was shaking.

"I'm going to take a step forward and place it on the ground," he said. "Is that okay?"

I gave him a curt nod.

As he stepped forward I changed my hold on my weapon—just as he'd taught me—and then watched as he knelt and placed the note on the dirt path. When he stepped back again, I changed my grip once more.

"It was a test," he said, and raised his arms in surrender. "All this—it was a test. To see if you two were ready. If you could do what it takes." His smile was grim, his voice flat, the look in his eyes confusing. Proud, but there was something else too. Disappointment? "Congratulations. You passed."

Elif took a half step forward and stopped. "It was a trick?"

"A test," he said again. "We all have to go through it. To make sure we can do the job. To see if we can pull the trigger. It's why I wasn't at the last two training sessions. So it would look like I didn't know what you were doing in there." He gestured toward the pub and then back at me and the weapon in my hand. "Lien, you can put the dagger away."

I shook my head. "How do we know you're telling the truth?"

"Trust me," he said.

Trust me. It was what he had said to me dozens of times in that basement or in the drills Henrik had put us through.

Trust me. Was he still fooling us? While Henrik had been training all of us, had Charlie been training *me*?

I shook my head, furious as tears sprang to my eyes. "I don't know if I can," I said.

"Lien." He sighed, his shoulders sagging. When he spoke again, there was something in his voice. An earnestness that, if it could be faked, was the greatest trick I'd ever heard. "Trust me. And if you can't, trust that." He gestured to the paper he'd placed on the ground.

I lowered my dagger a few inches, stepped forward, picked up the piece of paper, and unfolded it.

"'Elif and Lien,'" I read aloud for my sister to hear, my eyes moving from the paper to Charlie and back. "'Congratulations. A job well done. Go home, angels, and sleep well. Uncle Frannie.'"

Angels. It was our father's endearment for us. Charlie couldn't know that. Nor could he possibly replicate our uncle's particular scrawl.

An enraged sob burst from my throat as I crumpled the note. Elif lowered her useless gun and sank to her knees on the dirt path. Charlie began talking, but I couldn't hear him, the roar of my own fear and shock loud in my ears. I became light-headed, dizzy. My knees gave and, like my sister, I hit the ground.

"Lien," Charlie said, kneeling in front of me. "Take a deep breath and count to ten."

He reached for my weapon, and I gasped and sprang back. When he held up his hands again, I saw a flash of pain on his face and a red slash across his palm.

"I'm so sorry," I said, and finally lowered my weapon.

"No, *I'm* sorry," he said, his voice low. "I wish I could've warned you. I wish——" He exhaled and pressed his injured hand to his torso, putting pressure on it with his other hand. "I had to do it too, you know. A test. Mine was with my roommate. He almost didn't get the words out in time to stop me. I nearly slit his throat." He took in a long breath and let it out. "It was awful, but it proves our commitment to the cause, and how strong we are. Inside." He turned to address Elif. "You were brilliant back there in the pub. Your confusion and hesitance at first was natural. Your answers to my questions, the way you looked embarrassed to be out in a pub doing something you knew would bring you shame. And then when you started to flirt——" His cheeks reddened, and Elif looked down at the ground. "Well, you were very convincing. Whatever Liv taught you, you were a good student. If I didn't know better, I would've really thought you were interested in me. You'll have no trouble when it comes to doing this for real," he said. "And it will be easier, in a sense, when you go on a real job because you most likely won't know the man. Tonight's test was to see just how far the two of you could be pushed. If you could do the job regardless of who the target was. And you——" he turned back to me and the corners of his mouth lifted in a reluctant smile "——you didn't hesitate for a second. I'm not sure if I'm impressed or if I should be insulted."

I could tell he was joking. That he was trying to lighten the moment for us, but I wasn't ready for that and I stared down at the dirt path, watching as teardrop after teardrop fell into the dust.

"Lien——" he said.

"I killed you," I whispered, looking up at him. "I like you, and I looked you in the eye and I killed you."

He nodded. "You did what you were supposed to. Because anyone—*anyone*—could be a collaborator. Your friend, your cousin, your favorite teacher, the boy you know who shares his comic books… And that's what you have to remember."

I shook my head, stuck in the knowledge that had my gun been loaded, he'd be dead.

"You did good, Lien," he said. "You're a natural. Like Wonder Woman. Fighting for the good side. A life for a life."

But I barely heard the words after he called me a natural. I wanted to scream. That was not what I wanted to be good at. But that was the job. That was what was needed. That was how we would win.

A life for a life.

I sheathed my dagger, and shoved the crumpled note in my pocket.

I knew I should feel proud, but the truth was, I felt I'd actually failed and that this road I was on might not lead where I was hoping to go. But then I saw Tess's face again, the fear etched in her eyes. I felt the butt of the rifle slam into my head, the warmth of the blood dampening my skin. Maybe this wasn't the road I'd imagined—but maybe it would get me to my destination all the same.

I checked my watch and looked at my sister.

"We should go," I said. "It's almost curfew."

A natural.

Charlie's words clung to me as Elif and I hurried home, my entire body shaking with adrenaline, fear, and something else I couldn't identify. Pride? The idea that I was proud made my stomach turn. But I'd done the job. We both had. And there was pride to be had in that.

An image of Charlie's face appeared in my mind and I felt sick. Betrayed, even though I hadn't really been. At least not to the extent he'd made us believe at first. I thought back to the moment I'd seen that it was him. In a matter of seconds I went from confusion, to relief, to a sick and sad realization that hollowed me out and left me numb.

Charlie was a traitor.

Fear and a kind of anger I'd never experienced before had kicked in, and I'd pulled the trigger. When I'd learned it was a test, the anger had morphed into rage. I'd trusted him and he lied to me. I knew why. I understood the reasoning behind it. But still…how could he?

We arrived home several minutes before curfew, and Elif knocked on the door. A moment later we heard the cabinet slide out of place and the dead bolt unlock. Mama opened the door and ushered us in, checking us over from head to toe as we removed our coats and hung them.

"You took our ammunition," Elif said, her voice full of hurt and accusation.

I frowned, confused for a moment, and then my eyes widened. I'd been so absorbed in thinking about Charlie I hadn't bothered to give thought to our failing pistols. But Elif had worked it out, and she was shaking as she removed her gun and set it on the counter.

"I'm sorry," Mama said, her voice soft as she reached out a hand to her. "You must understand why."

"Do you know how frightened I was?" Elif asked, pushing her hand away, tears spilling down her face. "I didn't understand what happened. I thought we were going to die out there in the park. That Charlie would pull his own gun and shoot us both. And then he said it was a test and gave Lien the note and…" She crossed her arms over her chest. "It wasn't until we were walking home that I remembered you handing us our guns before we left, and how odd it was that you had them. That's when I figured it out."

"I would never tamper with your weapons normally," Mama said. "But you can understand why I was asked to surely?"

"Of course. I'm not stupid," Elif snapped.

I'd never heard Elif use that tone with our mother and watched the exchange in fascination, glad to not be the only one filled with emotion.

"I'm sorry." Mama's voice was soft, but firm. Resolute in what she'd done. "I was doing my part. You must have been frightened and confused."

"And angry," I put in, my tone hard. "I was made to decide if I could kill someone I know and trust. In fact, had my gun been loaded, I would have done just that. And then what? How would I have dealt with that? I can't even begin to imagine it. All I can do is see his face and feel sick that—" My voice caught.

"This was the point," Mama said. "What if you are faced with the realization someone you know and like is the enemy? What will you do? How will you respond? Will you let them go? What will it mean for others if you do? What will it mean for *you* if you do? And if you react, if you choose to take the life, how will you recover? Will it affect you going forward? Will it alter how you do your next job?" She took a step toward me, but I stepped back. She sighed, her shoulders slumping, tears filling her eyes now too. "It's a terrible lesson. A terrible job. And you girls are so young and incredibly brave to volunteer, but it may be too much to ask of you, and that's okay. It's okay to say you can't do it. No one will blame you."

I didn't say anything. I had no words. Instead, I stalked to the library and stood in front of the fireplace, unclenching my hands and holding them up, warming them in the heat from the flames and taking in slow, steadying breaths, trying to stop the fury that reverberated though my veins and rattled my bones.

Elif appeared beside me, her shoulder resting against mine. I felt her body rise and fall with measured breaths. When I dared to look over at her, I saw that tears still fell from her eyes, but there was a set to her jaw I recognized. She wasn't ready to give up.

And neither was I.

I sighed and sank against her. I hated being tricked, especially by someone I knew. Even if it was for a good reason. And that it was Charlie made it that much worse. Forevermore the look in his eyes when he'd heard that click would haunt me.

After dinner, a quiet and strained affair with barely a word spoken, Elif and I went upstairs to wash our faces, brush our teeth, and put on our nightclothes. But instead of going downstairs to the library, Elif sank onto her bed.

"Are you okay?" I asked from the doorway on my way out. All I wanted was to climb into my bed on the sofa and try to forget this day and the sick feeling in my stomach that no words of comfort or food had been able to displace. But the look on my sister's face gave me pause. "Elif?"

"I was so confused," she whispered, staring across the room with unseeing eyes, a little line creasing her brow as she frowned.

"About what?" I asked, taking a step toward her.

"Charlie."

I inhaled, not sure I wanted to hear about what happened inside the pub, but also wanting to comfort my sister.

"Do you want to talk about it?" I asked.

I'd wondered what had transpired, but we were both so distraught as we'd hurried home, I'd buried my curiosity beneath guilt and anger.

"I didn't notice him at first," she said. "And when I did, and I saw the bag…" She looked like she was going to be sick. "I thought it must be a mistake. He must happen to have the same bag as the target. But I looked around and—he was the only one." She looked up at me. "All I could think about was you. How much you like him. How much he seemed to like you. What were you going to do when you saw him? Would you be able to go through with it? Would I? How was I going to convince him I was interested in him when most of the time we've been around one another we hardly speak?"

I sat beside her as she intertwined her fingers in her lap and squeezed until her knuckles turned white.

"I thought about excusing myself and hurrying to find you so we could go home," she said. "But I remembered what Aunt Liv had said at that last training session we had with her. It could be anyone. Even someone we know and like. And then I remembered how Charlie hadn't been there at those meetings. Just us girls. And it made sense. They knew he was a traitor, so he hadn't been invited. But—" She inhaled a shaky breath. "That didn't make it any easier. It was Charlie. I felt scared, betrayed, and guilty."

"Guilty for what?"

"Flirting with a boy you liked. Even if I was being made to think he was bad."

Her face reddened then and a sick feeling filled my stomach.

"What did you do?" I asked quietly.

"I didn't have to do much, actually. He saw me and came over and...he was different. Harder. He looked mean almost, and his eyes kept shifting around the room. He wasn't the same as when he's with us." She shook her head, her own eyes narrowed as she remembered. "He asked me what I was doing there and I said what Aunt Liv suggested, that I was supposed to meet a friend but I didn't think she was going to show up. I smiled at him, told him I was sure glad to see him. Touched his hand like Aunt Liv suggested...laced my fingers through his." She shuddered. "As soon as I did that, his demeanor changed. He became attentive and moved his leg so it rested against mine under the table. And then I asked if maybe he'd walk me home. When we got outside, I suggested we take a walk in the park first. He seemed to like that idea a lot. It was—" Her voice broke. "Awful. Frightening. He was so different. I've never felt unsafe around Charlie, but tonight, thinking he was a traitor... I was terrified."

I nodded and leaned forward, dropping my face into my hands, letting the sob I'd been holding in come free.

"I shot him," I said, my body quaking as I succumbed to the guilt and fear and angst I'd felt out there in the park.

Elif's arms came around me and she pulled me to her and rocked me, whispering words to soothe me until the tension in my body began to dissipate and I melted into her, letting her body hold up mine.

"What if my gun had been loaded?" I asked a while later as we stared at the ceiling from where we lay on her bed.

"Then he would've gotten the death he deserved."

It was what Aunt Liv had said. But even Elif didn't sound that convinced in this moment. It was a hard argument to buy when it was someone I cared about.

"I keep seeing his face," I said, my voice a whisper.

"I imagine by the end of this, there will be many faces we have a hard time forgetting," Elif said.

We lay quiet with our own thoughts for a long while, letting her words repeat in our minds, washing over us, as we accepted what would be. Eventually we went back downstairs where mother sat at her sewing machine. But the usual hum was silenced and it took a moment to register the sight of her, her head on her arms, her body shaking as she cried.

"Oh, Mama," I whispered, and we went to her.

As I sank into the sofa to sleep finally, I pulled my blankets over my head and brought my knees to my chest, curling into a ball like a child. Mama turned the radio on low, and the familiar hum of the sewing machine started up and began to lull me.

"I'm sorry," I whispered in the dark, praying my words would carry through the night sky and land in the soft shell of Charlie's ear. "I'm sorry, Charlie."

But deep down I knew, were we to do it all over again, I'd still pull the trigger.

19

After the new year, we were given our first real liquidation assignment. As we made plans, mapping out the area around where we would attack, the country began to tilt and shift unfavorably around us.

While winter ushered in the frigid temperatures that paired so well with warm foods—thick stews laden with meat and potatoes, breads, tea, and coffee—rationing became stricter, flour supplies lower, meaning less bread to buy and to bake. Meat portions were slashed in half, tea coming in at a minimum, and coffee became a luxury item. If you didn't have a supply at home already, you weren't getting any in the foreseeable future.

There were some items that didn't matter for our small household. We didn't own a car so there was no need for gasoline, and we had more than enough clothing and shoes thanks to a mother who sewed and an aunt who gave us her castoffs. In fact, we had so much, we'd begun sorting it to be distributed among neighbors and other locals in need.

But there were other things that did matter. Like our radios. They posted signs first, warning it would happen. And then they came, banging on doors, demanding we turn over any and all radios in our possession. If you weren't accommodating, they pulled you out of your house and turned it over looking for one, oftentimes leaving with more than just the radio. Sometimes they arrested people. A few times they decided an example was to be made and shot someone outside their home.

We, of course, handed ours over without a fuss. The big one anyway. The smaller one Mama used to keep by her bedside table was hidden in a crude hole she'd made in a wall behind a picture frame.

The other change was the number of soldiers now shadowing our sidewalks. It was as if in a single night they had doubled in numbers. And they were suddenly less accommodating, less cordial, and much more forceful. Every day now I saw someone get stopped, searched, hauled off, or worse.

The only good thing in those first few days of the new year was a letter that arrived from Tess. Had it not been for the handwriting and a brief comment about her hair, I might not have believed it was from her. The words were spare, without her usual embellishments, and seemed carefully chosen, as if someone else might read it. She was well, she said. She and her mother had been given jobs cleaning an office building every evening. "It is nice to have a change of scenery and a sense of purpose," she wrote. She'd made some friends and hoped to see Fenna and I soon. As well as her father and brother, from whom they'd been separated when she and her mother were sent to an all-women's camp. My chest ached at the news. The four of them had always been so close. Being separated had to be frightening.

Elif and I were on our way to Aunt Liv's for some final instruction before we carried out our first job when I heard a shout down an alleyway and skidded to a stop. As usual, the person being pulled from their home was grossly outnumbered, four soldiers to the one woman, who was being accused and slapped as she cried and begged.

"Don't," Elif said.

I hadn't noticed my hand had moved to my waistband where my dagger had taken up near permanent residence whenever I left the house. I looked at my sister, and she shook her head. I shoved my hand in my pocket, gripping the little red bird instead.

"You can't fight every fight," Henrik had told us one day. "Don't be foolish. Your country needs you alive. Not everyone can do this work, or is willing. Be smart out there. If you can't win, walk away."

After watching for a minute more, my heart in my throat, my hands grasping the handlebars of my bike, I gave Elif a nod and we rode away.

When we arrived at the Vox residence, Elif in the lead, she stopped short, causing me to run into her back tire.

"Elif!" I said, but she waved me off and pointed. Parked in front of the house was a military vehicle emblazoned with the all too familiar Nazi symbol.

"What do we do?" she asked.

"She told us to come," I said, and glanced at the sitting room window that faced the street.

"Should there ever be trouble," Aunt Liv had told us early on in our training, "I'll place a green vase in the window. That's the signal not to come to the door, there's danger."

"There's no vase in the window," I said now.

But for a moment, neither of us moved.

"What if she didn't have time to put it up?" Elif asked.

"Then we're just two young women coming to see their aunt. They can't arrest us for that."

We parked our bikes and stepped up to the front door. For all my bravado a moment ago, my hand now shook as I raised it to knock.

"Ladies," Alard answered with his usual polite smile. "Please come in and have a seat. Your aunt will be with you momentarily."

He ushered us into the small sitting room off the foyer and we sat looking everywhere but at one another, as if too afraid to see the fear we felt mirrored in the other's eyes. We were never told to sit and wait here. If Aunt Liv was occupied, we were sent to the kitchen for a snack.

I shifted in my seat, my hand smoothing my skirt and feeling for the pistol beneath the pleats. When I finally dared to glance at Elif, I saw she was doing the same.

"Girls!" Aunt Liv said, her heels clicking on the floor as she entered the room.

I jumped and fixed a smile onto my face as I searched hers for clues. Her voice was friendly, but her expression carried a warning.

"Sorry to make you wait," she said, pressing a finger to her lips and gesturing toward the foyer where we'd just come in. In a whisper she continued. "I have an unexpected guest. I'm going to walk you through to the kitchen. Just smile, and if he asks questions, paste on that mask of naivete and answer politely."

"Yes, ma'am," we whispered, and followed her to the back of the house.

"I'm so pleased you girls could come by," she said loudly. "It's been a few weeks. You'll have to catch me up on what you've been doing. How's your mother?"

We reached the dining room, resplendent in the warm glow of the crystal chandeliers. At the head of the table in Aunt Liv's spot sat a stern-looking man with slicked hair, beady eyes that seemed to see everything, and that too-familiar dark uniform, the red sash on his arm making my stomach turn.

"General," Aunt Liv said, pausing as we walked through. "These are my nieces. Elif and Lien."

"Ladies," he said, and then turned back to the meal in front of him, dismissing us.

We were ushered into the kitchen where Elke was waiting with plates of food.

"Oh, girls," she said, rushing to us and hugging us, one after the other. "Come. Sit. Tell me how you are. It's been too long."

Like Aunt Liv, she spoke louder than usual, clearly trying to send the message that we were a normal sight in the household.

"I'll be back as soon as I can," Aunt Liv said quietly, and gave Elke a little nod before disappearing behind the door to the dining room.

While our aunt entertained her guest, Elke provided us with the necessary details of our upcoming mission. Who the target was, where he would be and when, and what we needed to get from him before we ran.

"It's a list," Elke said, her voice low.

"Of what?" I asked.

"People rumored to be harboring Jews. He will receive it at the pub from someone else. It's his entire reason for going there. You need to make sure he gets it, and then persuade him to go with you to the park. Got it?"

I sucked in a breath, met Elif's eyes, and nodded. We had it.

The general left, and Aunt Liv returned to the kitchen for a time before sending us off to the barn where Henrik was waiting with some last-minute instructions. To my surprise, Charlie was there too.

I hadn't seen Charlie since that night in the park and bristled when I saw him seated on the sofa, a comic in his hands.

"Hi," he said, his voice wary.

When I didn't say anything, he turned to my sister. "How are you, Elif?"

"I'm good, Charlie," she said. "How are— What happened to your eye?"

I peered through the dim light and saw that his eye was puffy and bruised.

"I got in a little tussle," he said to Elif.

"With whom?" she asked.

"No one," he said, getting to his feet. "It was a job."

Elif nodded and moved on to check in with Henrik, but I stood there, not knowing what to say, my body a swirl of complicated emotions.

"Are you okay?" I asked. "Did—did the job go well?"

His eyes met mine, and an overwhelming urge to hug him filled me. He looked pained and so very tired.

"He's dead, if that's what you're asking," he said.

I inhaled and stared down at my feet while he gathered his things, said goodbye to Henrik, and brushed past me, his hand grazing mine as he went. He stopped at the door and turned to meet my eyes again.

"Be careful," he said. "And Lien?"

"Yes?"

"Don't hesitate. Not for one second."

The job was to take place at the same location as the test with Charlie. Elif was once again dressed in our mother's clothing, sewn to fit, the too big shoes strapped onto her too small feet. I was once again armed, this time with a loaded gun. I'd checked more than once, the last time while my mother stood by watching, an exasperated look on her face before she took our hands in hers and told us to look out for one another.

"Be your sister's keeper," she'd said, looking from me to Elif and back again. "Both of you. Promise?"

"Promise," we'd said.

Her hands on ours squeezed hard, her breath escaping in a strange exhalation, as if there was more she wanted to say, but the words had been stolen from her. She nodded, looked from Elif to me, and then let us go.

We left on our bicycles, nerves causing us to pedal quick.

"Slow down!" an SS soldier shouted as we took a corner and nearly collided with him.

"Sorry!" I yelled as I swerved and nearly fell.

Gripping my handlebars tighter, I waited for him to tell us to stop. All it would take was one time. One search. One glimpse of our weapons and it would be over for us. But he didn't, and so we kept riding.

We left our bikes two streets up from the pub and walked the rest of the way, stopping just out of sight at the corner like we'd done before.

"Stop," I said, pulling Elif's hand away from the buttons she was twisting on her coat. One popped off and she pursed her lips.

"Shoot," she said, her eyes filling with tears as she tried to shove it in her pocket. But her hands were shaking, and it fell to the ground.

"Elif," I said, picking up the button and tucking it in my own pocket. "Are you sure you want to do this? We can go home."

Her eyes met mine and she blinked rapidly a few times, tipping her head back, trying not to ruin the makeup our mother had expertly applied.

"Yes. No." She exhaled and closed her eyes for a moment. "It doesn't matter. I'm going to do it. I just need a minute."

I reached out and took her hand, but she shook me off.

"Don't," she said. "Please. I'm too nervous and it will just make me cry."

I nodded. It was a feeling I understood well. After Madi died, being held only made me feel worse, the guilt and shame brought to the surface by kindness and love and human touch. And in times like the ones we were currently in, doing the things we were soon to be doing, it only heightened my emotions to be touched in a caring way. When what I really needed to do was shut myself off.

I stood staring across the street to the quiet park where I'd soon be hiding, just as I'd done before, but this time with what would most likely be a very different result. A shudder ran through me and I sucked in a breath.

"Lien?" Elif said. "Are *you* sure?"

For a long moment I couldn't meet her gaze. It was all well and good to say yes to the job. To the cause. To a life for a life. To make up for Madi's tragic death. To honor my friend and her family taken against their will from their home. But how could I possibly be okay with taking a life? No matter what someone had done or was planning to do in the future, how could I rectify the actions I was about to take with myself? Would shoving my feelings down like Aunt Liv told us to work? Or would they one day bubble to the surface and threaten everything I held dear?

"How can I be?" I asked finally. "How can any of us be sure? But I'm going to do it anyway. And I hope I can live with myself after."

I watched as she stood a little straighter, adjusted the strap of her handbag on her shoulder. "How do I look?" she asked.

"Ready," I said. "You remember the target's name?"

"I do," she said.

"Be careful in there," I said.

"Be careful out here," she said.

And then she squeezed her eyes shut in what we'd called a "double wink" when we were little girls, trying desperately to close just one eye like our parents and failing miserably. I "winked" back, and then watched her cross the street, open the door to the pub, and disappear inside.

It was cold, the frigid North Sea air sneaking under my clothes and numbing my fingertips as I walked across the park to my hiding spot. The grass was damp under my feet, what was left of the leaves from the trees gathered in wet mounds here and there. And it was quiet.

As a girl I'd often wondered if there were any place as quiet as Haarlem. I'd always found it peaceful, the wind lulling, the mist that seemed ever-present in the air a welcome kiss of familiar damp. But now...now the quiet was disconcerting. Every crack of a branch beneath my feet startling, the shrieking call of a passing gull making me want to shout out in fear.

I picked up my speed and ducked behind the same tree as before, finding the same notch in the roots to rest my feet between, the same branch to peek around at the pub. And I waited.

Time ticked by. Seconds became minutes and I grew weary, my body shaking with fear, cold, and exhaustion from standing in one position.

I peeked at my watch. It had been a half hour. I looked across the expanse of grass. People were coming in and out, but no Elif. Taking a step away from the tree, I moved my body, trying to feel my toes and fingertips again, stretching my back and shoulders. A crack behind me made me gasp, my heart leaping in my chest. I turned, scanning the brush for an animal or worse— a soldier. What I saw instead was a young man that looked to be about my age. He held a finger to his lips with one hand; in the other was a shovel. I nodded and stepped back into place behind the tree.

Over an hour went by before Elif finally emerged, stumbling a little in her heels, a gentleman on her arm. He pointed one way but she gestured toward the park and started walking, leaving him with a choice. He made the correct one.

Her laughter floated on the wind, forced, high-pitched, scared. The man followed, completely oblivious, his hands around her shoulders, around her waist, touching her hair, her breast. My grip on the pistol tightened. I wanted to shoot him now so he'd stop touching her, but they were still out in the open. Someone might see.

And then, just like when she was with Charlie, they were mere meters away. So close I could smell the alcohol coming off one or both of them, and hear my sister's little gasps of breath I recognized as the sound she made when she was trying not to cry.

Her eyes sought mine through the sparse branches before she

stopped and turned to him, keeping her body positioned to the left of the tree trunk like I'd instructed, and out of the line of fire. But unlike when she was with Charlie, this man took her flirtatious offer seriously, rushing in and pressing her to the tree I was hiding behind.

"Wait!" she cried out. "Stop—that hurts!"

But he only muttered his excitement and continued, ignoring my sister's pleas while I pressed my body to the tree and tried to move around the trunk without him noticing the branches moving or the gun pointing in his direction.

My footing was unstable, my nails clawing into the bark to keep me upright, my coat snagging and pulling against me. Elif's back was pressed against the tree, her face turned toward me, her eyes squeezed shut. That man's face was buried in her chest, one hand under her skirt.

I could only see the back half of his head, making the shot dangerous and nearly impossible. Nearly.

The discharging bang echoed through the trees, lingering in the bare branches, before dissipating on the wind as the world went quiet again.

"Li— Grietje!" Elif said, her voice scraping against my alias, verging on a wail.

My hand shook as I lowered my arm, the pistol warm from being fired, my body vibrating from the kick, the fear, the adrenaline. On the other side of the tree, Elif was pinned, the man slumped against her and sliding, taking her down with him.

I shoved the gun in my pocket, pushed my way through the shrubbery, and shoved at the man's shoulder. He was heavier than I'd anticipated and Elif, crumpled against the tree like a blood-spattered rag doll, her chest rising and falling as she cried silently, was too distraught to help.

The man finally fell to the ground and I hurriedly averted my eyes, not wanting to see the result of my actions, the sound of the gunshot still echoing in my ears. We didn't have time for both of us to lose focus. We needed to move. Now.

"Here," I said, looking around as I slid out of my coat.

So far no one seemed to be coming to investigate the noise. Gunshots weren't exactly a rare sound these days, but that didn't mean someone wouldn't come eventually, so we needed to go.

I held out the garment. "You need to put this on."

But she didn't move, her eyes screwed shut, her body shivering. She lurched suddenly and threw up in some shrubbery beside her and then began crying again.

"Elif." My own eyes welled with tears as I took first one of her arms and slid it in a coat sleeve, and then the other. I buttoned her up like I would a small child, and then grabbed her hand, frowning as I heard a crinkle.

She opened her closed fist. Inside it was the list we were supposed to retrieve.

"Good job," I whispered.

Her smile trembled, and I nodded my approval and grinned back.

"Let's go," I said.

As we turned to leave, I saw movement in the trees beyond and froze. The same young man I'd seen earlier moved into the clearing, shovel in hand, waiting to deliver the body to the pre-dug hole. I sighed and nodded, and then Elif and I hurried out of the park the opposite way we'd entered, while I wondered if I'd ever see this park the same way again, knowing graves had been dug into it, and that I'd supplied some of the bodies.

We walked two blocks, Elif wiping at the tiny droplets of blood on her face with the hem of my coat until I told her to stop fidgeting in case someone took notice and stared too hard. But no one paid us any mind as, chins tucked, eyes cast down, we circled around to where we'd left our bikes and rode home as quickly as we could without getting yelled at.

At the house, we parked our bikes and Elif hurried to the

door, knocking frantically, her gasps barely contained as I tried to calm her by rubbing her back. But she shook me off and knocked harder.

"Mama," she said, pressing her forehead to the door.

The lock slid out of place, and I sighed with relief as our mother's face appeared in the doorway and she pulled us inside. My sister threw herself into her arms.

She looked over Elif's shoulder at me, and my eyes filled as I shook my head.

"It was awful," I whispered. "He touched her. I don't know how much."

She closed her eyes and held Elif tighter.

"I can still feel his hands on me," Elif said, her slender body wracked with sobs.

"I know, my love. Let's get you out of those clothes and cleaned up. You'll feel better after."

I sat on the floor outside the bathroom as Mama drew a bath and helped Elif into the warm water. I listened as Elif told her about what had transpired inside the pub, her fear of the older man, and then her voice broke as she recounted how his rough fingers had torn at her blouse and reached beneath her skirt, grabbing at her thighs and touching the part of her she'd never even touched herself.

As her sobs echoed off the tiles, I pulled my knees to my chest, rested my forehead on them, and cried. For her. For me. And for the life I'd taken, regardless of what he'd done in the past, tonight, or planned for the future. He'd been alive, and I'd changed that. I'd altered his path, and possibly the life of his family, if he'd had one. These were the things Aunt Liv hadn't talked about. These were the things that would haunt me forever.

I was just glad I'd been numb in the park, my detachment probably the thing that saved us. Had I let myself feel the shock and guilt of taking a life there, we might not have left alive. But now...now I could allow myself the luxury of remembering the moment of clarity when I'd seen the shot, the horror of the back of the man's head exploding, and the sound of Elif's anguish in my ears.

Mama found me still crying outside the bathroom when she and Elif exited.

"Oh, Lien," she whispered, falling to her knees and gathering me in her arms. "Why didn't you come in?"

But I had no answer. At least none I wanted to share. The fact was, killing had been a lonely action, and my grief felt mired in solitude as a result. Only those who had done the same could possibly know the confusing feelings of triumph, sadness, and relief I felt. And neither my mother or sister could understand. And so there was no point in sharing. At least not on this night.

The evening passed as if I were watching it from behind a sheer curtain, the colors and sounds muted as mother moved about the house bringing us food, asking if we were okay, and tucking us into our beds on the sofas.

But as the hum of the sewing machine started up, I found I couldn't sleep. And after mother turned out the light and climbed into her own bed, her breath slowing as she fell into unconsciousness, I wrapped my quilt around my shoulders and climbed the stairs to the second floor.

I opened my younger sister's bedroom door and peered through the darkness at the belongings she'd so lovingly cared for. Everything had thrilled Madi. Nothing was too small or insignificant to receive her attention. I stepped inside and ran my fingers over her dolls, books, and various trinkets, the dust of disuse coating my fingertips. When I reached her bed, I crawled up onto it, pulling my quilt around me, and resting my face on the cool pillowcase. I inhaled, hoping for a glimpse of the scent that was hers and hers alone. But time had erased it, and I closed my eyes and let my tears soak the pillow beneath me.

Hearing a sound, I looked up and saw Elif's silhouette in the doorway.

"Come," I said.

She climbed in beside me, her hand slipping into mine, and a moment later, just like our mother, her breath slowed as the day's awful events finally and mercifully wore her out.

As I lay there, listening to my sister's soft breaths pushing against the dark of the night, I added her to my list.

A life for a life.

Madi. Tess. Elif.

I would fight for all of them.

20

After the first liquidation was done, we found ourselves pulled deeper into the world of Resistance work. "The real work" Annie called it. The dangerous tasks we'd trained for in the field and that dirty barn basement.

Along with this real work came a new team member. Jan was young, brash, loud, and had a crude sense of humor. He was constantly pretending to stab himself with the daggers he'd pull from the wall and play with. It annoyed Henrik, but the rest of us found him to be a breath of fresh air. Even Elif, who normally preferred a quieter type of boy, laughed at his conduct.

Annie took a real shine to him, though, which looked to be mutual by the way the two stared at one another when we were supposed to be packing dynamite sticks.

Jan's first assignment was with Elif and me. I was nervous. Though I enjoyed his constant mirth, I wondered if his noisy antics in the basement of the barn would carry into our job, making a dangerous situation worse, but if Henrik and Aunt Liv trusted him enough to bring him in, I supposed I should as well.

We were to set fire to a train car carrying supplies to the Germans. The information had come from one of Jan's contacts.

"How will we know which car?" Elif asked him as we sat at the massive table in Henrik's barn.

"It'll be marked," Jan said, packing a stick of dynamite.

"By whom?" I asked, peering at the young man, who looked to me no different from an ill-behaved schoolboy with his everready smirk and mussed hair. But Jan had a skill set suited to a soldier.

"One of their own," he said. "A traitor. Working for our side."

"And how do we know we can trust him?"

"Her," he said. "Because she's worked for us before."

"And that automatically means she's trustworthy every time?"

He stared at me as if determining what to say next, the thought that this double agent might betray him never seemed to have crossed his mind.

"It's a good question," he said, and my eyes widened, surprised by his admission. I'd expected an argument. "I'll have a friend check in on her."

"Thank you for considering the idea."

"My family was from Rotterdam," he said, his voice low. "If my father had considered another idea, they might all still be alive."

My hands, which had been winding twine around my bundle of dynamite, slowed and stopped. Jan looked up and met my eyes.

"My father didn't think we should run when the attack began," he explained, his voice uncharacteristically quiet. "He thought we should wait it out. Surely they didn't mean to bomb *us*. Not the Dutch for heaven's sake. When I questioned him, he accused me of scaring my younger siblings and sent me to my room, which was where my youngest sister came to tell me she agreed with me and wanted to leave. So, we threw some clothes and the fruit she'd sneaked under her blouse out the window, climbed over the sill, and made a run for it. You can guess what happened to my family who stayed." He sighed and rubbed his eyes. "The guilt we felt after... Anyway, I left her up north with some family friends while I committed to doing this work. It's the only thing that makes me feel better about deserting my family."

"But you didn't—" I started, but he held up a hand.

"I should be dead with them."

"But then your sister would be dead as well."

"And that is the only thought that keeps me going. Well, that and my terrible jokes. Anything to try and make myself feel the tiniest bit better."

I nodded, understanding now. Jan was just doing what the rest of us were doing—trying to survive in any way possible. After that day, I never found him loud or brash again.

In those days, we moved in the shadows before the sun came up and long after it had gone down, sneaking in and out of homes and buildings, passing information with a quick slide of a hand as we passed in the street, stood in line for weekly rations, and received goods with a manual for incendiary devices tucked beneath our butter allotment. We became actors, disguising ourselves with a variety of props: glasses, hats, stuffing we pulled from the throw pillows in Mama's shop. And with each successful exchange we were more confident, more daring, more willing to face the increasing danger.

In February, Elif and I received orders for another liquidation. Our second in as many months. Given what we'd found could be a precarious situation when it came to actually pulling the trigger, it was decided that until there was plausible reason to switch, Elif would always be the lure, and I would always be the shooter. The decision had been made during a rare Sunday dinner with Aunt Liv.

"You're sure?" she asked me as we were changing into our nightclothes in our bedroom.

"It's fine," I said from beneath the folds of my nightgown. "I'm the better shot."

"But—"

"I said it's fine." But my vehemence gave me away. It wasn't fine, and we both knew it.

After the first liquidation, I found I couldn't erase it from my mind, the images finding me at any given moment, most often when I lay in bed at night. I tried to shove the thoughts away, crawling onto the narrow settee beside Elif in hopes being near her would stave them off. But they found me in the dark, fueling nightmares that woke me and left me bleary and sad in the mornings. Gunshots yanked me from sleep, leaving me to stare into the inky blackness of the house, imagining dead eyes staring at me from the corners. And the sound of Elif's scared breaths echoed in my ears constantly. Mama would wake sometimes in the early-morning hours and find me sitting at the dining table, where I'd wandered when a dream had woken me, head on arms, fast asleep.

Time and time again I tried to bury the feelings of fear and guilt that intermingled like the roots of a tree, digging deeper into the earth, searching for solid footing so that it wouldn't tip.

"Now," Mama said, looking over Elif's makeup and outfit and giving her a nod, "don't get too caught up that you forget yourselves and head home instead of the safe house. It will be too dark to make it here safely, and you don't want to get caught dressed like that."

"We know, Mama," Elif said, giving her a kiss on the cheek. She wasn't happy we wouldn't be coming home after the job, and she wasn't alone. Despite being reassured someone would be there to let us in, Elif and I both worried that this might be the rare occasion there wouldn't be. Or maybe, because whoever owned the home didn't know us, they wouldn't let us in. Being caught out after curfew was dangerous. We could be taken to jail. Or worse, we could be shot on sight. But we put on brave faces, said what we could to comfort our mother, and ourselves, and hurried out the door.

The pub where we were to meet our target was farther south from the one we'd gone to before, but still near Haarlemmerhout Park, which was large and sprawling.

We stood out of sight, shivering as Elif fidgeted, twisting her fingers, her eyes darting from mine to the ground between us.

"What if he grabs me?" she said. "What if he touches me like—" She shuddered, and I reached out and wrapped my hand around her wrist.

"I'll be faster this time," I said. "I won't worry about being quiet or him seeing me. I'll just take the shot."

She nodded and wiped away the tear sitting on her lower lashes. "Okay," she whispered.

"Just lead him to the trees," I said, trying to make my voice sound soothing, which was hard when my teeth kept chattering. "I'll take care of the rest. I promise. I won't let you down."

She met my scared gaze. "I trust you," she said, and squeezed both eyes shut.

I squeezed mine in reply, and we exchanged a small smile.

"Are you ready?" she asked.

I swallowed and looked across the street to the park. I could suddenly feel the weight of the gun in my pocket, and the strap holding my dagger to my thigh felt tighter. But I nodded regardless. This was what I'd signed on for.

I removed my hand and she was gone, hurrying around the corner on silent feet and the whisper of her coat dragging across the bricks of the building we stood beside. I peeked around the wall and watched as she disappeared inside the door of the pub. A minute later I crossed the street.

It was colder outside than it had been the last time we'd done this. It wasn't easy to stay silent and still when you were scared, filled with a strange sort of excitement, while the cold wind licked at any bit of skin not covered by clothing.

I took my post, removed my pistol from my pocket, checked the magazine and counted the bullets, even though I'd checked right before leaving the house, and leaned against the large tree I hid behind.

The wind kicked up and I crouched down, tucking my chin into my scarf and wrapping my arms around my torso, eyes locked on the door of the pub, the second hand of my watch ticking beneath the cuff of my coat.

The crack of a branch nearby startled me and I nearly fell as I twisted around, searching through the branches of the shrubs hiding me. Two men in uniform wandered by, their steps slow, as if they had nowhere to be and nothing to do but be in this park at this moment. They were chatting, and stopped not twenty yards from where I hid while I alternately held my breath and exhaled slowly and silently into the leaves, praying neither noticed the puff of air floating up out of the shrubbery.

I craned my head to look toward the pub, bracing myself with my hand in the dirt and trying not to tip over. A shout from the opposite direction caused me to nearly lose my balance, and I watched as the two soldiers went to meet their comrade, the three standing on the dirt pathway talking and laughing.

"Dammit," I whispered. This would not do at all if they didn't move on.

I looked to the pub again. The door opened and a couple emerged, but the woman wasn't Elif. I sighed with relief and glanced at the men again. They had begun walking away from me and I urged them on inside my head, willing them to walk faster, to put as much distance as possible between the discharge of my gun and them.

They disappeared from sight, and I once more turned my attention to the pub door. Three men went in, one came out. My fingers began to ache from the cold, my knees from being crouched. I stood, still staying low, and moved my legs as best I could while first flexing the fingers of one hand, then the other. I was so preoccupied, I didn't notice Elif and her mark were walking toward me until I heard the crunch of leaves and the murmur of voices.

I nudged the safety off my gun, readying myself for what would come next, my heartbeat gathering speed in my chest as I listened to Elif's voice, high-pitched with nerves, her laugh shaky and brittle.

They were twenty yards away now, and I could see her eyes searching for mine through the brush as she simultaneously smiled and nodded at whatever the man with her was saying. And then I got a look at him. He was a small mouse of a man who was limping badly and seemed to be clinging to my sister not out of desire, but need. The look of distaste on her face screamed *don't touch me*. I braced myself.

"Slow down," he said, wheezing slightly.

Her eyes scanned the shrubbery once more, and then she turned her back to me and stepped to her left, giving me a clear shot.

My heartbeat thundered in my chest and echoed in my ears as I stared at the man, sweat rising on my upper lip as my palms grew clammy.

I took in a shaky breath. I could do this. I *would* do this.

I raised my gun and, knowing my aim was true, pulled the trigger.

His look of surprise as the bullet pierced the spot above his eye imprinted itself on my mind, and I watched as he folded into himself, dropping to the ground, the crack of the pistol still lingering in the air.

"Come on!" Elif reached through the brush and found my sleeve, dragging me into the open and then pulling me down the path the soldiers had been on not long before.

I stopped.

"What are you doing?" she asked, her face etched with fear.

"We can't go that way," I said, pulling her across the pathway from where I'd just been hiding, deeper into the woods.

"We'll get trapped if we hide in there," Elif said, and then her eyes widened at the sound of boots hitting the ground headed toward us.

"This way," a hushed male voice said, making me jump and my sister clap a hand over her mouth so she didn't scream. "Hurry."

The man looked to be our father's age, were he still alive, and wore a dirt-stained shirt and trousers. Clearly, he was one of the grave diggers. "The Cleaners," Jan called them. They dragged the bodies we'd shot out of sight and into the holes they'd pre-dug, covering them quickly before hunkering down nearby, waiting until it was safe to leave. Sometimes, we'd heard, they weren't able to escape until morning.

"I heard of a guy who had to lie down next to the corpse and cover himself with branches because the place was crawling with soldiers," Jan had told us once. I'd shuddered in response.

We followed the man deeper into the brush, and then he stopped and lifted a large, low-hanging tree branch where a hole sat empty.

"No," Elif whispered.

"There's no time," the man said. "It's this or get caught."

"It's okay," I said, squeezing my sister's hand and then reaching for the man, who helped me lower myself into the darkness.

It wasn't very deep. But that wasn't the point. The point was, it was a grave, and it took everything I had not to get sick at the thought.

I turned and looked up at Elif, who nodded and then allowed the man to help her as well. We knelt and then lay down in the soft, cool dirt face-to-face, heads resting on arms folded beneath them, legs intertwined, hands grasped tightly around one another's.

As the footsteps got louder, voices rising on the other side of the brush from where we hid, we stared at one another and then squeezed our eyes shut as branches were laid over us.

"*Stop!*" a voice yelled. "Come out of there! Who are you? Did you do this?"

There was a rustle, more footsteps, words in German I didn't understand, and then a shot rang out followed by the thud of a body falling.

I stared through the dark at Elif, her eyes only inches from mine. I could feel her trembling as she pulled our intertwined fingers to her and pressed them against her lips as she whimpered quietly. We jumped as footsteps shook the ground nearby.

"Any ID on him?" a man asked.

"Nothing. What do we do with him?"

"Leave him. We'll report it, and someone else can clean up the mess."

Their footsteps grew fainter, but neither Elif nor I moved. Without saying a word, we pulled ourselves even closer to one another, listening for footsteps and voices as the wind whispered through the trees, ruffling the foliage above us.

We slept in fits and starts, hidden beneath the branches of another man's grave, the earth cold and damp around us.

I tried not to think of the man who had helped us, and who had died because of it, or the fact that we were lying where a corpse belonged. In a horrid twist of fate, the hole dug for the enemy now cradled us, keeping us safe while we waited out the night, cold, frightened, and wishing for the light of morning.

For days after lying in another man's grave while the man who saved us lay dead just above, I felt haunted. The nightmares this time around were quiet images that felt like death, even though I couldn't see death. A dark space with light peeking through branches. And as much as I pulled at them, they multiplied and

I was unable to get out of the grave I'd stepped into, causing me to wake breathless and in a panic.

Other nights I dreamed I was at school, or my mother's shop, or the market. Sometimes the beach. But no matter where I was in the dream, I could hear a shovel not far away digging, and my sister's panicked breaths in my ear.

Thankfully the jobs we did in the weeks following were less traumatic. "Busywork" Aunt Liv called it. Forging of documents, delivering of information, and setting fire to another train. It kept me physically busy, which kept my mind busy, and eventually the nightmares dimmed and became less frequent. They still woke me when they came, but now they barely lingered, leaving me almost completely by the time I woke in the morning.

But a few weeks later, I was once again crouched behind a tree, waiting for Elif and the unsuspecting target trailing behind, hoping to slide a hand up her skirt and a tongue down her throat.

This one was younger than the others had been, and didn't waste any time going for what he thought he was being offered. They'd barely made it to the cover of trees before he had his hands all over her, all the while pulling her in another direction, away from me, and obscuring my shot by keeping her in front of him.

"No," Elif said, her voice stern but not too loud, not wanting to alert anyone. "Wait. Not over here."

I eased from my spot and kept to the edges of the brush, following along close enough to hear them, but not so close that he could see me.

"Shhh," he said. "It doesn't matter where we do it. Come on now. You promised. Don't play innocent now."

"I'm not. It's just—"

She gasped as he pushed her away, having caught sight of

me. I stood and raised my gun, but rather than turn and run, he charged at me.

I pulled the trigger but the gun didn't fire, a rare occurrence we'd been warned could happen with these old pistols. The mark rammed into me, sending me into the air before I crashed to the ground, my head hitting the dirt, the wind knocked from my lungs. The pistol was kicked from my hands, and he dragged me to my feet, his eyes glittering dangerously. He held me up by my coat.

"And who do we have here?" he asked.

Elif pushed him, and once more I was tossed away as though I were a rag doll. He turned and went after my sister who ran, but not fast enough.

"I'm going to get what I came here for," he said, his jaw clenched, teeth bared.

I heard the rip of fabric and Elif's whimper of fear and got to my hands and knees, scanning the grass and dirt for my pistol.

"No," Elif said. "Please."

Giving up on finding the gun, I pulled my dagger from its sheath and got to my feet. As I ran toward them on silent feet, Elif's scared gaze caught mine.

"Cover his mouth," I said.

Before he could turn his head, I jammed my weapon into his neck just like Charlie had taught me.

The sound of the gunnysack ripping, the feel of my blade sinking into packed hay, was nothing like shoving a knife into human flesh. My knees went weak as blood, hot and thick, spilled over his jacket, a strange animal-like sound coming from between his lips.

"Oh my God," Elif whispered as she jumped out of the way.

We watched him fall face-first into the tree he'd had her pinned against before tipping sideways onto the dirt, a dark puddle growing beneath him.

"Help me," I said, pulling his shoulder back to grab my dagger. His lifeless eyes stared up at me, but for once I didn't look. I pulled the knife free, wiped it on his shirt, and slid it back in its holster at my hip. "Let's go."

On our way to the safe house, I felt Elif's eyes on me. After we arrived, she used the bathroom first, and when I entered the bedroom we were to share for the night, I met her gaze.

"What is it?" I asked.

"You just… I've never seen you like that," she said.

"Like what?" I sat on the bed across from her with a frown.

"Like you didn't care or—you weren't affected." The crease between her brows deepened. "You stabbed him in the neck."

I took in a deep breath, images of the evening flashing through my mind, and then exhaled.

"I was scared," I said. "And *mad*. He hurt me, and he was going to hurt you. I couldn't find my pistol so I grabbed the dagger and…" I shrugged, unsure what to say next.

"It was terrifying," she whispered. "*You* were terrifying."

"I had to stop him. So I did."

Reluctantly, she nodded, not meeting my eyes. Then she lay down in the bed and turned her back to me.

No nightmares haunted me that night. No lingering feelings of guilt making me question my actions. There was only a single decisive thought: I was meant for this.

21

In early March, Elif and I volunteered for another sort of job. The extraction of a pilot who had escaped his damaged plane as it hurtled toward the ground, and had been hiding out in a town not too far from ours.

Reports from those harboring him weren't good. The town was crawling with soldiers, due to displacing many of the citizens to nearby cities and taking up residence, making getting the man out impossible so far. There had been several attempts, and two close calls.

"They move him constantly," Jan told us during a quick briefing the day before we were to go.

He had been part of one of the failed previous missions.

"You will have many eyes on you, so it is imperative you have your story straight for why you are there. In case you are stopped. And you most likely will be."

I'd looked to Elif across the table of the safe house we'd met up at, and we exchanged a glance. She raised her eyebrows, asking a silent question. After all we'd done already, I had no doubt we could manage the job.

I nodded.

The morning of the mission, I woke early and slid from my bed on the sofa. The hardwood was like ice beneath my feet, the fire Mama had made the night before long gone out.

My breath lingered like a cloud in front of my face before dissipating as I hurried from one rug to the next, much like Elif and I used to when we were girls, pretending they were islands and the floor in between was shark-infested waters, Madi, at two, toddling around us laughing, thinking we were hysterical. How I longed to go back to those days. The contrast to these ones was stark. Would the girl I was then recognize the one I was now, dagger strapped beneath dresses, a gun hidden in her pocket? I was positive the young woman I'd been would never have imagined she'd become this version of me. No, she'd dreamed of libraries that stretched floor to ceiling, smart clothes, and long nights writing even longer papers. Would I ever return to that version of me? Or had she been vanquished, as so many others had, by this war?

I rubbed the soles of my feet into the worn fibers and curled my toes, waiting until they warmed some before scurrying to the next rug and my house shoes, which I'd kicked off on the other side of the room from where I slept.

In the kitchen I put on the kettle and lit the burner, holding my hands up to the flame and urging the water to boil. We had an early day, and I hadn't been able to sleep in anticipation. I rationed out my daily allotment of tea, which was less than it had been last week, and continued to wait.

"Good morning," Elif said, rubbing her eyes as she entered the kitchen. "How'd you sleep?"

"I didn't."

"Me neither. I'm worried about today. There are too many opportunities for things to go wrong."

"We'll just have to stick to the plan as best we can and improvise when we need to. Hopefully by this time tomorrow we'll be on our way home, neither of us worse for wear."

But she didn't look convinced and I didn't blame her. This mission felt ten times more dangerous than luring men into the woods to kill them.

Thirty minutes later we'd had our weak tea, which we drank while it was still scalding hot to disguise the lack of flavor, a small bowl of warm oats each, and were dressed for the day. We wore plain, bulky dresses with layers of long-sleeved shirts that had belonged to our father beneath, trousers for added warmth, and our most worn pairs of shoes. As usual for this sort of job, our hair was twisted in plaits and our faces were left free of any sort of cosmetics. The entire effect made us look at least three years younger than we were, which was the point.

We checked we had the correct ID cards, I patted my pocket to make sure the little red bird was in its place, we bid our mother goodbye with the usual promises of staying alert and watching out for one another, and then we were on our way.

Our bicycles bumped over the cobblestones as we rode through Haarlem, our heads down, eyes darting in search of soldiers and pedestrians, doing our best to not draw attention to ourselves. We were just two young women out for a bike ride, our blond plaits flying out behind us, our layers of clothes hiding weapons.

It broke my heart to see how bleak the city looked. How barren. The already quiet town was so devoid of its usual sounds I nearly fell off my bike when I heard the sound of a trash bin being rolled down the sidewalk.

I'd just recovered, tightening my hands on the grips of my handlebars when an older man in uniform stepped out in front of us.

"Stop," he said.

"*Goedemorgen*, sir," Elif said, a tremor in her voice.

"Where are you two off to this morning?" His pale gaze

shifted from Elif to me as he seemed to take in every detail about us.

"We're off to visit a friend."

"At this early hour?"

"We don't have much else to do," I said, trying to keep the pointed tone out of my voice.

He peered at me and then stepped to the side with a sharp nod. "Enjoy your visit, ladies," he said.

As we pedaled away, Elif gave me a look.

"What?" I asked.

"You have to watch your tone."

It was not the first time I'd heard that in the past couple of weeks. And not just from her. We'd done a small job with Annie a few days before, and she'd raised her eyebrows at me when I'd practically snapped at a soldier she was flirting with as a distraction while Elif swiped a list of storage facilities for weapons off a clipboard at a building the Resistance was watching.

"Excuse my friend," she'd said to the young man who had turned irritated eyes on me. "She hasn't had much to eat today. You know how it is."

When we were a safe distance away, she gave me a look. "Are you trying to get us in trouble?" she asked.

I apologized and said of course not, but the truth was, I wasn't sure why I'd reacted the way I had. After the last liquidation where I'd been knocked down and Elif nearly killed, something had changed in me. A fury I was having a hard time containing, the flame burning low and fierce deep in my belly. I knew if I wasn't careful, I could end up getting myself and whoever was with me in trouble.

As we rode out of downtown and the homes got farther apart, I was able to breathe easier. We passed farms and a field that in the spring was filled with the bright, happy tulips the Dutch were so famous for, but now was just a long stretch of dark brown soil. I smiled, imagining it filled with color in just a few months.

We arrived in the small area of Hillegom and exchanged a nervous look as we noted the many men in uniform milling about the streets.

"They're everywhere," Elif said.

"That must be why they're having such a hard time moving him," I said, looking up and down the street. "Well, let's get to him, and then we'll figure out what to do from there."

We were to enter a small corner bookshop and ask to use the telephone. The owner was a member of the Resistance and, after looking us over, showed us where to find it.

Elif dialed the number and waited.

"Hi," she said. "Do you have a room available for the night?"

"No," I could hear a voice say. "Call back another time."

"Thank you," she said, and hung up. "Let's go."

That was the code for all safe houses. They were to say no if it was safe and yes, come on over, if they were compromised. That way, if a soldier had a gun to their head, it would sound like they were doing what they'd been asked.

In the clear, we headed to the address we'd memorized where a man had been hiding out for several days. A pilot for the RAF, he'd gone down near The Hague and had been slowly making his way north. The goal was to get him to Pas-Opkamp, the hiding camp in the woods of Vierhouten, a town east of Amsterdam. Referred to as the secret village, it supposedly had a handful of huts dug into the ground and hidden from sight by the forest. Once we got him out of Hillegom, the rest of the trip should be relatively easy. The problem was getting him out, though. Someone had sworn they'd seen him enter the town, and soldiers had swooped in and searched all houses and buildings. Two townspeople had been shot over the matter. How the safe house had managed to hide him I had no idea, but the situation was becoming dire and it was well past time to move him.

Double-checking the number beside the door, Elif knocked and we waited, keeping watch up and down the narrow alleyway. A curtain in the window next door moved, and I turned my head away and raised a hand to shield my face just in case.

A moment later the door opened, and we were ushered in by a middle-aged woman.

"Come," she said, gesturing for us to follow her into the dark home.

Darragh Walsh was Irish through and through, with an accent so thick I looked to my sister helplessly as I tried to understand a word he said.

"They'll never believe his papers if we get stopped," I said.

"I speak Dutch," he said—in Dutch. The Irish brogue was still there, but much less. Hopefully he wouldn't have to speak at all. "How will we leave?"

"I think I have an idea," Elif said.

My sister's idea was daring to say the least, and not for the faint of heart.

"We go to the market," she said, pointing in the direction of the small market we'd passed when we'd left the bookshop.

"What?" I said, confused at how this was a good idea. My confidence might be building with every mission, but I didn't have a death wish.

"The market is small," the woman of the house said. "There's nowhere to hide."

"That's the point," Elif said. "They're looking for someone trying to stay hidden. Someone staying to the shadows. Not someone out in the open."

We'd been informed that this was a last-chance effort to move the hiding pilot. There was movement happening from the Germans, and residents of Hillegom might soon find themselves homeless. If we couldn't get him out, he would be on his own, his chances of surviving not good.

I considered what my sister said and nodded slowly.

"Hiding in plain sight," I said, and looked Darragh over.

He wasn't particularly tall, his features as plain as ours, his clothing, clearly castoffs from someone bigger than him, were nondescript and baggy.

"There's a picture of you circulating," I said. "Probably from your pilot's license. Do you have it on you?"

He nodded and left the room to retrieve it. When he returned and handed it over, I nearly laughed. The young man in the picture was baby-faced and clean-shaven, his hair cropped close, eyes bright and eager. The man standing before us barely resembled the image. His hair was shaggy, he had a beard, his skin pale and lined. Even his eyes had dulled.

"Perfect," I said.

"Did you get the photo?" Elif asked the woman who nodded, opened a drawer, and removed its false bottom.

She handed over an envelope, and Elif removed the picture another member of the Resistance had come by to take, then took a book from the bag she carried, removing a false ID from behind the removable endpaper, and made quick work of attaching the photo.

"It needs to dry," she said.

"We'll have tea while we wait," the woman said. "I'm Agatha, by the way."

"Nice to meet you," we said, and offered the names printed on our fake IDs as we'd been trained. It was safer for everyone involved.

We drank tea while checking our watches and preparing ourselves for the task at hand—the enormous risk we were about to take. Darragh worked at memorizing our aliases in case he was asked, and we got our story straight about how we knew each other and where we were headed. When it was time, Elif, Darragh, and I got to our feet, took a collective breath, said goodbye to Agatha, and stepped outside.

It had begun to rain, large coin-sized droplets that splashed on the cobblestones and formed almost instant puddles.

Elif looked back at me, a look of panic in her eyes.

"It will be fine," I said. "Let's go."

We grabbed our bicycles, Darragh taking the one that had been left out for him by Agatha. Swinging our legs over the seats, we pushed off and headed for the center of town.

I counted the uniforms we passed as we went. One, two, five, ten. None of them even looked our way as they hurried to take cover from the sudden onslaught of weather.

We turned down the street that led to the market and saw the few vendors that had ventured out were packing up. Lack of a crowd that could afford their wares paired with the freezing rain wasn't enough to keep them out. The defeated looks on their faces tore at my heart. How I wished I had the time to stop and a few spare guilders to buy something.

Elif looked over her shoulder past Darragh, who rode between us, to me. She slowed.

"What do we do?" she asked.

I looked ahead of us. Three soldiers stood beneath the awning of a shop with wood covering its windows.

"We keep going," I said.

We rode past the three soldiers. One looked up and away, uninterested in the three poorly dressed citizens riding bikes like fools in the rain. We passed the next street where again, the men in uniform seemed less concerned with who was out and about than the amount of rain that was now coming down, little rivers of water bumping and zigzagging through the cobblestones.

My heart, already hammering in my chest, picked up speed as the end of the town came in to view. We were almost into farm country. Fifty meters to go and we'd be—

"Stop!"

Two soldiers came running into the street from a nearby doorway. I hit my brakes and felt the tires of my bike slide from underneath me, the handlebars slipping from my grasp as I went airborne before coming down with a bone-rattling thud, the cobblestones digging into my thigh and hip, a distinct snap reverberating through the hand I'd tried to brace myself on, my little finger bent beneath it, taking the brunt of the fall.

I sat in a wet heap on the ground, my tears mixing with the rain, the two uniformed men staring down at me.

"Grietje!" Darragh shouted my fake name as he dropped his bike and hurried to my side. "Are you okay?"

I nodded, taking stock of the tear in my trousers and dirt caked along the seam. I didn't even want to look at my hand, afraid of what I'd see.

"Is she okay?" one of the soldiers asked, his voice gruff.

"I think I broke a finger," I said, lifting the injured hand. Sure enough, my finger had already turned a spectacular shade of purplish-blue and was swelling.

"Oh no," Elif said, kneeling beside me.

"That looks bad," the other soldier said, bending to get a closer look. "Why don't you come with me."

I bristled, taking in his little blond mustache and pocked skin. My eyes darted to my sister.

"I'm just going to wrap it," he said. "Won't take but a minute, and then the three of you can be on your way."

None of the snappy retorts made their way to my lips now. In fact, all the confidence I'd gained in the past few months left my body as the three of us followed the two soldiers, looking nervously at one another as we went. We were so close. We just had to be smart and hopefully we'd be on our way again shortly.

"Sit here," the mustached soldier said to me, patting a seat.

We were in what had been a restaurant but looked to have been turned into an office space by the rearranged tables cluttered with pencils and paper and the boxes stacked against the far wall, each one labeled with words in German I couldn't read.

I sat where I was told while Elif and Darragh cowered by the door. I wanted to wave them off—tell them to go. I'd catch up. But before I could open my mouth, the soldier had taken my hand and was wrapping the smaller finger to the one next to it, and the pain was making me see stars.

"Where were the three of you off to?" he asked.

I swallowed. "Haarlem, sir."

"Is that where you live?"

"Mmm-hmm," I said, wincing as he wound more bandage in place.

"All three of you?"

"No," I said. "Our cousin, Tim, lives in The Hague." That was what it said on Darragh's forged ID. "We rode down to meet him here and are riding back to Haarlem. He's staying with us for a while."

"How come you're not fighting for the Führer?" the other soldier asked, taking a step toward Darragh and Elif. He was larger than the one wrapping my hand. His eyes suspicious. His demeanor threatening.

"I have a condition," Darragh said, keeping his face placid.

"Got your papers on you?"

"Of course."

He reached into his pocket and pulled out the ID card I'd so recently finished putting together. Elif's eyes darted to mine, but I held steady in my calm demeanor. I'd been instructed to list a condition should the question arise. But the soldier looking over the papers was taking his time, making me anxious that I'd got something wrong.

I leaned forward and gasped when the soldier tending to my finger tightened his hold.

"Almost done," he said, giving me a grim smile, his eyes moving to his comrade, watching the exchange intently. "Just need to tape it."

The soldier holding the ID card handed it back with a grunt and I breathed a small sigh of relief, looking over my shoulder at Elif again and noticing she'd slid her hand deep into the pocket of her dress where her pistol was hiding. I gave a slight shake of my head. Guns made noise. With all the soldiers in this town, one gunshot would have them all running our way. We were going to have to use daggers if we attacked.

The rip of tape startled me, and I turned back to the man tending to my injury. He placed a strip along the cut edge and pressed, making me squirm in my seat.

"We've been searching for a downed pilot who was seen entering town a few days ago. You three know anything about that?" he said, still holding my fingers, applying a bit more pressure.

"I've heard of it," Elif said. "But I can't say I know much about it. We don't live here."

"Thing is. Someone saw him come, but no one has seen him leave. Which means he has to still be here."

"Couldn't he have left in the night?" I asked, sliding my free hand beneath my skirt and into the concealed pocket where my dagger was.

"Not likely. We work in shifts. We have every inch of this place being watched at all times. But now here you three are. Three faces neither of us has seen before. Curious, don't you think?"

The pain in my fingers made it easy for me to work up tears.

"I don't know anything about a pilot," I said. "I swear it, sir. We're only here for our cousin. He's never been to our house so we rode down to show him the way and—"

"If that's true, then explain what this is."

Dread filled me as I turned to see the other soldier holding what looked to be a handkerchief.

Confused, I again looked to Elif but she looked as puzzled as me. Then I saw Darragh's face, which had paled. He took a step back.

"Funny thing," the soldier said. "I caught a British pilot a few weeks ago. He was carrying an identical one of these." He held it up so we could all see the map printed on a delicate material that looked like it might be silk. "These are escape routes." He traced his finger over several green lines before turning to Darragh. "This fell out of your pocket when you bent to help your...what did you say you were? Cousins?"

"Girls, run," Darragh said, rushing the bigger of the two men before he could pull his weapon.

I was yanked across the table by my injured fingers. But I was ready. My free arm arced around and I jammed the blade of my dagger into the soldier's neck. His eyes widened, his grip on me instantly released as he stumbled backward, trying to remove the blade as he went crashing to the floor.

"Elif!" I shouted, forgetting her alias.

She ran to where Darragh was wrestling with the larger man.

"Shoot him," Darragh said as a fist landed on his jaw. He fell with a groan as the soldier turned toward my sister.

"Aren't you a sly one, coming here dressed like an innocent lass." He took a step closer. "He said shoot. You gonna shoot? Where's your gun, little one?"

Elif's eyes darted to mine. I could see she hadn't pulled a weapon. If he ran at her, she'd have no chance to defend herself. He was nearly twice her size.

He glanced at me and smirked, missing the look my sister gave me. And her double wink.

"Go ahead," he said. "I can see you want to get your weapon. I'll be done with your friend by the time you pull it from Karl's neck."

I looked at Elif again, but she was watching the soldier in front of her, her eyes scanning. I didn't understand at first, and then looked down at her empty hands again, noticing her middle finger bent toward her palm, the silver tip of her dagger resting on its tip, the hilt hidden up her sleeve. A rush of energy filled my chest as the soldier turned and lunged at her.

I watched the dagger slide past her palm, her fingers wrapping around the hilt. In the blink of an eye she swung her arm

upward before all but disappearing from sight as the man engulfed her and the two of them fell to the floor.

My heart racing, I ran around the table and jumped over the
body of the soldier I'd stabbed. Ignoring his lifeless eyes staring
at the ceiling, I yanked my dagger from his neck and hurried
to help my sister. When I saw her small form squirming, trying
to get out from beneath her attacker, the relief caused my eyes
to sting with tears.

I stepped toward her, careful to stay clear of the growing
puddle of blood, and pulled on his arm just enough for Elif to
wriggle out from beneath him.

"My dagger," she said, staring down at the man whose life
she'd just taken, his blood staining the sleeve of her coat.

"Leave it," I said, grabbing her and holding her close for a
moment, our chests heaving against one another in relief.

Darragh had gotten to his feet and was rubbing his jaw.

"I'm so sorry," he said, looking around, an incredulous look
on his face. "But well done."

"We should go," Elif said, peeling her coat off and shoving it
behind a stack of boxes. "Before they notice our bicycles outside and come looking for these two."

Peeking out the door, we made sure no one was headed our
way before quickly exiting the building, closing the door, and
riding out of Hillegom.

We had just reached the outskirts of town when Elif shouted
at me to slow down.

I hit the brakes too hard, jolting my bicycle to a stop and
launching myself once more from the seat into the handlebars.
My breath caught and tears flooded my eyes as I inhaled in pain.

"Are you okay?" Elif asked, stopping next to me.

I wasn't. My hands were clenched around the grips, my injured finger throbbing, my breathing shallow, body shaking,
and my hips hurt from slamming into the metal frame.

The scene in the building we'd just left had been too close.

The sight of Elif disappearing beneath that man too frightening to bear. For several seconds I'd thought she was dead. He was massive compared to her tiny frame, and so much stronger.

"I thought you were dead," I whispered. "I thought—"

She reached for me, and this time it was she who pulled me to her. She was stronger than I remembered her to be. Her arms lean and hard from training for this job we'd signed on to do. It comforted me, knowing she wasn't the same meek girl I'd grown up with, but also scared me because her new assuredness made her braver. And her bravery nearly got her killed back there.

"Why didn't you use your gun?" I asked.

"Same reason you didn't," she said. "The noise."

"I was so scared. When he fell on you, I thought he'd killed you."

"But he didn't. I killed him," she said. "And now we need to get going. If those men have been found, they'll be looking for us. There's no time for dawdling."

Forty minutes later Haarlem came into view. At the familiar sight of my city, my back, the muscles bunched from the stress of expecting to get stopped with every push of the pedal, began to relax, shoulders sagging, legs slowing, my entire body inhaling long and slow.

We'd made it, but as we rode through the streets, I couldn't help but notice the town looked different somehow. As if, in our brief absence, it had shrunk. It had once been my entire world, but now…now it seemed smaller. Delicate. Precious. And I was different too. I wondered if it even recognized me anymore, its daughter, no longer as delicate or as precious as it, but wary, steeled, and dangerous.

I glanced at Elif. She looked—as I assumed I did—a little worse for wear and slightly shaken, but alive and mostly intact. She gave me a wistful smile.

Home. If only we could stay.

"Is this it?" Darragh called from behind us, and we nodded.

Our instructions were to get him on a train to Amsterdam and then to Vierhouten, where he would stay until it was safe to move him again. We sat in our seats, exhausted, barely able to talk, but unworried about his being hunted. The soldiers on this train were looking for Jews masquerading as something else, not downed pilots they knew nothing about. So when they asked for our registrations, we barely blinked an eye as we handed them over.

Originally, once we'd delivered Darragh to his final destination, we were to turn around and head back to Amsterdam for the night. But by the time we arrived, it was too near curfew.

"It's fine," said Berend, the man who ran the hidden camp. "We happen to have a few empty beds at the moment. Why don't we get you all something to eat, and then we'll show you where you can sleep."

We followed him through the camp, marveling as we passed the opening of a hut, barely noticeable in the dimming light, large swaths of branches obscuring it from view. He led us down into a third that was clearly the dining hut and served us three bowls of stew made of mainly cabbage and carrots, weak cups of tea, and a small heel of bread each.

"What happened to your hand?" he asked.

I explained I fell on it, and he nodded and pulled a box of medical supplies from beneath a table, offering to rewrap it for me. I accepted.

After we ate we were shown where we'd sleep.

"Darragh," Berend said, pointing to an entrance where the soft glow of light lit it from within. "You're here."

Darragh looked at Elif and I with a small, weary smile.

"You'll probably be gone by the time I wake tomorrow, yes?"

"Yes," Elif said as I nodded.

"How can I ever thank you?" he asked. "I nearly got us all killed and you—" He looked from me to Elif and shook his head. "You were incredible. When I was told angels were being sent

to retrieve me, I didn't understand—or believe it. But now..."
His eyes moved from our pale eyes to our hair. "I think I understand. Thank you both. You are braver than the toughest
soldiers I've ever met."

"Someone called us angels?" I asked.

He shrugged. "That's what Agatha told me. She said she'd
been told two angels were coming. I believe that's what your
group calls you? That's their code for the two of you."

"Uncle Frans," Elif murmured, and I nodded, understanding.

We woke in the morning before the rest of the camp and
hurried back to town and the train that would take us first to
Amsterdam, and then Haarlem. As the soldiers made their way
through the car, collecting and checking registrations, I looked
out the window, seeing our reflections ethereal and shimmering in the glass.

"Angels," I whispered.

22

A flurry of new jobs came in mid-March. Smaller things ranging from forgeries and planting incendiary bombs, to bigger things like moving an entire family and another liquidation.

After the job in Hillegom, Elif and I were split up as a team for a time for the sake of safety.

"People will be on the lookout for two young women who look similar to each other," Aunt Liv explained. "It's best the two of you aren't seen in public together for the next little while. We'll pair Elif with Annie, and Lien, you'll be with Charlie. And Jan will go between the two groups as usual."

It was pointless to argue. We were doing what was safest for the team. But it still felt odd to not prepare for missions with my sister, instead watching her walk out of the house alone, or waving goodbye to me as we exchanged a look of regret at not having one another to count on.

Not only was it strange not to be with my sister, but I hadn't seen Charlie in weeks, the last time having been in the barn when I'd gone for supplies. He'd been sitting on the sofa reading a comic book and I'd stopped in my tracks, unsure of what to say, and then hurried to the table to tell Henrik what I needed. When I'd left, Charlie was standing by the door.

"How are you?" he asked.

"Okay," I'd said, unable to meet his eyes as I searched for something to say. "How are you? Have you heard anything from your mother and sister?"

"I have. They're good." I looked up when I heard the smile in his voice. "They sent more comic books and some strange American treats. I'll have to bring them next time for you to try."

"I'd like that."

"Well," he said, suddenly looking as though he too now needed to search for words. "Be careful out there. Promise?"

I'd looked up then, meeting his gaze with my own. My lungs filled with air, my heartbeat quickening in my chest. I was warm, despite the chill drifting in from outside, a quiver of anticipation running up my spine. I'd forgotten how being near him affected me. The thrill at seeing that look in his eyes when he stared at me.

"I will," I said. "Promise."

When we met for the first assignment we'd be doing together, a job throwing firebombs into a building containing weaponry, there'd been a bit of awkwardness as we greeted one another and discussed the details of our plan. At the safe house after, we'd bid one another good-night and wandered off to our separate rooms. In the morning, I'd awoken before him and hurried out of the house as quietly as I could.

That day, five innocent men were executed in retaliation of the fire Charlie and I had set. My belief in the cause never wavered—I was always eager to be sent on a job—but the loss of innocent life because of something I'd done was brutal and hard to reconcile.

"Unfortunately, it's part of the job." Aunt Liv's voice had been grave when she spoke to us during a rare Friday evening dinner at her home a couple months earlier. "To make a dif-

ference, lives have to be sacrificed. Sometimes, even our own."
She'd sighed and given us a sad smile. "Try to do as I do and
compartmentalize it. Tuck it way. One day, never fear, it will
all come back to haunt you. Put it off as long as you can, dear
ones. Bury it deep."

That, I was used to doing.

To deal with the unwieldy feelings, Aunt Liv gave Elif and I
each a set of beautiful leather-bound journals.

"Sometimes stowing feelings is easier said than done," she told
us. "I've found writing them can give release. And afterward, if
the words are too painful and you wish to never see them again,
they provide a lovely fire to warm you with."

I'd nodded, thinking of the notebook I'd been writing in
whenever I needed to get feelings out. Before writing in it, I'd
never been one to keep a diary. Had never felt the need to tran-
scribe thoughts or feelings. But now, whenever I felt my emotions bursting at the seams of me, I pulled out that old notebook
and scribbled away.

On one particular evening, after a job that had gone perfectly,
I found myself considering what I'd become. It was almost as if
there were two of me. The one who carried out the deeds, and
the one who wrote about them afterward. One so engulfed,
the other distanced. I found the difference interesting, if not a
little bit disturbing, from where I'd begun to where I was now.

I have learned, I wrote, *evil cannot be bargained with, and to destroy
it, one must almost become it oneself. I tell myself it is temporary, but
I worry that it bleeds through. Who will I be when this is over? Will I
recognize myself at all?*

A few days later I stood outside a safe house door, my head
bowed beneath the hat I wore. I knocked and listened as always
for the sound of heavy boots coming toward me down the alleyway. One never knew when a house was being watched, a
neighbor growing suspicious and having called it in in hopes of
receiving a favor in return.

"Hello," Charlie said, opening the door.

"Hello, Charlie," I said, and stepped inside.

We stood in the entryway for a moment, not moving, just watching one another and being in each other's space. There was something so comforting about being near him. Maybe it was the confidence that never bordered on being egotistical. The patience he always showed us girls when we were unsure of something or afraid. Or just the way he never treated me like I was too young, too small, or too female. He respected me. Elif said once he was like the older brother we'd never had, but I was pretty sure my feelings were not of a familial nature.

"How was the walk over?" he asked, breaking the silence with a smile that washed over me and warmed me from the inside out.

I knew he wasn't asking about the quality of the walk, which was clear by the rain still dripping off my hat and coat. No, he was asking about any activity I might've seen on the way. And nearby clusters of soldiers. Anything we may need to work around.

"Calm," I said. "Nothing of note. What are we doing?"

He led me to the parlor, and we sat as the woman who owned the house came through and offered us tea while we discussed the job, which was another liquidation. A woman this time. I was surprised, and it must've shown because Charlie gave me a grim smile.

"Women are some of the best spies out there," he said. "They're very good at using their minds, as well as their bodies, like weapons." His cheeks reddened slightly, reminding me of how he'd sometimes get flustered when we used to train and our hands would accidentally brush.

"Where do we find her?"

"There's to be a meeting in the park. Very brief. She's delivering information she stole from her husband who has connections to the RAF."

"Who's she meeting?"

"Her lover. She's been having an affair with a German officer who told one of his buddies about the information she's been handing over. His friend happens to be a double agent for us."

I sighed. I could understand the women who did these things because they were homeless or starving, but this woman was the wife of an officer. She was likely neither of those things.

"Why wouldn't she just wait until they meet up again to give him information?"

"Her husband is back in town. This is her only opportunity to see him for a while."

"So what are we supposed to do? Get the information? Or just kill her?"

"Both."

"Are we killing him too?"

"Only if we have to."

The plan was to intercept her before she met up with her lover. She was the traitor. He was merely the enemy. One gunshot ringing out would be better than two. We had no idea how tight the time frame would be between her arriving at the park and meeting him, though; we knew only that they planned to meet before dark so that she wouldn't get stuck outside after curfew. But when before dark? Since the information had come in not that long ago, it could be anytime between now and sunset, which was only a couple hours away.

"There's a bench at the north end of the park where they meet and from what I was told, a good, thick cluster of trees and some shrubbery nearby. You'll need to get her to follow you behind the brush so you're out of sight."

I frowned. How was I supposed to get a woman to follow me? A low-cut blouse wasn't going to do it.

"How?" I asked.

"Say you lost your dog. Ask for her help finding it. Or maybe start in the bushes and call out. Say you've been hurt."

"I'll think of something," I said.

"Good. Then let's get what we need and go."

While Charlie checked his pistol, I hurried to the restroom and pulled my hair into two long plaits, making myself look instantly younger than my years. When I was done, I checked my own set of weapons and then grabbed a comb and a small compact off the shelf and pocketed them.

Thankfully the rain had subsided, leaving us with rivulets streaming through the streets and puddles on the sidewalks, the smell of damp stone and moss heavy in our noses. At the end of the street we split up, him taking the longer way around, me walking to the north end of the park, staying on the outskirts while keeping an eye out for the bench with the woman.

I didn't see either at first, and then I noticed the trees Charlie had been told about. In this part of the park, it was mostly grass with only a few trees here and there, except for the one larger grouping that had the area's one lone bench next to it. A bench that was currently empty.

Keeping myself obscured in the little alleyway behind a clothing store long since boarded up, I looked up and down the street, watching for a woman by herself. I checked my watch. It was nearly four. Sunset was around four thirty. We would be cutting it close.

I glanced around again and then suddenly there she was, stepping out from behind a tree as if she'd been hiding inside it. She wore a deep red scarf over her pale hair, and looked around as she quickly made her way to the bench and sat at its edge as if prepared to leave at a moment's notice. I rubbed my eyes hard, removed the comb I'd taken from the bathroom from my pocket, and pushed off the wall, heading toward her in a sprint.

She looked up at the sound of my footsteps, clutching her handbag, eyes wide with terror. I stopped, tripping over my own feet at the sight of her face. She reminded me so much of Tess, with her freckles and wide eyes, the same bow to her upper lip, she could've been her older sister or maybe an aunt. I forgot myself, forgot why I was there as I stared at her.

"Can I help you?" she asked, her eyes darting around the park.

I blinked, remembering why I was there, and shoved thoughts of my friend from my mind. This woman was not her. She was no relation of hers. She was, in fact, a traitor who would most definitely give up my friend's name if it meant she could get something out of it.

"Did you see him?" I asked, faking a sob and looking around frantically, pretending to search the area, my heart still racing at the physical similarities the woman had to my friend. In an instant, she'd made herself human to me and I had to fight to stay focused.

"See whom?" she asked, frowning as she glanced around.

"The boy," I said. "He took my handbag and ran this way. I know he must've come through here. I found my comb just over there." I showed her the comb and pointed.

"I'm sorry," she said. "I didn't see a boy."

"He—" I pretended to see something and hurried across the grass, pulling the compact discreetly from my pocket and pretending to find it on the ground. "See?" I said, holding it up. "He was here."

"Well, he must've come through before I got here," she said.

"Can you help me, please?" I asked. "The keys to my house were in there. My mother will be so angry if I've lost them again. Maybe he dropped them."

She checked her watch and sighed. Her clothes were nicer than what most people wore these days and seemed so out of place, but made sense if she was meeting her lover, even if only for a moment.

"I can help for a minute," she said. "But I'm sure your mother will understand if you explain the situation."

As she spoke, she stood and followed me behind the cover of

the trees where Charlie hid, waiting. I pointed to the ID card on the ground by him.

"My ID!" I said.

But as I bent to pick it up, rather than duck quickly so Charlie could get the shot off quick and we could escape, I hesitated for the briefest of moments, the woman's face, so similar to my friend's, lingering in my mind. I wanted it to be different. I wanted her to confess so that this time the night didn't have to end in someone losing their life. I wanted to not have blood on my hands. But at the sight of Charlie emerging from the brush, my body acted as if of its own accord, and I ducked. His gun discharged, the crack echoing off the trees, the bullet whizzing over me.

I heard a thud and Charlie raced past me. Kneeling beside the woman's body, he pulled her handbag open, removed a wad of papers, turned, and grabbed my hand.

"C'mon," he said.

We ran to the edge of the park and then slowed to a walk. I linked my arm through his and rested my head on his shoulder. We were just a couple out for a stroll before the dark of night fell.

It didn't take long for us to hear shouts and the thunder of boots hitting the ground from the direction of the park. We walked faster, reaching the other side of the street where we disappeared down alleyways that took us to the safe house moments before the sun set for the night.

"Are you okay?" Charlie asked as we ate a meager dinner of watered down stew.

I nodded, wiping a tear hovering on my lower lid with a trembling hand.

"I've never seen you hesitate before." His voice was gentle rather than accusing.

"She looked like Tess," I said. "I thought maybe if I gave her time to confess, she might. And then we could all go home alive for once."

He sighed and nodded, reaching across the table to take my hand.

"There have been a couple incidents where I've wished the same. Boys younger than me..." He rubbed his eyes. "An old woman once. It's hard. Impossible. And yet every time I pull that trigger. Am I a monster?"

I squeezed his hand hard and shook my head.

"It's them or us, Charlie. It's them or our best friend, our favorite teacher, a neighbor."

"I know," he said. "Still..."

"Still," I said, giving him a sad smile of understanding.

Still, it was awful. Still, it felt wrong, no matter how many pages of my journals I filled to justify my actions.

It was strange to be alone with Charlie at night. All our previous jobs had either taken place during the day or the safe house we'd gone to after had several other occupants. Tonight it was just us and the woman harboring us.

When we finished eating and cleaning up, we sat on either side of a small, shabby green sofa with hot cups of weak tea. Charlie pulled the papers he'd taken off the woman from his pocket and spread them out on the coffee table before us. Sure enough, there were several buildings of an airfield in England marked on a map. Charlie shook his head.

"I wonder if her husband had a clue," I said.

"I doubt it," he said, bitterness in his voice. "Like I said, women are masters at deception."

I peered at him. "I seem to remember a certain man tricking me not so long ago."

He looked at me, his brows drawn, and then understanding washed over his face. "It was a test, not a trick," he said.

"It was awful."

"It was." His voice was soft.

"Is that what you think of me?" I asked. "That I'm a master at deception?"

He tilted his head, a little smile taking the place of the usually serious expression he wore. I felt like I hadn't seen that smile since the days of training and swapping comics.

"No, Lien. I think you are incredible."

The words were simple, but the tone of his voice, the warmth in his eyes made me realize they were anything but.

He didn't move closer, but he turned so that he faced me.

"Right before I came here I had joined a similar cause in England. I met a girl. She was older. Exciting. I fancied myself in love." He sighed. "She turned out to be a German spy. We used to lie together at night and talk. I would tell her the things I'd learned. Turns out she was passing the information off to her comrades. When I found out—"

"Did you kill her?" I asked.

His chuckle was bitter.

"No. I thought about it. I had my gun turned on her. I couldn't do it, though, which she found amusing. I told her to leave." He ran a hand through his hair and leaned forward, resting his elbows on his knees. "A few weeks later she was part of a mission that got my best friend killed. When I heard I went after her, but it turned out she died that night too. A victim of her own attack."

"Charlie," I said, moving closer and lacing my fingers with his. "I'm so sorry."

His fingers tightened around mine.

"I thought she was like you," he said. "Strong, brave, smart… loyal. But there's no one like you, Lien. I've watched you go from unsure girl to this incredible woman determined to do what's right for all the right reasons. It's inspiring. And a tiny bit intimidating, if I'm to be honest."

His hands were featherlight as he brushed his fingertips over my face before running them over my hair. He stopped to pull the elastics holding the plaits in place and then gently undid each twist piece by piece.

I watched him as he worked, studying his furrowed brow, straight nose, the dark blue of his eyes, the scar that disappeared into his hairline. Reaching up, I ran my palm along his jaw, thrilling at the bite of his whiskers on my skin. A sensation I'd never felt before bloomed in the center of me and I moved closer, wanting more than his too-gentle touches.

"I want—" I said and then stopped, unsure what I wanted or how to even tell him.

His eyes met mine again, and I was sure I had never and would never see such longing ever again.

This time when he reached for me it wasn't as gentle.

Charlie's body was full of contradictions. Strong hands, soft lips, lean muscles hard beneath my hands, playful tongue teasing my mouth open so he could explore it more fully. I was aware of his every breath, gasp, and moan as my own less experienced hands trailed along the skin of his arms and neck.

After a time he pulled away and smiled down at me with a bashful grin. I suppressed a yawn and he chuckled.

"Let me walk you to your room," he said.

He put out the fire then held out a hand and helped me to my feet, leading the way up the stairs to where two identical bedrooms sat across the hall from one another. At the door to mine, he leaned down and kissed me once more.

"Sleep well," he said.

"Good night, Charlie," I whispered.

I shut the door, slipped off my shoes, and lay down on top of the quilt, the heat from the fire still lingering. It was quiet in the unfamiliar house. Too quiet. I missed the soft sound of Elif's breathing, the hum of Mama's sewing machine lulling me to sleep. I turned out the light, but when I shut my eyes I felt like I was floating off in a sea of black, unanchored, tetherless. I turned the light back on and sat up. A moment later I was standing outside Charlie's door.

"You okay?" he asked when he opened the door. He'd removed his sweater and socks and wore only his T-shirt and trousers.

"I know it's silly," I said, feeling my cheeks burn. "And I'm too old to be afraid of the dark, but it's strange not having Elif with me. We usually share a room. It's so quiet and dark and…"

"Do you want to sleep in here with me?" he asked. "I can make a bed on the floor for myself or—" He held up his hands in a sort of surrender. "We can share the bed. I promise to behave."

My cheeks, if possible, burned hotter. But I nodded and he stood aside to let me in.

He lay down and I lay beside him, unsure if I should face him or not. His soft "come here" answered the question, though, and I curled up into him, winding my body around his and tucking my head into his chest.

"Will you talk to me?" I asked. "Tell me something else about you that I don't know?"

"Hmm. Isn't it your turn to tell me something?"

"I suppose you're right. What do you want to know?"

"Tell me why you joined the cause."

I didn't realize I'd stiffened until he spoke again.

"It's okay. You don't have to. I didn't realize…if the reason is bad, you don't have to tell me."

I rolled away from him so that I was lying on my back, staring through the dark at the ceiling.

"It's okay," I said, my voice soft. "I've just never talked about it. I joined because of my sister."

"Elif?"

"No. My younger sister. Madi. Madelief."

"I didn't know you have a younger sister."

"I don't. Not anymore. Because I killed her."

The room went silent. I didn't wait for him to try and come up with a question. A why or how. The floodgates had opened.

"She was such a fun girl," I said. "Always laughing and playing, teasing and singing songs she made up. She could be naughty too, but we all thought the little tricks she played were funny. We indulged her. She was the baby. She was also always climbing and jumping off things. It was the one thing that drove my parents nuts. Since she could walk she would climb and jump, climb and jump. The days we walked to school or the market, my mother would have to constantly yell at her to stop jumping on the ledge along the canals. She almost fell in more times than we could count. One morning I had to walk her to school by myself. Elif had already left to study before a test, and mother had an early client coming in. The last thing she told me was to make sure Madi didn't get too near the canal."

I stopped for a moment to catch my breath, tears sliding down my temples, soaking my hair and the pillow beneath me.

"She was behaving at first," I said. "But then she couldn't help herself. Something about the water and the ledge always drew her to it. She wanted to be daring. She liked to scare us." I took a breath, remembering how irritated I'd been. How I'd wanted to walk away. "I told her to move away. To stop. I was going to tell Mama on her. But she didn't listen so I walked ahead, pretending I was going to leave her. And then it happened."

I squeezed my eyes shut, trying to block it out. But it didn't help. I could still hear it. Still see it.

"A person on a bike passed me too close and too fast. He must have gotten too close to Madi too because I heard her make a sound. A gasp, and then—"

Charlie's hand wrapped around mine.

"I heard a crack." I sucked in a breath. "I turned and looked around for her, but all I saw were strands of blond hair disappearing over the ledge. I was frozen—I couldn't move. But then I found my voice and screamed, running as fast as I could. It only took me seconds to get to where she'd fallen, but by then she'd disappeared in the dark water below." Tears continued to spill from beneath my lids. "I jumped in, but I couldn't see her. It was so cold my teeth were chattering, and I kept choking on the water. By the time someone found her and was able to pull her up, it was too late. She was dead. She'd hit her head on the cement. The doctor said she was likely dead before she hit the water." My body shook as tears flooded my eyes. "I try to forget. But every day I see her face when they hoisted her up out of the water. She was gray and lifeless, her lips white."

Charlie pulled me to him, holding me, rocking me, whispering words I couldn't hear into my hair until eventually I quieted, lulled by the deep timbre of his voice, the warmth of his body. I curled against him, trying to disappear into him.

"Lien," he said, "you didn't kill Madi. It was an accident."

I sighed. It was what everyone had said. What they all believed. But I didn't.

"I shouldn't have walked ahead," I said. "I should've had her in my sight at all times. And when I saw her hair... I shouldn't have hesitated. I should've realized—"

"You're not a superhero in a comic. Nor are you a psychic. You couldn't have known any of it would happen. And it just as easily could've happened while Elif was with her, or your mother. You were in shock—you did nothing wrong."

"Well," I said, bristling a little, "you asked why and that's my answer. After it happened I swore to myself I would never stand by idly for anything ever again. I would always be one step ahead. I would take charge, never be late, and help others every chance I got."

"Lien," he whispered and pulled me closer still, "I'm sorry that happened. I'm sorry you felt so helpless. But it wasn't your fault. Even if you hadn't walked ahead and could see her, it doesn't mean she wouldn't have slipped. If she was always being told not to go on the ledge and she did it anyway...that's her fault, not yours."

"But I was in charge of her."

"It's still not your fault."

He pulled back then, and I felt the loss of his closeness like a rejection until his lips found mine in the dark.

But no matter how much I wanted to believe him, to let him kiss my sadness and guilt away, as I drifted off to sleep, the strands of Madi's blond hair sliding over the ledge filled my mind and I knew I'd never believe I couldn't have saved her.

23

There was no season off-limits from the horrors of living in an occupied country. Summer came, and with it the sun, but the usual sights and sounds that accompanied were nowhere to be found. Streets normally filled with bicycles, the sound of bells chiming their chipper warnings, were empty as tires had been confiscated, the rubber needed for military vehicles. And the foot traffic, often heaviest at this time of year, was practically nonexistent, the citizens of Haarlem too scared to be out in case they were stopped for any small misdemeanor some kid in a uniform who was barely old enough to be called a man saw fit.

The few people who ventured to the beach, the parks, or the tulip fields were so intimidated by the soldiers already taking up residence, they were often seen trudging back home, the disappointment on their faces palpable. There was nowhere we could go anymore. No place we felt safe or free. Even our homes were subject to being searched whenever someone got the hankering to force their way in. If we protested, we risked jail. Or death.

With fewer people out and about, it also made it harder for us to do our jobs, as there weren't as many people to hide behind or blend in with. This was especially difficult for Annie, whose red hair had begun to stand out so much, she now had to wear a wig every time she was on a mission or keep it dyed, and hair color wasn't easy to come by these days. We'd learned the Gestapo called her "the girl with the red hair" and were keeping a keen eye out for her. We'd even once seen a sign tacked to a post offering a reward for information on her whereabouts.

"I'm famous," she'd said, proud to be seen as someone dangerous to the Nazi regime, a bag of hats from Aunt Liv over her shoulder.

Despite the increasing danger, though, the jobs kept coming. Some days I started out doing inventory at my mother's sewing shop, but by afternoon I was delivering a gun, forged registration papers, or a human to another location.

The Ten Boom watch shop a few stores down became one of our biggest drop-off and pick up points for Jewish citizens in hiding. The bedroom of one of the sisters in the upstairs apartment had been outfitted with a hiding place in the wall, the access to it through the bottom shelf of a bookcase. At any one time they could get six adults inside it, and had put a special buzzer under a counter in the shop to alert them upstairs to threats of being discovered. I'd never seen it used, but I'd seen the room it was in and couldn't believe how cleverly hidden it was.

When I returned to the shop, Elif peeked at me from the back room and waved me over. There were still restrictions on us going on jobs together, or even just being seen together when not on a job, and I missed her. In the evenings now, when we were both home, we caught up on the things we'd missed. She was still mostly paired with Annie, and me with Charlie. Jan bounced around between the two groups. He'd proved to be loyal and, more importantly, a valued and quiet ally during delicate missions. His knowledge of weapons rivaled Henrik's, he could always lighten the mood, and he and Charlie had become good friends—something Charlie told me in private meant a lot to him. But it was his way with Annie that endeared me to Jan the most. It was clear he was taken with her, and she with him, the way their eyes constantly met across any room, as though none of the rest of us existed.

"It's annoying," Elif said when I mentioned how sweet I found them to be.

"It's lovely."

"You only say that because you and Charlie do the same thing."

"I don't believe Henrik is seeing anyone," I said. She pretended to gag and threw a sock at me, making us both laugh.

I stepped into the room now and surveyed the thread spools lined up on the table.

"I went by the house before I came here," she said. "This came for you."

She held out a letter and I gasped and grabbed it, recognizing Tess's familiar scrawl. It had been so long since I'd received that first letter, I'd almost given up hope there would ever be another.

I sat in the chair and turned the envelope over in my hands, studying it as though looking for clues to why I hadn't heard from her in so long. I wondered if the return address, which looked different from the one before, had anything to do with it.

"She's in Germany," I said to Elif, who nodded, clearly having noted that herself.

I sighed and opened the envelope.

The pages inside were crinkled and dirty, grit rubbing off on my fingertips, and some of the words had been blacked out. I sat quietly, reading each side of the two-page letter, and then folded it and put it back in its envelope.

"What does she say?" Elif asked.

She said a lot. She was Tess after all. She could look at a piece of wood and make up a story about its life on earth; where it originated from, how it got to that particular spot, where it would go next on its journey. She could create something out of nothing, and I could tell she was spinning tales in her letter purely for my benefit. So I wouldn't worry. And so she wouldn't have to think about the truth of her situation, which we all knew couldn't be good.

"She and her mother were moved to another camp for women only. Her brother and father are still at the camp in Vught. She talks about the barracks. How they don't even have mattresses and have to sleep two to a bed of wood slats. There are fleas and rats everywhere. She said she made friends with one. She got another haircut and says it's much more manageable now." I recalled Tess's constant hair woes. How many times had she'd sworn she'd never cut it because the curls would be unmanageable?

I placed my arms on the table and laid my head down, great big gulping sobs shaking me. I felt Elif's arms come around me, her head resting on my back.

"I failed her," I said. "I didn't get there fast enough."

"Oh, Lien," Elif whispered. "You can't save everyone. Don't you know that by now?"

Elif spoke from experience. Her last job moving a family of three resulted in the father getting shot. The last one to go through the fence, his coat snagged on a nail and held him up for a second. A second that made all the difference, because at that moment a soldier exited a nearby barn, saw him struggling, took aim, and fired. Annie was able to get the others to safety, but she was shaken for days afterward.

Despite the truth I knew she spoke, I couldn't help wanting to be like the woman in Charlie's comic book. It was silly, I knew. And immature. But I knew heroes existed. I was surrounded by them. And even though I was doing the same work they were, I didn't see myself the same way.

I would have to try harder.

For the next few months, every job I was assigned I prepared for like never before. I studied maps and asked questions of the others. Had they been to that location before? Who ran the safe house? Best path to and from a certain shop? Was there a back door? Where? When? Why? Who? I needed to be ahead of whatever was to happen. To anticipate it from every angle. And be ready to act.

As the weather turned again, the sun disappearing behind the gray clouds of autumn, the cold winds off the ocean chilling our thinning bodies and making our bones ache, I was assigned a new job. My first liquidation on my own.

The others had done it already, and I was sure I hadn't been called on due to my size and age. I hated being the youngest in the group.

"It's not a bad thing," Charlie told me when I'd complained after Elif was sent out on her own only a week after he had.

"They treat me like a baby."

He'd pulled me close and kissed me, but I barely responded and pushed away, feeling as though I were being placated.

"They don't," he said, dropping his arms. "Who goes on what jobs depends on a lot of things. What other jobs may be happening at the same time, who's available, is a special skill set needed? Your time will come. Though I will admit, I wish it wouldn't. I don't like thinking of you out there on your own. It's dangerous and…"

"And what?"

He shrugged and looked away.

"Charlie."

"You are quite petite, Lien. You know that. You could be overpowered so easily."

I crossed my arms over my chest. "Now you're treating me like a child."

"I'm not." He pulled me back and wrapped his arms tightly around me so I couldn't get away again. "But I'm not going to stand here and tell you that it wouldn't kill me if something happened to you. And lately, I have to worry about that a lot. You prepare for jobs like you're on another kind of mission separate from the one assigned. I know you feel like you have something to prove. I worry that to make up for your imagined failings, you're going to get yourself into a situation you can't get out of."

"I'll be fine."

"We've all been incredibly lucky so far, Lien. I know other groups who have lost half their members. If we all make it out of this war alive, I'll be shocked. Please, don't let it be you who doesn't make it through."

I let him lead me up the stairs to his room then, and watched shyly as he lit a candle and shut the door. When his eyes met mine, there was a question in them. Inhaling, I took a step toward him, wound my arms around his neck, and pulled his head down to mine, kissing him more boldly than I'd ever done before.

His hands moved from my waist to the buttons on my blouse, undoing each one slowly, his eyes taking in every inch of my skin as it was revealed before he pulled the shirt away and tossed it on the chair in the corner. He got to his knees before me and removed my shoes and then slid my trousers off, his calloused palms skimming down my legs, my pulse racing as my want for him began to overtake me. I trembled as his mouth began making its way up, lingering in spots that made my knees weak and my breath quicken. And then he undressed himself, laid me down and, for a while at least, I forgot everything but me, Charlie, and the feel of our bodies moving together.

I woke before the sun the next morning and snuggled closer to Charlie, who slept soundly beside me. In sleep, he looked like a boy, the usual furrow between his brows gone, the serious line of his lips softened. I traced the scar that disappeared into his hairline and then turned over, wrapping his arm around me. He pulled me closer and kissed the back of my neck before falling asleep again.

As I lay beside this man I knew I loved but had never told, and might never get the chance to, I wondered that I was willing to risk losing what we had for a promise I'd made to a ghost. And yet I couldn't help myself. In my mind, there was only one way I'd ever find peace, and that was to be like the Wonder Woman of Charlie's comics. To step up and fight in every battle, to not give up, and to kill for the greater good.

A few days later I was on a train to Amsterdam, my pistol hidden deep in the secret pocket of my coat, dagger strapped to my thigh, out of sight.

I'd packed a small suitcase just in case the job took more than a day, the details of it mostly impossible to gather before the train sped me toward Haarlem's bigger sister city. I felt unprepared and anxious without being able to do my usual preparations, but determined to do a good job nonetheless.

My instructions were to check in with the safe house upon arrival and then make contact with the owner of a bookstore, who would have the information I needed to carry out the attack.

I dropped my case in the room I'd be staying in and had a quick cup of tea with Mara, the owner of the house, and an older gentleman who looked like he'd lost a battle with a cat, three tiny scratches running the length of his face.

"Fingernails," he said when he caught me looking. I was close. "She wasn't too happy to have been found out. She gave quite a fight before I put her down."

He looked delighted by his words, and I gave him a weak smile and returned to my drink.

I memorized the directions I received from Mara, which took me three blocks down and two over to a small bookshop facing a canal. I absorbed every detail I could as I went; the people meandering by, the soldiers standing on a nearby bridge scanning the meager crowds, the number of storefronts boarded up, and possible escape routes if I needed to run.

A bell on the door jingled as I stepped inside.

"Be right with you," a man called from somewhere in the back.

I glanced down at the display of books on a front table. They were all in German. I raised my eyebrows, wrinkling my nose in response, and meandered to a nearby bookshelf, trying my hardest to look like a browsing customer.

"Ah," a small man of nearly my height said, startling me as he came around the shelf. "There you are. How can I help you, miss?"

"I'm here to pick up a book I ordered."

He nodded and started walking to the back of the store again. "What's the title?" he asked over his shoulder.

"Little Women," I said. "It's a special edition."

He tripped, righted himself, and turned. His eyes swept over me and he gave a little nod, a slight grin on his face.

"Right," he said. "Well, I'll just go and get it then."

He disappeared into a back room and I slid my hand down into my coat pocket, undid the snap in the lining that obscured the hidden compartment, and wrapped my hand around the grip of my pistol. The seconds ticked by, punctuated by the thud of my heart.

I walked slowly to the front of the store, glancing from the doorway he'd gone through to the entrance of the shop, wondering if I was going to have to make a run for it. My eyes landed on the table of German books again, and I picked one up.

When the man reappeared, he smiled apologetically and held up the book.

"Sorry. It was beneath a box." He pressed his hand to his heart, clearly out of breath from his frantic search.

I smiled and walked to the counter and put down the book I'd grabbed, sliding it toward him. It was for insurance in case I was stopped and searched. Something Aunt Liv had suggested.

"They're likely to harass you less if they think you're trying to learn their ways," she'd said.

"This too," I said to the man.

He looked at the book, his eyes narrowed.

"Not this one," he said, and held up a finger. I watched as he went to the table I'd taken it from and exchanged it for another. "This one."

"What is it?" I asked, looking at the cover and wondering what it said.

"A how to speak German instructional," he said, his eyes full of mischief.

"Perfect." I smiled.

He rang up the books and then wrapped both in a sheet of brown paper and tied it with a string. As he handed me the package, he glanced toward the front door before looking back at me.

"I have to admit," he said, "you're not what I expected."

"Would you be surprised to hear that's not the first time I've heard that?" I asked, and he grinned.

"Be safe, miss," he said.

"I'll do my best, sir. Thank you."

I opened the door, the bell jingling, and stepped outside, running straight into a man walking by.

"Oh! I'm so sorry," I said, clutching the package to my chest.

"Look where you're going," a sharp voice barked at me.

"Yessir," I said and dared to look up.

My breath caught as the rest of my body went still.

"Diederik."

It was him. The boy who had sat behind me in science class three years ago, handsome and quiet and the subject of many of my innocent schoolgirl fantasies. Until the soldiers had marched in and he stood in salute to them. Until he let my friend and her family be taken away. Until he'd shoved the butt of his rifle into my forehead.

"Lien," he said, peering down at me.

An icy finger of fear slid down my spine as I studied him. He was taller, broader, and there was something more distinguished about him. The boy he'd been had gone, and in place was an intimidating man.

"What are you doing here?" he asked.

I peered at him. Was he going to pretend the last time we'd met hadn't happened? And yet, as he stared down at me, I realized that, yes, that was exactly what he was doing. And with no hint of remorse whatsoever.

"I'm visiting a friend," I said, pulling the lie easily from the reserves I had from previous jobs.

"Why were you in this bookstore?" He pointed to the shop behind me.

"I was purchasing books."

His eyes narrowed and he tilted his head, causing my heartbeat to pick up.

"We think the owner is passing information. Helping the Jews. Would you know anything about that?"

I forced a laugh. "I should hope not. I'm not in the habit of helping would-be traitors."

I could very well have been talking about him, but as I'd hoped, he missed the possible accusation entirely and eyed me even closer.

"And your friend?" he asked. "I seem to remember you wanting to help her not so long ago. She was a traitor. Her entire family was."

I waved a hand and shrugged, plastering a wistful smile on my face as inside I seethed, wanting nothing more than to pull my gun and leave him on the ground with a hole in his head.

"I was misguided," I said in a breezy voice. "Young and uneducated."

"And now you are not?"

"I am not."

The tenseness left his body in a long exhale, and he allowed himself a small smile.

"Well, that's good news," he said, and then looked almost

bashful. "I'm sorry for what I did. It was necessary, but I hope you weren't hurt too badly."

The gun in my pocket seemed to take on extra weight suddenly, but I forced my smile to widen.

"Barely a scratch," I said.

"Good." He pointed at the books. "What did you get?"

I couldn't tell if he still wasn't quite sure about me or if he was just curious. In case it was the former, I handed the package over, hopefully proving in doing so that I wasn't a threat, but praying he wouldn't call my bluff and open it.

My hopes were dashed when he pulled one end of the string and pushed the paper aside, his eyes flicking quickly over the copy of *Little Women* before landing on the German translation book, which made him visibly perk.

"Huh," he said, holding it up. "You are learning German?"

"*Ja,*" I said, with a slight nod. "I figured it was high time. Don't you think?"

"I do. And I'm impressed. Not everyone is on board with the new ideas."

"I can see their merit."

We stood for a moment, quiet. I slid my hands in my pockets, waiting to see what his next move would be, my fingertips brushing against the metal of my pistol. He smiled and handed the books back.

"Well," I said, anxious to be on my way, the reunion unsettling and I had more important things to get to, "it was lovely to see you again, Diederik. I'm glad to see you're well and—"

"Have dinner with me," he said.

"Excuse me?" My stomach turned over.

"It's been a while since we've seen one another. We must have so much to catch up on. And—" He pointed to the books in my arms. "Maybe I can help you with some of the more simple phrases. There's a nice place on Damrak that still serves a decent menu. Say, five o'clock?"

I arranged my expression into something I hoped conveyed both pleasure at being asked and disappointment at having to say no.

"I'd love to, but with curfew and all—"

"You'll be with an officer so it's okay. I'll walk you home after."

I smiled, knowing full well I'd never show up.

"What's the address?" I asked.

As I walked back to the safe house, my body thrummed with something I couldn't put my finger on. At first I wondered if I was frightened, but it didn't feel like fear. I wasn't in a hurry to get away, and my hands weren't shaking. Nor was I anxious. It was something else. Something that burned in my gut and gave me clear focus. I turned a corner and walked up another street, my pace clipped, my eyes darting. It wasn't until I reached out to knock on the door of the safe house that I realized my emotion.

Fury.

An anger so deep I could see now I'd buried it beneath the myriad other emotions that had taken over in recent years. Anger at Diederik for putting up those posters so long ago. Anger that I'd thought him a nice boy. And rage for what he'd allowed to happen to Tess.

I was let inside and hurried to my room and shut the door. Now my hands were shaking.

Sitting on the bed, I set the copy of *Little Women* in my lap.

At first glance it was just a book. I opened it, flipped through the pages, and ran my hands over the front and back covers, inside and out, my frown deepening as I searched and found nothing. Had I gotten it wrong? Had the shop owner? Was it a trick? Maybe there was a message within the pages. A code of some sort hidden in the letters? I started at the beginning and turned the pages one by one. I was halfway through when I noticed the top corner of the back endpaper had lifted. I gently pulled at it, watching as it peeled back bit by bit, revealing a handwritten message. There was an address for the target's home and then... I pulled the last bit of the paper away and stared down at the mark's name, my lips parting, my hands beginning to shake again. Not from anger this time. No, this time from fear.

The target's name was: *Diederik Claasen.*

24

I arrived at the restaurant a few minutes before five, my palms damp, my entire body on alert. Diederik was already there, waiting for me, his face breaking into the boyish smile I remembered from school. I exhaled and unclenched my fists, trying to make myself look relaxed and even excited to be there. With him. A traitor.

"You look wonderful," he said as he took my coat to hang on the back of my chair. I hoped he didn't notice it was slightly heavier on one side. But if he did, he didn't mention it.

"Thank you," I said. I was wearing the same blouse and skirt I'd been wearing earlier, but had changed my hair, leaving it loose and hanging down my back, and was wearing more makeup than I'd ever worn in my life. I'd been almost unrecognizable to myself when I'd left the safe house.

"Order anything you like," he said. "You probably haven't had a decent meal in a while. Or even been in a restaurant."

I could see he felt like a hero bringing me here. Feeding his poor old schoolmate must've made him feel powerful, and I wondered how gracious he expected me to be. It was part of my plan to let him think I was willing to be overly gracious. I'd left the top two buttons of my blouse undone and was prepared to flirt at every opportunity in hopes he offered me a drink back at his place where I'd find the perfect opportunity to sink the blade of my dagger into his carotid like Charlie had demonstrated once on the dummy in Henrik's barn. But I'd left the safe house early to scour for alleyways with exits on both ends, and if the invitation wasn't extended, I'd pull him into one with the premise of something highly inappropriate for a young, single woman. Of course, the only untoward business would be my bullet to his head.

I barely tasted a bite of my meal as I listened with half an ear while he regaled me with atrocious tales of spying on, raiding, and either sending Jews off to camps like he'd done to Tess and her family, or killing them outright.

"If only they understood what a stain on society they are. It would be so much easier," he said, taking a sip of the wine he'd ordered us. "Do you not like the wine?"

I'd only had one sip, and a tiny one at that. I was going to need to keep a level head and my faculties about me to get through this night. Alcohol blurring my ability to react wouldn't do. But I didn't want to raise any suspicions so I picked up the glass.

"I do," I said. "It's just been so long, I'm afraid if I drink it too fast it will go right to my head."

He smiled. "That wouldn't be so bad, would it?"

I smiled back and pretended to take a drink.

An hour and a half later he paid the check and helped me into my coat.

"I don't live far from here," he said. "Would you like to come over for a nightcap?"

I took a moment to pretend to think it over. "I really should get home…"

"I have food if you're still hungry. Maybe there's something there you want to take home with you?"

It was a sad sign of the times that he thought I could be so easily plied with food. I knew there were girls that could be. That would go there and do things they didn't want to because it was the only thing keeping them alive.

"Just the drink will be fine," I said, fighting to keep the bite out of my voice.

He opened the door for me, and we walked out onto the cold and quiet sidewalk, my hand tucked into his arm.

It had been years since I'd been out after dark without having to keep to the shadows. It felt strange to walk down the street in plain view of other soldiers who nodded at Diederik, unabashedly looked me up and down, and went on their way.

I kept an eye on street signs and my surroundings as we walked for two blocks before stopping in front of a stately canal view home with a brick facade and glossy black shutters flanking the many windows.

Diederik unlocked the door and stood aside. "Come in. Please."

I followed him upstairs to the main floor, taking in the understated elegance of the home.

"Is this your parents' home?" I asked, assuming it must be. It was much too nice for a man of his age to own.

He smiled and reached out to take my coat. I watched as he hung it in a nearby closet.

"No. It's mine. It used to belong to a Jewish doctor and his wife who were helping other Jews. Much like your friend's father." I wanted to slap him for having the nerve to say it, but instead forced my face to remain placid. "As a reward for hunting them down and delivering them to my superior, I was given their home."

"Well done," I managed to say, and took the seat he offered.

He removed a bottle of wine from a bronze bar cart in the corner and poured us each a glass of wine. The room filled with an awkward silence as he took swigs of his drink while I barely let the liquid in my glass pass my lips.

"Music," he said, and shot to his feet to put on a record.

As a familiar melody filled the room, he took my glass and pulled me to my feet.

"Dance with me," he said, wrapping one arm around my waist, taking my hand with the other.

Every part of me wanted to scream for him not to touch me. I tried to imagine it was Charlie. I reminded myself it was all part of the job and soon it would be over. But his hot breath on my neck, his clammy hand in mine, made my stomach turn over, and I pushed away from him.

"What's the matter?" he asked, grabbing my arm.

"I have to use the restroom," I said, looking up at him from beneath my lashes, hoping I looked embarrassed. "The wine…"

He exhaled and nodded.

"Of course," he said, stepping back and pointing. "It's right down that hallway. First door on the right."

"Thank you. I'll be right back. Don't go anywhere," I said, turning away and holding back tears as I hurried to the door he'd indicated, shut and locked it behind me, and stood in the dark trying to catch my breath.

I turned on the light and gasped. Diederik hadn't bothered to remove evidence of the previous owners. Their belongings were everywhere in here, from a floral robe to clusters of pink and lavender glass bottles lined up on a shelf for her, amber colored ones for him. There was a small, silver, heart-shaped frame with an image of the couple, a dried rose with a white ribbon tied around its stem, and a beautiful wood-and-glass case with pieces of jewelry inside. It was like a shrine…or perhaps a trophy case.

I sat on the edge of the bathtub and inhaled a deep breath, trying to steady my racing pulse. When I'd settled some, I leaned to one side and raised my skirt. Loosening the strap, I turned it so the weapon no longer rested on the delicate skin of my inner thigh but on the outside, making it easier to grab the moment I needed it. It was strange to not have my pistol within my reach, but the dagger would be much quieter. Even if he was able to get a shout out before his life drained from him, it was less likely to draw attention than a gunshot, making my getaway that much easier.

I wrapped my hand around the hilt, my fingertips brushing the familiar nicks in the wood, my thumb nestling in its spot, and unsheathed it. I held it in my hand, feeling its weight, comforted by its familiar curves and lines, and then slid it back in its holder and stood, taking another steadying breath as my skirt fell with a whisper back in place.

At the mirror above the sink I stopped and peered at my reflection, meeting the return gaze of my pale eyes. I barely recognized the face in the mirror. The uncertainty lurking in the gray-blue of the irises at odds with the resolve in the set of my jaw. I smoothed my hair, licked my lips to give them a bit of a shine, and closed my eyes as I drew in one last deep breath and held it.

A soft knock on the door sent a jolt through me.

"Lien?" Diederik called, his deep voice resonating through the door.

"Coming," I said.

With a last glance in the mirror, I ran my hand down my leg, giving the hilt of the dagger a last quick, reassuring squeeze, and then turned and reached for the door handle.

"Everything okay?" Diederik asked when I opened the door.

"Yes," I said and laughed softly. "I was just a little woozy from the wine and needed a minute."

"Can I get you a glass of water?"

"Yes, please. Thank you," I said, following him into the kitchen where again there were signs of the couple who had lived here before, including a ruffled apron and a box of cigars on the counter.

"Here you are," he said, handing me a glass.

He watched me as I took slow sips, my own eyes on his neck, mentally pinpointing the location of his most important artery. He was so tall, I'd most likely need to get him seated before I could hand him the ticket to wherever bastards like him went when they died.

I drained the glass, and he took it from me and set it on the table.

"Should we go back to the sitting room?" I asked. "Listen to more mus—"

His mouth was on mine before I could register what was happening, his body pressed against me, walking me backward until I hit the wall and cried out, my head ringing with the impact. I couldn't breathe as he bore down on me, his hands grabbing at my blouse and pulling it free of my skirt. I tried to bat him away, but my squirming only seemed to excite him more as he slid his mouth to my ear.

"I like a good struggle," he whispered.

My blood ran cold.

He pulled my blouse open with one hand, the buttons popping off and scattering across the kitchen floor. He yanked down the zipper of my skirt but it stayed in place thanks to the two buttons my mother had sewn on, keeping my dagger concealed for the time being. All it would take was for him to slide his hand down my leg to find the weapon hiding beneath it.

I pushed at his hands uselessly as he kept me pinned with his body, his hand moving from my waistband to my brassiere, squeezing painfully at my breasts, his mouth everywhere, kissing, sucking, biting. He was stronger than I'd anticipated, and I couldn't get leverage to employ any of the movements we'd practiced so diligently in the barn.

I tried reaching for the hilt, but he grabbed my wrists and held them above my head with one hand while the other made its way over my body, defiling the places I'd only let one other man touch.

As his mouth left mine and made its way down my neck to my chest, I frantically tried to think of a way to get free, but he was pressed so close against me there was no way to maneuver myself to kick or elbow him in any of the places Charlie had taught me so long ago.

When he moved in for another kiss, I bit down. He pulled away, raising his free hand to his mouth. There was a dot of blood where my teeth had broken skin, but to my horror he licked it, grinned, and leaned closer.

"That's it. Fight me."

His words reminded me of training with Henrik. Of feeling completely depleted, but having to go again because we were to fight until we were dead, or our attacker was. He had easily overpowered me already, but maybe if he thought I was trying to please him I could free up a hand. It was all I needed. One free hand.

I kissed him back now, biting him as he laughed and goaded me on before spinning me around, my cheekbone smashing against the wall. My arms were yanked behind my back and my skirt lifted.

I squeezed my eyes shut, waiting for him to see the dagger on my leg. Waiting for something else. Something worse. But the skirt fell back in place as the distinct sound of a zipper being lowered could be heard.

"Diederik," I said, panting, exhausted, tears hovering on my lower lids. I had never been more scared in my life. I was stupid to have come here. I couldn't beat him, and he was about to take something I wasn't willing to give him. Not while I was still alive anyway.

I felt my skirt raise again, but the hand holding my wrists had become sweaty and he was having trouble maintaining his hold on me and getting his pants down while keeping my skirt up. This was my chance.

I pulled down hard with one arm. It slid free, and I grabbed my dagger and twisted around.

There was no ripping of fabric like there'd been with the dummies. Just his quick inhalation of breath as my blade sank into his skin, his eyes widening in surprise as warm blood spilled over my hand and his.

He finally let me go and clamped his hands over the wound, taking a step back, his eyes filled with confusion as the blood gushed down the front of him, torrid and red.

He sank to his knees and grabbed at me again, desperately, catching my arm and pulling me with him as he fell backward. I landed half on him, his grip on me still tight, until it wasn't. Until it went slack. Until understanding filled his eyes and then disappeared behind the cloud of death.

I didn't move, my chest heaving, my eyes glued to him, not believing he was really dead. I waited for him to blink, to make a move, to throw me off him. But the amount of blood drenching his shirt and pooling beneath his head and shoulders confirmed he had not survived the blow. He was gone.

I slid off and leaned against him, unable to move, sitting in his blood in the middle of the floor. I began to shake, deep, quaking movements that jarred me and made my jaw ache. I gathered my knees into my chest and began to cry. Quietly. Sorrowfully. In relief.

When my body finally stilled, I rose and looked down at him. His eyes were open, his lips parted as if for a last breath. Sighing, I wiped the dagger on my bloodied skirt, lifted the hem, sheathed it, and went down the hall to the bathroom to clean up.

The blood wouldn't come off.

I had stripped down, dumping my ruined clothes in the tub and scrubbing at my skin in the lukewarm spray of the shower with a bar of soap and a washrag. But the blood had stained my hands and arms, saturating my skin.

The thought that he had somehow become part of me made my stomach heave and I slipped, hitting my knee on the side of the tub as I hauled myself over it, and barely made it to the toilet where I threw up the entirety of my restaurant meal. As my body calmed, I caught sight of my fingernails, Diederik's blood caked beneath. With a sob, I doubled over and retched again.

When I felt well enough to stand, I shoved my dirty clothes into the trash bin, rinsed again in vain in the shower, threw the washrag in the bin with my soiled clothing, and went in search of something clean to wear.

I had to force myself not to be sick again when I found a woman's full wardrobe piled on what looked to be a guest room bed. Diederik hadn't disposed of anything. He had just lived among their things as if perhaps they were gone on holiday and he was taking care of the place. Or maybe he'd enjoyed knowing he ruined their lives, and walked through the house proudly gazing upon the many trophies.

On bare feet, I padded back to the living room and sat on the sofa, determining my next moves. Unlike the liquidations done in various parks, there was no one coming to clean up this mess. It was part of the risk that came with the job. There wasn't always someone to remove the body. Sometimes you just had to let it lie where it fell and run. But because I'd done this after dark while a curfew was in place, I was trapped in a house with the dead body of a German soldier. I could leave and, if caught, play embarrassed. Say I was out visiting my boyfriend and it got late. But what if they made me take them back to where I'd come from?

I glanced toward the kitchen where I could just see one of Diederik's shoes from my place on the sofa. Shuddering, I checked the time. It was after nine o'clock. I could either take my chances getting to the safe house by slipping through the shadows down alleyways I'd checked earlier, or wait until morning when I could mix in with whatever pedestrians were making their way through town. I decided on the latter and made a bed for myself on the sofa with a blanket I pulled from a closet.

Rolling over so I didn't have to see the body, I curled into a ball and tried to erase the feeling of his hands on my body. I was hurt in places I'd never imagined, my skin tender, torn, and bruised. I tried to keep the tears from coming. It was over. There was no need to be scared anymore. I'd stopped him.

But I almost hadn't, and the thought of what might've happened if I'd not gotten my hand on my dagger caused my body to shiver uncontrollably, and I buried my face in the blanket and cried until I fell asleep.

I woke before the sun after a fitful night of sleep on a stranger's sofa, folded the blanket and put it away, and grabbed the bag of bloodied clothes, shoving some clean ones from the pile in the guest room on top. Should I be stopped, I could say I was donating or selling.

I washed and put away the glasses we drank out of the night before. All other traces of me cleaned or hidden away. Whoever found him would wonder who had done this. Perhaps the soldiers we had passed after we'd left the restaurant would tell of the young woman they'd seen him with. Perhaps not. Regardless, I'd been careful to make sure I looked nothing like I normally do with my hair worn down and my face slathered in cosmetics. This morning I was back to normal, hair in plaits, face devoid of the eyeliner and lipstick from the night before. I looked pale, plain, and harmless.

"It's your secret weapon," Aunt Liv had told Elif and me once.

We blended in, our faces blank slates, invisible.

I took a last look around, avoiding Diederik's body and his unseeing eyes staring at the ceiling, the dark pool of blood shimmering around him, and hurried down the stairs to the front door, the sack of clothes over my shoulder. At the landing I took in a deep breath, letting it out as I opened the door and stepped outside.

I didn't hurry, not wanting to call attention to myself. I was just one more weary citizen going about her business.

The air was cold, the wind whipping beneath my layers, the silence so deafening I barely dared to breathe as I followed the maze of streets and alleyways I'd memorized before, dressed in a dead woman's clothes, all the way back to the safe house.

I knocked the special knock, trying to keep myself from glancing around in case anyone was watching and thought I looked guilty of something. A moment later Mara opened the door and ushered me in.

"You look like you had a bad night," she said as I slipped inside the darkened house. "Tea?"

"Please," I said, dropping the sack of clothes, pulling a chair out, and easing my aching body into it.

As the water boiled, she sat across from me at the table.

"Did it go okay?" she asked.

An image of Diederik's malevolent grin as he leaned into me, my hands pinned over my head, flashed in my mind.

"Mmm-hmm," I said.

"You got what you needed?"

Another image, this time of my dagger, blood spilling dark and red down his shirt and over my hand. "I did."

She peered at me. "And did he?"

I exhaled, my fingers trembling. I clasped them together and shook my head. "He did not," I said.

"Good."

She poured the tea and set a steaming cup in front of me with a thin slice of bread that smelled faintly of cinnamon. We sat together, not saying a word, her providing me with company until the shaking had mostly subsided and I could finally get to my feet to retrieve my things and make my way to the train station.

"Oh," I said as I caught a glimpse of myself in the mirror over the bathroom sink.

I was covered in bruises. Fingertip-sized purple marks dotted my jawbone, my neck, my wrists, and various other tender places lower down that were thankfully covered by clothing.

"Here," Mara said, standing in the doorway, a scarf in her hand. "It will cover some of it."

I nodded gratefully and wrapped it around me, taking a last look at my reflection before shouldering my small bag.

"Thank you," I said. "For everything."

"Be careful getting home, dear."

Chin tucked into the scarf, I made my way to the station, boarded, and stared out the window at the passing farmland as the train scraped along the tracks from Amsterdam to Haarlem. No one bothered me. No one even sat next to me. The soldiers that strolled through, eyeing everyone with suspicion, barely glanced my way. As usual, without makeup and fancier hair, I'd resumed my invisibility.

In Haarlem I got off the train and stood on the platform, unsure where to go as people pushed past, disembarking and boarding, unaware of the young woman trying to hold herself together, her facade starting to crumble.

I didn't want to go home yet. Didn't want to take this feeling into my house. Didn't want to frighten my mother or Elif with my appearance. I considered going to Aunt Liv's, but it was too risky. And so I went to the only other place I knew I'd find comfort.

Charlie's look of delight at seeing me turned instantly to one of concern as his eyes took in my appearance, and he pulled me inside. "Oh my God. Lien. What happened? Are you okay?"

I reached for him as my knees gave, and together we sank to the floor where he drew me to him and I clung, unable to get close enough, clawing at him as though I could somehow disappear inside him where it was safe and warm and away from all other people.

I wanted to tell him what happened. Every horrible detail. Every awful second. The fear. The disgust. The panic that I would die by that man's hands. But I was scared. Worried he would think differently about me, knowing another man's hands had touched where only his had before. Worried he would question my decision to go to Diederik's residence. Maybe he would think I wanted to go. That I'd hoped for something romantic to happen, and it was my own fault that I was attacked.

And so I didn't tell him who the target had been, only that he was stronger than I'd anticipated and I hadn't been able to use my gun. And because we didn't go to his bedroom that day, he never saw the far reaches of the bruises Diederik's hands had left on me, and never guessed I'd been damaged in less visible ways by the interaction. Until it was too late.

25

"You're sure," Mama said, standing before me, arms crossed over her chest.

"Yes, Mama. I'm fine," I said, avoiding her stern gaze.

Since arriving home from Amsterdam the week before, quiet and withdrawn, bruises dotting my skin from my head to parts of me I hadn't dared show anyone, our mother had been watching me more carefully. She knew something was wrong and could tell by the way I winced when I moved certain ways that I'd been hurt, but the extent of it I'd only been able to tell my sister in a terse conversation the day I came home as we changed into our nightgowns and she saw the marks on my ribs and back. I knew she of all people would understand after what she'd endured on our missions. She'd listened quietly, tears filling her eyes as she grasped my hands, my voice flat as I recounted each moment with painstaking detail. Details I hoped to one day forget. Moments I wished I could burn from my mind. Touches I wanted erased from my body.

Afterward she hugged me carefully while I promised I was fine and pulled away. It was just another job. A terrible one. But there would be more that were just as bad or worse. No need to get worked up over this one.

"That's not true, though, Lien," she said. "It was someone you knew. That makes it much worse."

"He was a bad person," I said. "He got what he deserved."

She peered at me, but I turned away, putting up a wall, unwilling to let it affect me any more than it already had. Her tears were enough. I didn't—*couldn't*—fall apart over this. Over him. I wouldn't allow it. There was work to be done, and I would not let him be the reason I couldn't do my job.

But for many days after, the memory of that night found me, catching me at inopportune moments, waking me in the middle of the night, causing me to lose track as I counted fuses, ammunition, or mapped a route.

I was setting the table one evening when my mother ripped the seam of a skirt she was sewing. The sound of the fabric tearing took me instantly back to that night, and the plate in my hand slipped and crashed to the floor, exploding into shards.

I got dressed as an afterthought, oftentimes forgetting to put on socks or finding I'd been wearing an article of clothing inside out all day. If I brushed my hair and teeth, I didn't remember doing so. And as I left on a simple mission to deliver a piece of information, I was halfway down the alleyway walking toward the main street when I realized the note was in my hand, not tucked away.

When Charlie came by to check on me a few days after my encounter with Diederik, I barely hugged him, shrinking away. I watched as he exchanged a look with Elif, but didn't bother to say anything. They were overly concerned. I was fine.

"Elif told me about the bruises on your back," he said after she'd left to give us some space. "Lien—"

"I'm fine. I told you he pushed me against the wall. That's what they're from."

"And the ones on your ribs?" he asked.

I glared at him. Clearly Elif had told him a lot.

"We struggled for a while," I said. "I have some bruises. They'll heal up in no time. Please stop worrying, Charlie. I'm okay. Truly."

But even as I said it, images of Diederik's face as he pinned my arms over my head flooded in, the sound of my blouse being ripped open, his breath hot in my ear, his mouth and fingers everywhere. I could still feel him against me and hear his hateful words in my ear.

Thankfully, Charlie let it go. But my mother wouldn't.

"You're paler than usual and you look frail," she said now, surveying me in the kitchen as I prepared to go out on a job.

"Everyone looks like that these days," I said.

It wasn't a lie, but I knew I looked worse than usual, my inability to eat much making me wan and oftentimes dizzy.

"Can't they send someone else instead?"

"No, Mama," I said. "This is *my* job. I can do it."

"I know you *can*. But should you?"

I sighed, grabbed my jacket, and slipped into my shoes. "I'll be home tomorrow."

I met Charlie and once again we snuck through the shadows, firebombs hidden in the cloth sack he carried, softly jostling as we hurried to a residence on the outskirts of town.

"Are you sure no one is home?" I asked, staring up at the darkened windows of the attached house where a known collaborator lived and had been conducting recruitment meetings.

We'd been sent to relay a message. One that would leave him homeless. Payback for helping remove many in our community from their own homes.

"That's the information we were given. Their neighbors might be in, though, so we'll need to be mindful of that."

Crouching low, I followed him to the house and then stood watch while he picked the lock of the back door and opened it.

Since we were targeting a specific room, we'd been told to go in and make sure the fires were set, rather than lobbing the bombs at the second-story windows and hoping the flames reached the room before the fire department was called.

We hurried up the staircase and looked for the office, finding it at the end of a narrow hallway.

"Ready?" Charlie asked.

I nodded.

We lit the bombs and tossed them from outside the door. But as I watched, the flame on mine went out, the bomb dropping to the floor and rolling into the corner as Charlie's exploded, sending a wave of heat toward us. I turned away, but as soon as the heat was sucked back inside, I ran in.

"Lien, no!" Charlie shouted.

I had no idea why I'd run into the burning room. It was a novice mistake, one Henrik had warned us about.

"Throw it and run. If it doesn't light, leave it. It could be a trick of the fuse, hiding the flame. You won't see it until it ignites. But if the flame goes out, it's not worth the risk. Don't be stupid."

But here I was, being stupid as I grabbed my unlit firebomb and threw it into the center of the fire. The explosion threw me back into the glass doors that led to a tiny balcony. Not thinking, I pulled one open. Finding oxygen, the fire lurched toward me and I screamed as my sleeve lit.

"What are you thinking?" Charlie said, appearing beside me. He patted hard at the burning fabric, snuffing the flame out, and then pushed me backward. "Go. Jump!"

I looked at the wall of fire before me and then turned to where Charlie was pointing. From where we were, we could leap to the lower roof of the neighbor's house. Without waiting to be told again, I scrambled up onto the railing and jumped, landing hard and then sliding down the angled roof until I had to jump again to the ground below. Charlie landed beside me and then pulled me by the hand around the side of the house. But as we left the yard I stopped.

"Lien," he said, his voice a warning, the smell of smoke in the air. "What are you doing?"

"We have to warn the neighbors," I said, and then ran toward the other house. Charlie beat me to it, though, and pounded on the door.

"Fire!" he yelled, banging his fists. "Wake up! Fire!"

He yanked me away from the burning structure and out of sight, our feet pounding into the soft grass, our breath coming in short bursts as we ducked behind a line of trees.

"Stay here," Charlie said, and then hurried back to the house.

A moment later he returned.

"They got out," he said. "Let's go."

At the safe house he gently peeled the singed fabric from my raw and blistered arm and applied an ointment supplied by the house owner while I bit onto a towel to keep from screaming.

"Thank you for going back to check that the people got out of the other house."

"I knew if I didn't you'd fret," he said as he wrapped a bandage around the wound. "I just don't understand why you ran in that room. You know better than that."

I shrugged. "The flame went out on the fuse. I had to make sure I did my job right."

"But that was dangerous, Lien. And incredibly stupid. You could've seen it wrong. The flame could have been too small for you to see from where you were, and the bomb could've exploded in your face. What were you thinking?"

His words were harsh, but instead of crying, I steeled myself.

"I was thinking I said I'd set fire to that room," I said. "And so I did."

To me it seemed a valid excuse for my recklessness, but two days later I had another mishap.

The job, another liquidation, was no different from any of the others we'd done. Elif went into the pub, I waited in the trees. But when I saw the target...

He was tall and blond and had a smirk on his handsome face that reminded me so much of Diederik that I found myself paralyzed, unable to move, even as he led my sister down a different path and pushed her to the ground, his hand covering her mouth. As she struggled against him, her screams muffled, I couldn't raise my arm, my finger slipping from the trigger.

The man yelled out and I blinked, watching as he pulled his hand away to look at it. There was blood on his palm, and he reached back and smacked Elif across the face, leaving a smear of red on her cheek.

"Lien!" she screamed, forgetting in her terror to use my alias.

He turned and saw me, and as he got to his feet, Elif scrambled to her own, her hair in disarray, her face tear and blood streaked. Getting hold of myself, I raised the pistol. He saw the gun and grabbed Elif, shoving her in front of him, but he was taller than her, and I was a sure shot.

"Duck," I said, my voice hard.

She squeezed her eyes shut, bowed her head forward, and I took the shot. His look of surprise before he crumpled to the ground at once satisfied and repulsed me.

"Come on," I said, gesturing for Elif to follow me into the trees. "We have to get out of here."

But she didn't take my hand. She merely followed, her eyes darting to me every so often as we hurried through the shadows to the safe house.

"What?" I said as we sat at the spindly kitchen table we'd become oddly familiar with. We'd spent so much time in this particular house, it almost felt like we lived here.

Elif sat across from me, her eyes narrowed, her lips pressed into a straight line.

"You could've killed me," she said in a hushed voice. "And

why did you wait so long? You had a clear shot when he was on top of me."

"He was moving too much," I said, looking down into my watery tea to avoid her accusing glare.

"You're lying."

"He— It wasn't a good shot."

"I saw you lower your arm!"

"Girls."

We both jumped at the urgent whispered voice of the home-owner. She pressed her finger to her lips and then left the room again.

"It wasn't a good shot," I said again, my voice quiet and insistent.

"I don't believe you. I saw your face. You looked like you'd seen a ghost."

"I was just concerned for you. I wasn't sure—"

"I know he looked like Diederik."

The room went silent as we stared at one another. I shook my head, trying to deny that was what had affected me, but tears filled my eyes and I swiped at them angrily.

"Lien." She reached across the table, but I pulled my hands back, clasping them in my lap.

"It was just an off night," I insisted.

"That could've gotten me killed. And certainly got me hurt."

I glanced at the smear of blood now dried on her cheek. I felt sick as I recalled him hitting her and bolted to my feet. Finding a dishrag at the sink, I wetted it and then knelt beside my sister, gently wiping at her face until the blood was gone and all that remained were the tears streaming down her face as my own eyes filled and blurred.

"Lien," she whispered, grasping my hand. "You're not fine. That was a reckless shot to take, and you know it."

I bowed my head, resting it on her knee, my shoulders heaving as I cried.

"I'm so sorry, Elif," I whispered. "I'm sorry. I'm sorry. I'm sorry."

We slept side by side that night, grasping one another's hands, our tears dried, our bodies spent from fear, anger, and exhaustion. She'd forgiven me, but as I listened to her breathing slow, I wondered if I'd ever forgive myself.

We returned home the following morning, and when I came downstairs after washing up and changing into clean clothes, Charlie was waiting for me, my mother and Elif nowhere to be found.

"I came to see you," he said. "Elif told me what happened last night."

I hung my head, ashamed, embarrassed, and angry with myself.

"He looked like someone I knew," I said, my voice low. "It won't happen again."

"Ever since that job in Amsterdam you've not been yourself, Lien. I know you told me what happened, but I'm starting to think you didn't give me the whole story. It's the only explanation I can come up with for why you seem so different. You're jumpy, and you tense up when I hug you." His eyes reddened as they filled with tears. "I thought it was me. I thought maybe you didn't feel the same about me anymore. But now...now I think it's something else because I know you would never let harm come to your sister. And normally you wouldn't jump stupidly into fire. So please, talk to me. Tell me what's happening. Or what happened before."

I sighed and sank into one of the four remaining dining chairs. Charlie sat across from me, hands folded on the table, listening as I tried and failed, and then tried again to tell him what had happened the night I met Diederik Claasen for dinner.

"You can trust me, Lien," he said, reaching across the table and taking my hand.

I stared at him, hearing his words, letting them sink in as I met and held his gaze. Those warm blue eyes with all their depth and understanding and love looking back at me.

I sighed. I knew without doubt I could trust Charlie. That he would never hurt me and would hold whatever I told him close to his heart and protect it. But that didn't make it easier to say the actual words. To open my mouth and release them. I was frightened. What if he thought differently of me? I wouldn't be able to bear it.

But despite that fear, haltingly the words came. I told him about the house, the drinks, and the bathroom. And then I told him about the sound of my clothing being ripped, the feeling of my skin being touched and torn and clawed. Hot breath, my head and face slammed into the wall, my vision blurred and spinning, unable to catch my own breath, all the while thinking this was it. He would take me, and then he would kill me. Or maybe he'd kill me as he took me. And then the dagger in my hand. The feeling of his blood spilling over my hand, and the look in his eyes as the life left him.

Charlie didn't move. He didn't say a word. He simply sat, his eyes both sad and angry as he listened. When I was done, he waited until I let him know it was okay to touch me.

"You need to step away from this for a while," he said quietly as we sat on the sofa, my head on his chest, his arms wrapped around me. "You're too dangerous right now. Too raw and hurt. You need time."

I wanted to fight him, to tell him he was wrong. I was fine. He couldn't tell me what to do. But I knew he was right. I was anxious all the time these days. I barely slept, barely ate the little food we had, and I had made stupid, life-threatening mistakes.

I nodded into his shirt and he held me tighter.

The following day, while Elif headed out on an assignment with Annie and Jan, I threw the straps of my cloth bag over my shoulder and followed Mama out the door to her shop.

Customers were practically nonexistent these days, most wearing what they already had, unable to afford new, or not wanting to venture out due to the number of soldiers stationed on our particular street. As it happened, we had one customer come in, a wealthy neighbor of Aunt Liv's, who asked to have several garments altered to fit her diminishing size.

"This is not the way I thought I'd lose weight," she said, standing still as mother pinned in the waist of a dress. "But I'll take it."

I pasted a smile on my face and bit my tongue.

On my second day, in a fit of anger at having to be there rather than helping in the Resistance effort, I overturned a basket of fabric swatches and threw a spool at the wall. Mama, usually so patient and quiet, kicked me out of the shop and wouldn't let me come back until the next day.

"I don't know what's gotten into you," she said as she held the door open. "But you need to go home now. You'll draw attention acting like that, and we can't have anyone snooping around in here."

Her tone, one I'd remembered from my childhood when I threw a particularly explosive tantrum, stopped me in my tracks. After a tense evening of avoiding one another, I returned the next day and sat in the back room doing as I was told.

When there weren't customers, Mama and I cut fabric into squares, which she then sewed together into blankets that were given out to those in need. I cleaned shelves, counted thread spools and logged the numbers into a supplies book, reduced prices, dressed and redressed the mannequin in the window, and dusted and swept the floor. After five days I was itching for something else to do.

"I'm sure I'm fine to go on an assignment," I said from my post behind the cash register.

"You woke screaming last night," Mama said, and shook her head.

I sighed and went back to counting straight pins.

Saturday I wasn't expected to go into the shop and was surprised when Mama decided not to go in either.

"If they need anything, it can wait until Monday," she said. "I thought maybe we could have a picnic in the garden."

"With what?" I asked. Our cupboards were mostly bare.

"Alard came by early this morning," she said, pointing to a basket on the dining table.

I jumped up from the sofa, nearly stepping on Charlie, who sat on the floor, and slapping Elif's hand as I flew by. "A basket from Aunt Liv!" I said.

She hurried over. When I lifted the lid, the aroma of bread wafted upward, and Elif and I both moaned. We spread the contents on the table and then stood back in awe. It had been a long while since we'd seen so much food all at once. There was a loaf of bread, a small bottle of milk, a large cube of butter, three carrots, ten small potatoes, two cans of evaporated milk, a wedge of cheese, and most precious, a small bar of chocolate.

"How?" Charlie asked, standing beside me, rubbing his eyes.

"All those parties," Mama said. "She pays a lot of money to bring these items in, which brings the soldiers to her house. And information."

"Incredible."

We saved half of everything, and then took the other half outside to the garden where Elif and I spread out a blanket. The four of us sat, taking tiny bites of our servings, trying to make it last as long as possible. Afterward, Mama and Elif went inside while Charlie and I lay on our backs on the blanket, holding hands and staring up at the blue sky. Were it not for the constant buzzing of planes and my stomach grumbling for more food, it would've felt like any other spring day.

"How was the shop this week?" Charlie asked, his thumb making small circles on my palm.

"Boring."

He chuckled. "Good. I think you need boring for now."

I shot him a look and he widened his eyes.

"Do I need to remind you why?"

"No," I said, pulling my hand away and crossing my arms over my chest.

"Are you pouting?" he asked. I didn't have to look at him to know he was grinning.

"No." I tried to be irritated, but found I couldn't keep the smile from my face.

He pulled me to him, placing a kiss on my forehead. "Just give it some time," he said. "A little bit longer at least. You can read and sleep, help your mom, and rest. I can even bring you a stack of comic books if you like."

I grumbled something incoherent and he laughed.

"Was that a yes?"

"I suppose," I said.

"And didn't you say sometimes you write thoughts in a notebook? Maybe that would be helpful."

I glanced up at him and he smiled. "You're awfully adorable, Charlie."

"I adore you, Lien. And I want you to be well. You need to take care of yourself. For you, and for the rest of us who need you around. But especially for me."

I grinned and he kissed me.

"Yuck," Elif said from the back door. "Can you two stop that for a minute?"

We looked up at her.

"Mama and I are going to run those new blankets you two made to the Ten Booms. We'll be back soon."

As soon as the door clicked closed, I got to my feet and reached out to Charlie.

"Where are we going?" he asked.

"Bed."

"Lien, are you sure?" he asked, resisting the tug of my hand. "I'm afraid it will just remind you."

I wrapped my arms around his waist, tipping my head back to stare at his handsome face.

"I can still feel his hands on me," I said. "I need yours to make me forget."

For the next two weeks, I did exactly as Charlie had suggested. When I wasn't at the sewing shop, I reread my favorite books, wrote in my journal, slept, and went through my belongings, making piles of clothes that no longer fit to be given away or had holes to be sewn.

I was standing in the center of Elif's and my bedroom one evening, determining what to go through next in the dim light from a candle, when my mother walked in and sat on my bed.

"How are you?" she asked.

I'd spent the whole day with her at the shop and was surprised by the question. It had been a good day.

"I'm okay," I said, and she nodded.

"You seem less angry. Less... I don't know. Sad, I guess."

I turned and looked at her, and then sank down beside her and took her hand in mine as I lay my head on her shoulder. While she sat quietly next to me, I told her about the night I killed Diederik. Recounting the details a second time came slightly easier, now that I'd told them to Charlie. Though it was no easier to watch her react to the story than it had been him.

"I still think about it," I said. "It's hard to put it out of my head. But I feel calmer now. What happened was—" I sucked in a breath, images and sounds starting to flood in. But I stopped them and exhaled. "Frightening. Awful. I thought I was going to die. But somehow I didn't. Even through everything he was doing, I kept my wits about me. I remembered my dagger. I knew if I could just get my hand on it, I would be okay. And so I let him be distracted by all the awful things he was doing, and as soon as he eased his grip, it was over."

"You are so brave, Lien," she said. "I don't know anyone who could've stayed so focused in that situation." A sob stopped her from saying more, and I hurried to wrap my arms around her. "I'm just so proud of you for being so strong," she said.

"I learned that from you."

She held me close and kissed my cheek.

"I want to go back to work," I said, and held up my hand as her mouth opened in what I assumed would be a protest. "I've been thinking about it. About what happened to me that night and…if I can prevent that from happening to anyone else. If I can liquidate the men who would do those things and save other girls from being hurt that way, then I want to. And I will."

She sighed and leaned into me.

"I've never been so proud of you girls," she said. "It's terrifying watching you both leave on these assignments that no young woman or man should have to deal with. As much as I want to stop you every time, I won't. Maybe one day I'll regret that, but the world needs women like you. Women willing to risk everything to save as many others as they can."

She hugged me close again, her tears dampening my face, and then stood to leave.

"Mama?" I said, my voice small.

"Yes?"

"Would you mind sitting here with me for a while?"

She smiled and climbed onto the bed beside me, our backs against the wall, her hand reaching for mine.

"Nothing would make me happier," she said.

26

In February of 1944, as the war continued to rage around us, we were ravaged of our resources, including any remaining able-bodied men, who were sent to the German forced labor camps, leaving only the elderly, the women, and the children to fend for themselves.

Food, scarce before, was even less available now as each citizen was granted only a small portion of bread a day and a helping of soup consisting of cabbage leaves and potato skins—if you were lucky. Meat was nonexistent unless you were a soldier, but every so often shavings that used to be bagged and sold to dog owners could be bought to be added to stews. They were hard to come by, though, and many times spoiled.

Thankfully for us, Aunt Liv was still entertaining top officials from time to time, leading her to receive more food than most. Leftovers were given to her staff, her brother, us, and the rest of our small team. It wasn't much, but it was more than most had. Between that and our still-producing garden, we were hungry, but not starving. This year more than ever, though, we all looked forward to the warmer months when the crops in the surrounding farms became available to barter for.

In March, Annie, Jan, Elif, and I were sent to Amsterdam on two separate missions, Annie and Jan to liquidate a high-ranking official, Elif and I to make an exchange of information at a bookshop I happened to be familiar with.

We traveled in twos, arriving at the safe house we'd be staying at within a couple hours of one another.

"I'm gonna go check out his route," Annie said, adjusting the now ever-present wig covering her red hair. "Jan?"

He nodded and stood. "Shall we bring you ladies back an ice cream? How about a warm *stroopwafel* fresh off the grill?"

Elif groaned. "You're so mean, Jan."

"Can't you just smell it?" he asked.

"Why do you do this to us?" Annie asked.

Jan was always talking about food. His favorite dish his *mam* made. His favorite dish his *oma* made. What he would eat at that very moment if he could, and then asking the same of us.

"I miss food," he said. "Imagining having it again keeps me going."

"Imagining having it again just makes me hungry." Annie pushed him out the door, calling over her shoulder as they went, "We'll be back soon."

While they scouted their target's route to and from work, Elif and I left for the bookshop.

It was bittersweet walking into the store where I'd run into Diederik for the very last time. It had only been months, but it seemed like a lifetime ago.

The bell on the door jingled like I remembered, and I was happy to see it looked exactly the same, though the owner looked worse for wear with a bruised and swollen cheek, and a small bloodstain on the cuff of his sleeve.

"Ah," he said with a smile when he saw me. "So you made it after all. I wondered and hoped."

"I did," I said, returning his smile. "Thank you."

"I'm glad it went well."

While I wouldn't exactly describe that night as having gone *well*, I just nodded and offered the book we were there to "exchange," and then pretended to peruse the shelves while he went to the back to put it somewhere safe.

The bell on the door sounded, and I turned to see two men in uniform enter, their sharp stares darting from me to Elif. I gave them a well-practiced demure smile and turned back to the shelves, my heart racing in my chest as my eyes met Elif's over a row of books in the next aisle over.

When the shop owner returned, he slowed for a moment at the sight of the new customers, his smile wavering.

"Can I help you find something, gentlemen?" he called.

"Just looking," the one said.

"How about you ladies?" the shop owner asked.

"Do you have something with romance?" Elif asked, smiling shyly when one of the two soldiers looked her way.

"Indeed I do, miss. Right this way."

He led her to another section, raising his voice a decibel as he asked her what kind of romance she was looking for while I continued to run my fingers along colored spines, pretending to browse as I kept my eyes on the men in uniform. Should either of them make a move for their weapon, I was prepared to grab Elif and run.

"I'll take that one," I heard Elif say. I peeked around the corner and watched her follow the shop owner to the counter to pay.

"Ready?" she asked me a moment later, her book wrapped in brown paper, a string tied around it. A wave of familiarity at the whole scene washed over me, and my knees weakened for a moment. "Grietje?" she said, using the name on the falsified paperwork in my pocket.

I snapped to attention. "Yes. I'm ready. Shall we go then?"

As we turned to leave, a deep voice said, "Stop."

I glanced at my sister who turned wide eyes at the officer stalking toward her, his hand outstretched.

"The book," he said.

She frowned and handed it over as my heart lodged itself in my throat.

"Sir?" she said as he tore the paper off, the string floating to the floor.

He flipped through the pages once, and then again, before ripping the front and back endpapers away and pulling the cover clean off, revealing...nothing but pages.

He shoved it at Elif, glared at the shop owner, signaled to his comrade, and they stalked out of the store.

"Thanks again!" Elif called as she grabbed my arm and pulled me from the store.

We were down the street before she tapped her belly and a hollow sound emerged. Somehow, while we were in the shop, the owner had passed her the book we'd come for, and she'd managed to slip it beneath her dress.

"You never fail to surprise me," I said, and linked my arm through hers.

When Annie and Jan returned, the four of us scrounged together a meager meal and drank weak cups of tea while playing cards and trying to keep our voices down. Not an easy task with Jan and Annie around. The two of them were incredibly competitive, mostly with each other, which led to pretend outrage followed by passionate kisses that had Elif and I covering our eyes.

"Please spare us," Elif said.

"I think we shall," Annie said, getting to her feet and taking her boyfriend's hand. "See you gals in the morning."

With the two of them gone, the house was quiet. We cleaned up the cards and the dishes, washed up separately in the bathroom, and sank into twin beds across from one another in the bedroom across from the others, where soft sounds and a creak-ing bed made us cover our mouths and giggle.

Despite the brief moment of terror at the bookshop, it had been a good day, and for once when I closed my eyes and drifted off to sleep, my mind wasn't clouded with thoughts of what had been, but instead, hope for what might come.

Over breakfast the next morning, Annie asked from behind Jan's hand, which she'd been playfully biting, "You two off on the first train then?"

"Yes," I said, shaking my head as Jan pulled her from her chair onto his lap. "You two ready for today?"

"Always," Jan said.

"Always," Annie repeated, and kissed the tip of his nose. "In fact, I need to get changed. Wanna help?"

They ran off and I caught Elif's eye.

"Thank you for not being like that with Charlie in front of me," she said.

"I'm starting to feel like we're doing something wrong," I said.

"You mean you don't bite his knuckles?" she asked, smirk-ing. I felt my face heat.

"Well, not at the breakfast table anyway," I said.

Her laughter, something I hadn't heard in what felt like years, would follow me through the day, standing in stark contrast to the horrors that transpired that afternoon.

We took our time packing up the few things we'd brought for the brief trip, not in any hurry to return home to a cold house or the sewing shop where we'd undoubtedly spend hours reor-ganizing something mother deemed important, just to keep our minds busy and off our hungry stomachs.

"Got the book?" I asked Elif, who patted the bottom of her bag in response.

Mrs. Dekker, the owner of the house, was knitting in a well-worn rocking chair in the sitting room. We stopped and chatted for a while and were thanking her once more before we left when someone pounded on the front door.

"Stay here," Mrs. Dekker said as she hurried from the room.

We stared at one another with wide eyes, listening as our hostess answered the door.

"My goodness," we heard her say before she was cut off by a loud wail.

"Is that—" I said, looking at my sister, but she was already on her feet and I rushed to follow.

"Annie," she said, seeing their friend in the entryway. "What's happened?"

Annie's face was pale beneath the dark brown wig, her back pressed to the door.

"Jan," she whispered, and her eyes filled with tears.

"Where is he?" I asked. "Did he— Was he—" I didn't want to say it. Captured. Shot. Dead. None of the options were good.

"I have to go back," she said, pushing off the door.

"Back where? Annie, where is he?"

She sniffled and wiped her nose on her sleeve. "We were near *Vondelpark*. I was on the bike and I took the shot, but my pistol failed so he took it. I saw the man stumble and grab his side. I thought it was over. But then he turned around and fired back and Jan..." She covered her face with her hands. "He was hit. He fell and—I didn't know what to do. I was afraid if I stopped, if I turned around, I'd be shot too, so I kept riding. I came back here and—" She stared at us in horror. "I left him there. I left him on the ground bleeding. I should've gone back. Oh my God." She turned and grabbed the doorknob. "I have to go back."

Elif shoved her foot in front of the door. "You can't," she said, her voice firm. "Someone might recognize you. Lien or I will go." She glanced at me and I nodded.

"I'll go now," I said.

While Mrs. Dekker led Annie to the sofa, I pulled Elif aside.

"What if he's not there?" I asked.

"Then either the Germans have him or someone took him to the hospital." By the look on her face, I could tell she felt as I did—that it was most likely the former. "Be careful." She squeezed my hand.

I slipped out the front door and made my way to the large public park Annie had mentioned. I knew there was a hospital and another safe house not far from there and hoped to find Jan at one of those two locations. I headed toward the park first in case he'd never gotten up from where Annie had seen him fall.

Unsure which street the incident had happened on, I zig-zagged from one to the next until I saw a cluster of people and a stain on the cobblestones in front of a restaurant and strained to hear what was being said.

"Awful, isn't it?" a voice said from behind me.

I turned to see an older woman staring at the group as well, her fingers clutching the cross hanging from her neck.

"I didn't see what happened," I said.

"Young man got shot. One minute he was on his bicycle, the next he was on the ground." She shook her head. "Wish I could say it's the first time I've seen something like that, but lately I've seen it all too often."

"Did the Germans take him?" I asked.

"Probably, but I didn't see. Somehow he got to his feet and disappeared down that street." She pointed to an alleyway.

I chewed my lip and swore silently as I looked where she pointed, seeing several spots of blood marking the path he'd taken. Annie would never be satisfied if I reported he'd dis-appeared down a street and hadn't gone looking for him. She would probably come back and start knocking on doors.

The woman must've noticed my distress because she gave a glance around and leaned in. "Are you a friend of his?" she asked.

I didn't answer.

"Well, if you were a friend, you might like to know that I

heard the young man was taken to the hospital. I mean, I can't be sure. It may just be a rumor but…"

I squeezed her arm. "Thank you," I said, and rushed off in the direction of the hospital nearby.

Minutes later, out of breath, my legs weary from running, I pushed through the doors of the hospital and raced to the front desk near an Emergency sign.

"Can I help you?" the receptionist asked, looking startled by my entrance.

"I'm looking for—" I stopped. Saying his name, alias or real, would connect us. "A young man," I said. "I don't know his name. He was shot and I helped bring him here, but I don't know where they took him."

"Oh," she said. "Right. I believe he was taken to Emergency. Someone there should be able to locate him for you."

She pointed to the Emergency Department sign down the hall.

"Thank you," I said, and hurried away.

As I pushed through the door, I noticed a large man leaning against the wall, a bloodstain covering half his shirt.

"Excuse me," I said. "Was it you who brought in the young man that was shot?"

"I am," he said. "Do you know him?"

Like with the woman earlier, I wasn't sure what to say so I said nothing. Like her, he seemed to understand.

"They took him back a little while ago, but I haven't heard anything. He was alive and talking when we got here, though, if that helps."

"It does. Thank you."

"Excuse me, sir?"

We looked up to see a young nurse with bouncy blond curls heading toward us. She glanced at me and then addressed the gentleman again.

"I'm so sorry to inform you, but the young man you brought in has died."

"Oh," he said. "Right. Well..." He looked to me. "I'm so sorry."

The nurse turned to me.

"Did you know him?" she asked.

There was something in her voice that made me uneasy. A forcefulness behind the almost cheerful inquiry. I shook my head and she turned back to the gentleman, pulling something from her pocket as she did.

"I found this on him. Is it okay if I hang on to it? In case it's his next of kin?"

I looked at the picture she held up and sucked in a breath. In her hand was a photo of Annie.

"It's fine with me," the man said. "Like I said, I didn't know him."

She nodded. "She has such lovely red hair," she said, and tucked it back in her pocket. "Well, I'm sorry I didn't have better news." She gave us both a nod before disappearing down the hall.

"Well," the gentleman said, looking down at me. "That's that, I suppose. I'm sorry about your—" He caught himself. "About the young man."

I swallowed. "Thank you for trying to help him."

He touched my shoulder, and then ambled off down the hallway, leaving me to wonder how the hell I was going to tell Annie.

The walk back to the safe house was long, my body flush with emotion as I thought about Jan at the kitchen table this morning, teasing us in his usual fashion, some part of him touching Annie at all times. As unsure as I'd been about him in his early days on the team, my adoration for him grew quickly. He was the light we'd all needed when so often we were surrounded by darkness and doom. I remembered the night we'd all had to spend in a ditch after blowing up a train car, the Gestapo swarming the area moments after the sound of the explosion filled the air.

I would miss him and his jokes, his constant talk of food and music and the things he'd got up to as a boy.

But no one would miss him like Annie, and my heart ached as I knocked on the safe house door and waited to be let in.

"How's Annie?" I said as soon as Elif opened the door.

She shook her head. "Did you find him?" she asked.

I sighed and nodded.

"Oh no," she whispered.

I stepped into the entryway. "A man brought him to the hospital but..."

"But what?"

I jumped at the sound of Annie's voice and turned to see her standing in the doorway to the kitchen, her face blotchy and wet with tears.

"Annie—"

"No," she whispered, shaking her head. "Don't say it. Please don't say it."

"I'm so sorry, Annie. He didn't make it."

Her face crumpled and she slid to the floor, her slight body wracked with grief. Elif sat beside her and held her close. I sank into a chair at the table, my body cold as I listened to Annie cry, realizing what happened to Jan could happen to any of us. At any moment it could be me lying lifeless in that hospital. Or worse—Charlie or Elif.

My breath quickened as the fear I so often pushed aside filled me. Every moment we were out there, weapons hidden beneath our layers, information slipped beneath sleeves and tucked in our hair, throwing firebombs and tangling with men much larger than us, we were risking harm, jail, or death. We'd escaped it so many times, we'd become numb to the fact that it could happen to us. And now it had. One of our own was gone.

After a while, Elif helped Annie upstairs to the room she'd

shared with Jan. When she returned to the kitchen a few minutes later, she reported that Annie had fallen asleep.

"Good," I said, and motioned to the chair beside me. "There's
something else I didn't mention."

"What is it?"

"A nurse that helped with Jan told the gentleman who brought
him in that she found something in his pocket. It was a photo
of Annie."

"So?"

"There was something about her... She commented on her
hair. She asked if she could keep the picture, in case it was his
next of kin. The man said yes, and I didn't argue because I
thought it might seem suspicious."

"Damn," Elif said. "We should get out of here. What if you
were followed?"

We woke Annie, and an hour later the three of us were on
a train back to Haarlem. When we disembarked, we headed
straight for the Vox property and the barn.

"She'll need to go into hiding," Henrik said, glancing at
Annie, who was sitting on the sofa staring unseeing across the
room. "Color her hair, stay out of sight. At least for a while."

"Where will she go?" I asked.

"Liv will work it out. She'll be fine here for now, though."
The look of sadness in his eyes belied the gruff rumble of his
voice, and for the first time I saw what Mama had always talked
about in regards to her old friend. "You two should get out of
here now. Before you worry your mother."

We took turns hugging Annie. She'd always seemed so tough.
So untouched by the things we did. But this...

"I'm so sorry, Annie," I said. "Take care, okay? Be safe."

I stepped away and Elif took my place, murmuring into her
friend's ear and holding her as she began to cry again.

"We'll see each other soon," she said as she pulled away.

As we made our way through the field to the dirt road that ran behind the Vox property, I looked at my sister.

"Do you think she'll be okay?" I asked.

I couldn't imagine recovering if Charlie died. And if anything ever happened to my sister... I shuddered at the thought.

Elif linked her arm through mine and pulled me closer. "Will any of us be after all this is over?"

27

With Jan gone and Annie in hiding for the time being, the demands on Elif, Charlie, and me increased.

Throughout spring and into summer, it seemed we were constantly on the move; hiding, passing information and weapons, setting explosives, and acting as executioners without trial for the accused.

I began spending more nights with Charlie. Each moment in his arms was that much sweeter, that much more frightening, as I began to cling, committing to memory the way he lazily traced the curves of my body with his fingertips before desire swept over him and his touch became greedier, how his legs felt intertwined with mine, and the feel of his chest rising and falling beneath my hands as he lay spent beside me. The realization that what we had was special—and could be gone with one shot fired from someone's gun haunted me. And I could tell he felt it too. He held me longer, closer, stared more intently, and kissed me with the sort of desperation born from fear.

As summer slid away and fall returned, rumors of an imminent attack by the Allies bolstered Nazi efforts to defend what they'd taken. Areas in the northern part of the city were evacuated, the displaced roaming for somewhere to harbor, and the stadium the professional football team played in was leveled to make way for a defensive line.

In the southern part of the city, a wall called Mauer-Muur was built in Haarlemmerhout Park, and several checkpoints cropped up all over town, making getting in and out and around the city more difficult and dangerous than ever.

The most unnerving part was how the streets cleared. Thousands of Dutch collaborators throughout the country, we learned, had packed up and left for Germany. But in the end, it was all for naught when the rumored attack by the Allies turned out to be true and the mission failed, disappointment blanketing Haarlem with a heaviness it was hard to get out from under.

Annie returned to the fold in early October, but she wasn't the same. The feistiness had all but gone out of her without Jan around to tease and goad her, and her determination to do well on missions became less urgent and more careless, because she, it turned out, cared less. I understood in my own way. Though I hadn't cared about Diederik, the loss of a life of someone you knew was a shock to the system. The three of us rallied around her, trying to keep her spirits up and her mind focused, and being extra vigilant for the times she wasn't.

With continued Ally attacks, more German soldiers were brought in constantly to fortify defenses. A railway strike called for by the Dutch government in exile in London worked for a while to keep them out, but the Nazis just reacted by using their own trains—and retaliated by stopping all inland shipping—a move that brought our meager food supplies to a standstill.

And then they took our electricity away.

As fall limped its way toward winter, it was clear to all that it would be a tougher one than usual to get through, as temperatures had already begun to drop to record lows.

By November shipping had resumed, but the canals and rivers had frozen over, making it impossible for the boats to take food to the towns as the coldest winter in my nineteen years descended upon us.

Our only saving grace, as we scoured our cupboards for something we might've missed, was Aunt Liv. A week before *Sinterklaas*, a plain wooden box arrived with a note: *Wishing you all well. Stay safe. In good health. Olivia.*

Inside was a tiny brisket, potatoes, carrots, brown beans, a sachet of dried herbs, oats, a tin of tea, and most precious of all, two small bags of flour and sugar, and a bit of butter.

"Butter," Elif said, grabbing it and holding it to her chest. "Can we make bread?"

"We most certainly can," Mama said.

We ended up making three small loaves, one for us, and two for our neighbors on either side. One, an older couple who used to watch us when we were girls, and the other, a family of five suffering greatly with too little for so many. Any extras we had always went to them, and it was a thrill to be able to bring them a pot of hot soup and bread with butter.

But while we survived on Aunt Liv's charity, circumstances for others in town became more desperate. Hundreds of women packed up their silver and whatever else they owned and took perilous treks to the country in hopes of trading for food. But by then, many of the farmers had already traded so much of what they'd produced, people were turned away, many to die on their way home, their malnourished bodies frozen where they fell.

Stores were broken into as people looked to steal whatever they could find. The shots that rang out came daily now, soldiers not bothering with imprisoning people, but rather executing them in the streets where they stood.

By the time *Sinterklaas* came that year, it was clear many of us wouldn't make it to spring. Starvation was imminent for many, disease rampant, and freezing temperatures exacerbated it all. There would be no celebration this year. There was nothing to celebrate. Even the fact you were still alive wasn't necessarily something to be grateful for when there was no food to be had.

On Christmas Day, Charlie came over and he, Elif, mother, and I passed the time by playing card games on the floor in front of a fire made from what was left of the dining room table. We were bundled in coats and scarves beneath our blankets, trying to distract ourselves from the hunger we felt as we'd saved our allotment of food for the day to have for dinner.

While Charlie kept the fire going, Elif cut the few spindly carrots we'd saved and I sifted through the potatoes, finding five decent-sized ones and cutting off the moldy bits. Mama pulled the plates from the cupboard and a bottle of wine from its hiding place beneath a floorboard.

"I think we could all use a little of this," she said, removing the cork.

We ate our meal in front of the fireplace, telling stories of Christmases past and laughing as we recalled the worst gift we'd ever received from a distant relative, the alcohol warming us from the inside and turning our cheeks and noses pink.

"I wish we had dessert," Elif said, reclining on the floor in front of the sofa she slept on at night.

"Oh!" Charlie said, getting to his feet. "I almost forgot."

He hurried from the room, disappearing into the foyer, and returning a moment later with the bag he'd brought. Inside was a can of sweetened condensed milk.

"Wherever did you get it?" I asked, picking it up and marveling at the mere sight of something that had once been a staple in our home.

"It was in a small box of food Alard delivered."

Mama poured it equally into four teacups and then we sat once more in front of the fire and slowly spooned the creamy liquid into our mouths, savoring the taste of something sweet on our tongues, each of us lost in our own thoughts.

When the fire was nearly out, we piled blankets on the floor for Charlie and climbed onto our sofas. By candlelight, Mama read us the same Christmas story she'd been reading since we were babies, and as we'd done then, we fell asleep to the comforting sound of her voice, my fingers intertwined with Charlie's, the roar of planes flying overhead through the darkened skies.

In the coldest January I could remember, I hurried through town running errands. First to the sewing shop to retrieve supplies for Mama, who was now working from home doing small repairs by hand for whoever needed her services, which wasn't many people these days. And second to Aunt Liv's to deliver some information I'd received the day before.

There were few people out, the temperatures dangerously low. Even the soldiers were scarce now.

I passed a man prying the windowsills from the front of his house. Beside him on the ground were several shutters he'd already removed. As I approached, he stepped in front of his belongings, the tool in his hand ready to strike if need be. I lowered my head and hurried past.

He wasn't the only one I'd seen scavenging for wood to burn. A few days before I'd seen two young boys removing street signs from town. Several homes and businesses were missing their roofing material. And the wooden benches from the park had been broken down and carried away, many of the trees chopped down, their foliage gathered.

I let myself into the shop, and grabbed one of the small fabric bags hanging on a hook in the back room and filled it with the thread colors my mother had asked for, as well as a box of straight pins and another of needles of different sizes. When I had everything she'd asked for, I locked up and headed for the Vox residence.

I didn't notice the smoke until I was almost to the front gate of the grand house. I stopped and stared, not understanding at first why the hazy air was thick with acrid plumes blowing in the wind.

"Lien."

I turned and frowned in confusion at the sight of Charlie disguised as an old man, hiding not far away, gesturing for me to come closer.

"Get down before they see you," he said.

I looked past the gate at the estate where several military vehicles were parked in the driveway, men in uniforms going in and out the front door. Two of the upstairs windows were smashed, black smoke billowing out. A chill went up my spine, and I ran to where Charlie was.

"Aunt Liv," I said quickly. "Is she inside? Do they have her?"

He shook his head. "I got here a few minutes before you. I haven't seen her or Alard... I've no idea if they're inside. If someone else is responsible and these guys came to help. Or if she was found out and—" He stopped, his eyes meeting mine.

"Don't say it," I said, staring in horror at the house. "What do we do?"

"The barn?" he asked.

"Do you think Henrik's in there?" It was highly possible Liv's brother had no idea what was happening at the main house. In the basement of the barn it was hard to hear anything outside. "Maybe Liv is with him. Should we go around the back?"

At Charlie's nod we extricated ourselves from the shrubbery and hurried down the street to the path that cut through a wooded area between the Vox residence and the home next door. We kept low until we reached the dirt road that ran behind the property, then pushed through the gate and made our way to the rear of the barn.

From our hiding spot we could see the greenhouse was smashed in, the plants inside brown and lifeless from the bitter cold. Beyond it the back doors of the house stood open, smoke seeping out, the wind sweeping it across the yard.

"Come on," Charlie said, taking my hand and edging us along the side of the barn.

When he reached the corner he stopped, his grip tightening, his body tense. He turned to look at me, his eyes filled with an expression I'd become familiar with the past couple of years. It was a warning. One I couldn't heed. I inhaled, and as I breathed out, I peeked around Charlie and the corner of the barn.

Nothing could've prepared me for the sight of Henrik lying in the grass, his already bent body twisted in a pool of blood, his head at an odd angle, his neck slit. Beyond him, near the gate to the backyard, was another body. At first I couldn't tell who it was, but then I saw the tie of the apron blowing in the wind. Elke.

I whimpered and my knees buckled, threatening to collapse beneath me.

"We need to get out of here," Charlie said.

"But Aunt Liv..."

"Lien—"

"Charlie."

My voice was small. Desperate. My eyes filled with tears. I knew it was too late. If she were alive, the others would be too.

Charlie's hand tightened in mine, and I nodded. It was time to go. We weren't safe here any longer.

With a last look at the house, I followed him across the pasture and out the gate to the dirt road beyond. As we walked, my hand in his, vision blurred, I wondered the same thing I had so many times before. Was this the end we'd all find? Was death the price we would pay for standing up for what we believed to be true and just?

In our pursuit of righting the wrongs inflicted by others, I'd often considered the consequences for being one of the "good" guys. Winning didn't always mean a life lived after the fight was over. Perhaps, like so many soldiers who had fallen already, I was just another name to one day be forgotten. Just one more body to be buried.

28

Aunt Liv's death left us all gasping a little for breath. It wasn't just that she'd provided food, it was her calming sense of clarity. She was always able to see beyond what was in front of us. Before wealth had cloaked her knowledge of how cruel life could be beneath fur and jewels, she too had spent time in ditches and hiding in plain sight. She knew what we were only just learning. The lessons that would follow us. The wisdom and skills we would glean if we only paid attention…and stayed alive.

With her death also came fear. Were we now in danger? Could the men at the grand residence trace us back here? Aunt Liv had always been so careful, using the fake names on our forged identification papers. But what if it hadn't been enough? What if someone had talked? What if one of the kitchen staff had spilled our real identities in the hope they'd be spared?

"We'll need to be extra careful now," Mama said. "Don't go out alone if it can be helped. Always be armed."

"What about our missions?" Elif asked. "Are we— Is this done?"

"I imagine Frans will put someone in place to continue what

Liv was doing. Until then, though, I want you both to stay inside as much as possible. *Please.* I can't lose you girls. I just can't."

Her voice broke, and I hurried to her and wrapped my arms around her shoulders. We'd always been in danger, and she'd always known this. But the death of our beloved aunt, a woman who had survived more than we could fathom, brought the fear to the surface. Made it real in a way it hadn't been before. We were all vulnerable. And we might not all make it out of this war alive.

Elif's eyes met mine. She blinked back tears, but I was numb. The news the day before from Charlie, who had been able to get information from one of Aunt Liv's neighbors, had left me shaken, my mind paralyzed in a carousel of terrible thoughts about what her last moments had been like. She'd been found beaten and tied to her bed, a single shot to her head.

"And the others?" Mama had asked, her voice low.

Charlie had glanced at me before answering. "Alard was shot in the doorway, three staff members were found locked in the pantry—all shot to death. And then, as Lien must have told you, Elke and Henrik—"

Mama held up her hand and nodded. She didn't need to hear again.

"Can I do anything?" he asked.

Mama wiped a tear from her cheek and took a long, deep breath. "There's nothing to be done now," she said. "We'll wait to hear from Frans. Until then, the three of you and Annie are to stay out of sight as much as possible."

"I have a piece of information that needs to be delivered," Charlie said.

"When?"

"Today."

She sighed but nodded wearily. "Be quick about it, then come back here. You're welcome to stay with us as long as you want.

Without Liv to pay rent or supply food…and then your room-mate…" She gave him a sad smile.

His roommate, who worked within another cell of the Resis-tance, had failed come home the week before and he still hadn't heard if he'd been taken, or was dead. The absence of the other man weighed on him, and he'd grown anxious, losing sleep as every sound put him on edge.

"You're very kind," he said. "Thank you."

"You're family, Charlie. No thanks needed."

Uncle Frans did not show up the next day, or even the one after that, but word arrived via courier in a telegram addressed to mother, his familiar scrawl all we needed as identification.

"What's it say?" Elif and I asked, rising from where we sat playing a card game with Charlie.

"'My Dears,'" she read. "'My condolences. I am unable to visit as hoped. Please take care in my absence. Be mindful of one another. And remember to treat time with care.'"

I frowned and looked at Elif, whose expression mirrored mine.

"What does he mean?" I asked. "Treat time with care?"

"It's a code," Charlie said, getting up from his seat. "May I?"

Mama handed over the letter, and I watched as his blue eyes scanned the words.

"Time is spelled with a capital *T*," he said, holding up the page for us to see.

"But what could he mean?" Mama asked.

"Time," Elif murmured, tapping a finger against her chin. "Time… Oh!" Her eyes were bright as she took us all in. *"Time."*

I shook my head, not understanding.

"The watch shop. The Ten Booms. We know they've been in-volved for years. I'll bet he means for us to connect with them."

"Elif," Mama said, reaching for her hand, "you're brilliant."

She blushed and shrugged. "You all would've gotten it even-tually."

"Very clever indeed," Charlie said, giving her a nod and making her turn a deeper shade of red. "The Ten Booms. We'll have to check in first thing tomorrow."

The freezing temperatures only intensified, and it was no longer surprising to come across bodies frozen in alleyways, the park, and on the way out to the farmlands. Women, their bodies emaciated from a diet of food scraps and tulip bulbs, stopped on the side of the road for a moment of rest and found they couldn't go on. Too tired to open their eyes again, too weak to call for help, the frost of their last breath settling on their lips and skin, freezing them where they sat, turning them into beautiful statues glistening with death.

Homes went up in flames when owners built fires and fell asleep, their bodies too worn from starvation and cold to see the spark that jumped from the fireplace, catching on a blanket or a rug and sending the whole place up, sometimes taking the neighbors' homes with it.

Missions, assigned directly from Uncle Frans now, became harder and harder to carry out. Safe houses had been discovered, leaving fewer places to hide. If we had a job that needed to take place after dark, we risked being left in the cold for the night. It had happened to me twice, and the second time, after taking cover in a woodshed and its family of mice, I lost my little toe to frostbite.

I was sleeping late one morning, dressed in three layers of clothes and buried beneath a pile of blankets, when I woke to the front door slamming shut. Thinking it was a gunshot, I was instantly on my feet, my pistol in my hand.

"It's me," Elif said, coming around the corner and stopping in her tracks, arms raised.

"I thought I heard a gun," I said.

"It was the door. Sorry."

Shaking, from cold or fear, I couldn't be sure which, I sat and stowed my pistol back under the sofa.

"Where's Mama?" she asked.

"Checking the garden," I said.

Most everything was frozen or dead, but every so often we checked in case there was a small miracle. We'd found a beet one day that had somehow been missed in months previous. It was buried, but as Elif used a small shovel to dig into the frozen ground, its round head had shown itself and she'd given a shout and ran inside with it.

"Is everything okay?" I asked my sister as I climbed back under the bedding.

"No," she said, and opened the back door to call to our mother.

"What is it?" Mama asked as she came inside, shut the door, and moved the bookcase back into place in front of it.

"The Ten Booms was raided last night. Casper, Betsie, Corrie, and a slew of others were arrested."

"Oh no," Mama said. "How did you find out?"

"People were talking about it in line."

Mama glanced toward the kitchen, momentarily distracted by the thought of food. "Was there bread today?"

Elif shook her head.

"Did anyone happen to hear where the family was taken?"

"No," Elif said. "I tried asking discreetly but—"

A pounding on the door startled us, and we all grabbed for our weapons.

"Stay here," Mama said, and hurried to the door.

I glanced at Elif who stood ready with her gun on the other side of the wall from the foyer while I'd taken cover behind the sofa our mother slept on, prepared to shoot whoever came through the doorway.

But a moment later Mama returned with Charlie, who had been gone since the day before on a job with Annie. He looked ravaged. Delirious almost. He couldn't stop moving, flexing and clenching his fists.

"They've got her," he said.

"They have who?" Elif asked.

But I knew from the look on her face she knew. We all knew.

"Annie," he said.

"What happened?" Mama asked.

"We had to go through the checkpoint at Mauer-Muur. The place was swarming with soldiers. It was like they were looking for someone or on a mission to gather anyone and everyone they could for no reason at all. There was a truck there half filled with people when we arrived." He ran a hand through his hair. "We split up to be safe. She went ahead of me. She insisted, and I didn't think anything of it. Everyone had to go through regardless. We were just two more faces, and with her hair dyed, I knew she didn't stand out more or less than anyone else. But then I heard a shout, and they were dragging her from the line. She didn't even…"

I'd only seen Charlie get emotional a few times since we'd known one another. The first time after receiving a letter from his sister in America. They had always been close and having not seen her in years, he was suddenly hit with a wave of homesickness reading about her life there.

"It seems silly to say I'm homesick," he'd said. "I've never lived there. It's them I miss. The home I had with them."

The other two times were when we told him Jan had died, and after the attack on the Vox property. Like they were to us, Aunt Liv and her brother had been special to Charlie. They'd taken care of him in place of his real family, and the loss left a hole in all our hearts.

As he stood beside me now, his hand in mine, his face ashen as if he was watching Annie being taken all over again, a single tear rolled down his cheek.

"She didn't even what?" I asked.

His sigh was a shudder and he shook his head. "She didn't even look back at me."

"She didn't want them to know she wasn't alone." Mama's voice was quiet.

"Can we find out where they took her?" Elif asked.

"We should have someone on the inside. Hopefully we'll hear something."

"Dammit," I whispered.

"I should go," Charlie said.

"What? Where?" I asked, clinging to his hand now. I didn't want him to go back out there. Disguise or not, it wasn't safe. Especially not now.

"I still have to deliver the information I have." He kissed my head. "There's a contact that might be able to get it out for me. Don't worry. I should be back soon."

As he adjusted his wig once more, he turned back to the three of us.

"Don't ask around trying to find out where Annie is. The more people asking, the more likely they'll figure out who she is and that we're connected to her. If they haven't already."

He kissed me then and left.

We were restless after he departed, wandering around the downstairs picking up and folding blankets, dusting, rearranging dishes. After a while, Elif and I went upstairs. We'd been slowly going through the things in our room, making piles of what we no longer wanted, clothes that didn't fit that could be given away or repurposed, their stitches torn out, the material used to make blankets or clothes for smaller children in the neighborhood should the electricity ever come back on and Mama was able to use her sewing machine again.

Charlie arrived before curfew, out of breath from having delivered what he needed to. And while he built a bigger fire, using the wood from Madi's old bedroom door, we gathered what we could for dinner.

The following day word came that Annie was in the city jail. A week later we found out she'd been transferred to a prison in Amsterdam.

"At least she hasn't been sent to one of the camps," Elif said.

But I wasn't sure if prison was the better option. Prison was where they tortured people for information, and Annie had a lot. Names of Resistance members to start with.

Throughout the next weeks there was a lot of whispered conversations circulating through the underground about trying to break her out. A couple of guards at the prison were double agents, and the hope was to come up with a plan to sneak in a wig and pretend she was another prisoner being transferred. Once they smuggled her out, she'd be brought to a safe house.

The day it was planned for we sat inside our home, no one talking, barely daring to breathe as we waited to hear that she'd been safely transferred out and was free. Unfortunately, they'd made the plan for a day too late. Or at least several hours too late. When they arrived for their scheduled shifts, she'd already been removed from her cell and the grounds.

Uncle Frans arrived to deliver the news himself that evening.

"She was taken out to the dunes," he said. "They shot her there."

Beside me, Charlie's head bowed as Mama gasped and Elif's sorrowful moan filled the room, leaving me hollow with grief for our spirited redheaded friend.

29

By April, the only positive news we had was the warming of the weather. The canals had thawed and food, though still painfully scarce, was more plentiful than it had been. Especially with the shorter ration lines, as hundreds had perished during the worst of the winter months, leaving Haarlem to feel a bit like a ghost town.

The electricity was still turned off, the nights still cold, but the days were comfortable enough now that we didn't have to walk around our own homes beneath several layers of clothing anymore. And with the return of spring, vegetables began to sprout in the garden.

I was pulling weeds out back, while Charlie, who had officially moved in with us, read in father's old favorite chair with the door open so we could chat. Elif returned from the sewing shop, where she'd gone with Mama earlier in the day to open the doors and give the space a good cleaning. And to check for any job requests delivered for us through the secret slot in the back door.

"We need to go to Amsterdam," she said quietly, glancing at the homes around us as she handed me the note she'd retrieved.

I read it over quickly and handed it to Charlie, who frowned as he looked at it and then handed it back to Elif. Another family needed to be moved. There were rumors someone was hiding Jews in the neighborhood they were in, and they needed to get out before they were found.

"Why can't they just leave them alone," I whispered, yanking a weed from the soil and throwing it in the pile I'd made.

But if they hadn't by now, I knew they never would. Not unless they were made to stop. And while we heard of small successes by the Allies almost daily now, the end of the war still seemed to be a long time away.

We arrived in Amsterdam the following afternoon, changed into our disguises at the safe house, and hurried back out to reach our destination.

"That one there," Elif said with a discreet nod. "Four down, red brick, white front door."

I looked up and down the street. "There's five of them?" I asked.

"Dad, mom, and three kids. I think we should split them up."

I nodded my agreement. Five people plus us would stand out these days. Splitting up and reconvening at the next location would be safest.

"There are fewer soldiers about than I expected," Elif said.

There were two pairs, one to each side of the street, neither walking particularly fast or with purpose.

"Do you think it's a trick?" Elif asked, peering at the two soldiers walking our way, chatting and almost casual looking. "Trying not to worry anyone so they'll let their guards down?"

"Seems like it. Let's go around back and have a look."

We crossed the street and turned down a narrow pathway that led to the green area behind the rows of houses. Little yards with gardens, wrought-iron benches beneath trees newly green with the budding of spring, marked the back side of each home. It was obvious it had once been pretty, but neglect had created overgrowth, and trash that was usually taken away was piled in corners and spilling out onto doorsteps and pathways.

We walked along the center path that separated one row of properties from the other, slowing as we passed the house the family was in, and taking in any details that stood out before exiting through the other end where we turned back down *Willemsparkweg* so we could walk by the front once more.

We passed two of the soldiers, but they didn't bother to look at the two old women we were disguised as.

At the corner we stepped out of sight and watched to see what the men did next. Were they patrolling this street or merely walking through? At the opposite corner, they turned and disappeared down the next street.

"What do you think?" Elif asked. "Come back tomorrow?"

"Come back tonight," I said, my eyes narrowed as I looked at the house. "Then tomorrow as well."

For the next twenty-four hours, we watched the house on *Willemsparkweg*. Sometimes together, sometimes on our own, switching out clothing, changing hairstyles, wearing glasses and not. Sometimes we carried shopping bags, other times we pulled a small wagon filled with random items from the safe house.

We kept a list of things we noticed; soldiers seen, how many of them, times they appeared, times they seemed to go through a changing of the guard, citizens out and about, and so on. We listened and we watched as best we could, and then we went back to the safe house to set our plan.

The following day, after checking our weapons and the forged documents we had for each member of the family, we were ready.

There was no set time for when they were to expect us, but we decided a midday hiding in plain sight strategy would be best.

We could split into three groups, one parent taking one child, Elif going with the other parent and child, and me with the last kid. It was a beautiful day, and people would be out more than usual, trying to enjoy the fresh air and the sun on their faces.

We were dressed as ourselves for the job. Young, wide-eyed women with plaited hair and shabby clothes. We looked like no one and everyone, which was exactly the point. I checked my pistol one last time, put it in the inside pocket of my coat, and nodded.

We arrived at the corner of *Willemsparkweg* separately. Elif went first and headed to the back of the row of houses. A few minutes later I walked down the street, eyes focused on the ground, just a timid young woman on her way to see a friend. As I passed the two soldiers we'd seen the day before, one glanced at me while the other didn't even bother. Breathing a sigh of relief, I continued down the sidewalk and up the steps of the house where I stepped out of sight beneath the brick arch of the porch and knocked.

The lock clicked and the door opened a crack.

"Yes?" the elderly woman on the other side asked.

"I'm here for a delivery," I said.

Her eyes widened slightly at the words, and she opened the door and let me in. As soon as the door shut and locked behind me, she rang a little bell sitting on a table in the entryway.

"My sister should be at that back door," I said.

"Come then," she said, and led me through the house to the back where she undid several locks and peeked out.

"I'm here for a delivery," I heard my sister say. A moment later we were standing in a small, dimly lit kitchen together.

Like everywhere else, all the curtains were drawn, the only light inside coming from some well-placed candles.

"Why don't you have a seat," the woman said. "They'll be down shortly."

Elif sat, but I couldn't. My body was filled with adrenaline.

I wanted to get on with it. Of all the jobs we did, this was the one I liked the least. Seducing men and leading them to their deaths was easy. Throwing firebombs was a bit of a thrill. But moving humans in broad daylight…the margin of error was terrifying. The potential body count horrific.

I heard a shuffle in the hall and stood taller. A man entered the room, and I could hear his intake of breath.

"Lien?" he said.

I recognized the voice but couldn't place it and took a step forward, gasping when he too took a step, his face coming into the light.

"Mr. Aberman," I whispered.

My beloved teacher pulled me into a hug. A sob caught in my throat as his familiar scent filled my nose. How often I'd thought of this kind man and his family, wondering where they had ended up, fearing the worst. Seeing him now, my heart nearly burst from happiness and relief. He was alive. Tired and worn, his face having aged since we last saw one another. But then, what must he think of me? I was clearly not the same girl he had known only years before. My arms no longer carried schoolbooks and notes for friends. They were scarred from fire, fingernails in constant need of cleaning, weapons hidden beneath my clothing. Could he even see the girl I used to be? Did she exist any longer?

He let me go and turned to give Elif a hug.

"Have you been here all this time?" I asked.

"No," he said. "We went south first and stayed with a couple different friends. Then north. Landed here at the end of last year. We try not to stay too long in any one place. We even separated for a while. I took the older kids while Rachel took the little one. We're hoping this next stop is the last one." He smiled at the old woman. "Lotte here has been a wonderful hostess, but we've put her in danger for long enough."

"I just can't believe it's you," I said. "I wondered and hoped and—"

"Oh my goodness."

I turned at the sound of Rachel's voice.

"Are you girls—" She looked at her husband who nodded. "But—surely the two of you aren't the ones taking us...are you?"

"We are," Elif said, getting to her feet. "We've been doing this work for years now, so please just trust us and we'll do our best to get you where you need to go."

Mrs. Aberman hugged her then, and when it was my turn, she held fast, a sob shaking the two of us.

"I just can't believe it," she said with a soft smile.

Just then a little girl with a head of dark curls hurried into the room and hurled herself into her father's arms.

"Is that Bo?" I asked.

"It is," Mr. Aberman said.

The two older kids entered the room next. They were nearly as tall as me now and I smiled at them, wondering if they'd recognize me.

"Lien?" Lara said, taking a hesitant step toward me. At my nod, she launched herself at me. "I thought I'd never see you again." She looked up at me, her eyes bright with tears. A moment later Isaak joined us.

"Who that?" Bo asked from her father's arms.

"That's—"

"Grietje," Elif said, her face suddenly serious.

I sobered. "Right. For this I'm Grietje. And this is Fern." I pointed to my sister.

"And you're the Clarks," Elif said, pulling their forged registration booklets from inside her coat.

I checked my watch. "I wish we could talk longer, but we have a small window when the soldiers out front switch with two others and it would be great if we could avoid walking directly past any of them."

"How will we do this?" Mr. Aberman asked. "We're such a large group."

"We'll split up," Elif said. "Each parent with one of the two younger kids and then one of us with Isaak, the other with one of you. One group out the front, the other two out the back within minutes of each other. We'll make our way across the park separately, and meet at the new residence. You are to take nothing with you. Your belongings will be brought to you later. Hopefully no one will even notice us. We'll just be people out for a late afternoon stroll at the end of a beautiful spring day."

Elif and I excused ourselves then to take a look out both the front and back. Lotte followed me.

"They're good people," she said.

"I know," I said, and unlocked the back door to have a look outside.

There was a couple sitting on their patio two doors down, but other than them, the space was empty. I shut the door.

"Are you family?" I asked, and she shook her head. "Well then, it's good of you to take them in."

"This is what I do," she said.

I nodded in understanding. This was what I did too.

Elif and I returned to the kitchen and found five expectant faces looking back at us.

"Put this on," Elif said to Mrs. Aberman, handing her the blond wig she'd stuffed in her coat.

Lotte stood in the hallway as we filed out and kissed each of the Abermans—or Clarks—on the head as they passed. "God-speed," she whispered.

Elif led Isaak to the front door, and his parents both rushed to hug him.

"Listen to Elif—I mean Fern," his dad said. "She'll do her best to keep you safe."

Isaak nodded, giving his parents a solemn look.

"Okay?" Elif said to him, her hand on his arm.

"Okay," he said.

She turned to me and our eyes met and held. I squeezed mine shut in a double wink that she returned, and a moment later they were gone.

I led the others to the back door.

"I'll go with Mr. Aberman," I said, smiling at Bo, who sat secure in her father's arms before looking to Rachel. "You follow a minute later with Lara. Stay at a distance, look like you're out enjoying the day. Smile. Don't look around too much. Follow us to the park. Once we get there, if no one is following us, we should be in the clear the rest of the way."

She nodded and pulled Lara closer to her before tilting her head up to kiss her husband and then Bo.

"Be good for Daddy, little one," she said, choking back a sob as she then met her husband's eyes. "Be careful."

"Stay close," he said, and kissed her again. "It's going to be okay."

I squeezed Rachel's hand, gave Lara a quick hug, took a breath, and opened the door.

"Let's go," I said, and turned the knob to the back door.

It was quiet as we walked through Lotte's garden to the pathway splitting the two rows of homes. From the houses around us came the faint sounds of their residents moving about inside. I ducked my head and kept walking.

When we reached the corner we stopped, leaning into the brick wall of the building beside us as we watched Elif and Isaak cross the street heading away from us. When they made it to the other side safely, I gave a quick look behind me to where Rachel and Lara were just starting our way, and then signaled to Mr. Aberman that it was time to move.

As we crossed the street, a woman with a heavily made up face came toward us, crossing in the other direction. She glanced at me. Then Mr. Aberman. Then Bo. Her eyes moved past us and focused on something else, narrowing as though trying to get a better look—or wanting to be sure. As soon as she passed us, I reached up and tugged on Mr. Aberman's sleeve.

"Be ready to run," I whispered.

A moment later a high-pitched shout split the air. "That's them!"

"Go!" I said, and turned to see Rachel and Lara stopped at the corner behind us, their eyes wide as they stared at the woman pointing at them, not knowing what to do. "Run!" I yelled.

Our feet were like thunder on the cobblestones as we raced toward the park, Mrs. Aberman and Lara close on our heels. I could see Elif and Isaak already toward the middle of the lawn, Elif keeping her wits about her and not calling attention to them by breaking out in a run as well.

A shot rang out. Then another. Both hit the building beside me, sending a spray of brick into the air. I turned my head away as I was showered with debris. Bo whimpered in her daddy's arms.

"It's okay, sweetheart," he whispered as we ran harder, leaving the city and entering the park.

Another shot. Dirt exploding near Mr. Aberman's foot as the bullet missed its target.

I pulled my gun from my pocket.

"Go," I said. "Get to Elif. I'll catch up."

I turned and planted my feet, pistol raised, waving at Mrs. Aberman and Lara to keep going. As they passed by, the soldier running at me paused, momentarily confused. Should he shoot mother and daughter or the young woman aiming a weapon at his chest? While he wrestled with the decision, I took the shot and watched as his body jerked back, his legs slowed and buckled, the shock in his eyes fading as he fell.

But the soldiers coming up behind him got me moving again. I took another shot, hitting the next guy in the leg. He stumbled and fell as I spun and took off in a sprint to catch up with the others.

"Head for the trees," I shouted between breaths as I caught up to the group, indicating to where I'd just seen Elif and Isaak disappear.

It was getting dark. Between that and the cover of trees ahead, I would have a better chance at liquidating as many soldiers as I could while Mr. Aberman and his family kept going. But by the increasing volume of their footsteps behind me, I could tell they were gaining ground. We needed to move faster.

"Hurry," I shouted.

I heard a shot and then a grunt beside me followed by a muffled scream.

"No!" I said, watching Bo fall from her father's arms and tumble to the ground.

"Bo!" Rachel screamed, reaching for the little girl.

"I've got her," I said. "Help him."

"Samuel!" she said, reaching for him with one hand, the other one still in Lara's while I scooped up Bo.

"It's just my arm," he said.

"Keep going," I said.

Elif waited ahead of us, and I saw that she'd sent Isaak on. He stood half-hidden behind an overflowing trash bin on the other side of the park, watching his family run for their lives. We were so close. Just a little farther, and Elif and I could join forces fending off the men gaining ground behind us.

Gunfire.

"Duck!" I shouted, curling myself around Bo like a shield, her little body bouncing in my arms, her breath coming in huffs in my ear, hands grasping at the plaits in my hair.

Another shot. The dirt beside me exploded. Another one and a chunk of tree splintered off and landed in our path.

The next shot came from in front of us, and I stumbled and slowed. Were we surrounded?

"Come on!" a man yelled. "Hurry!"

I peered through the dimming light, not understanding what

was happening and confused at the familiarity of the voice. And then he stepped into the clearing and I gasped.

Charlie.

As I wondered how he'd come to be there, I began to falter, the little girl in my arms growing heavier by the second.

Mr. Aberman stumbled and fell, pulling Rachel with him, ripping her hand from Lara's, who screamed in panic. "Mama!"

As they scrambled to their feet another shot rang out. I didn't hear where it landed. Didn't understand the jolt of fire at my center as I shifted Bo on my hip, too distracted by the commotion, the sound of footfalls from behind and ahead of us, the shouting and gunfire coming from two different directions now.

I could see Charlie's face furrowed in concentration, and several feet away Elif and—I frowned—was that Uncle Frans? They each stood, guns in hands, motioning for us to keep coming. Keep moving. Don't stop now. Beyond them I saw Isaak being ushered into a car by another familiar face, one I'd seen in passing several times as we slipped notes to one another in the streets over the years.

Charlie's eyes met mine and I smiled, Bo slipping a little from my grasp. We were nearly there.

I saw Charlie begin to smile back, but then something else crossed his face as a deep burn filled my belly—a look of anguish as I began to lose my grip on Bo, who slid down my body to the ground. I tried to hold on, but my strength was melting away. I tripped over her, my knees buckling...my breath fading. I looked down, seeing now what Charlie had. A red stain growing across my abdomen.

"No," I whispered as pain ripped through my center. "Bo!"

I reached for the little girl again, yelling out as another bullet ripped through my shoulder.

My knees hit the ground hard and Charlie ran toward me, his

mouth open, shouting words I couldn't hear, a tunnel of black closing around him, until he was gone and the world finally and mercifully went quiet.

30

July 1945

The sun shone high in a cloudless sky, its rays sparking off shop windows. The few that were open barely had a thing to sell, trying to entice the happy-faced Canadian soldiers with the items they had left.

But for every shop that was able to open its doors, there were two more that couldn't. The Ten Boom watch and clock shop was closed. Several restaurants, as well as every flower market, the fields producing next to nothing this year with so many of the bulbs scavenged for sustenance during the winter, would probably not open until next year, if ever again.

Haarlem was an odd sight these days. Elated but ravaged faces walked the streets, looking for connections, old friends, and familiar sights and sounds. Our every emotion was quick to appear and overflow, too fragile to find an in-between space. Oftentimes people were seen crying as they spoke quietly on a corner, eyes darting, waiting…expecting…fearing it was all a joke. The Germans were coming back. Any minute the rumble of tanks on our cobbled streets would come, the strike of boots returning and shaking us to our cores.

But they didn't come. They never would again.

So much had been lost here. A way of life. A sense of security. Entire families.

I hadn't heard from Tess again. I prayed it didn't mean anything. I prayed I'd hear a knock on our door one day and find her on the other side. But the more time that passed, the less likely I knew it was that it would happen, and my grief made me fold in on myself some days, stealing my breath, crushing my heart.

I inhaled, breathing in the sacred scent of fresh bread from a nearby bakery. A gull called out to another overhead as a rare bicycle, its tires intact, glided by. And then a sound I hadn't heard in years stopped me in my tracks.

I rounded the corner to the square and stared up at the great old church, listening as her bells once more chimed inside her tower. Around me others stopped as well, their faces lifted, eyes filled with wonder and tears. How simple a thing, the toll of a bell. But its absence in the past five years had been resounding. Its full, round tones that had filled the streets and echoed warmly for miles missed more than we knew. I smiled as I looked around at all the people who had stopped to listen, and then continued on my way once more.

The handsome facade of the Aberman house was a welcoming sight. The curtains, closed for years, were thrown wide in every window now, letting the light, long kept out, pour inside.

I knocked on the door.

It had been three months since the attack in the park. Two months since the war had finally ended and the Germans and their collaborators had been sent home, jailed, or executed. In their place were large, handsome Canadian soldiers with chocolate bars in their pockets and an easy laugh. They'd swooped in near the end, driving the enemy finally, mercifully from our town and bringing truckloads of food.

Of course, I'd missed all of it, laid up in a hospital in Amsterdam recovering from two gunshot wounds, one to the shoulder, and one to my abdomen that had resulted in the removal of my uterus. I'd cried when I'd found out the Nazis' horrific war had taken away my chance to ever have children. But I knew so many who had lost so much more. Their homes, their livelihoods, their families, and in many cases, their lives.

There was a click, and then the door swung open and my favorite teacher stood before me.

"Lien," Mr. Aberman said, his voice soft, his face lighting up with a smile. "It's so good to see you. Come in. Please. How are you feeling? All healed up now?"

I stepped inside the familiar space, breathing in the smells of food cooking and the sounds of dishes clanking together in the kitchen.

"I feel okay," I said, running a hand across my stomach as I so often did now. Beneath the fabric of my shirt I could feel where the skin had been stitched, the still-red scar healing from where the bullet had entered my body.

"Rachel," he called, "look who's here."

Mrs. Aberman peeked around the corner, a pot and towel in her hand. She smiled, her eyes filling with tears as she brought the towel to her heart.

"Lien," she said, and rushed forward to give me a careful hug. "How are you, dear? You look well. Are you feeling okay?"

She led me to the kitchen table and put the kettle on for tea.

"I'm still sore, but the doctor says I'm healing."

"Good. And your mom and Elif? How are they?"

"Mama's back in the shop full-time, though it's a lot quieter than it was. But she loves it there. It's her space. And Elif is looking into attending university in the fall."

"And you?" Mr. Aberman asked. "What about your studies?"

It was an odd time for those of us who had been attending school when the war began. Many had continued to take classes as they could, where they could—until the teachers were no longer available or the kids were no longer able. But there were thousands like me who had stopped going altogether. It was hard to determine what to do with us. Return us to where we'd left off? Excuse the missing years and let us move on? Test and place us based on some sort of scoring system? Hadn't we all been tested enough?

But where did that leave us then?

"I'm not sure," I said. "I haven't thought about my future in a long time. The lessons I've learned in the past five years are not the ones I was expecting, and I'm not sure if they've served me, or hindered me in some way. I've done things..." My voice broke and I couldn't finish my sentence, which was just as well because Isaak and Lara came sprinting into the room then and threw themselves at me.

"Children," Mr. Aberman said. "Careful. Please. Lien is still healing."

"Sorry," they said, guilty looks passing over their excited faces.

"It's okay," I said, hugging them both in turn. "Goodness, I'm not sure I'll ever get used to the fact that you're both as tall as me."

"Taller," Isaak said with a smug grin.

I laughed and nodded.

"That you are. How are you both doing? Glad to be home?" I asked.

As they rattled off all the things they'd missed, Lara took my hand and led me outside to their garden where they'd spread out a blanket with books and a deck of cards scattered across it.

I smiled at the familiar sight. Despite all that had changed, they had stayed exactly who they were, and I was reminded once again of how resilient humans could be.

"Lien," Lara said, breaking through my thoughts, "are you okay?"

I sniffled and wiped my eyes. "Yes. I'm just so happy to see you all here again. In your home. I missed you."

"Will you ever sit for us again?" she asked.

"You might be too old for that now. Maybe I could just come over like I have today and visit?"

"Or we could go to the park," Isaak said. "Maybe we'll find another hurt bird."

I smiled. I'd forgotten about that bird. I wondered how he'd fared, or if he had perished like so many others in that park.

After a while I wandered back inside and found Rachel slicing up some fruit.

"I could hardly believe it when he brought it home," she said, her eyes wide as she pointed to the coveted apple. So many things were still scarce these days. Getting a piece of fruit felt like a small miracle.

"We had one last week," I said. "I swear I've never tasted one so sweet."

She held out a slice but I shook my head.

"Thank you. But I wouldn't dare deny someone a slice." I sighed then and looked around. "Is Bo...?"

Mrs. Aberman smiled. "She's upstairs in her room. She woke from a nap while you were outside."

"May I see her?"

"Of course." She wiped her hands on her apron. "Come on. She'll be happy to see you. We talk about you often."

"You do?"

"Oh yes. You're the girl that saved her life. She calls you her angel."

I paused on the steps, my breath catching in my throat.

Mrs. Aberman looked down at me. "Are you okay?"

"Yes." I forced a smile. "I'm fine."

We continued up the narrow staircase and stopped on the second-floor landing. To the right a door stood open, the sound of a small girl singing to herself floating into the hall.

"Look who's here," Mrs. Aberman said.

Bo looked up from the dolls she was playing with, her tumble of dark curls swinging along her shoulders.

"Hello there," I said.

"Hi," she said, her voice soft.

She wore a navy blue shirt with embroidered white flowers scattered across it and a pair of shorts.

"Do you remember me?" I asked.

"You're my angel. You had an accident." She pointed to my stomach.

"You're right. I did. You had one too." I pointed to her stomach.

She grinned and pulled up the front of her shirt, revealing a small pink scar that marked where the bullet that had ripped through me had lodged in her. Thankfully, my body had slowed the speed enough that her injury ended up being minimal, and she'd barely needed more than a few stitches, unlike me.

I untucked my blouse and lifted the hem, showing her my own pink scar. She stepped forward to get a closer look, and then reached out and touched her fingertips to the wound.

"We're the same!" she said, her eyes wide with delight as they met mine.

I looked to Mrs. Aberman, who squeezed my hand as I blinked back tears.

"We are the same," I whispered to Bo.

"Want to play?" she asked, holding out a doll.

I grinned. "I'd love to."

As I knelt, I reached into my pocket. "I have something for you actually."

Her brown eyes widened as she saw the little red bird in the palm of my hand.

"This was my sister Madi's favorite toy in all the world," I said. "She was in my pocket when you and I got hurt, and I fell on her, which made her get hurt too. See?" I pointed to a crack where the tail had broken off and been glued back on. "She can't be played with much now."

"Because her tail might fall off?" Bo asked.

"Exactly," I said. "But I thought maybe she could sit in your window and keep watch. If you want."

Very carefully, so as not to disturb the glued tail, Bo lifted the little bird from my hand. I watched as she climbed onto her bed and gently set it on the windowsill, its beak pointing out and up at the sky, watching—just as it had in Madi's so many years before.

Bo hopped back down and sat before me once more. She picked up the doll she'd been playing with and handed me another.

"Thank you," she said, her wide brown eyes meeting mine.

"You're welcome."

Mrs. Aberman left us then, and after a while, I returned downstairs to find the older kids still outside, and the elder Abermans preparing dinner.

"Did you have a nice time?" Mr. Aberman asked as I wandered into the kitchen.

"I did. Bo is so sweet," I said. "She doesn't even seem to be bothered by all that happened. And the older kids are sure happy."

"Kids are tougher than they look," he said. "We all are."

"Would you like to join us for dinner, Lien?" Mrs. Aberman asked as she set plates on the table.

"I'd love to, but I'm meeting Charlie," I said, pulling out a chair and taking a seat.

"Are you okay, dear?"

I glanced at husband and wife and saw them both watching me, eyebrows knit with worry. I sighed, my shoulders sagging, and sank farther into the chair. "I can't stop thinking about Madi lately," I said.

Mrs. Aberman set down the last plate and sat beside me,

reaching for my hand. Mr. Aberman sat across from us, giving me an encouraging smile.

"You nearly lost someone young again who you love," he said. "Of course you're reminded of Madi. I would be surprised if you weren't."

I nodded. "It's just... When I started all this—the work for the Resistance—I told myself I was doing it for her. To make up for not saving her. I would save others who needed help. That was the mission I told myself I was on. I would save them by killing the people who would see harm come to them." I squeezed my eyes shut, a menagerie of the faces I'd killed passing through my mind. "It was hard at first. Frightening. And then it got easier, and I started to forget why I was doing it. I became confident. Cocky. I forgot Madi. I forgot Tess. I started doing the job for me. It made me feel powerful. All these horrid men, lured by Elif, wanting to do terrible things to her. Wanting to do terrible things to anyone they could. Until I took their lives. I was proud. And then..."

I pulled in a shaky breath, and Mr. Aberman put his hand on top of the one his wife had linked with mine.

"And then what?" he asked, his voice soft.

"When I was in the hospital, I watched people taken from their beds never to return. Or I'd look over in the morning to find my latest neighbor had passed in the night and lay silent and still beside me. It didn't matter to me if they were Dutch or German, it was life. And life is precious. You can have it one moment, and the next you could slip and fall and hit your head, sliding beneath the water never to return to the surface." Tears spilled over and down my cheeks. "I can't stop thinking of the lives I've taken. I can't stop seeing their faces. Were people saved because of a life I took? How can I know for sure? Where is the documentation to prove it? Without it, I fear I'm no better than the other side. I set out to make a difference. To be the difference. But I don't feel as though I've done anything but prove ugliness and hatred comes in all shapes in sizes. And I hated them. I hated them for the people they tortured, the lives they took, and my country that they'd pillaged. But did their actions excuse mine?"

Mr. Aberman sighed and leaned back in his chair, running his hand along his jaw as he nodded thoughtfully.

"We've all had to make tough decisions during this war," he said. "War provides a devastating education, and there's no way to really know if the choices we make are the right ones at the time we have to make them. The fear I felt leaving our home in the middle of the night with my wife, two children, and a baby. The things that could've gone wrong... But I knew if we stayed, we'd be put on one of those trucks and who knew what we'd encounter or where we'd go. So we made the decision to flee, hoping and praying it was the correct one. But every day we wondered. Every day until we stepped foot back in our home. Lien, what you did. The choice you made...there may be no documentation to show how many lives you saved with your brave actions, but have no doubt—you saved lives. And there are at least five pieces of proof. Two are sitting at this table with you. You risked your own life for us. You used your own body as a shield for Bo. We were trapped in that house, and you risked everything to get us out. Thank God you were confident. Thank God you had all the experience behind you. We might not be here right now if not for you and Elif. We owe you *our* lives. And that alone should show you how right your choices were."

His eyes were full of tears now, and he wiped them on his sleeve and continued.

"I know Madi's death left you feeling like you were at fault. I know you've been struggling to make up for that every day since. But you weren't responsible, dear girl. You were never at fault for what happened to her. It was an accident, pure and simple. And you're not responsible for Tess being taken either.

Nor anyone else. None of this is your fault. It was war. And you were a soldier. A soldier defending her country. That's it."

I stared blindly down at my hand, enfolded in Mrs. Aberman's, my eyes blurred with tears.

"Madi would be so proud of you," Mr. Aberman said, his voice soft. "So would your father."

The tears spilled over then, and the two of them came around the table and wrapped their arms around me as I cried.

"Mama?"

We looked up to find Bo, Madi's red bird in her hand.

"Why sad?" she asked me.

"I miss my sister," I whispered, managing a small smile for the girl.

"Here," she said, and lifted the bird to my cheek where she softly pressed it into my skin. "She kisses you all better."

In an instant I was thirteen again, sitting at the dining table while my mother placed a bandage on the knee I'd scraped and bloodied. Madi ran in the back door to check on me, little red bird in hand.

"Here," she said, lifting the bird's beak to my cheek. "Kisses to make you feel better."

I pulled Bo to me and hugged her gently.

"Thank you, Bo," I said.

The telephone rang then, and Mr. Aberman rushed off to answer it as Bo ran off, calling for her siblings.

"It rings almost ten times a day now," Mrs. Aberman said. "Ever since he said he'd love to come back to teach in the fall."

"I'm so happy for him," I said. "He must be thrilled. He's such a good teacher and the students love him."

"He is quite happy. Already driving me crazy with lists of books he must get, lessons he can't wait to impart, and assignments he's excited to assign. I almost feel sorry for his first class!"

We laughed and it felt good. As though the action had broken loose something dark and set it free.

"I have something I want to give you," Mrs. Aberman said. "I'll be right back."

When she returned, she held out a slender, brown leather-covered book.

"I don't know if you've ever kept a journal," she said, and I grinned.

"I have," I said, taking the beautiful book in my hand, my fingers sinking into the soft and supple cover. "I have quite a few actually."

"So you can use it?"

"I will fill up every inch of its pages. Thank you. It's lovely."

I left the Aberman house lighter than when I'd arrived, smiling as the bells of the great church began to chime again, echoing off the buildings, filling the town with her music once more.

I turned the corner to the alleyway that led to our house, thinking about the Abermans, and digging in my pocket for my key.

"There you are."

I grinned at the familiar sound of his voice and looked up to see Charlie leaning against the front door, a flat package wrapped in brown paper in his hands.

"Don't you still have a key?" I asked, looking up at him.

"I do, but I thought I'd wait for you here. Where did you go?" While he let us in, I filled him in on my day.

"I'm glad you went," he said. "You seem lighter. Happier."

"I feel lighter and happier."

"Good," he said, and held out the package. "This came today."

"What is it?" I asked, eyeing him with a suspicious smile.

He'd gotten a fresh haircut and wore a pair of my father's old trousers Mama had taken in for him, and a new T-shirt. As always, his jaw was shadowed by whiskers, and his eyes sparked with mischief as he watched me. I followed the line of the scar on his face into his hairline. It had faded since the first time

I'd seen him, but there were others now. Some above the skin, some deep below.

"Open it," he said, prompting me.

I tore the paper open and slid out a brand-new comic book.

"It arrived in the post today," he said, grinning like a kid. "Shall we go upstairs and read it?"

Upstairs. To Madi's room. It was where I'd spent most of my time since coming home from the hospital. I'd been uncomfortable on the sofa, but didn't want to go all the way to the third floor to Elif's and my room. And so I'd found myself standing on the threshold of my little sister's room, the door long gone, used for firewood, her belongings still exactly where she'd left them five years later.

After a week of sleeping in her bed and staring at her walls all day, one by one I began to pick up the toys she'd loved. The items she'd claimed as treasures. The things that she'd chosen to represent who she was and would one day be. As I touched them, dusted them off, and replaced them, I allowed myself to really remember her. The blond hair, paler than both Elif's and mine. Her eyes, more blue than gray. The pale skin dashed with a sprinkle of freckles across her nose and cheeks. And her laugh, the sweet, husky giggle that belied her age and made her seem wiser than her years.

I allowed the pain of losing her to engulf me. I cried angry tears into her pillow at night. I begged forgiveness in the early-morning light that streamed once more through her window. And slowly, surely, I began to heal. Imagining her words of encouragement in my ear. *You can do it, Lien.* I could almost feel her breath warm against my skin.

I looked at Charlie, and then at the house around us, which had been restored as it had once been, minus a few pieces of furniture and several books we'd sacrificed for fire. I'd spent so much time inside these walls in the past several years.

I glanced down at the comic book again.

"Why don't we go to the beach instead?" I said.

We walked hand in hand down the familiar streets and through the park. And for once, instead of remembering the death I'd seen in a certain corner, the attack in a particular doorway, which windows of which homes and shops had been smashed in, or the dark uniforms that had lined the sidewalks like looming shadows, I focused on something else. The man beside me, his fingers laced through mine, the sun on my face, and a future still not known, but full of hope once more.

EPILOGUE

There were times when I forgot. Hours and days that went by without once thinking about the horrors I'd seen, or even the ones I'd inflicted.

But for years, like a crushing blow, the memories came flooding back in, the nightmares creeping from hiding places like soldiers marching in from the shadows, stealing the breath from my lungs as I woke gasping for air, old injuries, physical and mental, aching in my skin.

In the early days after the war ended, wc were still trying to survive. Trying to find where to get food, and looking for familiar faces in the streets as we wondered who had survived and who had been taken from us. There were many funerals in those days. The war had ended, but the fallout lasted long after.

Eventually the lights came back on, and the heat with it. More and more shops reopened, and families returned home, thin, pale, worry seemingly permanently etched on their faces.

Queen Wilhelmina ordered the bodies buried in the dunes exhumed. Annie, along with hundreds of Dutch soldiers who had been executed in the rolling, sandy hills, were relocated to a cemetery built just for them. There was a large ceremony after the last body was buried, and then Elif, Charlie, Mama, and I had a quiet service to honor Annie, laying all the red flowers we could scavenge on the grave of our feisty, redheaded friend.

In October of 1945, our mother was contacted by Aunt Liv's attorney. Apparently she'd left the entirety of her estate to us.

"I thought there wasn't anything left," Elif said. The fires hadn't done much damage to the actual home, but anything of value had been taken.

"Most of her wealth was kept safe in several banks," Mama said. "And then there are the three homes she and Hugo owned. I'll have the attorney sell those and add that sum to the rest of what she left us." She'd smiled sadly then. "Oh, Liv. Still taking care of us even in death."

When all was said and done, we were left with a sum that meant none of us would have to work for a very long time if we so chose. As it happened, we all had other goals, none of which was to sit idle and while away our beloved aunt's money.

Elif left for university in Amsterdam the following year. Mama leased the shop space beside hers and expanded her store. And Charlie asked me to join him in London where he was returning to university to continue his studies.

"What would I do, though?" I asked one night as we lay in his bed, my head on his chest.

"Go to school. You wanted to be a barrister when we met. Do that. Or just walk around the city all day and meet me for dinner. I don't care. Just come with me."

But I hadn't thought about my future in years and wasn't sure becoming a barrister like my father was still my dream. And I wasn't comfortable going without a plan for myself. I needed to find my place in the world, and tagging along after my boyfriend, I was positive, would not get me there.

"I'll visit," I said. "Often."

He'd rolled me over then and pinned me to the mattress.

"Promise me," he said, staring into my eyes before moving down my body, kissing my skin as he whispered, "Promise. Promise. Promise."

With Charlie and Elif gone, and Mama busy at her shop with a new assistant employed to do all the spool counting and fabric folding, I found myself spending my time writing in one of the many journals I'd acquired, working in the garden, and wandering the outskirts of our city, always returning to one particular brick building.

"Who are you here to see?" the woman at the front desk asked when I finally deigned to go inside.

"Whoever is in charge," I said.

She'd frowned but hurried off, returning a few moments later with an older woman with gray hair and glasses.

"How can I help you?" she asked.

I told her I wanted to help. The orphanage was filled with children misplaced by the war. No one knew if they still had parents, or how to find them if they were alive.

"What can you do?" she asked.

"I can write letters, ask around, travel and search if need be. I'm resourceful, and can do whatever you need me to."

And so I did. For the next two years I searched for families, aiming to reunite children with parents, or with family members willing to take them in. I wrote letters to other orphanages and rejoined siblings. I traveled to France to bring a young boy to his father who'd thought he'd died in a camp with his mother.

"What are these?" Charlie asked one day when he'd come home to Haarlem for a visit. He was lying on my bed staring at the ceiling while I put away a pile of clean clothes. I'd taken over the entire third floor room by then, and had a pile of journals stacked on my bedside table.

"Journals," I said.

"Are they all written in?"

"All but the top one. It's new."

"What do you write about?" he asked, raising an eyebrow. "Am I in here?"

He pretended he was going to open one, and I laughed and launched myself onto him.

"Don't you dare, Charlie Mulder," I said and bent to kiss him, knowing he'd never resist me. With a groan, he dropped the journal to the floor and rolled me over.

"When's your mother going to be home?" he whispered against my neck as he reached for the buttons of my blouse.

Later, we lay with our limbs entangled, him wrapping strands of my hair around his finger as I drifted in and out of sleep.

"Now that you've had your way with me," he said, his voice deep with exhaustion, "will you tell me what you write in all of those journals?"

I ran my fingers down his chest. "I write about the war. What it was like. The things we did. How it felt to do the job we did." I shrugged. "Moments. Images I remember. I needed to get it out, so I started writing."

"I'd love to read them sometime."

"Maybe," I said, my voice quiet. "Maybe someday."

As the years went by, I continued my work at the orphanage. We'd found all the family we could for the children in residence and now set about finding new homes and new families for those who had lost everything. It was an exhausting and emotional job, but when we found that perfect match, there was nothing better.

Charlie graduated and moved home to teach at a small university in Haarlem. We found a flat and moved in together, laughing as we learned who could cook what and where to put what furniture.

Marriage was something we didn't speak of. At least not seriously. Everyone seemed to expect it would happen sooner or later, but I wasn't in a hurry. The fact that I couldn't have children of my own made me feel that maybe it would be unfair to Charlie, despite how often he told me he was okay with it.

"You know for a fact how many kids out there need a good home," he'd told me during our last argument about it. "If I feel the need to be a father, we can adopt."

But it wasn't as easy a decision for me. The loss of Madi, though it no longer haunted me, had scarred me. I'd lost a sister. What would it be to possibly one day lose a child? The thought was too much to bear. Thankfully, though, Charlie didn't push. He continued to love and support me.

Upon Elif's graduation the following year, she married her longtime boyfriend, George. They had met their first year of university, and he was exactly who I would've picked for her had I been given the choice of every man in every country. Tall, good-natured, and clearly smitten by everything she said and did, he made her laugh and was her biggest supporter, constantly asking if we'd seen her newest painting any time any of us came to visit.

"And he holds me," she told me one day as we sat in her kitchen sipping tea. "When I have nightmares. He holds me so tight until he squeezes them away and I fall back to sleep."

They made a lovely couple, and a year after their wedding they had their first child and settled in Amsterdam where she managed a gallery part-time, spending the rest of her days at home with her daughter, and painting, which she'd returned to with a flourish.

Mama enjoyed her new life running back and forth visiting us and Elif, doting on her only granddaughter.

I kept in touch with the Abermans. The two eldest kids were both at university now, while Bo was still navigating primary school.

Fenna had married and moved to London. She had two children and called often, begging me to come visit her.

"They won't leave me alone, Lien. Save me. We'll go shopping and get a room at the Ritz and drink champagne in bed."

To amuse her, I once set it up with her husband, showed up on her doorstep, and we did exactly the thing she'd wished for. It was expensive, and worth every penny to see my old friend and reminisce about our schoolgirl days. And Tess.

It wasn't until the summer of 1945 was wrapping up that we got answers about our dear Tess. Her father and brother, who had spent years in the camp in Vught, returned home together, looking like so many others before them. Traumatized, malnourished, and haunted by the things they'd experienced. When we heard they'd returned, Mama and I put together a basket of the food we could spare, and went to their house where we met up with Fenna, and the men told us all they knew about Tess and her mother.

"After they were moved, we didn't hear much. Weren't even sure they were receiving all our letters," Dr. Abrams said. "Thanks to my being a physician, we got certain benefits. Mail was one of them. But a year after they'd gone, we didn't receive any more letters from either of them, and of course began to worry. Again, thanks to my position, I was able to ask around. Turns out they were part of an escape plan." He stopped, his voice catching on a sob. "They were shot and killed."

Fenna's hand slipped into mine and I squeezed her fingers, unable to meet her gaze as I sat there, shocked. I had oftentimes assumed the worst, and then silently berated myself for thinking such things. But war had taught me well. The longer someone's silence lingered, the more likely it was that silence was all we'd ever hear from them again.

Dr. Abrams invited us to go up to Tess's room. "Nothing has changed. I can't bear to touch any of it yet, but if there's something in particular you'd like to take, I know she would've wanted you girls to have it."

Fenna and I sat for a long while side by side on Tess's bed, our backs pressed to the wall like we used to do, our feet hanging off the edge. We cried thinking of our friend trying to escape the hell she was in. We laughed remembering how sweet and funny she was. And then we told some of our favorite Tess stories before we each chose an item to take home with us. For Fenna, it was a photo of the three of us. For me it was her little green compact that had sat dusty and unused for years. When I opened it, I half expected Tess's reflection to stare back at me.

After some deliberation, I also took the heart I'd made as a child from the corner of her window, the red now bleached a pale pink by the sun, our initials faded to almost nothing. When I arrived home, I affixed it to the window in our living room, where it remained—offering memories of my beloved friend—for many years thereafter.

The year I turned twenty-nine, Charlie was offered a position at Oxford. I sat in shock on the edge of our bed.

"Is it over then?" I asked.

He frowned. "Is what over?"

"Us."

"What are you talking about? You'll come with me, of course."

I opened and shut my mouth. "But I've got a job. And we're not married. Not that we need to be but—"

I stopped talking as he pushed me back onto the bed.

"Then marry me, Lien. Don't you think you've made me wait long enough?"

"Me?" I said. "I'm not making you wait."

"You kept saying you didn't know what you wanted for your life. I thought you meant..." He ran a hand over his face, and I was surprised to see two pink splotches arise on his cheeks. "I thought that applied to me as well."

I reached up and pulled him down to me. "For a professor at Oxford, you're not all that smart." I kissed him. "I don't mean you. I know what I'm doing with you. I just wonder about my work at the orphanage." So many of the children misplaced by the war had either been adopted or had come of age and moved on. The service I had provided for years was no longer needed, and I'd been relegated to a desk job answering phones and filing papers.

"Perhaps your time there has come to an end," Charlie said, his voice soft. "Maybe it's time to find a new mission."

"But what?"

"I don't know. But you can think about it in our new Oxford home and as you introduce yourself to the neighbors as Mrs. Mulder."

We married a month later in a small ceremony. Elif was there of course, Fenna and her family came, and Mama, the Abermans, and several other friends and loved ones.

As Charlie settled into his new teaching job, I found a nearby orphanage at which to offer my time. Initially I tried to ignore the stirring in my belly when I held the babies, soothing their crying and rocking them to sleep. But a year later that call hadn't stopped.

"I want to adopt," I told Charlie over dinner one night.

He stared at me for a long while and then nodded. "Let's adopt," he said. "A baby or a small child. Maybe a teenager?"

"The overlooked ones," I said.

Over the next two years we moved into a bigger house and adopted two children—siblings Levi and Mila. Fourteen and fifteen respectively, they remembered just enough of the war to have nightmares, but not enough to be tormented.

There were many hard days as we tried to blend ourselves together to form a family. Now Charlie and I weren't the only ones who needed comforting at night when the nightmares came, or space to ourselves when our emotions were too raw to speak about. But as much as I still needed time alone, I found myself craving it less and less, the sound of family pulling me toward them, not away. And then there was the day I held Mila

as she cried over something someone said to her at school about
her hair.

"No one's ever taught me how to do anything more than
brush it and pin it back," she said, patting her frizzy, long tresses.
"But I'm terrible even at that."

Thinking of my old friend Tess and her constant fight with
her own tresses, I unraveled my hair from the bun I wore and
taught her how to plait, my breath in my throat as she wrapped
her fingers around the thick strands and twisted over and over
again until she had it. I hadn't even noticed Charlie had come
home and was standing in the doorway, his briefcase in hand,
watching, a soft smile on his handsome face.

The children grew and left us too fast, both finding their
voices and a path of their own. With no one to look after anymore, I got antsy. Charlie suggested taking a month off to travel.

"Let's go see a bit of the world," he said as we lay in bed one
night. "We've always said we would."

"Where would we go?" I asked.

"America?" he said. "New York? California?"

It was in California, on tiny Balboa Island, that I found myself standing in a gift shop staring at a stack of brightly colored
journals. I grabbed two, and spent the rest of the day writing.

I wrote for days until I'd filled one and had to start the other.
By the time we left, I'd filled three more notebooks.

"Is it more about the war?" Charlie asked.

I nodded, but said nothing more.

Charlie went back to work, and I busied myself checking in
with the kids and getting the house back in order. But every
morning and every night I opened whichever notebook I was
currently working in and wrote more. By the time the clock
turned its back on 1966 and we welcomed in 1967, I had a stack
of notebooks full of words.

On New Year's Day I slid a heavy box across the floor to
Charlie. "Here," I said.

"What is it?" he asked, peeking inside.

"My journals."

"I can finally read them?"

I shrugged, exhausted mentally. I had wrung myself out on those pages.

"If you want. I'm positive it's just a bunch of drivel. Sappy prose that's no match for your Oxford brain."

"My wife doesn't write drivel," he said, pulling me onto his lap. "Can I really read them?"

"Of course. Just, be gentle."

For the next month, every time I saw him he had his nose buried in one of the notebooks.

"Don't you have papers to grade?" I'd ask. "Don't you have a quiz to prepare? Shouldn't you be leaving for your meeting now?"

He'd just shoo me away and turn the page.

"It's a book," he said one morning, yawning as he poured coffee into a mug and sat across from me at the table.

I looked around. "What's a book?"

"Your notebooks, Lien. It's a book."

"It's not a book," I said. "Who would want to read that? It's depressing."

"It's not depressing. It's your story. It's our story. And Annie's and Jan's. But mostly it's yours and Elif's story. And it is wild, and agonizing, and so painfully beautiful."

His eyes welled as he said it, and I had to look away. There was so much I'd allowed to flow from me on the lines of those pages. Things I hadn't talked about to anyone. The fear, the sadness, the guilt. The details of what it felt like to stand alone in the dark and freezing night, frightened, waiting for my prey. The feel of a pistol discharging. The sound of soldiers' boots as I waited to be found. The moment my dagger sank into Diederik's skin.

I shook my head, but he nodded.

"It's up to you," he said. "I know several people in publishing here. I've even been asked to write my own account but—it would never be as perfect as what you've already written." He stood then and bent to kiss me. "Think about it."

At first I didn't want to. I pushed the idea from my mind. But it followed me. Poked at me. Woke me in the middle of the night and nagged at me.

I called Fenna. I called my mother. I even reached out to Uncle Frans who was retired and living in London.

And then I called Elif.

"Can I read it?" she asked, her voice quiet. Hesitant.

I delivered it all in person a week later, leaving the special box Charlie had bought especially for them on the floor of her sitting room. For the entire week I was visiting, it didn't move an inch.

Two weeks later as I finished my afternoon tea, there was a knock at the door. When I opened it, the box was on the front porch, set there by a courier, a note attached.

Charlie's right, Elif wrote. *This is a book, Lien. And it's beautiful.*

There were several parties when the book came out a year and a half later. Newspapers asked to interview me, Charlie, Elif, and even Mama. It was the end of the sixties, and a civil rights movement had started, its focus on equality. I was asked to give talks. To tell what we'd done as women fighting for our country. As girls giving up our dreams for the ones who came after us.

On a beautiful, snowy winter's day, I came in late after giving a talk for a room full of female students in a lecture hall at Oxford. Charlie, who had sworn he was going to don a wig and sit in the back row, had left the light on in the kitchen and a slice of cake with a note on the table for me: *Well done, Wonder Woman.*

I covered the cake, and walked down the long hall to where my Superman waited for me.

As I climbed in bed, careful not to jostle Charlie, I grinned at the book that lay open across his chest. It was mine. He had started reading it all over again a few days prior.

"How can you read that thing again?" I'd asked.

"Are you kidding? Have you read the part where the girl sets a firebomb that ignites too fast and she has to jump out a second-story window onto a neighboring roof?"

I'd laughed, running my finger over the scar the flames had left. It was funny now. It hadn't been at the time.

I picked the book up, marked his page, and closed it, staring at the cover with a smile. It was a photograph my father had taken of Elif and I when we were young girls. We were riding away from him on our bicycles, bumping over the cobblestones of Haarlem, our long, blond plaits flying out behind us.

As I slept that night, I dreamed I was spinning, my bare feet pressing into the cool grass of the garden at our childhood home, arms outstretched, hair whipping around my face. Faster and faster I went until, dizzy, I fell to the ground, splayed on my back, the world turning around me.

A hand touched mine and I looked over my shoulder at Elif, her face so like mine, a piece of grass stuck to her cheek. I smiled.

Small, soft fingers wrapped around my other hand and I turned, grinning at Madi with her flushed cheeks and pale blue eyes, so alive and filled with mischief.

"What should we do now?" I asked her.

She turned her head so that she was staring up at the sky, and I watched her, tracing her profile with my eyes, committing it forever to my memory. And then she turned to face me again, a giggle cascading from her lips as she got to her feet and pulled at my hand.

"Let's keep going, Lien. Let's see what comes next."

★ ★ ★ ★ ★

AUTHOR NOTE

I was ankle-deep in my first round of edits for my debut novel, *The Flight Girls*, when best pal and fellow author, Jamie Pacton, sent me an email. "Write this book" it said in the subject line. Inside was a link to a newspaper article about Dutch sisters Truus and Freddie Oversteegen. I read the article, and without a second thought decided I had no choice.

I had to write that book.

To be clear, this is not a retelling of the Oversteegens' story. It is not the tale of the very real and very courageous sisters who, at the ages of fourteen and sixteen, joined the Dutch Resistance and seduced and killed Nazis and Dutch collaborators. Rather, this is a book inspired by their bravery. By their determination, loyalty to their country and countrymen, and pure grit. There are similarities, yes. A red-haired girl with the same fate, the variety of jobs done, a watch shop, and a family that actually existed and aided in harboring Jews, and a small, quiet village by the sea with wind so cold in the winter it cuts through your clothes, no matter how many layers you wear. But *Angels of the Resistance* is a work of my imagination, with details from a real town and real people fictionalized in a way I hope will intrigue you, the reader, to research their story on your own. Because such bravery deserves recognition.

ACKNOWLEDGMENTS

The sophomore slump. They don't call it that for nothing. But add to that the dark and foreboding cloud of a pandemic descending upon you, your normally quiet house now filled with the constant call of "MOM!" as we try to navigate school from the kitchen island, and a world filled with worried eyes above masked mouths and noses, the news murmuring terrible statistics in the background.

It took me three tries. Three complete rewrites to find this story. And as I agonized, I had the two best cheerleaders an author could ask for. A huge, massive THANK YOU to both my agent, Erin Cox, who, despite an overwhelming schedule, is somehow always available to pick up the phone to calm me, encourage me, and pass on wise words of wisdom—AND my beloved editor, Emily Ohanjanians, who helped me dissect this story time and time again until we found it, fell in love with it, and cried actual tears over it. You are brilliant and incomparable. Somehow you always know what I'm trying to say despite the pile of crap words I send you. Thank you to you both. How

I got lucky enough to work with two amazing women, who have since become my friends, I will never know. I adore you. Who's buying the cake?

Family is everything to me, and I certainly wouldn't be here if not for my parents, Pete and Sharon, and bonus parents, Al and Margaret Ann. Thank you for loving me and supporting me, being excited for me, and buying many, *many* copies of my book (parents, am I right?). And my siblings. Sharice, Dianna, Peter, and Marisa. I never want to know a day without the four of you in the world. No one makes me laugh like you weirdos.

Special thanks to my two best writer pals, Jamie Pacton and Dan Hanks. The former, who navigated the writing trenches with me early on and prevailed! And who's read nearly every version of every idea I've ever had—and is still my friend despite that. And the latter, who showed up one day with offers of the writing sprints that saved my flagging spirit and this book. Your wise words were appreciated. Your pathetic attempt to beat me at the "worst song ever" game was ridiculous. Thank you both eternally.

To Danny, who listened to me tear down and rebuild scene after scene, sitting by as I talked it out over and over again, trying to find clarity while interrupting his TV shows. Thank you for your patience, thoughtful ideas, and all the links you sent pertaining to whatever new harebrained ideas I came up with.

And to the greatest loves of my life, Jackson and Sofia. I hope you remember me one day as fun and loving, and not the weirdo sitting cross-legged on the sofa in a knit hat and two-day-old sweats, covering my ears to block out your voices so I can concentrate on the sentence I'm obsessing over. Thank you for being interested in my stories. For thinking I'm kind of cool. And for making me laugh every day. I'm so proud to be your mom. You're the best thing I ever did.

Lastly, but most importantly, THANK YOU to the readers. Thank you for choosing this book. It is my honor to have you spend your precious time reading my words. I hope you'll come again.

ANGELS
OF
THE
RESISTANCE

BY NOELLE SALAZAR

Reader's Guide

mira

1. This novel explores some of the unseen but important "ordinary heroes" during World War II. How else did ordinary people help in the war effort?

2. Did you learn anything new about World War II from this story?

3. Did you have a favorite character in this novel? If so, who was it and why?

4. Lien has many great examples of strong, educated women in her life, from her own mother to Mrs. Aberman to Mrs. Vox. How do you think her exposure to these women has helped shape her character?

5. How have the losses of her father and younger sister shape Lien's character at the beginning of the story? How do her experiences throughout the novel shape her further?

6. Lien wishes to help in the Resistance effort, finagling her way into dangerous assignments. What did you think of her tenacity? Was it brave or foolish?

7. How do Lien and Elif respond differently to the trials and tribulations they experience throughout the story? Did you identify more with one sister than the other? Which one, and why?

8. Did the story unfold as you would have expected, or did anything surprise you?

9. What did you think of the ending? Did Lien's life turn out how you would have hoped after the war? How about the other characters'?

10. If you were to make a movie out of *Angels of the Resistance*, which actors would you cast?

What inspired you to write *Angels of the Resistance*?

I love reading stories about women during WWII. The Oversteegen sisters were especially intriguing to me because of the nature of the jobs they did, and at such young and impressionable ages. How terrifying it must have been to make the kinds of choices they did. How brave. And while this isn't their story, it is certainly inspired by the work they did, their tenacity, determination, and love of their country and countrymen.

This is your second novel. What were the major differences between writing your debut, *The Flight Girls*, and this one?

The biggest difference was time. I had all the time in the world to write my first novel. Book two was bought as a proposal, which came with a deadline—and was written during a pandemic. (Not—ahem—highly recommended if one has the choice.) The lovely part of writing a second novel is the lessons you learned from the first. It wasn't easier. If anything, it was harder. But I had experience under my belt. I knew the process. I caught mistakes quicker. I knew story structure better. And I had confidence. I'd done it before. I could do it again.

What's the question you get asked most by readers? What's your response?

Where do I get my stories. When it comes to historical fiction, I am inspired by real human stories. For The Flight Girls I found a short but sweet book on the Women Airforce Service Pilots (WASP) and was smitten with the anecdotes of their time serving. For Angels of the Resistance I was sent an article about the Oversteegen sisters. For a 1920s jazz era book I'm working on, it was my own family's early Seattle log boom beginnings that caused a story to develop. As far as other genres I one day hope to delve into, a lot of those ideas come from a scene in my life. A terrible breakup. A young girl quietly following my son around a candy shop. A young woman coming into her own.

What was the most enjoyable part of writing this novel? The most challenging?

I loved getting to know who Lien was and exploring her relationship with her sister and mother. The most challenging part was trying to decide what I wanted to include in the story. How to keep it somewhat true to what the Oversteegen sisters experienced. This is not meant to be a true telling of their time working for the Resistance, merely a story inspired by them. There are some similarities between their story and this one, and many differences. They did live in Haarlem. It was just the two of them and their mother. And there was a redheaded girl. Hannie Schaft worked with the Oversteegen sisters and was caught and executed in the dunes days before The Netherlands was liberated.

Haarlem plays such a huge role in this novel, and really comes alive on the page. Have you ever traveled to Haarlem? What can you tell us about it?

I had the good fortune to travel to Haarlem in early 2020 (right before the pandemic began). Haarlem is a small and beautiful town near the North Sea in The Netherlands. It is quiet. Winter is bitterly cold (I wore three layers every time I went out). The people are lovely. There are bicycles absolutely everywhere you look. Good food, the sound of the church bell, the startling screech of the seagulls, that amazing Dutch architecture. There is a simplicity to the area. An elegance and gentleness. Three days there wasn't nearly enough, and in winter, there were no tulips to be seen. I should probably go back...

Do you have a favorite scene or passage in the book? What is it and why?

I love the scene where Lien shows up at target practice. I love her defiance, determination, and confidence in her own skill. I am also completely in love with the entire epilogue. Full circle moments slay me every time.

What kinds of books do you most enjoy reading?

There is no one particular genre I like over another. What I love is to be entertained. Torn apart and put back together again. I love to laugh and cry and get furious at an author for the emotional roller coaster they put me on. I love a good rom-com with characters that remind me of my own friends. I like suspense that fools me all the way until the end. A good sci-fi with amazing action scenes. Fantasy with a world I want to travel to and amazing characters I can't forget. Vampires. Nostalgia. Talking foxes... If a book makes me laugh AND cry—I will buy whatever that author writes next.

If you could give aspiring authors one piece of advice, what would it be?

Write. Everything. Down. Writers are collectors of life's most minute details. The way a person walks, the way the air smells, the light as a storm comes in. Notice these things, put words to them, write them down. I am constantly hearing book titles in conversations. I collect names I see or hear. I have scenes develop in my mind during movies, while driving, or as I fold the laundry. I write them all down. A scene I imagined many years ago, that had no place in any other book idea I've had, found its place in Angels of the Resistance. I had no idea if it would ever go anywhere—and then as I came to the terrible Diederik scene, I realized I'd already written his outcome. Write everything down.

Can you tell us anything about what you're working on next?

I am currently working on three different projects. A historical fiction set in 1920s jazz era Seattle. A women's fiction book I started with a friend that tells the story of two best friends and a spectacular house. And a YA I have dreamt of writing for nine years and am finally getting to see come to life on the page. I'm incredibly excited for all three.